THE
HARROWED PATHS

WARHAMMER HORROR

• THE VAMPIRE GENEVIEVE •
by Kim Newman

DRACHENFELS
GENEVIEVE UNDEAD
BEASTS IN VELVET
SILVER NAILS

THE WICKED AND THE DAMNED
A portmanteau novel by Josh Reynolds, Phil Kelly and David Annandale

MALEDICTIONS
An anthology by various authors

INVOCATIONS
An anthology by various authors

ANATHEMAS
An anthology by various authors

THE HOUSE OF NIGHT AND CHAIN
A novel by David Annandale

CASTLE OF BLOOD
A novel by C L Werner

DARK HARVEST
A novel by Josh Reynolds

THE OUBLIETTE
A novel by J C Stearns

SEPULTURUM
A novel by Nick Kyme

THE REVERIE
A novel by Peter Fehervari

THE DEACON OF WOUNDS
A novel by David Annandale

PERDITION'S FLAME
An audio drama by Alec Worley

THE WAY OUT
An audio drama by Rachel Harrison

WARHAMMER HORROR

THE HARROWED PATHS

GRAHAM McNEILL | LORA GRAY
RICHARD STRACHAN | STEVEN SHIEL
NICK KYME | DARIUS HINKS
JAKE OZGA

WARHAMMER HORROR
A BLACK LIBRARY IMPRINT

The Colonel's Monograph first published in 2019.
'Bone Cutter' first published in *Black Library Events Anthology 2019/20* in 2019.
This edition published in Great Britain in 2021 by
Black Library,
Games Workshop Ltd.,
Willow Road,
Nottingham, NG7 2WS, UK.

10 9 8 7 6 5 4 3 2 1

Produced by Games Workshop in Nottingham.
Cover illustration by Rachel Williams.

The Harrowed Paths © Copyright Games Workshop Limited 2021. The Harrowed Paths, Warhammer Horror, GW, Games Workshop, Black Library, Warhammer, Warhammer Age of Sigmar, Stormcast Eternals, Space Marine, 40K, Warhammer 40,000, the 'Aquila' Double-headed Eagle logo, and all associated logos, illustrations, images, names, creatures, races, vehicles, locations, weapons, characters, and the distinctive likenesses thereof, are either ® or TM, and/or © Games Workshop Limited, variably registered around the world.
All Rights Reserved.

A CIP record for this book is available from the British Library.

ISBN 13: 978-1-78999-286-1

No part of this publication may be reproduced, stored in a retrieval system, or transmitted in any form or by any means, electronic, mechanical, photocopying, recording or otherwise, without the prior permission of the publishers.

This is a work of fiction. All the characters and events portrayed in this book are fictional, and any resemblance to real people or incidents is purely coincidental.

See Warhammer Horror on the internet at

blacklibrary.com

Find out more about Games Workshop
and the worlds of Warhammer at

games-workshop.com

Printed and bound by CPI Group (UK) Ltd, Croydon, CR0 4YY

WARHAMMER HORROR

A dark bell tolls in the abyss.

It echoes across cold and unforgiving worlds, mourning the fate of humanity. Terror has been unleashed, and every foul creature of the night haunts the shadows. There is naught but evil here. Alien monstrosities drift in tomblike vessels. Watching. Waiting. Ravenous. Baleful magicks whisper in gloom-shrouded forests, spectres scuttle across disquiet minds. From the depths of the void to the blood-soaked earth, diabolic horrors stalk the endless night to feast upon unworthy souls.

Abandon hope. Do not trust to faith. Sacrifices burn on pyres of madness, rotting corpses stir in unquiet graves. Daemonic abominations leer with rictus grins and stare into the eyes of the accursed. And the Ruinous Gods, with indifference, look on.

This is a time of reckoning, where every mortal soul is at the mercy of the things that lurk in the dark. This is the night eternal, the province of monsters and daemons. This is Warhammer Horror. None shall escape damnation.

And so, the bell tolls on.

CONTENTS

The Colonel's Monograph *Graham McNeill*	9
Five Candles *Lora Gray*	97
Tesserae *Richard Strachan*	115
Ghost Planet *Steven Sheil*	133
Pentimento *Nick Kyme*	167
Bone Cutter *Darius Hinks*	197
Into Dark Water *Jake Ozga*	219

THE COLONEL'S MONOGRAPH

Graham McNeill

My name is Teresina Sullo, and these will be my last words.

This is not hyperbole, nor do I intend for you to read them as melodramatic, for I abhor exaggeration when more often than not, truth is drama enough.

I am reclusive by choice, and in my long life have made only a very few close friends. Those generous souls I am fortunate enough to count as such, together with my late husband, would describe me as a venerable woman of quiet reflection, sober judgement and principled methodology. It can safely be said that I am a private person, not normally given to outpourings of emotion.

I want you to hold to that as you read further.

This record exists only so that no matter what slanders may be aired upon the occasion of my death, you will understand the truth of the matter.

Though I suspect you will not thank me for that truth.

* * *

I write by candlelight within the walls of the Cardophian Repository, which is to be found within Servadac Magna, the sector capital of Yervaunt. Presently, I sit at an ink-stained desk in the office of the Archivist Primaris, a position I was privileged to hold for three decades until my retirement.

If you are unaware of the Cardophian Repository, allow me to briefly illuminate you. It is a venerable institution that has occupied its present site for the last four millennia, established in the last year of M36 to preserve the history of our world and its surrounding subsectors. Its grand structure is a much-lauded example of post-Akkadian Gothic, and boasts many fine collections of early Imperial histories, Ecclesiarchical art and, regrettably in light of current circumstances, an irreplaceable collection of pre-Apostasy illuminated manuscripts.

But I digress – an inveterate habit of mine, which I must now attempt to curb as there is little time left to me, and I fear my resolve may falter if I delay overmuch. Thus, dear reader, with my bona fides and distaste for inflammatory rhetoric established, please believe me when I make the following statement:

I encountered true evil at Grayloc Manor.

To any who knew me, it ought to have come as no surprise that I accepted Garrett Grayloc's invitation to catalogue his late mother's collection of antiquarian books.[1] I was, of course, familiar with the colonel's patronage, what with her many donations, though I had only ever dealt with her factotum, and had never met the woman in person.

Her beneficence had resulted in fevered speculation among

---

1 Colonel Elena Grayloc of the 83rd Yervaunt Voltigeurs (a light regiment of the Astra Militarum with a long and storied history of heroic actions in this sector and beyond) was well known as a collector of artefacts on the campaign trail, many of which she subsequently gifted to the Cardophian Repository prior to her death.

my staff as to what other books and esoterica the colonel might keep, for her private collection was rumoured to be extensive and comprised of volumes of such antiquity that simply to touch them would result in their complete disintegration. I discouraged such talk, but my acceptance of her son's request was driven in no small part by my own curiosity. You will, no doubt, be aware of the many idioms dedicated to the downfalls such sentiment inspires!

Devotion to work has been my lodestar for as long as I can remember, a guiding light, set in the firmament of my being by the Emperor, blessed be His name. This devotion has weathered all that time and life has placed in my path, even the terrible events that later transpired at Grayloc Manor.

It is this devotion that brings me back to the repository tonight.

I had been gainfully employed by the Cardophian Repository in one capacity or another for over a century. Taken on as a scrivener's inker at age thirteen, I diligently and methodically worked my way up through the archival hierarchies of academia – as vicious (if not as bloody) as any battlefield in the neighbouring Ocyllaria subsector – to reach the lofty rank of Archivist Primaris.

Under my supervision, dedicated teams of archivists, lexicographers and data-miners shouldered the burden of a historiographical establishment of the means by which the great campaigns of Lord Militant General Hexior Padira III would be recorded. Twenty-six years after the completion of that work, our labours were rewarded with an honoured footnote in *A History of the Later Imperial Crusades* – a matter of considerable pride to all of us.

In time, I would lead efforts to archive the sermons of Cardinal Saloma.[2] This, in particular, was a thankless task, given the

---

[2] Cardinal Saloma was a hero to the people of Yervaunt after she led an army of the faithful alongside the 83rd Yervaunt Voltigeurs against the forces of the Archenemy in the latter years of the forty-first millennium.

aged prelate's penchant for never committing anything to paper or slate from that campaign, and the paucity of corroborating records following the humidity crisis of the Great Ingress.

But, as had become increasingly clear to me over the decades, Imperial archiving is a task for the young and fortitudinous. My health had begun to suffer from many years of breathing in fixative particulates and preservative chemicals, and the surgeries effected upon my lungs were only partially successful in undoing the years of damage.

And as debates about various methodologies of archiving continued to rage between the conservatory factions, it was decided by those with no appreciation for the importance of things like mass deacidification or print permanence that it was time for me to finally put aside my quill and hang up my frictionless proxy-gloves.

With one hundred and thirty years of life behind me, and an unknown number ahead of me, I was retired from my post. I received full honours, and a statue with a passable resemblance to me was erected in one of the moderately traversed galleries. My husband thought it made me look severe, but I saw only devotion in the sculptor's craft and was much taken with its likeness.

Though I at first resented this enforced retirement, I quickly took to the more leisurely pace of life, and found time to read purely for pleasure, without the need for cross-checking, data-sorting and fastidious indexing. The simple joy of a well-told story became my pleasure as I rediscovered the works of dramaturges like Philaken, Gorso and Shakespire.

Though I was no longer employed by the repository, I nevertheless consulted with its archivists on a regular basis, for my expertise still had value. Many of this world's nobility sought out my discerning eye to establish the veracity and value of their family's heirlooms, Imperial Charters and genealogical writs.

Retirement was treating me well until the day Teodoro died.

I had recently returned from the long and tiring task of systemising the database of criminal records in the nearby port city of Hesarid. It had been a weeks-long endeavour that allowed for the proper cross-referencing of various evidentiary records and resulted in the perpetrators of seventy-six unsolved murders finally being brought to justice.

The day after I returned to Servadac Magna, I said goodnight to Teodoro, and retired for the evening, leaving him reclining in his favourite chair by the window with his first edition of *The Spheres of Longing*.

When I awoke the next morning, I was alone, and made my way downstairs to our parlour. There, I found him still sitting in his chair, with the book open on his lap. Tears streaming down my cheeks, I pulled a chair next to his and finished the verses he had been reading. I had loved my Teodoro from the moment I first met him, and now he was gone, I felt a yawning emptiness in my heart.

The medicae later told me Teodoro had suffered a ruptured brain aneurysm, causing a subarachnoid haemorrhage that likely killed him before he even knew it was happening.

He did not suffer, which is the only consolation I was able to take.

The weeks following his death are grey and empty to me, as though the records of that time were consumed by waves of grief as caustic as the radioactive storms said to have erased the ancient library of NeoAleksandrya. I can recall little from that time save for the condolences and support of friends, which I am sure were welcome, but could do nothing to heal the void within my soul.

Into this void arrived Garrett Grayloc's petition in a monogrammed envelope of vellum embossed with his family crest; a Tetrarch Prince from a regicide set.

The letter within was succinct, the handwriting uneven and alternating between left and right leaning, not the neatly kerned and leaded script of a scrivener servitor. I was impressed by the personal touch, even if the new master of Grayloc Manor wrote with a brusque tone that could be interpreted as somewhat condescending. At this time, I did not know if Garrett Grayloc had served in the Astra Militarum, but clearly a measure of the mother's military mien had passed to the son.

I have not the time to reproduce the full letter, but in summary, it requested I travel south to Vansen Falls and present myself at Grayloc Manor, where I would assist with the cataloguing of the late colonel's library. Together with a generous fee, a groundcar would be placed at my disposal as well as whatever else might be necessary for the swift completion of the work.

Like a drowning sailor clutching a lifeline as they sink for what they know will be the last time, I seized the opportunity. I wanted to lose myself in work, to devote myself to my craft so thoroughly that it would numb the grief I was feeling.

I immediately drafted my acceptance.

The following morning, a groundcar was waiting for me: a Kiehlen 580 from the previous century. I had travelled enough in my years to appreciate the comfort and craft of fine engineering, and this was just such a vehicle. The interior was deep red, of a soft leather that would make the seven-hour journey south to Vansen Falls far more tolerable.

The driver was a brutish and, thankfully, mute servitor-chauffeur, which alleviated the need to engage in small talk, an activity I abhor and with which I have little skill. Spared the need to communicate, I opted to spend the journey reading what little information I had been able to gather concerning the late Colonel Grayloc and her family.

But soon after leaving the outskirts of Servadac Magna proper, the landscape took on a curious quality I had not previously experienced, and I found myself unable to concentrate fully on my research. I had often travelled the environs of the city with Teodoro, and we had delighted in the untamed splendour of the landscape. Now it seemed altogether more desolate and threatening, as though nature were on the verge of reclaiming what humans had taken for themselves.

Each time I returned to my reading, I was troubled by the feeling of an unwholesome gaze upon me, a sense of being appraised in an altogether predatory manner. In my youth, I was more often aware of this sensation, as are the majority of my sex, and though it had been some time since I had known such scrutiny, the feeling was instantly recognisable. In the end, I put aside my papers, and simply concentrated all my awareness on my surroundings.

The ground grew steadily higher as the Kiehlen left the tamed flatlands of the interior and climbed towards the wilder coastal mountains. Farther out from the city, weed-choked ruins pressed close against the cracked and curving highway, while the encroaching forests pressed looming shadows over the glass of the groundcar's windows. Red bracken and rust-gorse spread beyond the treeline like spilled blood, and the few agri-collectives I saw appeared singularly barren, with a uniform aspect of dilapidation clinging to the prefabbed dormitory blocks and silos within.

When a rise in the road brought the mountains into view above the deep woods, my strange feeling of unease was only heightened. The slopes were too bleak and their summits too lofty, as though they had been deliberately raised to such heights as to keep their secrets hidden from all but the most determined seeker.

Numerous gorges and ravines cut the landscape of our route, and the ancient iron bridges always seemed too rusted and neglected for my liking. The road dipped again, becoming a rockcrete causeway traversing a lightless stretch of mist-shrouded marshland to which I took an immediate and instinctive dislike. Frothed industrial scum lay upon the surface of the marsh, and I wondered what secrets might lie hidden beneath its brackish waters.

At some point in this long crossing, the sway of the groundcar, coupled with the oppressive gloom of this stretch of the journey, lulled me into a fitful doze. I am a light sleeper at the best of times, and insomnia has been my constant companion since I entered my eleventh decade, but something in the uniform bleakness of these surroundings dragged me down into sleep. Whether it was the nagging thought of unwholesome things hidden beneath the marsh or my already heightened unease, I do not know, but the dream that bled into my consciousness was of a tenor I had rarely experienced before.

I have no memory of sleep claiming me. One instant I was looking out over the marsh, the next I was deep in the dream. Even as I recall the details now, the fear still sets a cold hand in the pit of my stomach.

It began slowly, almost pleasantly; a sensation of drifting downwards into darkness. This was not threatening, rather it was welcome, like drawing a favourite blanket tight on a cold night. Then the quality of the darkness *shifted*, and what was once comforting became threatening. Enclosing. Suffocating.

...cloying wetness forced into my throat. Paralysing cold sliding over my limbs. Pinning me in place.

...heavy weight pressed upon me. White linen fabric at my neck. Tightening. Choking.

...a voice whispering in my ear. Obscenities.

...icy fingers reaching into my chest. Closing upon my heart.

*...**let me in**...*

I woke with a start, slumped against the car door and unable to draw breath. I tried to speak, but the air was locked in my lungs. My heart raced. No words would come. Paralysis still held me in its grip.

I could only stare at the burnished metallic curve of the servitor-chauffeur's skull.

Slowly it began to rotate on its spinal axis.

I felt the desperate urge to flee, like an animal caught in a hunter's snare.

I could not bear to see the servitor's face. I knew it would be terrible. The ravaged features of a drowned man vomited back into the sunlight after years in the foetid darkness below. Its flesh would be like jelly, bloated and rank with decay, the eyes devoured by sightless things of the swamp in spite for their exile to the inky blackness below.

But it was none of those things.

It was Teodoro, smiling at me.

'Let me in,' he said.

And then I awoke, *truly* awoke.

Only with great difficulty was I able to control my breathing and reassure myself that I had not woken from one nightmare into another. Eventually, I convinced myself I was no longer dreaming, but for the hour it took to complete the crossing of the marsh, I kept my attention fixed on the groundcar's interior. The leather texture of my seat, the gleam of chrome on a door handle, the throb of the powerful engine, the rumble of tyres on the road.

Anything to keep my gaze from wandering to the dreadful view beyond the glass.

As the Kiehlen climbed back into the wooded hills, I allowed myself a measure of relief, but it was to be short-lived as the coastal mountains reared up so darkly and precipitously that they seemed ready to fall and crush me beneath their immensity.

Clearly the dream in the marsh was still crawling within my skin!

It had made me susceptible to dangerous leaps of imagination, so I took a series of deep breaths and recited my favourite catechisms from the *Imperator Beneficio*.

The journey to Grayloc Manor was greatly unsettling me, but the comforting words of the *Beneficio* calmed me as they always do. As I have previously set down, I consider myself a rational woman, not given to flights of fancy, but this journey was filling my head with ill thoughts and dark imaginings.

The road then passed into a sheer-sided valley, and the temperature within the Kiehlen dropped so sharply that, with great reluctance, I was forced to instruct the servitor-chauffeur to engage the vehicle's thermal generator. Eventually, after an interminably long descent through the cold valley, the enclosing rock opened up and I beheld the dramatic vista of the western ocean spreading to the far horizon.

The road looped steadily downhill until we crossed a narrow bridge of black steel to enter a coastal township of such charm and beauty that it all but took my breath away, after the maudlin character of the journey.

This was Vansen Falls, and it sprawled pleasantly on the inner slopes of what had once been an impact crater blasted in the planet's bedrock over ten thousand years ago. The rising of the ocean and its erosive powers had collapsed the western portion of the crater wall, allowing water to rush in and form an almost perfectly circular bay, with two jutting promontories to the north and south. An Imperial temple of black stone, hewn from the surrounding mountains, sat precipitously on the northernmost promontory, its spire curiously crooked and stark against the pale blue of the sky.

Across from the temple, on the opposite promontory, was Grayloc Manor.

My first impression was of astonishment, for the dwelling was far larger and more ornamented than I had expected for a soldier. In my years archiving the records of the cardinal and lord militant general, I have had the opportunity to converse with many who served the Imperium as warriors, and even the most senior of those never lived so grandly.

As if in contrast to the temple opposite, Grayloc Manor was primarily constructed from white marble, with flashes of colour worked into its domes and the long magenta banners hanging between its fluted pillars. The high portico of its entrance was grander than many Imperial shrines, and spreading out from the well-manicured gardens were expansive vineyards that tumbled to the shoreline in waves of undulant greenery. Gilded follies, like ornamented birdcages, dotted the slopes overlooking the sea, and I immediately pictured myself seated within one, reading *The Brothers Carmassi* while sipping a sugared tisane.

The little I had been able to learn of Colonel Grayloc, on the journey to Vansen Falls, spoke simply of meritorious service in campaigns fought throughout the neighbouring Ocyllaria subsector, but the sources were maddeningly light on details. She had been awarded the Honorifica Imperialis, but I could find no specific citation. She had been granted leave to retire with full honours, and again I found no explanation of why so senior and capable an officer would be allowed to withdraw from the battlefield at a time when the threat was so great.

Wars against the Archenemy had been raging throughout the Ocyllaria subsector since before my birth. I had never known a time without war, or without the sons and daughters of our world being tithed for the Astra Militarum. Each time I saw the transports climbing to the bulk carriers in orbit I felt a strange mixture of emotions: guilt and sadness that Teodoro and I had chosen not to have children who might serve the Emperor, yet also relief that we would never send them off to die on some far-flung battlefield.

The groundcar purred smoothly through Vansen Falls, allowing me a closer look at the town itself. Its stone and timber structures spoke of a period of human habitation that predated the Imperium, and the people I saw on its streets were tall, clean-limbed and healthy. Their eyes followed the Kiehlen as it swept past.

The road curved up and around the southern peninsula, and soon the tyres crunched on the gravel driveway of the pale house as we came to a halt before its main entrance, an imposing double door of pale blue timber. The servitor-chauffeur disengaged the drive mechanism and got out to open the door for me. I did not look at it for fear of what I might see. The memory of my dream in the marsh was still fresh in my mind. My limbs were stiff from so long in the back of the car, so I was grateful to finally stretch my legs.

The view was quite spectacular, and a path of embossed paviors led a weaving path down the stepped slopes. The crash of booming waves upon the cliffs drifted up to me, and I took a deep breath, tasting chill air freighted with a faint salty tang. I also smelled fresh-turned earth, and the ever-so-slightly acidic tang of the offshore Mechanicus geocore platforms that marred the horizon with a faint petrochemical haze. I turned as I heard the doors opening behind me.

A man in his middle years wearing a crisp tunic-suit of pressed white linen descended the steps to greet me, his hand extended. I had never met him, but the resemblance to his mother, the colonel, removed all doubt as to his identity.

'Mistress Sullo,' he said. 'Welcome to Grayloc Manor.'

Garrett Grayloc pre-empted the servitor-chauffeur's efforts to bring my few bags within, and hefted them with the casual ease of a man not used to others waiting hand and foot upon him. I had, as was my habit, travelled light, but to see the lord of Grayloc Manor bearing my travel cases within his home immediately created a favourable impression of the man.

He set down my luggage, and I took a moment to look around.

The vestibule was high-ceilinged with a curving stone staircase leading to the upper levels and a number of arches leading into other rooms. To my left was a receiving room with white sheets draped across the few remaining pieces of furniture, while to my right was an expansive ballroom large enough to host hundreds of guests with ease. Like the receiving room, its furniture was also draped with white sheets.

The structure of Grayloc Manor was very fine indeed, but my initial impression was that it was absent of the usual finery one expects in such a dwelling; the accoutrements of deep history and long centuries of familial acquisition. I was reminded of the time Teodoro and I had been the last guests to leave an isolated hotel in the northern mountains, as its solitary caretaker worked diligently to shut the building up before winter snows closed the roads.

A single portrait hung opposite the main entrance, a large oil painting depicting Colonel Grayloc standing alongside her command vehicle – a Salamander, I believe. The colonel was depicted in her combat uniform, the fabric torn and bloodstained, her boots caked in mud. The bronze of her breastplate was dented by numerous hard-round impacts, and her battered helmet lay broken at her feet. In one hand she held a power sabre, a plasma pistol in the other.

A trooper's lasrifle was slung across her shoulder.

Clearly Elena Grayloc had not been one to avoid the crucible of combat.

As naturalistic as the rest of the painting was, I felt drawn to her patrician face, framed as it was with silver hair that hung loose to her neck. Her expression was aristocratically aloof, yet weary, and her vividly rendered eyes were a rich golden-green that conveyed a sense of her unwavering purpose.

The resemblance between the colonel and her son was striking, though the younger Grayloc's features possessed less of a war-hardened edge to them. His blond hair was thinning at the temples, but he retained an air of youth to him that appeared natural and not the result of a regime of juvenat treatments.

'I hope your journey was without incident, Mistress Sullo,' said Garrett Grayloc.[3]

I struggled to think of how I might convey how disquieting a journey it had been without sounding ridiculous. I did not wish my host to form an adverse impression of my faculties from the outset, so decided to keep what I had felt to myself.

'It passed most uneventfully,' I replied, 'which is exactly what I hope for whenever I travel, Lord Grayloc.'

'Most excellent. Now, uneventful though it was, you must be tired. And please, call me Garrett. My mother was the one who obsessed over rank and title. Thankfully, something I didn't inherit.'

His words were unusually forthright and strangely accented with a curious lilt I could not easily place.

'Is that an off-world accent I hear?' I asked. 'Daranian, perhaps?'

'You have a good ear, Teresina,' he said. 'Oh, do you mind if I call you Teresina?'

'It would seem only fair,' I answered, and he smiled in return.

'I was born on Yervaunt,' he said, 'but grew up on Darania,

---

[3] Such was Mistress Sullo's reputation for precision in recall that her former colleagues attest that any conversations thus recorded would likely have taken place exactly as set down here. However, in light of her subsequent actions, the possibility exists that this missive was penned as a form of exculpatory record.

learning how to manage the family's inter-system trade networks from my father. I had no impulse to join the Guard, much to my mother's disappointment.'

He shrugged, as if realising he had let slip a confidence to a stranger, and smiled again.

'Come, let me show you to your room,' he said. 'Assuming I can find it, that is. I'm still finding my feet around here. It's been decades since I set foot in this house.'

Garrett moved to retrieve my luggage, only to find the servitor-chauffeur had followed us within, and now held both my bags.

'Ah, yes, I suppose I should let Kyrano attend to your luggage,' he said with an embarrassed smile. 'I believe he knows the layout better than I do.'

'Kyrano?' I said. 'I was given to understand it was normal practice for servitors to be shorn of their past identities.'

'In most cases, yes, but Kyrano here was senior colour guard in the 83rd,' explained Garrett. 'Threw himself on a greenskin bomb to save my mother's life some fifty years ago. Most of his body was destroyed, as well as his brain, but still he never let the regimental standard fall. My mother said his last wish was to continue to serve. *Only in death does duty end*, you know? Throne, but I must have heard that story a thousand times as a boy.'

I nodded, and took a moment to more fully study the servitor.

Its kind are woven so deeply into the Imperium that they have become virtually essential to its continued workings, yet they are all but invisible. That their names are erased along with their history further pushes them out to the margins, and I wondered then, as I wonder now, what horrors we perpetuate on our own people for the sake of convenience and functionality.

This half human, half cyborgised servitor was bulked out with combat augmetics, but it was clear the individual had been of considerable size even before the Adeptus Mechanicus remade him. Though dressed in smartly functional attire of pale blue tailored silk, Kyrano looked more like an underhive thug in a borrowed suit. The lower half of his face was obscured, or had been replaced, by a moulded bronze plate that exuded thin wisps of gaseous breath. The remainder of his features were expressionless, one eye having been replaced with what looked like a field-installed augmetic. What little skin remained on his face was pockmarked with what I guessed were shrapnel scars from the bomb that ended his service.

'Perhaps after I have settled into my room, we might reconvene in your mother's library,' I suggested.

Garrett nodded, and I saw relief wash through him. I was reminded that I was only here thanks to the death of his mother. Clearly a complex play of emotions existed between son and mother, though I could not guess how complex at this time. Whatever troubles may rear their head in later life, I am told it is hard to entirely shake the bonds or dysfunctions that grow between parents and their children.

'Yes, of course. I expect you're eager to get to work.'

'Indeed I am,' I said. 'Your mother's collection was a source of great interest to us at the repository, and I would dearly love to see it for myself.'

Garrett gave a shallow bow, and said, 'I hope the room proves comfortable, but instruct Kyrano should anything not be to your satisfaction.'

'Thank you,' I replied, as the servitor began climbing to the upper levels of the house.

I followed Kyrano upstairs, before turning to ask one last question at the turn on the landing.

But Garrett Grayloc had already gone.

Kyrano led me to my room along a series of wood-panelled corridors floored with worn and stained carpets. The notion of a servitor with a name still sat strangely with me, but I was too struck by the air of neglect I saw throughout Grayloc Manor to fully understand just how wrong that was.

We passed a wide set of doors that gleamed with a vivid red lacquer.

'Is that the colonel's library?' I asked.

Kyrano nodded, but did not respond. I wondered if it had the capacity for speech at all.

A little farther along the corridor we reached the room I had been assigned, and I was grateful to close the door behind me and be done with the mute servitor. The chamber was indeed functional, much larger than I had been expecting, but I shall not waste time on its description, save to say that its furnishings had the musty smell common to items having been kept in a basement, an impression only heightened by the folded white sheets piled on a threadbare chaise longue beneath a cracked window with a view of the ocean.

After settling in to my room and taking some time to refresh myself after the journey, I sat at an antique desk and took some time to more fully acquaint myself with the colonel's history from the files upon which I had been unable to concentrate during the journey here.

Colonel Elena Grayloc had commanded Guardsmen for seventy years, earning almost every battle honour it was possible to win and drawing admiration for both her military conduct and intellectual achievements. During her time in the Astra Militarum, she was a prolific writer, composing numerous treatises on regimental tactics and leadership that are still required reading at the Yervaunt schola progenium.

She also became something of a collector, amassing a wealth of rare texts from her many victorious campaigns and shipping them back to the library in Grayloc Manor.

It seemed her star was in the ascendant, with her promotion

to the rank of lord militant general or, some whispered, even lord commander of the sector, all but assured.

Then the Archenemy launched a counter-attack that few within high command will openly speak about or even acknowledge. It has since become known as the Dawn of Dark Suns, a night where the stars reportedly went out and the bonds between regiments of the Astra Militarum were sundered as they have not been since the age of the Great Betrayal.

A dearth of reports exist that chronicle the Dark Suns campaign, in part because so few survived it.[4] It is impossible to obtain confirmed casualty figures, but I have heard rumours that over thirty-six million Guardsmen were lost in that one disaster.

Colonel Grayloc had led her soldiers in a fighting retreat that lasted nearly three years of gruelling guerrilla warfare and desperate survival against the odds.

Her regiment, which had started out fifteen thousand strong, finally returned to Imperial space numbering a mere two hundred souls. For her meritorious service, Colonel Grayloc was awarded the Honorifica Imperialis, though as I have previously recorded, I can find no specific citation as to the exact circumstances surrounding the action that led to this award. The colonel was granted a discharge with full honours, and retired to her estates on Yervaunt, where she would live out the last fifteen years of her life as a recluse, emerging only rarely to attend regimental functions and low-key philanthropic events.

I checked my chrono and saw that ninety minutes had passed since my arrival.

Gathering the papers spread across the desk, and returning each document and report to its assigned place within my folders, I then rose with a groan as my back twinged painfully. The

---

4 Many of the survivors of this benighted campaign were subsequently confined to the lunatic wards of the Hospice of Cardinal Saloma Arisen. As of now, only one yet survives.

chirurgeon has told me often enough that sitting too long at a desk is not good for me – an occupational hazard of the archivist – so I began a series of stretches.

As I worked through exercises to loosen the muscular cramps around my vertebra, I took a moment to admire the shrine on the opposite promontory through the window. It was a fine structure, and I resolved to walk around the crater to offer prayers at my earliest opportunity.

Until then, I decided it was time to visit the colonel's library. I pulled my long silver hair back into a ponytail and opened the door to my room.

Kyrano was standing right outside.

The servitor stood motionless, his bulk filling the doorway.

'Throne!' I cried, stepping back.

I was struck by the sudden sense he... *no, not he, it* had been waiting for me.

When I recovered my composure, I said, 'Excuse me, I wish to visit Lord Grayloc's library now.'

The servitor did not move.

I repeated my request, and this time the lens of its right eye whirred and clicked, its iris dilating as if in appraisal. Reluctantly it seemed, the servitor decided it would move. It bowed its head and stepped aside. I closed my door as I moved past it and walked the short distance towards the red lacquered doors.

As I stood before them, all thoughts of how I had admonished my staff for their fevered speculation as to what might lie within Colonel Grayloc's library were entirely forgotten. I felt giddy at the prospect of beginning my work and learning what lay within.

I gripped the handles, took a breath and pushed the doors open.

The library of Grayloc Manor was perhaps smaller than I had expected, but what it lacked in scale, it more than made up for in content. Its high ceiling was vaulted with square coffers, the interiors of which were decorated with repeating patterns of square-cut spirals that drew the eye around the space, no doubt as its architect intended.

Another portrait hung opposite the entrance, this one stiffer and more formal than the one hanging in the vestibule. This depicted Colonel Grayloc, now clad in the rich dress greens of the 83rd Yervaunt Voltigeurs, staring imperiously out of the canvas. She stood beside an archaic map table piled high with scrolls, and with a gilt-edged book tucked in the crook of her arm. The colonel's weapons – the battered lasrifle, plasma pistol and power sabre – were hung on polished wooden plaques beneath the painting. I wondered if they were still functional.

Tearing my gaze from the colonel's visage, the first thing that struck me was the faint smell of age and preservatives, of powders, and the hum of precise temperature controls. Light diffused from the upper skylights with the crisp quality of polarisation, and cast a pleasingly warm illumination. Where the few parts of the house I had recently seen appeared somewhat neglected, no expense had been spared in the library's upkeep.

Elaborately carved walnut shelves lined every wall, rising from floor to ceiling, and each shelf groaned with potential. Books of all ages, dimensions and descriptions were neatly stacked in a pleasing array of colours and sizes, each a portal to knowledge and understanding.

A rush of sensation and memory surged through me; of my youth as an inscriber and conservator of damaged manuscripts, of weeks spent in the basement archives of the repository hunting down one elusive piece of corroboration, and the simple joy of finding a lost book that had been mis-shelved centuries before.

I have been intimately connected with the written word for as long as I can remember, and it has always elicited in me the deepest of emotions. My father taught me to read with his mother's torn and stained copy of the *Imperial Infantryman's Uplifting*

Primer (only much later in life did I realise those stains were her blood). Growing up, I learned never to ask for playthings or confectionaries, but my mother would never say no to a new book.

Tears pricked the corners of my eyes, and I exhaled slowly to calm the sudden and unexpected recall of youth.

'It's quite something the first time you see it, isn't it?' said Garrett Grayloc, emerging from the space between two shelves with an armful of books. He set them down perilously close to the edge of the table with a carelessness that set my conservator's soul on edge. I hadn't known he was there, and quickly reasserted a measure of control upon my emotions.

Only now did I notice the collapsible packing crates lying stacked in one corner of the library. A handful had already been assembled, and a quick mental calculation told me there were not nearly enough to contain even a fraction of the library's books.

'It is impressive,' I agreed. 'Is everything here physical?'

'Yes, my mother didn't hold with data-slates, even in the Guard. Claimed if it wasn't set down on paper then it wasn't real. Always hand-wrote everything.'

I moved through the space, resisting the urge to run my fingers down the spines of the books just to feel the texture of cracked leather and gilt binding.

'That will make my job easier,' I said.

'Good, the sooner this is gone the better,' he replied, hefting another armful of books from a nearby shelf. I resisted the urge to tell him to be careful. These were his books, after all.

'Gone?' I said, a flutter of panic welling in my breast. 'I'm not sure I understand.'

Garrett nodded. 'Yes, was my letter not clear on the nature of your engagement?'

'It spoke of a desire to have your mother's collection catalogued,' I said. 'Nothing of the purpose behind that effort was mentioned.'

'Ah, that was remiss of me,' said Garrett, pointing to the stacked crates. 'Just so we are clear from the outset, it is my intention to sell the entire collection.'

'Sell it?' I said, aghast. 'Why?'

Garrett sighed and said, 'My mother possessed many qualities, but sound financial judgement was not one of them. Our family's trade dealings have enjoyed Imperial Charter for over two thousand years, ever since Fydor Grayloc first broke Uglork Splitfang's blockade. Our fortunes have risen and fallen with the tides of war, but we have always maintained a solid fiscal foundation from which to do business. Unfortunately, many of our most lucrative trading partners are in systems now lost to us beyond the Great Rift, and the maintenance of an inter-system fleet of ships is ruinously expensive.'

'This collection is likely priceless…' I said.

'Which is why I wish you to catalogue its contents and place a fair market value upon each volume it contains,' said Garrett. 'It has recently become clear my mother lived far more extravagantly than any of us suspected, and her debts are what might be charitably called calamitous. I had to release what staff remained and begin selling off the furniture to keep the bailiffs from our doors so you might complete your work.'

That surprised me. My admittedly limited knowledge of Colonel Grayloc was that she had lived simply in Vansen Falls until her recent death (I had, as yet, not read anything that revealed how that end had come). I wondered how she had incurred such catastrophic debt, but refrained from asking so indelicate a question.

'My father has made it clear that he will see everything in this house down to the last nail sold before he liquidates any of our business assets to pay my mother's arrears,' continued Garrett. 'And neither he nor I wish to hold on to reminders of the past.'

I could understand the reality of the situation, but part of me rebelled at the notion of selling so important a collection. The shelves of the house Teodoro and I shared had been replete with books, and the thought of ridding ourselves of any of them, even volumes we knew we would never again read, filled us with horror.

But these were not my books, and all of us have things that connect us to pasts we would be better off letting go. I could not know what bad memories lurked in Garrett's family histories, nor what painful associations his mother's books might have for him. If ridding themselves of these books was what they needed of me, then who was I to judge them for that?

'Very well,' I said. 'I will begin immediately.'

'One last thing. You may be aware that my mother was also something of a writer.'

I nodded, and Garrett continued.

'She mainly wrote military books, but she also contracted with a local printer to publish a few collections of poetry and, if you can believe it, romantic verse. I'm told she even wrote a passably reviewed novel.'

I hadn't known that, and Garrett read my expression.

'I know,' he said, 'it surprised me too.'

'Assuming they are here, do you wish those books set aside?'

'Throne, no!' said Garrett. 'I've no interest in them, but there was one book the staff mentioned that she never published.'

'What was the book?'

'I'm told it was a memoir of sorts,' said Garrett. 'A monograph.'

'A monograph? Do you know the subject?'

'I am given to understand it describes the events that led up to the Dawn of Dark Suns.'

With my task laid out before me, I threw myself into cataloguing the colonel's collection that very night. Garrett Grayloc gave me carte blanche to conduct the work in whatever way I saw fit, so my first week was taken up by systematising a methodology;

breaking the effort into genre, author, subject and style, which would allow me to classify each text according to its veracity, age and condition.

Immediately, I saw it would require many weeks if not months to complete this task, but I cared little for the time it would take. Immersing myself in the art of my profession would be intensely satisfying, as it had been too long since I had rolled my sleeves up, snapped on frictionless proxy-gloves and donned an appraiser's loupe.

Each shelf was identified by a numbered ceramic disc set within the shelf edge, but they appeared to be placed at random – or at least I could find no pattern to their placement. For example, shelf sixty was next to shelf three, which was adjacent to eleven and twenty-nine. Each night I sought to work out the system of numbering, to no avail.

If there *was* a sequence, I could not find it.

The collection itself encompassed a wildly varied span of time periods and styles. The bulk of her books were, as was only to be expected, of a military nature. Over the coming weeks, I catalogued no fewer than two hundred copies of *Tactica Imperium*, and ninety-four copies of *The Uplifting Primer*, each with a subtly different bias to their contents, depending on the fighting style of the regiment that printed it.

Equally common were planetary histories of the worlds on which the 83rd had fought, and I grouped these together, reasoning that the more complete each collection, the greater value it would possess. I cross-linked those to other books describing the various regiments and commanders the 83rd had fought alongside. Presumably these had been exchanged between officers in the field, and while some were blatantly hagiographic in nature, they offered fascinating windows into human cultures across the Imperium.

Naturally, most of the military books were concerned with the fighting histories of the Astra Militarum, though a few touched upon the legendary heroes of the Adeptus Astartes. The *Book of Five Spheres* described the dogmatic warfare of the Imperial Fists, while a series of twine-bound pages purported to be one of the sole surviving excerpts of the Prandium Consul's *Codex Astartes*. My favourite of such books was a tome clothed in animal hide and penned by an unnamed warrior of the White Scars: *Hidden Chronicles of the Chogorian Epics*. I kept returning to this book, and such was the skill of the writer that I felt I could taste the wild salt flats of the Chapter's homeworld.

Religious texts were also common, and I collated numerous editions of the sermons of Sebastian Thor and Dolan Chirosius. I even found a mildly heretical volume in the form of a book of catechisms said to have belonged to Cardinal Bucharis before his fall to apostasy. I recorded numerous textbooks as well; legal doctrines mainly. *Corpus Presidium Calixis*, various planetary versions of the *Book of Judgement* as well as books of natural philosophy such as Drusher's *A Complete Taxonomy of Gershom*, Linnaeus' *Nemesis Divina,* and the medico-anatomical texts of Crezia Berschilde.

I also recorded a great many biographies of Imperial heroes. Some, like the individual chronicled in *To Serve the Emperor*, described acts of bravery that were almost beyond belief, while others, like a first edition of Ravenor's *The Mirror of Smoke*, broke my heart anew.

Most of the texts were valuable and of considerable age, dealing primarily with human institutions, which was to be expected in the library of an Imperial hero, but a great enough proportion delved into subjects that were less expected and would no doubt create a stir when listed at auction.

These risqué volumes were mostly concerned with the cultures of xenoforms: *Dogma Omniastra*, *Greenskins and How to Kill Them*, *Aeldari Perfidy*, *Obscurus Analects of Xenoartefacts*, and

Locard's seminal *Biophage Infestations*. The possession of any one of these works might not raise too many eyebrows, but to see so many gathered together was certainly surprising, though I put the colonel's possession of so many texts of this nature down to the maxim of *know thine enemy*.

Frustratingly, the one book I saw no sign of within the library was the colonel's monograph. Any record of the Dawn of Dark Suns would be of incalculable worth, and the completist heart of my archivist's soul longed to study its contents.

What knowledge might it contain? What *secrets?*

I was working on the assumption that the book depicted in the portrait hung at the entrance to the library was the volume I was seeking, reasoning that the colonel would keep such a book close to her person at all times. Its binding bore a specific pattern, a golden circle with a rippling line bisecting it horizontally and a cruciform arrow running through it, parallel to the book's spine. The symbol was unknown to me, yet I felt it held the key to locating the book. I confess, in my eagerness to find the colonel's monograph, I did not stop to consider *why* it might have been hidden.

The system of categorisation (such as it was) that existed within the library did not obviously suggest a section in which I might have found the monograph, but then, I had not expected it to reveal itself so easily.

It would be hidden in a way that would be obvious only to Colonel Grayloc herself.

In lieu of a dead woman's instructions, it was going to require time and patience.

My nights at Grayloc Manor were restful, and the insomnia that so often plagued me abated almost entirely after a few nights. At first, I put this down to the ocean air or simply exhaustion from spending so long in the hermetic vault of the library.

How naive that now sounds.

For the most part, I did not dream, and modesty forbids me to record in detail those few I *did* have. Suffice to say, they were entirely pleasant memories of intimacy with Teodoro that saw me awaken with my skin sheened in sweat and the breath hot in my throat.

I miss my husband more than I care to describe here, but I pushed thoughts of him to the back of my mind. I was not yet ready to face the full weight of grief, and work was my way of keeping that loss at bay for a time. Perhaps that was cowardly, but each of us face loss in different ways, and this was mine.

Between cataloguing the colonel's books, I began exploring my surroundings.

The grounds of Grayloc Manor were extensive, though much of its grand finery had been overtaken by nature now there were no groundsmen to maintain it. Its best years had passed, but I saw enough to wish that I had known the gardens in full bloom or that it might one day be restored. But, as with all things, every moment of neglect makes any former perfection harder to reclaim.

I discovered a hedge maze with winding pathways overrun by creeping weeds and bracken. The hedges had grown so high and crooked that no cheating was possible, but the decrepitude of age has not withered my recall, and I easily divined the path to its centre.

There I discovered a tall statue wrought from a curious, pinkish material that somewhat resembled coral, yet was smooth and pleasing to the touch. It featured an abstract figure dressed in flowing robes with proportions and features that were curiously ambiguous. From certain angles it resembled a beautiful man, while from others I found it to be a woman of superlative comeliness. Its outline was protean, as though the statue had once been pliant and had settled naturally into this shape, as opposed to being sculpted by chisels and smoothed by rasps. A marble bench that mirrored the curve of the cratered bay partially encircled the statue, and I lost many an afternoon in contemplation of this figure's elusive truth.

No plaque existed to offer clues as to the statue's identity or creator, and when I asked Garrett Grayloc, he told me it was something his mother had brought back from an ocean world of floating cities. Beyond that, he could offer no further clues as to its nature.

Beyond the maze, there was a hexagonal landing platform with the regimental emblem of the 83rd all but obscured by the jetwash of aircraft. It sat next to a small hangar I felt was built perilously close to the edge of the cliff. Peering inside, I saw the hangar was now home to the Kiehlen 580 groundcar that had brought me here. Whatever aircraft the colonel might once have possessed had clearly been sold already.

I took most of my meals upon the sun-dappled patio to the rear of the house or within one of the many vineyard follies. During one mid-afternoon perambulation, I discovered steps running from the lowest of the follies that zigzagged down a precipitously steep cliff to a small jetty artfully concealed in the rocks at its base, though I saw no evidence of a boathouse.

Kyrano served my food, and I gradually became somewhat used to the limping servitor, often throwing out rhetorical questions to it whenever a particularly knotty taxonomic issue presented itself. With no voice or mouth it of course gave me no answers, but the very act of questioning often led me to the answer I sought. I still found myself uneasy whenever it spent any amount of time in my presence, but its strength was a boon when I required heavy crates of books moved.

Of Garrett Grayloc, I saw little, save for on those few occasions he entered the library to enquire as to my progress. He was frequently distracted, which I attributed to dealing with creditors and the settling of his mother's affairs. He would, each time, enquire as to whether or not I had found the monograph, and left disappointed when I answered in the negative.

His tone was always casual, but the tension behind his words was hard to miss. With every question I became more and more convinced Garrett Grayloc already had dark suspicions as to what might be contained within his mother's memoir.

I tried not to speculate what that might be, but I am only human.

Could it be the unabridged story behind her citation for the Honorifica Imperialis?

Perhaps the truth behind the stars going out?

Or something more sinister?

After three weeks of constant work, even I conceded that a break beyond the bounds of Grayloc Manor was required. As the sun rose on the twenty-second day after my arrival in Vansen Falls, I dressed in a loose-fitting tunic of pale green and pulled on a pair of sturdy walking boots, intending to hike around the rim of the crater to the Imperial shrine.

The wind blew in cold from the ocean.

Rain clouds gathered on the horizon.

I set out early, following the road the Kiehlen had taken through the town. The sun was bright, but low cloud cover rendered the sky washed out like grey dishwater. The air bore the crispness of oncoming winter, but I had a long padded coat that kept me warm as I descended the curve of the crater.

The stiffness in my back had eased a great deal, and there was a vigour to my step I had not felt in a long time. I saw only a few of the town's inhabitants as I entered its outskirts, and though they nodded in greeting, they kept on about their business. I did not find this unusual or rude, for only those with pressing desires were about at this hour.

The buildings of Vansen Falls were old indeed, older even than many in Servadac Magna, and the texture of their walls was gnarled and eroded by salt winds from the ocean. They were, nevertheless, characterful, with no two alike, and a variety of heights and widths that made each one unique.

I had brought my sketchbook, and though my works will never be hung in a gallery, I take great solace in the act of sketching a fine landscape or a handsome building. I saw many buildings I would happily draw, and resolved to take another day to do just that.

The smell of baked bread and fresh-brewed caffeine drew my attention to a quaint, timber-framed eatery built of greenish stone, with rippled-glass windows. A projecting sign named the establishment as Gant's Confectionary and Recaff Emporium. I entered and was delighted to find the interior was just as rustic as the exterior.

'Greetings of the day, ma'am,' said the owner, an aproned man with a ruddy complexion and a welcoming demeanour. 'Zeirath Gant, at your service.'

'Greetings be upon you, sir,' I replied. 'I was on my way to visit the temple on the headland, but the rich aromas from your establishment diverted me.'

The majority of our conversation had no bearing on what was to follow, but when I introduced myself and spoke of my task at Grayloc Manor, Gant's demeanour abruptly changed.

He nodded and said, 'Ah, yes, young Master Grayloc, a terrible business. Lost his mother the same night we lost the temple.'

The significance of his latter remark escaped me at the time.

I still did not know how the colonel had died, but I sensed the soul of a gossip within Mister Gant and suspected he would be all too ready to share what he knew.

'May I ask how the colonel died?'

'A terrible business,' said Gant again. 'A boatman found her body broken on the rocks below her mansion when the storm abated. Poor woman.'

I vaguely recalled friends in Servadac Magna telling me of a brief and intensely powerful storm ravaging the western coasts last month, but I had been adrift in the fog of Teodoro's loss at the time and had cared little for anything beyond my misery.

'The storm?' I asked.

'Indeed. Thunder and lightning such as I have not seen in all my days. Biggest storm to hit the Amethyst Coast in seventy years.'

'Most likely she was taking the air and slipped while too close to the edge…' I said.

He hesitated before answering. 'That's certainly what the local authorities concluded.'

'You don't sound particularly convinced by that. Do you believe foul play was involved?'

'I couldn't possibly say,' replied Gant.

'Throne!' I said with extra drama. 'You don't think she was… *pushed*?'

'I don't know, Mistress Sullo,' said Gant. 'Not the done thing to give air to idle speculation, is it?'

'No, of course not,' I agreed. 'Though the mysterious circumstances surrounding the colonel's death have all the ingredients of grand melodrama performed in the Theatrica Imperialis, don't you think? A devoted Imperial servant potentially murdered under the cover of the biggest storm to hit the region in nearly a century. A grieving son newly returned from off-world.'

'Truth is often stranger than fiction,' he answered.

'How so?' I asked.

Perhaps he sensed the intensity of my interest, for his gossiper's soul would say no more. So I thanked him for the conversation, settled my bill and went on my way. Fortified by a hot mug of caffeine and a sugared pastry that was deliciously sweet, I passed through the centre of the town, where I came upon a single wall of basalt atop a raised plinth.

Upon this wall were inscribed hundreds of names, some dating back thousands of years. I paused to read them, and quickly realised this was not a monument to memorial, but of honour. These were the sons and daughters of Vansen Falls, young men and women who had been called to fight for the Imperium. I did not linger, but simply made the sign of the aquila and bowed to the wall before moving on.

The curve of the bay took longer to circumnavigate than I had expected, and the gradient of the streets made the climb steeper with every step. By the time I reached the windswept promontory I had climbed a considerable distance and three hours had passed, but my limbs were filled with such energy that I felt I might have ascended yet further.

Clearly the sea air was working wonders upon my constitution.

A path of black flagstones crossed the wild grass of the promontory.

At last I beheld my destination.

Now I understood the significance of Mister Gant's remark about the temple.

From the road, en route to Grayloc Manor, the temple had appeared quite normal, but now I was closer I saw it was a ruin. I had thought it constructed of black stone, but that blackness was not the natural quality of any material, rather the effects of searing fire. I approached the building, casting wary glances up at its crooked spire as the wind howled over the headland and a light smirr of rain began to fall. The dark clouds I had seen at daybreak gathered in sullen thunderheads on the horizon, but I could not tell if they were advancing or retreating.

The fire had scorched the masonry to its very bones. Nothing timber remained and the heath surrounding the ruin glistened with reflective motes of coloured glass. The temple had been roofed with steel trusses and stone tiles, less than half of which had survived.

For all intents and purposes, the building's shell was intact, but looking through the yawning portal where only splintered fragments of its doors remained, I saw the interior had been comprehensively gutted. I crossed the threshold, feeling a dank chill seep into my bones. The temperature within the temple was markedly colder than without, so I pulled my long coat tighter about myself.

Smashed timbers littered the interior, pews for the faithful charred to ash and ruin.

Alcoves that once contained reliquaries were now filled with melted wax from votive candles like glistening pools of blood.

Drizzling rain drifted down through the broken roof and wind sighed through the empty window frames. It whistled mournfully around the destroyed temple, and sadness touched me at the thought of this house of worship lying abandoned and forgotten.

That emotion was swiftly replaced by anger as I saw a blackened statue of the Emperor lying fallen across the altar. The Master of Mankind lay in a pool of light shining through the temple's last remaining window.

The sight so distressed me that I hurried out.

By now the weather had worsened, but even the cold rain and bitter wind was better than remaining in the dark of the temple's ruin. I could not bear to re-enter the temple, so walked a dispirited circle around its perimeter.

On the far gable looking over the endless ocean was a glassaic window. The rest of the temple's windows had been destroyed, but this one had somehow survived. It depicted the Emperor of Mankind atop a burning mountain of Old Earth. His holy primarchs surrounded Him, armoured demigods in crimson, gold and cobalt.

It must have been magnificent in its day, but the fire's heat had warped the glass, distorting the Emperor and the figures around Him. Once they had been glorious and inspirational, but the glass had run molten, twisting their faces into hideous leers and making them monstrous.

I could not bear the sight of them so transformed, and turned away as the sensation of being observed crawled up my neck.

I looked around, but could see no one nearby.

Only when I turned towards Grayloc Manor did I catch sight of my observer.

Standing on the opposite headland, a solitary figure shrouded in white.

Distance and the fine rain drifting in off the ocean hazed the abyss between us. Scraps of damp mist coiled about my ankles as I took a step towards the hooded figure. Something in the way it held itself made me think it was a woman, but I could not be certain.

The low sun prevented me from seeing a face in the shadows beneath the hood, and some ancient, primal part of me was grateful for the mercy of that.

Its head tilted to the side, like a bird on a branch curiously regarding its next meal.

I felt a chill travel the length of my spine as the angle of its neck passed beyond what any human bones ought to be capable of. I saw the back of its hood was stained red, and lines of crimson bled slowly down the length of its shrouded body as I watched.

I wanted to step back, but a warm sigh brushed across my cheek, like the intimate breath of a loved one. Reaching up, I felt the sensation of callused fingertips slipping down my neck. The feeling traced the line of my collarbone, and my heart beat a little faster. I could not move, and the cold of the promontory faded as a pleasurable warmth spread through my body, tingling along my limbs and into my loins. My lips parted and

I let out a shuddering breath as the most potent of my recent dreams surged in my memory.

A voice in my head was telling me to avert my gaze from this woman, but the youthful vigour infusing my body smothered it.

The warmth was too welcome. The memories too powerful.

I closed my eyes and took another step forwards.

'Ma'am!' cried a voice, and my eyes snapped open.

A dizzying sense of vertigo seized me as I looked down and saw my feet were at the very edge of the cliff. But for this shouted warning, I would have stepped into thin air and fallen hundreds of metres to a grave of jagged rocks below.

Just like Colonel Grayloc...

I stumbled back from the edge, and the healing warmth fled from my flesh. The day's cold – hard and piercing – stabbed painfully into my limbs. I turned to face the source of the cry that had undoubtedly saved my life.

A figure, as dark as the one across the bay was light, stood in the doorway of the temple. He was tall, broad of shoulder and powerful, carrying something long and club-like.

The figure took a step from the temple, and the breath eased in my chest as I saw it was a heavyset man dressed in threadbare priestly vestments. The object he carried was no more threatening than an umbrella.

My breathing began to return to normal and I turned back to Grayloc Manor.

The figure was gone.

I struggled to find both my composure and my voice as the preacher came towards me.

'Did you see it?' I said at last.

'Ma'am?'

'The figure across the bay,' I said. 'A figure in white.'

He shook his head, and I could see he thought me quite mad.

'Ma'am,' he said, his voice a mixture of concern and wariness. 'Please, come away from the edge.'

I was only too happy to put greater distance between myself and the sheer drop.

'My thanks, sir,' I said as I set foot on the flagstone path again. 'The mist confounded me. I fear I would have stepped to my death but for your warning. You have my thanks.'

'I am at your service,' he said with a slight bow. 'I am Father Calidarus, the preacher here. Or at least I was until last month.'

I shook his hand. The skin of his palm was rough, the hand of a worker.

'Teresina Sullo.'

'A pleasure, ma'am,' he said. 'Are you visiting Vansen Falls?'

'I am undertaking some archiving work at Grayloc Manor,' I said, nodding towards the temple. 'Can you tell me what happened here?'

'Ah, yes, a terrible business,' said Calidarus. 'It happened during last month's storm. A bolt of lightning struck the steeple in the middle of the night. The flash started a fire that gutted the temple before anyone could lift a finger to save it.'

'How awful,' I said. 'Will it be rebuilt?'

'In time, yes. We have secured some funds locally, and the diocese is securing donations from neighbouring parishes. All being well, Militarum pioneers will soon arrive to demolish the old structure in readiness for the new.'

'And this happened on the same night Colonel Grayloc died?'

'I believe so, yes,' said Calidarus.

I spoke with Father Calidarus for a little longer, affording my racing heartbeat the opportunity to slow, while learning more of the history pertaining to the temple. None of which is germane to this record so I shall omit it for the sake of brevity. Though, looking at the length of this missive so far, achieving brevity may already be impossible.

My return to Grayloc Manor took considerably less time than my ascent to the temple, and by the time I arrived I had reserves of energy I had not expected. The rain that threatened to fall in waves did not come, but the clouds overhead remained looming and low, a taste of what was in store.

I reached the headland opposite the temple, and paused to look back over the bay.

Strangely, the temple still looked intact. Encroaching night and distance conspired to render it completely normal, as though the lightning had not hollowed it out. Thinking back on that moment, I wonder at how easily we are taken in by the *desire* to see things the way we would wish them, and how wilfully we ignore the reality of what only becomes obvious with the benefit of hindsight.

As I entered the vestibule of the manor, Kyrano was waiting for me with a linen towel.

The material was freshly warmed, and was at first welcoming, but something in the quality of its texture made me curiously reluctant to press it to my face. As I patted my arms and skin dry, Garrett Grayloc descended the stairs.

He smiled to see me and enquired after my time in Vansen Falls.

'It was most instructional,' I said. 'I sampled the sweet delights of Zeirath Gant's establishment, then visited the temple across the crater.'

'Ah, yes, a terrible business,' he said, and the oddly echoing sentiment, which so closely recalled Gant's earlier remarks, sent a curious frisson over my skin. He seemed distracted, and excused himself with a curt bow of his head.

As he departed, I handed the towel back to Kyrano and said, 'Garrett?'

'Yes?'

'Is there anyone else staying at the manor? A woman perhaps?'

A shadow passed over his features, so swiftly I cannot to this day be certain I saw it.

He shook his head and gave me a bemused smile that was not at all convincing.

'No, Teresina,' he said. 'It's just us.'

I returned to my room and locked the door behind me. The bed had been made and fresh water placed in a ewer on the dresser. Fresh flowers, vividly red-leafed Fireblooms, stood proud in a vase and filled the air with a heady, musky bouquet.

A little too potent for my tastes, but not unpleasant.

The day's excursion had left me tired, though not so much as I had expected. The chill damp of the fine rain still clung to me, so I stripped off and took a warm shower in the adjacent ablutions cubicle, taking the time to wash my hair and massage the cold from my bones. By the time I emerged, the space was filled with warm steam and the mirror opposite was fogged with condensation. Soldiers often speak of the simple pleasure of a warm meal on the campaign trail, but for me there was no greater comfort than a warm shower and the feeling of once again being clean.

Wrapping the towel about myself, I wiped a patch of the mirror clear and began applying a moisturising cream to my face. After a few minutes I leaned in, pleased by what I saw. I was no youngster, but I was still a striking woman, and did not feel aggrieved at what time had wrought upon my features.

But... was I imagining it, or were the crow's feet at the edges of my eyes marginally less pronounced? My fingertips traced the line of my jaw. The skin felt tighter to the bone, taut and vital. I ran a hand through my hair, and my eyes narrowed. During my seventieth year, my hair had swiftly turned from a rich auburn to the silver it is today.

My roots were tinted the faint brown of my youth.

I have never been overly concerned with the visible effects of ageing, but the sight of smoother skin and my natural colour returning was far from unpleasant. I have had only mild juvenat treatments over the years; procedures to maintain bone density, neural regeneration, and transfusions to counteract the natural degeneration of vital tissues, but nothing cosmetic. I did not know how this was possible, but to see an echo of the young woman I had once been was pleasing in a way I can scarcely describe.

My vain contemplation was cut short as I heard the sound of my door closing.

Was there someone in my room?

I eased to the door and pressed my ear to the wood. I could hear nothing save the patter of rain on the window glass and the creaks and groans of an old house settling for the night. Warmth evaporated from my skin, and I shivered as cold air seeped in from the room beyond.

Gingerly, I pressed open the door a few centimetres and peered through the crack into my room. I glimpsed the lace curtains at the window twisting and dancing, blown and billowed by soft wind through the cracked glass. I altered the angle of my head to see that the door to my room was closed. I breathed a sigh of relief.

I knew I was being ridiculous and pushed the door open, stepping boldly into the room.

At first it appeared as though everything was just as I had left it, but that initial impression was soon dispelled.

The damp tunic and undergarments I had left wadded in a bundle on the floor by the bed were gone. Laid on the bed were fresh clothes, but they were not mine.

The fresh-pressed uniform of an Astra Militarum colonel was laid out with the precision of an officer's servant. A worn battle-jacket of deep green lay next to a pair of faded fatigues and a peaked cap of black and red. Leather boots polished to a mirror finish sat with the toes tucked under the low-hanging bedspread.

A tray of food was set upon the antique desk opposite the bed. A plate of rich, pinkish meat, brightly coloured vegetables, and a cut-crystal decanter of what looked like amasec. I have been vegetarian for most of my life, and the meals Kyrano had served me at Grayloc Manor had respected this.

Why now was I being served rare steak?

Next to the decanter was a worn and tattered book, like something an officer might carry to record their thoughts on the campaign trail. The leather of the spine was cracked as though it had been bent back many times, its pages curling up at the corners.

The cover was a faded red, and bore the monogram *M.R.* in faded gold leaf.

I lifted the book and opened it to a random page.

It was not, as I had first dared hope, the colonel's monograph; rather it was a journal of sorts. I immediately recognised what I was looking at: a plan to organise, categorise and order the collection of books in Colonel Grayloc's library, the first entry of which dated back thirty years at least. I had been preparing plans just like this in the month I had spent here.

I pushed the tray of food away and poured a drink from the decanter. As I had suspected, the liquid within was amasec. A fine vintage, too. I flicked through the book, seeing references to numerous books I had already catalogued. Some were books I had not yet encountered, while yet others were ones that appeared to be in languages I could not read.

I lit the desk lumen as night finally closed in.

Isolated in my little island of buzzing light, I lost myself in the intricacy of the writer's process. His handwriting was meticulous (the tone and style of writing made me reasonably confident the author was a man), the methodology impeccable, and his singular devotion to the task at hand reminded me of my own perfectionism.

Much of the journal was given over to a detailed account of the colonel's collection, though alongside the lists of books were occasional annotations by the author on its very nature. Most of these were simple observations on the rarity of certain tomes, but others could be read as admonishments to the colonel for even possessing them. The tone of these observations ranged from simple remarks to commentary that would likely have earned a stern rebuke had the colonel read them.

Had the colonel seen them?

Was that why *M.R.* was no longer the curator of this collection?

Some of his notes I could well understand, for as I have mentioned, more than a few of the books were of a questionable nature. Around the halfway point through the journal, I noticed a distinct change in the tenor of the notes, coinciding with the arrival of a book or books that featured more than once in *M.R.*'s notes.

Its name appeared variously as *The Elegy of Valgaast*, *Lament of Valgaast*, and also *Valgaast Theogonies*, though I could not be certain if these were three separate books or a single volume, given that each title appeared to have been sourced from a different planet and every title appeared to be a translation of the same root words.

I had not seen any of these works, nor any reference to what the name might mean.

Whatever its truth, the book or books had clearly upset *M.R.* to a degree I found hard to fathom. Matters were complicated by the fact that it was clear his mind was unravelling the deeper into the book I went. *M.R.*'s handwriting, which had been neat and even at the start, was now ragged and spidery by the time I reached the journal's midpoint. I saw smudged blots on the page (the writer's quill too laden with ink) and frequent scratched-out words. As I drew to its end, more than a few pages had been ripped out, and much of what *M.R.* wrote was virtually illegible.

One portion I *could* read appeared to make reference to the destruction of the temple, while another hinted at a scandalous memoir I could only imagine was the monograph Garrett had spoken of. I found several trembling notes that spoke in terror of something known as the *Inamorata*, though, like Valgaast, no hint was given as to what that might be.

By now, the moon had passed its zenith, and my eyes were heavy from peering too long at the handwriting of a very disturbed individual. It had been many years since I had worked this long into the night, and though some trace of the youthful vigour I had felt earlier today remained, I knew I would be fit for nothing come the dawn were I to deny myself at least a few hours of sleep. I moved the Militarum uniform onto the chaise longue, next to the piled linen sheets. Resolving to query Garrett on why such clothing had been laid out for me, I climbed into bed.

I hoped I might dream of Teodoro again.

I did not dream of my late husband.

But so deep and swift was my descent into sleep that I can recall little of how my dreaming began. I vaguely recall a sense of comfort, of being enfolded in warmth, like a babe in arms swaddled in a favourite blanket. Tight and binding, holding me safe and protected.

But that tightness soon passed from comforting to constricting.

I struggled against the sensation, but I couldn't move. Something was pressing against my face. I tried to move, to roll over, thinking I was still dreaming. I tried to draw breath, but what felt like a heavy cloth was pulled tight over my mouth.

I smelled stale, shuttered rooms and the dry mustiness of age-stiffened fabric.

I tasted dust and dead flowers.

My eyes flickered open as it penetrated my consciousness that this was no dream. I saw only dull whiteness, the thick warp and weft of coarse linen.

A shroud...

I tried to sit up, to push the sheet from my face. My legs and arms were pinned in place, bound tight with more of the rough fabric. It chafed my ankles and wrists as the cloth pulled tighter against my face.

Somewhere, a light bloomed, stuttering and weak; the desk lumen. It silhouetted a heavyset form just beyond the suffocating cloth, its outline blurry and indistinct. I tried to scream, but a wadded bolus of moist cloth forced itself down my throat like a hungry snake.

I gagged, fighting for breath.

Greyness hazed the edges of my vision.

...***let me in***...

My chest heaved, desperate for air, but there was none to be had.

I felt rough hands at my neck, callused flesh and metal. Thrashing on the bed, my body spasmed in fear and desperation. I couldn't breathe, I couldn't move.

And then the choking blockage was withdrawn. My back arched as I drew in a breath that felt like fire in my lungs. The greyness retreated from my vision.

I felt the vice grip on my extremities release.

Frantic, I kicked out and reached up to tear the cloth from my face. I scrambled up the bed as my vision adjusted. Hot, acidic fear surged up from my stomach.

Kyrano stood at the edge of the bed, holding twisted sheets of white linen cloth like a garrote. They clung to him like the toga of a planetary senator or the king of some pre-Imperial feral world.

His immobile face gave no hint of murderous intent, but in the flickering light of the desk lumen his face was daemonic. Sick with loathing and fear, I frantically pushed myself away.

I fell from the opposite side of the bed, gashing my head on the corner of the dresser beside it. Warm blood ran down the side of my face as I lay, stunned, on the floor. I heard the servitor's heavy footsteps as he circled the bed, moving towards me.

Panic seized me, and I tried to pull myself up, but my limbs were dead weight, numb from their constriction. Instead, I crawled frantically beneath the bed, clawing my way forwards with my fingernails until I emerged on the other side.

My mind was clearing, and my legs ached as blood flowed back to my feet.

I could already feel bruising swelling my wrists and ankles.

Pushing myself upright, I stumbled weakly towards the open door. The corridor beyond was lit by the pale light of the moon. I lurched along its length to where Garrett Grayloc's room was located.

I paused at a turn in the corridor to see if I was being pursued.

I whimpered in fear as Kyrano stepped through my door, pulling rumpled sheets of linen from himself as though tearing free of a cocoon. Our gaze met, but I saw only the bland horror of a dispassionate murderer who barely even notices his victim.

But instead of following me, the hulking servitor turned and walked in the opposite direction, as though he had accomplished whatever it was he had set out to do.

I waited, breathless, at the turn as he disappeared into the darkness of the house.

Tears streaming down my face, I slid down the wall and wept.

The following day, I told Garrett Grayloc everything that had transpired during the night.

'Are you sure he was *attacking* you?' he asked as he poured me a hot cup of herbal tea.

I could scarcely believe he was asking me that.

'Perfectly sure,' I replied, holding out my wrists and leaning my head back.

Garrett drew in a breath as he saw how bruised and grazed both were.

'Damned peculiar behaviour,' he said, taking a seat at the dining room table. 'Perhaps he's stuck in a service loop.'

'A service loop? What are you talking about?' I said, the anger at my assault still burning hot in my chest. 'He tried to *kill* me!'

'Of course I see how you might think that,' said Garrett, holding his hands aloft as he saw my eyes widen. 'Wait, hear me out, Teresina. You said one of my mother's uniforms was laid out on the bed, yes?'

I nodded, too furious to speak.

'And there was a meal of rare steak and amasec on the desk?'

I nodded again as Garrett ran a hand across his chin.

'I think I see what happened,' he said. 'Kyrano's always been a bit glitchy, but it's got worse since my mother passed. You see, and I realise now that it might have been a trifle inappropriate, but you're actually sleeping in my mother's room.'

I could barely believe what he was saying.

'I'm sleeping in your *dead mother's room*?' I said, struggling to keep my tone even.

'Well, it seemed like the most expedient solution, given that it hadn't yet been closed up, though I see now that was somewhat foolish. I apologise for that.'

I should have turned and walked away right there and then. I should have immediately marched down into Vansen Falls and arranged passage back to Servadac Magna.

But I did not, and I still wonder at how easily I was convinced to remain.

Taking my silence as consent to continue speaking, Garrett said, 'So I wonder if perhaps Kyrano was confused, and thought my mother was, well, not dead. Hence the meal and the clothes.'

'I've been here nearly a month,' I pointed out. 'Surely he must have known I was not her?'

'One would think so, but who *really* knows what goes on in the mind of a servitor? The machine-spirit moves in mysterious ways within its servants, after all. Now, I think what happened is that Kyrano–'

'Stop calling him that,' I snapped. 'Whoever he was before, that thing is a servitor now.'

'Of course, yes,' said Garrett. 'You're right, of course. I'll have another room prepared for you immediately. I shall see to it personally.'

'What are you going to do about the servitor?'

'There's a man in town,' said Garrett. 'Not a tech-priest as such, but he has a knack with cybernetics. Used to work in the vehicle pool as part of the enginseer cohorts. Maintains most of the old cargo-eights around here. I'll have him take a look at Kyr– the servitor today, do a fresh memory-cache scrub.'

'Fine, but do it today or I am leaving.'

'Absolutely. No question,' said Garrett. 'And please, take today to rest and recover. Whatever it was that happened in the night must have been traumatic.'

I bit back an angry retort to *whatever it was*. While Garrett Grayloc was in the mood for concessions, I had one last thing to ask him.

'Do the initials *M.R.* mean anything to you?'

He thought for a moment before answering.

'It could be Montague Rhodes, why?'

Unwilling to yet disclose the existence of the monogrammed journal I had studied last night, I decided obfuscation was the best course of action.

'I found his initials in a number of the colonel's books,' I said. 'Who is he?'

'I believe he was the custodian of my mother's library,' said Garrett.

'*Was?*'

'Yes. He retired soon after my mother's death. I heard the poor fellow was quite distraught at her loss. He and his wife still live down in the town, I believe.'

I nodded, now knowing how I would spend the rest of this day.

I left Grayloc Manor as soon as I could and walked back down into Vansen Falls. Garrett claimed to have no knowledge as to where exactly Montague Rhodes lived, but I had a good idea of where to start.

Making my way to Gant's Confectionary and Recaff Emporium, I purchased another sugared pastry that felt deliciously comforting and engaged in awkward small talk until I found a way to enquire after Colonel Grayloc's previous librarian.

'A terrible business,' he said, leading me to believe that this must be a favourite phrase around Vansen Falls. 'Poor fellow. Was never the same after the colonel died, Emperor rest her soul.'

'What happened to him?'

'Books were his life, you see, Mistress Sullo,' said Gant. 'He'd curated her books for decades, knew that collection inside out. When Master Garrett came back and announced he was going to sell them off, well, it quite broke the fellow's mind.'

'As you say, a terrible business,' I said, with enough of an upwards inflection that Gant might feel the urge to continue.

'Indeed it was,' agreed Gant. 'Poor fellow lost his mind. Too aghast at all the colonel's books being scattered to the wind, I suppose. Can't remember the last time I saw him. Only ever see his wife, Odette. And even then, rarely.'

I nodded and said, 'The thing is, Master Gant, I've encountered a rather knotty issue in my cataloguing, and it would be most helpful were I able to consult with Master Rhodes. Do you happen to know where I might be able to call upon him?'

* * *

Gant was indeed able to furnish me with an address, and after only a mild diversion in the twisting streets of Vansen Falls, I found myself before a sturdy door of pale wood set in a low, clay-tiled cottage overlooking the ocean on the northern curve of the crater. Smoke issued from a leaning chimney, and I could not help but be slightly unsettled to see that each of the windows was shuttered, and that the shutters had been nailed into their frames.

My first knocks went unanswered, but I persisted, suspecting that the cottage's inhabitants would not be the sort of people to wander far from their place of sanctuary.

Eventually the door was opened by an elderly woman who wore the cares of the world upon her face. She eyed me suspiciously, her appraisal visibly swift and brutal.

'What do you want?' she said.

'I'm sorry to disturb you, but are you Odette?' I asked.

She nodded, but volunteered no further information.

'My name is Teresina Sullo, and I would very much like to speak to your husband.'

Odette's expression, already wary, hardened to outright hostility and she began to shut the door in my face. I stepped in close to prevent its closing.

'Please,' I said. 'I need his help.'

'He can't help anyone,' said Odette. 'Not any more.'

I had one last gamble before the door was closed for good.

'It's about Valgaast,' I said.

The interior of the cottage was dark, which was only to be expected given that its heavy shutters were kept permanently sealed. I felt as though the light that entered with the opening of the door was an unwilling guest, one that gratefully fled with its closing.

Odette led me to a sealed room towards the back of the cottage and hesitated before it.

'You won't get anything from him,' she promised. 'No one does.'

'I need to speak with him,' I insisted.

'You can speak, but he won't be answering.'

I couldn't help but feel she was offering me a last chance to withdraw. Even now I wonder how things might have transpired had I done so.

'Please,' I said.

She sighed, lifting a key from a pocket at her waist and unlocking the door.

The room beyond was musty and stifling, and the stench filled me with the urge to flee, for I sensed nothing but reeking madness within and a life sustained at a cost not worth paying.

I looked back at Odette. She bore the expression of a woman trying to quell something entirely intolerable. Reluctantly, I stepped inside and felt my gorge rise at the thickness of the air, as much a prisoner within as the old man slumped in a chair before an empty hearth.

No daylight reached this room, and only a pair of tallow candles set upon the mantle provided any illumination. Montague Rhodes sat with his back to me, staring into the cold fireplace as if hoping flames might spring forth to consume him and the cottage both. From the doorway, I could only see the top of his hairless pate, wrinkled and spotted with age.

'Master Rhodes?'

His head tilted a fraction at the sound of his name, but he did not turn nor rise from his chair. I had known men and women who had, through age or injury, been forced to abandon their vocations and who had swiftly sunk into depression or listlessness. But, according to Garrett, Montague Rhodes had only recently left the colonel's employ.

Surely he could not have sunk so low so soon?

Slowly I approached his chair.

A low stool was set in front of the old man's chair. I circled it and sat down before him.

He lifted his head and I gasped at the horrid ruin of his face. I had hoped to converse with him, archivist to archivist, but I now saw that would be impossible.

Montague's eyes had been destroyed, gouged out of his skull. The flesh around his sockets was raw and mutilated with deep-ploughed furrows, tearing wounds cut by ragged glass and sealed with sutures. My hand flew to my mouth, horrified at the scale and severity of his wounds; wounds I knew with an absolute certainty I cannot now explain were self-inflicted.

His thin body was swathed in woollen blankets, and I saw his protruding hands were restrained by thick leather straps. My gorge rose as I saw the fingers of his left hand were gone, only ragged stumps remaining beneath a filthy bandage. The image of him hacking them away with the same bloodied glass that had taken his eyes flashed into my mind. His right hand still possessed its digits but they were broken and useless, as though he had punched them against steel until the bones within had been reduced to powder.

'Master Rhodes?' I said again.

He did not answer, but swung his head towards me, like a burrowing creature suddenly aware of nearby predators. His cracked and dry lips parted and he drew breath. A soft sound began in his throat, and I leaned closer to hear what he had to say.

His jaw fell open and I recoiled as I saw the ragged wet nub of lacerated meat that was all that remained of his tongue. This was no surgical incision, but the result of frenzied slicing with something jagged and not quite sharp enough to cut cleanly. The inside of Montague's mouth was filled with poorly healed stab wounds and broken teeth.

'Throne!' I cried, almost falling from the stool.

I turned towards Odette.

'Emperor's Mercy, what happened to him?'

'That manor at the top of the promontory happened to him,' she said, circling her stricken husband and stroking his head. 'The books he read. The colonel's very own words. The things she saw, things she did. *The things she brought back...*'

'I don't understand.'

'Colonel Grayloc, they say she was a hero, yes?'

'She is,' I said. 'She was able to fight her way back to the Imperium after the Dawn of Dark Suns when all others fell.'

'So many died,' said Odette. 'Did you never wonder *how* she made it back?'

'By all accounts, Elena Grayloc was an exemplary leader, and her soldiers were some of the very best.'

'The 83rd were good soldiers, some of the very best,' agreed Odette. 'But no one is *that* good. They all should have died. No one could have lived through that, but *she* did. She and those she trusted to come with her, *no matter what*. Imagine what that cost her, how much of her humanity she would've had to surrender along the way.'

'How do you know all this?' I asked.

Odette knelt beside her husband.

His head turned this way and that, as if straining to hear a far-distant song. I wondered how much he could understand of what we were saying.

Odette gently placed a hand on his arm and said, 'My Montague, he found her memoirs.'

My heart leapt with excitement I did my best to conceal.

'He found the colonel's monograph?'

'For all the good it did him.'

'What do you mean?'

Odette rose from her knees and said, 'I've heard about you, Mistress Sullo. You're going through the colonel's books, yes?'

'Yes. Garrett Grayloc intends to sell them to cover his mother's debts.'

Odette moved around the back of her husband's chair and rested her hand on his shoulder.

'You should leave this place,' she said to me. 'Now, while you still can. I ought to have warned you earlier, but I couldn't leave my Montague. The books… the things he read… they drove him mad, you see. The horror of learning what happened out there in the Ocyllaria subsector, it broke his mind. The day it was finally too much… he came home, the words just spilling out of him in a flood, like he couldn't stop it. He was saying awful things, vile things…'

'What things?'

'Things I won't repeat,' said Odette, and I saw a memory of the most hideous slurs imaginable pass over her face. 'He knew he was saying them, he was weeping the whole time, but it was like he couldn't stop saying them. He kept trying to stop, but the words inside kept boiling out of him.'

I could see revisiting these memories was traumatic for Odette, but I needed to know what had happened, what Montague had found.

'Did he ever mention Val–'

Odette's hand snapped out and clamped over my mouth. Her skin tasted of fish and the stale sweat of a locked room.

She glanced down at Montague and shook her head slowly. 'Don't say it.'

I nodded as she lifted her hand away and continued.

'So he's ranting and raving like a madman, and *that* word you were about to say comes out of his mouth. No sooner does it pass his lips than he gets up and smashes his fist into the mirror. Breaks it to pieces and picks up a long shard like a carving knife. Takes it to his tongue first, then his eyes. All the time I'm screaming and trying to stop him, but he's stronger than he looks and he throws me off. No sooner are his eyes and tongue gone than he's looking for parchment and quill, like what was in him was trying to find a way out, *any way out*. He starts scratching random numbers on a page he'd torn from his old journal. As soon as he's done, he takes the same glass that cut out his eyes and tongue and hacks his fingers away back to the palm. When he realised he couldn't do the same to the hand he had left, he just punched the wall until it was nothing but bloody flesh and bone fragments.'

All through Odette's tale, I sat incredulous, transfixed by the horror Montague Rhodes had wrought upon his own flesh.

'What could have been so terrible that it would warrant such horrifying self-mutilation?'

'I don't know,' said Odette. 'I don't *want* to know. And neither should you.'

'Do you think something similar happened to the colonel?'

Odette's eyes narrowed. 'What do you mean?'

'I heard she fell from the cliffs of the manor during the storm,' I said. 'Perhaps her death wasn't an accident? Perhaps she too was afflicted by these... *visions*, and that drove her to hurl herself from the cliff?'

Odette gave me a look of the kind I had not seen since my days in the scholam when the drill abbots were displeased with me.

'You're half right,' allowed Odette.

'What does *that* mean?'

'It means the colonel's death wasn't an accident, but it wasn't a suicide either.'

'So what was it?'

'Boatman that found her said her head was mostly gone, split wide open, and empty like a cracked egg.'

'Those cliffs are high. The impact of landing could easily explain such a wound.'

'That they are, but the boatman is ex-Guard,' said Odette. 'He saw more than one commissar perform a summary execution.'

Odette saw my look of confusion and said, 'Point is, he knows what a gunshot to the back of the head looks like.'

I did not linger much longer in that awful cottage, and the memory of Montague Rhodes still sends a surge of revulsion through me, though now I have a better understanding of what motivated him to take the mirrorglass to his face.

As I stood in the doorway of the cottage, Odette pressed a folded sheet of paper into my palm and said, 'Take it. I don't want it in here a moment longer. Maybe it'll help you, or maybe you should just burn it.'

She retreated and closed the door before I could ask any more.

I felt desperately sorry for Odette and her husband, but I stepped quickly away from their cottage, wanting to put as much distance between myself and the despair that lay within like a sickness. I could feel the dank texture of trapped air leaving my lungs with every step I took and each breath of sea air.

I was not yet ready to return to Grayloc Manor, so made my way to Gant's emporium. I intended to purchase a hot mug of caffeine, hoping to impart some warmth to my limbs and to drive away the ice that had settled in my bones. I needed time to process all I had learned from Odette's tale. How much of it could be true, and what did it mean?

I took a seat in a secluded booth at the rear and nursed my drink, now understanding how little I really knew, and how much more there was to Colonel Grayloc's life.

Could the colonel have been murdered?

If so, by whom, and why?

What terrors were concealed within the monograph that had driven Montague Rhodes to inflict such terrible injuries upon himself? What danger was I in just being here? And, most important of all, could I endure what he had not?

Those were questions I could not answer with my limited knowledge. I sipped my drink and reached into the pocket of my robes to lift out the journal and see if any new insights might reveal themselves. I thumbed through its pages until I came to the ragged edges at the gutter where two of its pages had been ripped out.

Unfolding the paper Odette had handed me, I laid it flat next to the torn edges.

Its edges perfectly matched up, unequivocally establishing its provenance.

The paper had been crumpled since being torn out, and dried bloodstains were smeared across it. I could imagine Odette, having balled up the page in grief, standing before the hearth and debating whether or not to throw it in the fire. I wondered why she had not, as I wondered why she had thought to pass it on to me.

The page was filled with a repeating series of six numbers.

The handwriting was familiar to me, the frantic etchings of a damaged psyche. Like the later writings in the journal it was hard to read, but given the circumstance in which these numbers had been set down, it was a miracle any of this was legible at all. What could be so important about these numbers that the last remaining scraps of sanity the old man possessed had driven him to record them after stabbing a glass dagger into both his eyeballs?

I stared at them for hours, willing them to reveal their significance. Running a finger over the paper, I felt the rough texture of its pressed fibres, the raised ridge-lines of dried ink.

Was there a sequence or order to these numbers?
Was there a sequ–
And then I knew.

* * *

After speaking with Odette and seeing the ruin of her husband, I had little desire to return to Grayloc Manor, but the promise of what I might discover were my suspicions correct was too great to resist. The sun was well past its zenith, and I felt no warmth from it as a stiff gale blew in from the ocean.

The curve of the crater spun ocean spume into vortices of mist and seawater, such that I felt as though I was walking uphill through a veil of tears. Looking out to sea, it was clear the storm that had long threatened to break overhead now seemed on the verge of unleashing its fury. Though it was only mid-afternoon, the sky was the textured grey of knapped flint, and the dark clouds over the ocean were racing to the coast at a rate of knots.

I glanced back at the temple on the opposite headland, its lonely spire stark against the clouds. Now that I knew the truth of its condition, it was impossible not to feel the absence of the Emperor's presence in Vansen Falls.

'The Emperor protects,' I whispered as I approached the manor, but the memory of the destroyed temple made my words ring hollow. I saw no lights within the manor, all its windows as black as the void of space.

Taking care to make as little noise as possible, I entered the manor like a thief, not wishing to attract any attention. I hoped to test my theory undisturbed, and the approaching storm abetted me in this as a peal of thunder rumbled overhead.

The house felt deserted, which perfectly suited my purpose as I climbed the stairs towards the library. A sudden burst of rain beat a tattoo against the windows. Howling winds whistled around the eaves.

Darkness held sway within the house. No lights were lit, but I knew my way around enough not to need more than the last of the day's light spilling in through the rain-smeared windows. Swiftly, I made my way to the red doors of the colonel's library.

I paused to listen at the door, but could hear nothing more than the creak of settling timbers and rattling roof tiles. Satisfied the library was empty, I entered and closed the door behind me.

Thunder rolled again, louder this time.

A flash of lightning illuminated the colonel's formal portrait and the weapons beneath it.

Taking a moment to quell my rising anticipation, I let out a shuddering breath and unfolded the paper Odette had given me.

1, 6, 15, 28, 45, 61.

My time in the library had given me a deep familiarity with its layout, and I made my way to the shelf inset with the numbered ceramic disc labelled with a 1.

I laid my fingertip against it and felt the tiniest sensation of potential movement. Taking a deep breath, I pressed the disc, and my heart leapt as I was rewarded with a soft click, like a tumbler rolling in the barrel of a lock. Moving from shelf to shelf, I located each number in turn and pressed. Each time, it clicked with the sound of a turning key.

Despite everything I had learned and my growing sense of standing at the edge of something I could barely comprehend, I could scarce contain a giddy sense of excitement as I stood before the last shelf.

I pressed the disc marked 61 and waited.

For long seconds, nothing happened. All I could hear was the rising winds encircling Grayloc Manor, but then I heard the ratcheting clockwork sounds of an elaborate mechanism coming into some preordained configuration.

I turned to see a portion of the floor sliding back to reveal a set of stone steps leading down into darkness. A flash of lightning illuminated a short stairwell. The musky bouquet of Fireblooms wafted up from below, and I had the impression of a much larger space beneath.

I had found what I was looking for, yet still I hesitated.

My mouth was dry. Suddenly I wasn't sure I *wanted* to know what lay below.

Was this where Colonel Grayloc kept her monograph?

Surely so secret a room was too great a precaution for any book, even one so singular?

What else might the colonel keep hidden below? What was it Odette had said?

The things she brought back...

But I had come too far to turn away now, so I descended into the darkness with hesitant steps, each one feeling like it might be my last.

Dust lay thick on the stone floor of the room below, and the musty air of something spoiled was hard to miss, even over the potency of the Firebloom petals that lay scattered like confetti. My nose wrinkled at the smell – like soured fruit or an overpowering perfume.

The room beneath the library was akin to a study, lit by an oil-fuelled storm lantern that threw dancing shadows upon walls lined with shelves. Most of these were empty, but those that were not held disturbing statuettes carved from a strange greenish soapstone whose grotesque and monstrous anatomies were thankfully obscured by the gloom. A few books stood in splendid isolation, as though some past librarian – Montague perhaps? – had come upon them and not dared remove these particular volumes of forgotten lore.

The remains of packing crates and scraps of wax paper lay discarded in a corner, telling me that whatever books and artefacts had once lined these shelves had long gone.

But where were they now?

My skin crawled just to look upon the books that remained, for the texture of their bindings was, even in this low light, impossible to mistake for anything other than skin.

Why would a colonel of the Astra Militarum possess such things...?

I could not bring myself to touch any of these books and thus learn their titles. Just being near them made me feel unclean and violated in the most profound way.

But worse than the hideous books, the fundamental *wrongness* of this space was impossible to ignore.

I knew from my time at Grayloc Manor that the dining room lay directly beneath the library. This space should not be able to exist. So blatant a violation of the natural physical laws set my teeth on edge and the contents of my stomach churning.

I could not bear to be here, but nor could I leave.

My body was at war with competing sensations of revulsion and the desire to know more.

My heart beat fast in my chest as I walked an ever-decreasing circle around the single table and chair in the centre of this impossible space. The lantern cast a fitful illumination over two books laid upon the table as though awaiting a reader to unlock their secrets. I felt unhealthily drawn to these books, as though an invisible cord linked me to them and was being wound tighter with every step I took.

No, these books weren't waiting for just any reader, they were waiting for me.

Denying the inevitable seemed pointless at this stage, so I pulled the chair back and sat down, feeling like my entire life and career had led me to this time and place.

The first book was thinner, and appeared to be a nondescript accounting ledger, while the second bore a cover stamped with the aquila and skull symbol of the Astra Militarum. While researching the campaigns of Lord Militant General Hexior Padira III during my time at the Cardophian Repository, my team and I had studied countless commanders' records kept in just such books.

Though it wasn't the same book as painted in the colonel's portrait, it bore the same circular symbol pierced by an arrow that book had possessed. I felt certain that this was the book that Garrett Grayloc and I had long sought.

Reluctant to touch this item, I instead lifted the ledger and scanned its contents.

The pages were arranged in columns and were filled with titles, dates, amounts of money and locations. It took the recognition of unwelcomely familiar titles I had seen in Montague Rhodes' journal for me to realise what I held. I looked up at the empty shelves as a rancid knot of horror made a clenched fist in my belly.

This was a record of the various locations to which the books in this study had been despatched. Some had been sent off-world to fellow connoisseurs of the perverse, others to hive nobility across Yervaunt. But a great many had been sent to the Cardophian Repository.

The texts in the library above were occasionally risqué, sometimes ill-advised to own, or borderline illegal, but every title I could bear to read in the ledger was utterly proscribed, a heretical book that would see its owner immediately executed for even knowing about, let alone possessing.

The things she brought back...

Colonel Grayloc had spread a host of blasphemous books throughout the subsector like a virus, and altogether too many were housed in *my* repository. Who knew what damage they were doing or how many innocents had become tainted by the heresy they contained?

I was hyperventilating at the scale of Colonel Grayloc's treachery, and I put the ledger back on the table as my eyes drifted to the larger book. This had to be the monograph Garrett Grayloc had spoken of, and though I absolutely did *not* want to look at what lay within, I knew that I must.

I had to have an explanation. I had to know *why* Colonel Grayloc had chosen to collect these hideous books and wilfully spread their blasphemous knowledge.

She was a hero of the Imperium, and her betrayal was a knife in my heart.

Tears streamed down my face as I opened the colonel's monograph and began to read.

I have studied the writings of many great men and women, the words of saints and traitors alike. Throughout my life, the written word has made me laugh, made me weep, brought me joy and pierced me with sorrow.

In all its forms it has brought me knowledge, wonder and escape.

The monograph of Elena Grayloc was the first book I wished I could unread.

It began innocuously enough, but soon descended into madness.

I cannot bring myself to set down every hideous detail of what was recorded in that damned book, a mercy for which you should be thankful. I suspected there were many journals before this, ones that dealt with the logistics of commanding a sector-wide campaign, but I never found them. By the time the words in the monograph had been written, however, the very worst canker had taken root in Elena Grayloc's soul.

Her descent into treachery began sometime after the liberation of Heliogabalus, a hive world where a debased pleasure cult had taken root in the noble family of an Imperial commander named Aphra Verlaine. The corruption had swiftly spread to his ancestral allies, ultimately resulting in a devastating civil war that spilled over into neighbouring systems.

Elena Grayloc had led her Tempestus Scions in a decapitating strike against Verlaine's palace, fighting their way to his throne room through hordes of shrieking cultists whose bodies had been transformed by grotesque surgeries and mutagenic drugs. Elaborate descriptions and detailed anatomical drawings of the foe were recorded in the monograph, abominations and things of such horror that it seemed impossible they could live beyond a single breath.

With the death of Aphra Verlaine, the Archenemy forces fell into disarray, the tide of the war turned, and Heliogabalus was liberated.

I cannot say for sure how her fall to darkness began; an artefact taken from the palace that carried with it some taint, a wound that festered and corrupted her from within. Or mayhap some psychic spoor of Verlaine's was laid within her skull that day. However it came to pass, when Elena Grayloc left Heliogabalus, it was as a servant of darkness.

Perhaps learning from what had befallen Aphra Verlaine, the corruption began to spread slowly through the regiment with a subtle insidiousness. A number of new martial customs and practices were established in every company, practices that allowed the evil of Chaos to corrupt every Guardsman within the regiment: tainted litanies of battle, blasphemous iconography, and a broadening of the rules of engagement that encouraged debauched conduct in the aftermath of battle.

With every campaign, the behaviour of the 83rd grew ever more hideous, with Colonel Grayloc overseeing scenes of mass murder, torture and depravity I could scarcely bear to read. Their victims were men and women, mothers, children and babes in arms. All were mere sport for the soldiers and officers of the regiment, their bodies simply canvasses upon which they wrought the most monstrous of evils.

Colonel Grayloc saw to it that her regiment was deployed on the front lines of the most hellish warzones, theatres of conflict where the terror of their debasements and horror of their actions could more easily be concealed. Each victory against

Archenemy forces saw yet more artefacts and tomes concealed from the quarantine teams of the ordos and despatched in secret to Grayloc Manor.

Perhaps to the very study in which I now sat.

My skin crawled at the thought of sitting in a room where so many cursed tomes and blasphemous artefacts had once been stored. What evil had seeped from their pages and into the very air? Was that what the Fireblooms were to conceal, the rank stench of perfidy?

I looked up from the flickering light cast by the storm-lantern, fear making me see monsters in the shadows on the walls and hear the muttering of the damned in the rumbles of thunder coming from the library above.

I had no wish to return to the colonel's monograph, but I felt compelled to read more.

On and on it went, revelling in heinous excesses. A carnivale of grotesqueries followed in the regiment's wake until finally, at the height of the terrible wars in the Ocyllaria subsector, the rumours surrounding the truth of Colonel Grayloc's regiment came to a head.

With mounting horror, I read of the colonel's frustrations as the net closed in on her corrupted regiment. Her every effort, combined with the fury of war and the capriciousness of the warp, had conspired to conceal their depravities for longer than ought to have been possible, but eventually the truth of their utter corruption could not be denied.

Imperial agents of the Holy Ordos, combined with elements of the Adepta Sororitas, at last moved against Colonel Grayloc, but it was already too late.

Sensing her enemies closing in, Elena Grayloc committed the ultimate betrayal of her species. Thankfully, I could not fully understand the nature of what she did, nor how she did it, but it seems clear she used the tainted artefacts in her possession to call for aid from the dark prince she now called master. Her words described this moment of apotheosis thusly:

'...a wondrous veil fell across the world, a shroud of Night, a tide of darkness to devour the slaves of the rotting corpse god. It rolled ever on, a black tide that spilled like tainted seed to corrupt the land with its glorious boon. And when it had supped all the life and vigour of this world, it reached up into the heavens to quench its endless thirst, and, one by one, snuffed out the stars as easily as I might douse a candle flame.'

I could barely draw breath by this point. Tears streamed down my face as the full extent of what Elena Grayloc had done became clear.

She had caused the Dawn of Dark Suns and killed everyone who knew of her sins.

The deaths of millions of men and women of the Astra Militarum lay upon her soul. Their blood was a red ocean upon her hands.

And her superiors had unwittingly rewarded her for it!

The sickness in my gut was almost too much to bear.

My heart pounded within my chest. Blood thundered in my ears.

Every time I thought I could not bear to read more, my eyes were irresistibly drawn back to the silken pages.

I took a deep, calming breath that helped not at all. I needed to know more.

After her monstrous crime, Colonel Grayloc returned to Yervaunt and, for a time it seemed, sought to curb her unholy appetites. I imagine they were harder to conceal without a war to cover the excesses of blood and depravity. But the blight on her soul would not be so easily restrained, and Grayloc Manor became a locus for those of like desires. Gatherings of the wicked and the damned became common. Dubbed *Maraviglia*, these were days-long debauches of sense-heightening drugs, unnatural couplings of orgiastic intensity, and ritualised murder that sent such jolts of revulsion through my mind that I feared for my very sanity.

I read accounts of men and women variously described as sensationalists, gourmands, profligates, epicures and libertines, who journeyed from afar and even from off-world to partake in the colonel's wild debauches. The descriptions of seething flesh, blood, bodily fluids and vile acts made me sick to picture them.

These guests came to the hidden jetty at the foot of the cliffs or arrived under cover of night at her cliffside landing platform. The descriptions of these *Maraviglia* defied belief, and the *activities* described were so outrageous and so unimaginable that I now understood the calamitous nature of the colonel's debts.

With trembling fingers, I closed the colonel's monograph.

I covered my face with my hands, weeping and shaking with the horror of what I had learned. My eyes were tightly shut, but upon the inner surfaces of my eyelids I saw only screaming faces twisted in lust, in anguish and in agony.

Each arrhythmic crash in my chest made me fear for my life. The rush of blood through my head felt like hammer blows upon my skull.

Then I understood that the pounding noise was not just in my head.

Heavy footfalls were descending the steps from the library.

I took my hands from my face, too terrified to move.

A brutish outline filled the doorway, a glowing storm-lantern held aloft before him.

Kyrano.

I rose from the chair on shaking legs as the servitor strode towards me with relentless purpose. He had already tried to murder me once before, and I knew I was powerless to stop him from succeeding this time.

'Please,' I begged the cybernetic as he approached.

I screamed as loud as I could, filling the small space with my anger and terror. It did no good, and Kyrano cared nothing for any noise I made. For all I knew the servitor and I were the only two souls left alive in Grayloc Manor.

Where was Garrett Grayloc? Had the servitor already murdered him in his sleep?

Was this *thing* still enacting Elena Grayloc's deviant orders beyond her death?

The servitor circled the table, and I could already imagine how his hands would feel around my neck as they crushed my throat. He would kill me with no remorse, no passion, and no care for the evil of what he was doing.

My legs spasmed with frantic tremors, the muscles twitching as my anger at this fate railed against the paralysis of terror. I pushed back from the table, thankful for its scale, as I circled in the opposite direction to the approaching servitor.

I could not hope to fight him, but perhaps I could delay him or, at the very least, hurt him.

Leaning over the table, I snatched up the storm lantern. Kyrano reached out to grab me, his fingers closing on my sleeve. Thankfully, his fingers had no real purchase, and his grip slid free. For a moment, it seemed I saw frustration in his one remaining eye, a hooded, flinty thing that had peered into the heart of true evil.

Glancing towards the stairs leading back to the library, I tried to imagine how quickly I could cover the distance. Could I outrun Kyrano?

He was not fast, but he was utterly relentless.

I judged my chances poor, but what other choice was there?

Feinting one way, I bolted for the stairs. Faster than I would have believed possible, the murderous servitor came after me. I heard the thud of his booted feet behind me and reacted with an act of instinctive self-preservation.

I swung the storm lantern like a club and managed to smash it against the side of his metalled skull. Burning oil flared in a sheet of bright orange fire. It filled the hidden study with light, and engulfed the servitor's upper body in flame.

Pools of burning oil landed on the table and hungrily spread to the two books. I hurled the smashed remains of the lantern to the floor and ran for the stairs, taking them two at a time. I did not look back, and heard the servitor thrashing around the study.

I had not thought servitors capable of feeling pain, but was in that moment glad it seemed not to be the case here. I hoped the flames would consume Kyrano and whatever was left upon the shelves.

Smoke followed me up the stairs, and I took a shuddering breath as I emerged into the library. Rain hammered on the skylights and a forking bolt of lightning split the sky. I drew in sucking breaths of air, wondering if I could somehow seal off the study and trap the murderous servitor below.

A flare of light behind me told me I had no time.

Kyrano was climbing the stairs after me. The flames had burned away much of his suit, revealing the scorched skin of his torso. Beaten metal gleamed through pallid skin criss-crossed with crude surgical scars that looked as though they had been inflicted as much to hurt as to heal.

I turned and ran for the library doors, pausing as I saw the stern face of Colonel Grayloc staring down at me from the frame of her portrait. Even then, in full knowledge of her monstrous deeds and the millions of lives she sacrificed, I could see no hint of that evil lurking in her eyes. She appeared to be every inch the Imperial hero she was believed to be. That such depravity and such a black and soulless heart could hide in plain sight behind a mask of civility and a veneer of civilisation was the true horror.

Evil walked amongst us and we knew it not.

Thudding footsteps galvanised me into action, and I ran to the portrait to seize the weapons hung beneath it. I have no love of firearms, but Teodoro and I both held to the view that every Imperial citizen ought to at least maintain a basic competence with weaponry.

The weapons were old, and neither had likely been fired in years.

I could see the plasma pistol had no powercell in place, so snatched the lasrifle down from its mount, quickly hauling back on the charging lever by the trigger guard. Even a Whiteshield knows to strip an unknown weapon down before risking pulling the trigger, but that was a luxury I could not afford.

The lasrifle hummed as power flowed into its firing mechanism, but any hopes of using the weapon died as the powercell registered as empty. I wanted to weep with frustration.

I dropped the lasrifle and took up Colonel Grayloc's power sabre. I thumbed the activation rune at the pommel. Even if its charge was depleted, I could at least swing it and hope its edge was sharp.

Footsteps sounded, and I gagged at the thought of the servitor's rotten-meat body touching me. A deafening rumble of thunder crashed overhead. I thought I heard my name. The blade sparked to life. I screamed as I spun around and swung it with all my strength.

The energised edge struck flesh, carving through meat and bone, muscle and organs. Blood sprayed from the wound, a catastrophic amount jetting from ruptured flesh. It sprayed my face, blinding me. I ripped the blade loose and lifted it high, ready to strike again.

I blinked away the blood in my eyes.

I had not killed Kyrano.

I had killed Garrett Grayloc.

His body lay on the floor of the library in a vast lake of blood, split from collarbone to pelvis. I backed away in horror at what I had done. His head turned to me, incomprehension flickering in his eyes as the last vestiges of life left him.

'No... no... no...' I cried, as though forceful enough a denial might undo this murder.

I saw him die in front of me, and looked up as I saw Kyrano approach. Smoke and flames lit the library behind him, and he no longer had his storm lantern. I saw him register the presence of Garrett Grayloc's body, but could not tell what reaction – if any – his master's death had upon him.

Still holding the colonel's sword, I ran for the library doors, barrelling through them, breathless and horrified at what I had done. My entire body was shaking with fear and revulsion. What had I done? I had killed an innocent man! I bent double and expelled the contents of my stomach on the floor.

I wanted to sink to my knees and curl up into a ball. I wanted this tide of horrible things to stop, to leave me alone. My mind could not cope with so many nightmarish revelations, with such bloodshed and murder.

Looking back into the library, I saw Kyrano bend to lift the lasrifle from the floor where I had thrown it. He expertly swapped out the empty powercell for a fresh one and rose smoothly as he snapped back the charging lever to render it lethal.

Even armed with the power sabre I could not fight a deadly killer armed with a rifle.

'No,' I said, but this time the word was not said in reaction to an accidental murder, rather it was a declaration that I would not end my days squatting and afraid.

Pushing myself upright, I ran for the staircase that led down to the vestibule.

* * *

I emerged from Grayloc Manor into a thunderstorm of epic proportions. Bruised clouds of lightning-shot darkness pressed down on the landscape, and a deluge set to drown the world fell from the sky in howling torrents. The power sabre spat and hissed as I half ran, half stumbled around the corner of the building.

Looking out to sea, the storm was even more impressive.

Purple and blue columns of lightning battled on the horizon and the normally calm bay within the crater raged against the coastline. I saw ships smashed to tinder at their moorings, and pummelling waves broke against structures hundreds of metres from the shoreline.

Across the headland, the temple was in flames, and not even the downpour could quench the conflagration. And was it my imagination or did I see the figure of a man in priestly vestments within, vainly attempting to fight the blaze?

I could think of no more apt a metaphor of my time in Vansen Falls.

I turned the corner, heading for the cliffside hangar where the Kiehlen 580 groundcar was housed. If I could just get the car, I could escape this nightmare. I passed the winding path leading to the follies, and stopped at the entrance to the maze as I saw my path to the hangar was blocked.

Kyrano stood illuminated in the glow of the burning manor. Flames leapt from its gable windows and billowed high from the shattered skylights in the library.

I had stupidly assumed the servitor would blindly follow me, but of course he would take the more direct route. He must have anticipated I would run to the hangar and had chosen a route to intercept my flight.

His augmetic eye blinked red and he marched towards me, seemingly untroubled by the horrific wounds wrought upon his body. The rain slicked his ruined flesh, and he held the colonel's rifle across his chest. My strike with the storm lantern had wounded him terribly, the burning fuel devouring his dead skin and leaving him all but crippled.

But even crippled he would easily kill me.

His pace was unrelenting. Not fast, but fast enough to catch me no matter where I ran.

Heading for the follies seemed foolish, so I turned and entered the maze. My only hope was that Kyrano did not know its paths. Or even if he did, that I could navigate them faster and emerge while he was still within.

Perhaps then I could reach the groundcar and escape.

I plunged into its tangled depths.

The rain beat down as I pushed deep into the maze, washing my face of tears. My feet slipped on the muddy paths, and several times I fell as I lost my footing. Thunder crashed, but even over its echoing rumbles, I could still hear Kyrano following me.

I blundered through the maze, scratching my face bloody on grasping thorns and deactivating the sabre's blade. I had no idea how much power was left to it, and saw no need to drain what little remained until I needed it.

I struggled to focus as I ran, remembering the times I had navigated the maze and committed its paths to memory. I prayed to the Emperor I was remembering things correctly, and that Kyrano had not seen fit to walk within or learn its many twists and turns.

It was perhaps a vain and desperate hope, but it was the only hope I had.

I pushed onwards, turning and pressing ever deeper into the maze, not knowing if any turn would bring me face to face with the servitor. I gripped the sabre tight, ready to swing it again if I saw him. My hands were shaking, and I tried to keep the memory of Garrett Grayloc's ruptured body from my mind. I knew that if I let thoughts of what I had done consume me, then I would be overwhelmed and lost.

At last I emerged into the centre of the maze, and let out a strangled cry of relief.

The strangely androgynous statue of pinkish coral gleamed in the rain, its surfaces slick and dripping with water. I stumbled forwards and all but collapsed onto the marble bench encircling it, gasping for breath.

I needed to move. I needed to get back out to reach the groundcar.

But I had nothing left to draw upon. My reserves of strength and resilience were spent.

The driving rain and crashing waves were oddly muted through the crooked hedgerows of the maze, but I could hear a curious sound, the source of which I could not at first identify.

A splitting sound, like hairline cracks spreading through a pane of glass.

The tenor of the sound changed, becoming the wet sucking noise of something being pulled from the cloying grasp of a swamp. The rain was beating down harder now, and another flash of lightning bathed the sky in violet light.

My memory flew back to the long causeway traversing the hideous marshland that so disquieted me on my journey to Grayloc Manor. My mind flooded with images of dead and misbegotten things festering unseen in the dark.

I turned slowly as I felt a growing sensation of warmth behind me.

Now I understood the source of the sound, and the fraying weave of my sanity begin to unravel yet further.

The statue at the centre of the maze was *moving*.

It rippled with a grotesque internal movement, its once rigid structure now pliant as though the torrential rain had softened it. No longer did it appear to be made of ridged and nubbed coral, but of pinkish folds of layered flesh that were unfolding like a night-blooming flower. It stretched and swelled, as if something confined within its moist innards was struggling to push itself free.

Like a newborn pushing against the membrane of an egg sac…

Even as I watched, the stretched *skin* of the statue tore in a jagged, vertical line. Blood and fluid spilled from the rent, and the stench of burnt sugar drove me to my feet as the mass of the statue peeled away like meat no longer supported by a skeleton.

Embedded within the folds of flesh were splintered bone shards, scores of gleaming teeth and discarded networks of veins and half-digested organs.

And in the centre of this mass was a bent and crooked figure.

Its wrinkled and ancient skin was wet and slathered with a clear, amniotic slime, like the princeps of a battle Titan removed from its command tank. The awful thing faced away from me, and I saw a blasted hole in the back of its head like a gunshot wound. Threads of light and gossamer-thin flesh held the skull together, and but for them, the creature's cranium would have collapsed to ruin long ago.

Long silver hair clung to its hunched and twisted back, and beneath the translucent skin, I saw a spine that had been shattered by some ferocious impact.

Like falling from a cliff…

The thing turned to face me, and its awful, ravaged appearance was horribly familiar.

The patrician features, the eyes of rich gold-green…

Elena Grayloc.

I fell into the maelstrom of her eyes.

She was the most beautiful human being I had ever seen.

Young and filled with the vitality only those who have never known loss can possess. This was Elena Grayloc before her long years in the Astra Militarum, an idealised version of the person she believed herself to be.

Her eyes met mine, and the sound of the storm was instantly replaced by the soft sound of gentle waves lapping on a beach. Sunlight bathed me, and I trembled at the feeling of a silken touch winding its way around the back of my neck.

'Auburn suits you,' she said in a whispered voice.

I looked past her and saw that I now stood on a golden beach, with an ocean of cerulean blue stretching out before me. A copper sun warmed my skin and the sound of a child's laughter drifted from somewhere just out of sight.

Elena Grayloc slowly circled me, her fingertips trailing down the length of my arm.

I followed the movement, and the breath caught in my throat as I saw how smooth my skin had become. I lifted my hand, turning it over and marvelling at its flawless youth. My nails were cherry red, my palms supple.

Reaching up to my face, I ran my hand over my cheeks and neck.

Like my arm, the skin was taut and porcelain smooth as it had been in my youth.

'You're beautiful,' said Elena Grayloc, stepping back to admire my physique.

Only then did I realise I was naked, and one look down at my body revealed that all the ravages of age had been undone. Flesh that sagged from muscle was once again tight, the spots and blotches of age had vanished, and a strength flowed through me that I had not known in decades.

'Intoxicating, isn't it?' said Elena Grayloc, seeing my cheeks flush and my chest rise and fall with unbridled excitement. 'How swiftly we forget the vigour of youth. How easily we accept the decline of age and think it normal. But it doesn't have to be that way.'

The youthful energy filling my limbs and my heart and lungs was exhilarating. I felt the urge to wield this incredible power;

to run, to fight, to couple with beautiful people until dawn crested the horizon. Such power was mine, had *always* been mine, but the passing of the years had stolen it from me without me even noticing.

No, it was worse than that. I had *let* it go.

I had foregone those pleasures of the flesh, denying my senses the experience of what it meant to be human. I looked back on the ascetic path my life had taken and felt a boiling wave of anger fill me.

'You can have it all again, Teresina,' said Elena Grayloc, stepping towards me and holding up a jagged shard of glass. I saw myself reflected in its silver depths, my once stern and lined face softened and young again.

The colour that had only recently begun to seep back into my hair was now fully restored. My lips were once again full, my cheekbones clearly defined and my eyes alive with the vitality and promise of youth.

'What is this...?' I said, and even my voice was renewed.

'It is *life*,' said Elena Grayloc. 'And it can be yours again. You have a mind of brilliance and flesh I can make whole again. If you let me...'

She reached out and placed her hands on my flat stomach. I felt motion stir within me, and gasped as the potential of new life fluttered in my once again fertile womb. My hand slipped protectively to the idea of a swelling in my belly, and tears pricked the corners of my eyes.

'Yes,' said Elena Grayloc. 'We will put that womb of yours to good use.'

I frowned at that, but she moved in close to me, and I forgot her presumption.

Her hands slipped around the small of my back, and my own hands laced themselves naturally around her neck. We stood facing one another like lovers.

We moved closer, but I could not say who was pulling who.

Elena Grayloc was beautiful in a way I had never experienced before. I wanted to know what she tasted like, how her skin felt upon mine. The scent of Fireblooms filled my senses and the heat of her skin was like a furnace on me.

I ran my hands through her hair, feeling the fused and melted shards of skull, the rubbery texture of overcooked meat under my fingertips. Fused brain matter and bone. Flash-boiled cranial fluids spilled over my hands.

I didn't care. I wanted to be with her, to lie upon the warm sand and let her sink into my flesh, to let her know me completely.

She felt my exploration of her shattered skull and said, 'The bastard killed me, you know.'

'Who?'

She ignored the question as her lips brushed against my ear. 'Came up behind me as I wrought destruction on His temple. Shot me in the back of the head and then threw me from the cliff. But you can make me whole again, Teresina. You can give me my life back.'

'Anything,' I answered.

Something inside me was screaming, a silent prisoner with no voice in a cell with no window.

I knew I should listen to it, that what it was shrieking was vitally important, but the power surging through my rejuvenated flesh was too strong, and too desperate to cling to this rebirth.

'Let me in,' said Elena Grayloc. 'My body is too broken, its hurts too deep to heal. The cocoon of my *Inamorata* has sustained me, but its power is fading. You have a mind I yearn to inhabit, a body I *can* renew. A body I *have* renewed. You feel it already, don't you? The siren song of youth. It calls to you with all the promises of immortality, yes? Let me in and I will show you things you could never imagine, experiences you could never know.'

She leaned in and kissed me, and I felt the warmth of her tongue part my lips.

Its texture was rough, its wriggling motion pushing deeper into my throat.

I gagged as I tasted the reek of warm earth, the scratching texture of insect-like cilia as they wormed her tongue down my throat. The heat of Elena Grayloc's body changed from pleasurable warmth to a burning fire. I felt as though my flesh was slowly melting, becoming soft and malleable as she pressed herself against me.

The hardness of her fingers sank into the softness of my hips, pulling us together as though to press us into one body. I tried to resist, but her grip was locked to my flesh. Her tongue was no longer a tongue, but a writhing, frond-tipped proboscis that exuded a sickly sweet sap within me.

My stomach churned with motion, and again I felt the promise of new life. I felt the skin of my belly stretch as something new and living pulsed with sickening vitality, but this would be no innocent child, it would be a sickly parasite that would draw the life from me with every beat of its filthy heart.

My body could be young again, but would this be the price I must pay?

Not like this! Not like this!

Too often we look back on our lives and wish we could have our time again.

To do better, to do more, to walk the paths not taken.

But I have loved and I have learned. I have done my best to pass on my experiences to others. And in that I have no regrets.

In the end, I think that was what saved me.

Regret was what Elena Grayloc was counting on, a sense of my wasted potential that could be realised if I would only offer my flesh to her. And, yes, I sometimes thought of how the course of our lives would have been different had Teodoro and I chosen to have children, but I never once considered our choice to be a mistake.

But surrendering to Elena Grayloc would be the costliest mistake of my life.

She felt my resistance and her fury was terrible to behold. She clung to my hips, her fingertips like hot pokers burrowing into the bone of my pelvis.

But my anger was the equal of her desire.

I dug my fingers into the shattered edges of her skull and pulled, furiously tearing chunks of hair-covered bone away.

She tried to pull back, but our lips were still locked together. I bit down on her proboscis tongue, sawing my teeth from side to side. The fleshy organ burst apart in my mouth, and I tasted warm fluid like stagnant swamp water. Rank clots of putrid blood made me gag as I now pushed her away.

I sank to my knees, bent double, and retched up a torrent of black pulsing *things* that burrowed into the sand to escape the glare of the sun's light. My stomach heaved again, disgorging a host of wet, slithering creatures like eyeless glossy eels.

My hands were bloody to the elbows, and I looked up at Elena Grayloc.

Not as she *wished* she had been.

But as she *was*.

In the blink of an eye, I was once again in the maze. Hammering sheets of rain drenched me to the bone. I was on my knees, holding sodden chunks of softened pink bone in my hands, from which hung thin wisps of silver hair.

Elena Grayloc loomed over me, her veil of glamours stripped away. The fleshy cocoon was draped around her like a shawl, and her broken body writhed in a final act of transformation. Violet light suffused her rippling flesh as it budded new limbs like pulsing tumours, extruded new organs and swelled with a power bolstered by what she had so very nearly stolen from me.

What I had so very nearly *given* her...

Her eyes were no longer rich gold-green, but a terrible, predatory neon-yellow.

'You could have had it all!' she shrieked, her face angular and daemonic. It was no longer human, yet possessed an alluring beauty that both repulsed and entranced my senses at the same time. I threw aside the gelatinous mass of brain and skull fragments clinging to my fingers and rose to face her.

'I do not want what you have to give,' I said, knowing she was going to kill me.

A succubus denied cannot allow those who reject it to live.

Her arms were slender, hooked things, her fingers no longer recognisable as human, but fused together like the claws of some mutant crustacean. She reached for me, ready to tear me apart, but then her head lifted and I saw a towering fury enter those coruscating eyes.

'You!' she shrieked. ***'Faithless coward! Come to finish what you started?'***

I twisted my head and through tears of frustration and rainwater, I saw Kyrano enter the heart of the maze, the lasrifle still held at his chest. He lifted his hand and fastened his grip around the bronze plate covering the lower half of his face.

I had no idea what he was doing until I saw the servo-muscles grafted to his arm flex.

He pulled at the plate, slowly prising it from his skin. Blood poured down his face as medical sutures and tissue grafts tore loose from their bone anchors. I saw the effort and agony it was taking Kyrano to tear it loose, his organic eye filled with furious determination.

Finally, the plate came loose in a welter of blood. It trailed an arc of viscous fluids, fused scraps of flesh and powdered bone fragments. A snaking length of rubber hose trailed from Kyrano's gullet, an oesophageal implant that was part rebreather, part digestive tract.

The servitor dropped the plate and ripped the tube from his throat. Yellowish stomach acid and intestinal fluids dribbled from its frayed end as he pulled it free. His exposed mouth was a ruin of splintered teeth and rotten gums. He shouted something with the tenor of a command, but its meaning was lost in a wet horror of bubbling blood and phlegm.

It was a death rattle and birth cry all in one.

I could not understand what he was saying or if what he was shouting were even words.

If they were, then they were the shrieks of a damned and tortured soul.

He shouted again, and this time I understood him.

Get down!

I dropped to the mud of the clearing as Kyrano shouldered the lasrifle and opened fire. A storm of blitzing las-fire filled the air, every bolt aimed with pinpoint accuracy. The servitor walked calmly forwards, the colonel's rifle blazing on full-auto.

Elena Grayloc came apart in an explosion of gore.

Half formed and melted bones exploded in the searing heat of the las-fire. Rotten meat vaporised in stinking clouds, and her monstrous limbs tumbled away as they were cut from her in the unending fusillade.

Eventually only a swaying trunk of bloodied meat remained.

Kyrano pumped shot after shot into Elena Grayloc's remains until the weapon ran dry, the powercell whining empty and the charging lever racked back against the breech.

Nothing remained that was recognisable as having once been human.

A lasrifle might not be the most powerful weapon in the Imperial arsenal, but at close range and in the hands of a skilled shooter it was devastating. Kyrano slung the rifle and spat a mouthful of black and oily phlegm at Elena Grayloc's vaporised corpse.

I had no real idea of the diabolical means by which she had sustained her life, but I felt sure nothing could survive such thorough destruction.

I rolled onto my haunches and squinted up through the rain.

Kyrano stood above me, a thick hand held out to me. His misshapen jaw struggled to form the shape of words.

'Am. Not. Servitor,' he said, and those three words told a horrifying narrative of cybernetically enforced slavery.

He hauled me to my feet, and I looked into his eye, now seeing life and soul filling the void behind it, a soul freed from what must have felt like an eternity in a lightless gulag.

'She did this to you,' I said, and he nodded. Perhaps it was the rain or perhaps he wept; I could not tell and would not shame him by asking.

I gestured towards the burnt ruin of flesh spread out in the mud.

'Is it over?' I asked.

Kyrano looked back to Grayloc Manor and shook his head.

'Not. Yet.'

We drove the Kiehlen 580 from the hangar and I watched through the rear window as Grayloc Manor burned. The storm had blown out with the colonel's death and the flames were eager to devour her ancestral home. Between us, we emptied two dozen canisters of promethium throughout its structure, taking particular care to ensure that every volume in the library would burn to ash.

Orange flames lit the night as we drove away from Vansen Falls, and I felt a particular symmetry had been achieved now that both promontories were home to fire-struck ruins.

I shall not fill these pages with the mundane details of the journey back to Servadac Magna, save to elaborate upon some gaps in my knowledge that Kyrano was able to fill.

Speaking was still difficult for him, for his transformation into cyborg had not been gentle, and the psychic blockers that had kept him mute and servile were akin to burning nails hammered into the centre of his brain. With Elena Grayloc's death, their intensity was waning, but it would take time for him to fully recover, if he ever would.

He told me of how he had seen Elena Grayloc on the headland on the night of the previous storm, arms raised as if conducting its wrath. While her attention was fixed on whatever sorcery she was conducting, the agony of his burning nails had receded just enough for him to take the colonel's plasma pistol from the library and get close enough to her to put a single, overpowered shot through her skull. Such a wound ought to have killed her instantly, but her dark masters were not yet ready to release their mortal avatar.

Just as she re-established psychic control, Kyrano had kicked her from the cliff with his last independent thought. He had no knowledge of how she had come to be encased within the *Inamorata*, but it seemed clear to me that Garrett Grayloc was not the innocent I had feared when I killed him. I could only surmise that he had been a willing participant in his mother's scheme of rebirth. It was impossible to know for sure, but it was difficult to believe he had not been party to events at Grayloc Manor.

And the night I had woken to find Kyrano standing at my bed with what looked like a garrotte of twisted sheets in his hands? He had not been trying to kill me, he had been *saving* me. Elena Grayloc's malign influence permeated the entire house, and in her deathly, regenerative state, it seemed her mind roamed the site of her death with only fragmentary knowledge of what and who she was.

Seeing a stranger in her bed had likely stoked a murderous rage in her.

Kyrano had heard me choking and had rushed in to save me, and had in turn found himself the object of the colonel's psycho-kinetic fury.

Had the figure I had seen on the headland been a phantasm also conjured by her gestating nightmares? It was the only explanation I could think of, but who can know the minds of the mad or the designs of one fallen to the Ruinous Powers?

Who would wish to...?

I slept some of the way, exhaustion and the after-effects of adrenaline leaving me alternately weeping, angry, cold, terrified and determined.

The sun was cresting the horizon as the spires of Servadac Magna came into view.

'Where. To. Go. Now?' asked Kyrano, working his jaw from side to side.

I had given the matter careful consideration on the journey back.

Events at Grayloc Manor would eventually come to light. Investigators would find the corpse of Garrett Grayloc and perhaps they might even be able to positively identify him. It wouldn't take long to trace a line from him back to me, so we only had a short window in which to act.

Both books in the hidden study had been destroyed, but I remembered enough of what was contained in the ledger to know that the colonel's poisonous collection had spread far and wide. We would not be able to reach them all, but we could at least make a start.

'The Cardophian Repository,' I said.

And now we come full circle.

The candle is almost burned down, and this missive is complete.

Now you know the truth of what happened at Grayloc Manor. Now you know the truth of the Dawn of Dark Suns.

I warned you that you would not thank me for these revelations.

Kyrano has almost finished his task, and the acrid reek of promethium fills the repository.

We spent the day gathering as much as we could fit onto an old cargo-8 and, using my access codes to the repository, which were still valid thanks to my regular consultations with the staff, entered and poured the flammable liquid wherever I could remember books of the colonel's being deposited.

I lament that I can see no other way to rid this world of Elena Grayloc's corruption, for who knows how far the malign power in her books has spread? It pains me to do this, for I have many fond memories of this building. But for all we know, every book on every shelf might be infected with the horrors Colonel Grayloc brought back from the howling darkness she found in the hostile void of space.

Nor are Kyrano and I exempt from this purge.

He lived with her taint in his mind for decades, and if I touch my hand to my belly, I fancy I can feel a tremor of movement. I cannot be certain, but the chance that Elena Grayloc was able to pass on something of her treachery into my flesh is too great a risk.

No, this must end tonight.

I look up and Kyrano nods. Our task is almost at an end.

I doubt this record will survive, for Kyrano is nothing if not thorough.

The truth of setting this down, then, is that it has only been for me.

Catharsis perhaps. Or maybe it is something more, something I cannot express but feel must somehow be recorded, even if the reasons for that are entirely selfish.

Once an archivist, always an archivist, I suppose.

Kyrano has lit the flare.
It burns so very bright.
So, too, shall we.[5]

---

[5] Inquisitorial Note: The above confession was discovered in the burned ruins of the Cardophian Repository on Yervaunt. How it survived the fire that destroyed the rest of the building is a matter of some interest, as the murderer, Teresina Sullo, and her servitor accomplice were thorough in their application of flammable accelerants. How much of this record can be considered truthful is impossible to verify at this time, as both bodies found at the site bore signs of deep psychic manipulation. It is our recommendation that their remains be contained and transported securely to the nearest ordo facility for further psycho-forensic examination. We also recommend that this record be sealed to Omicron-level clearance and that investigations begin into Grayloc Trading Cartel. A last recommendation is that an interrogation be undertaken of the sole survivor of the campaign colloquially known as the Dawn of Dark Suns at the earliest opportunity. Ave Imperator!

FIVE CANDLES

Lora Gray

In Havisa's dream, her fire was not fading. She was young and strong again, blazing bright as she always should have, an unstoppable force, spear in hand. A beautiful, terrible Aqshian warrior...

Havisa coughed herself awake, jerking upright where she'd fallen asleep on the stool beside her narrow bed. Smoke stabbed her lungs and eyes, acrid and stinking of scorched rushes and burning timber. *Haze.* She couldn't see. *Fire.* She could barely breathe. Hacking and swearing, pain lancing through her arthritic hip, Havisa limped to the door and shouldered it open.

Smoke chased her outside, choking out the sunlight, the whole world dim and sallow. Or perhaps the sun had never brightened fully that day. It was why she had lit her candles that morning, after all. Dawn had seemed too feeble to chase away the death magic. It did no good to tempt fate when she was all alone and so far from the village. Havisa had lit her candles and had fallen asleep, leaving them unattended...

A timber popped and Havisa backpedalled, shielding her face. Flames licked up and out of the narrow window. Everything was burning...

Havisa smacked herself. 'You fool.' Ignoring the grinding protests of her hip and back, she grabbed the empty bucket beside the door. 'You stupid, old fool.' Gaping at that fire wouldn't extinguish it.

Hobbling and huffing, Havisa hurried to the withered stand of trees and into the scrub-strangled gully beyond. Her eyes stung – from the embers, she told herself, not tears – and her lungs clenched, but she ran as fast as her body could carry her, until her knee finally buckled. She skidded down the bank of the gully, a flail of arms and ragged skirts, into the ruddy muck at the bottom. The bucket splashed into the water beside her. Havisa reached for it.

On the opposite bank, a dark shape rose from all fours.

He stood, a young man, tall, thin, dressed in black and backlit against the sallow sky. His cheeks were unshaven and patchy, jaw jutting from beneath the scruff. His hair was a mangy tangle that sprouted a pair of flies when he lifted his head.

Any other time, Havisa would have demanded to know who he was, why he was here on her land, but she didn't have time to wonder. Her whole world was going up in flames.

Havisa plunged her bucket into the shallow water.

'You stink of smoke, old woman,' the stranger said, his voice a deep, uneven timbre.

'Of course I "stink of smoke!"' Havisa lost her grip on the bucket, coughed, and cursed. 'The house on the hill there, my house, is burning!'

'And you're going to extinguish it all by yourself?'

'It's not going to put itself out!' Havisa hiked her muddy skirts to her knees and turned to amble up the embankment towards her house. Had she been younger, she could have carried twice as much water. Had she been younger, maybe she could have asked this stranger for help without fearing judgement or pity. But she wasn't young any more, was she? She was old, too weak to do anything properly...

Havisa didn't anticipate the stranger's hands when he grabbed her by the scruff and shoulder and hefted her up and over the lip of the gully. Havisa stumbled, water sloshing onto her feet, and sputtered, but the stranger was already loping past her, carrying his cloak, knotted into a makeshift water bladder, over his shoulder.

Havisa's pride stung, but she was far too frantic and winded to protest. By the time she reached her house and tossed her meagre bucket of water onto the flames, the stranger was already sprinting towards the river again, a trough in his arms, for whatever good it would do. A single room didn't take very long to burn.

She did her best to quash the fire, throwing armfuls of dirt onto the flames when they licked their way out of the narrow window, trying to smother rogue embers with her cloak, but finally, she resigned herself to save what she could. She darted inside, through the crackling flames and haze. She had only just retrieved a small sack of silver and her precious spear from its place beside the door, when the roof shuddered and collapsed inward.

Havisa careened from the rush of searing air, cinders biting into the exposed flesh of her arms and face as she fell, panting and coughing so violently she felt as if her lungs might lurch up and out of her throat, wet and blackened. She closed her eyes, struggling for oxygen, her skin prickling, her entire body throbbing from the running, the falling, too much smoke, exhaustion.

Heartbreak.

She concentrated on the pain. Not the loss. Not the horrible, gnawing grief of seeing the last remains of her sad little life burning to nothing. What did she have now? She had no friends;

they'd all died as Aqshians should, gloriously, the heat of battle consuming them when they were young. Her fire had never been as fierce as theirs and she'd committed the cardinal sin of surviving, of growing *old*. She was a coward. Useless. Where would she go? Who would have her now?

Gritting her teeth, Havisa sat up, resolutely grinding an ember into the back of her hand to keep her focused. A shadow fell over her. Havisa started, but it was only the stranger, stepping past her and grunting as he heaved the water from the feed trough onto the smouldering ruins, though the fire was already dying. The crumbled roof had smothered the worst of it, and the dead earth surrounding her home wasn't going to feed it further.

Hands on his knees, the stranger panted, tongue lolling from his mouth a moment before he turned to Havisa and asked, 'Do you live here all by yourself?'

Havisa scowled. It was easier to embrace anger and pride than sadness. Gripping her spear, she grunted and pulled herself to her feet. 'What business is that of yours?'

The stranger shrugged and sniffed, scratching absently at his matted hair as he straightened. 'If there are bodies to bury, now would be the time to do it – while there's still daylight.'

Havisa snorted. 'There is no one else.' Nobody in the village would have her. She narrowed her eyes. 'Why did you help me? Who are you?'

'I'm Eudon.' He smiled, a small tick of his lips that was more amused than friendly. 'And you're welcome.'

'I didn't ask for your help.' Havisa turned her head and spat. 'What do you want?'

'Is it a crime to help an old woman?'

Havisa laughed bitterly. Her lungs pinched a warning. 'That depends on the old woman. I don't recognise your accent. Why are you here?'

Eudon turned to peer past the smoking heap of her hovel

towards the foothills swelling to the east. 'I bring news of what they're calling the necroquake. The death magic. You've heard of Shyish's curse, haven't you, old woman?'

'Havisa!'

Eudon cocked his head as if weighing her reaction before smoothing the air with his fingers. 'My apologies. Havisa.'

Havisa prickled a moment longer before grumbling, 'Of course I've heard of the death magic.' She had seen the unnatural mists that scattered dead field mice and birds in its wake instead of dew, bloody footprints on the riverbank from animals with too many toes. She had heard the far-off shrieking in the night and the voices moaning in languages she'd never heard before.

'That is why I am here,' Eudon said. 'I must find the nearest village and warn them of the threat. The danger coming is worse than any of you could possibly imagine.'

Havisa considered Eudon. He could be lying, but his boots were worn and scuffed, his clothes a shamble, dusty from weeks of Aqshian roads. He looked well travelled, at least. 'Well,' she said, rolling her shoulders, wincing at a crick deep in her neck, 'if you were looking for the village, you were going the wrong way.'

'It's fortunate I found you, then, isn't it? Perhaps we could travel together. After all, you'll need to go to the village yourself now, won't you? There's nothing for you here.'

Havisa puckered her mouth, a lingering cough wracking her aching chest. The thought of facing that village full of young warriors, who did nothing but scoff and sneer every time she ventured anywhere near them, made her gut sour. If they ever discovered she'd burned down her own house because she'd fallen asleep... Perhaps she should stay there, among the charred remains of her life, and accept the fate she'd made. Maybe she could somehow redeem herself by dying nobly in the night, battling the evil death magic when it came to feast on her old bones, a final burst of courage.

But how could she simply throw her life away?

The shame she felt was so heavy, her voice trembled when she finally said, 'I don't need your company or your protection.' She turned and swallowed past a knot in her throat. 'But I owe you for your help.' She tightened her hand on her spear and began to amble down the narrow path, away from what had once been her home. 'Come on then. What are you waiting for? An invitation?'

Havisa was trying to remember the name of her nephew – her late sister's son who lived in the next village over, beyond the foothills to the east, the only family she could think of that might be obligated to take her in – when Eudon asked, 'Have you heard of the Black Dog of Mhurghast?'

'A dog? No. I haven't heard of it.' Havisa reaffirmed her grip on her spear, leaning heavily into it as she walked. The afternoon was already fading, and though Havisa was fairly certain they would reach the village by sundown, they didn't have much time, especially if she was going to send word to her nephew.

'The Black Dog of Mhurghast is no ordinary animal,' Eudon said, falling into step beside her. She still couldn't decide if she was grateful or irritated that he hadn't once complained about the pace she'd set. 'It is a huge beast. Terrible. Cursed by Shyish. It moves silently in the darkness, waiting for hapless travellers to feast upon. Its eyes are red as blood, its appetite ferocious. They say if you happen upon it at a crossroads at midnight, it will devour you.'

Havisa laughed a little too loudly before coughing. Damn that fire and its smoke. Damn her ancient, crippled lungs. 'Is this what you're going to tell the village council? A story meant to frighten old women and children?'

Eudon stepped in front of her, his long jaw tense and set. He smelled sour as he leaned close. 'It's no story,' he said, his breath rotten. There was a strange, excited light in his eyes, as if he was waiting for her reaction. As if he was playing a horrible trick, telling a joke only he understood. 'The Black Dog is very real. You should never underestimate the powers of Shyish.'

Havisa squinted up at him. 'And you shouldn't underestimate Aqshian women. Even the old ones.' Havisa lifted her spear, of half a mind to crack Eudon across the shins, but she only huffed and shoved her way past him to continue down the path.

Was he laughing at her? Mocking her? She wouldn't play the old fool for this young stranger. She wouldn't be the butt of his joke. She'd get enough of that in the village. Squaring her shoulders as much as her stooped back would allow, she lifted her chin and quickened her pace.

She didn't tell Eudon what she saw from the corner of her eye. As the sun began its descent, she did not mention the strange, four-legged shadow that disappeared when she turned to look at it directly. A glimpse of a dark muzzle bursting with teeth. A curved, bristling back. Long legs trotting, keeping pace with her.

Waiting.

By the time the council gathered in the village hall, night had fallen. Tapers flickered on every sill and tabletop, a hundred wax pillars, their flames straining upward and chasing the shadows from the corners of the long, narrow room. A hearth blazed on the back wall, well stoked and crackling steadily. The council sat before it, their backs stiff and proud as they listened to Eudon.

From her place in the far corner, Havisa shifted and begged her bad hip to finally pop. The stool they'd given her was squat and full of splinters. If it hadn't been for Eudon insisting that she be there, they wouldn't have given her a seat at all. She was the oldest by at least thirty years and she hadn't missed the sneers, the snickering whispers. *Feeble*, they muttered. *A coward. Weak.* Havisa passed her fingertip through a nearby flame, letting the snap of pain remind her: she was Aqshian, whether they liked it or not.

'I have seen entire villages destroyed by mist,' Eudon was saying. 'Dead children, their corpses floating above their beds, drained of blood and still clutching their mothers' cold hands. There are plagues of locusts and vermin, beetles with the faces of skulls. Entire crops wither overnight. Cows give blood instead of milk. Starvation claims those the death magic doesn't consume completely. The curse of Shyish is intensifying. The death magic is unstoppable. And it's coming this way.'

Tension thickened and Havisa watched as Damiel finally shifted in his tall council chair. Leaning forward, he propped his hand on his knee. 'Do you think we've been spared Shyish's curse?' he said, and there was a forced grit to his voice that Havisa suspected had more to do with the fact he'd only just grown a full beard this past winter than any earned gruffness. 'We've seen the effects of the death magic.'

'Then you know why you must come with me,' Eudon said. 'If you travel east, to the crossroads, you might buy yourselves a little more time. If you hurry, you might be able to ferry your families to safety. The passage through the mountains shouldn't be too difficult from there.'

'Difficult.' Ruka, her long braids swinging, snorted a laugh. 'And why should we trust you? How do we know you aren't an agent of Shyish yourself?'

Eudon paused, his shoulders coiling dangerously. 'If I wanted to harm you here, in your village, I would have done so. The death magic you've seen here is only the beginning of the storm. It's sweeping over the land so quickly you'll never be able to defend yourselves. I've seen it happen time and again.'

Ruka stood slowly, her eyes glittering in the firelight, livid scar a puckered slash on her left cheek as she stepped toe to toe with Eudon. She was a full head shorter, but her voice was fierce when she said, 'Do you really think we can't defend ourselves? We are Aqshian. We aren't all as feeble as this old woman you've chosen as your travel companion. *We* are not cowards.'

Indignation sparked deep in Havisa's breast and she stood, one hand braced against the wall to keep her arthritic hip from buckling. 'I've seen the death magic myself! That is, I've heard it. At night. And there are tales of a black dog!'

One by one, the council scoffed and turned away from her. Havisa was left sputtering, torn between fury and shame, her gnarled fingers curling against the wall. She met Eudon's eyes, expecting scorn, but his expression was curious, perhaps even kind, the firelight flickering warm and red in his eyes. He only looked away from her when Damiel stood.

'As Ruka said, we are well defended here.' Damiel smiled. The expression was strained. 'We are far from helpless.'

'No.' Eudon turned to him. 'No, I suppose you aren't. And I fully understand why you would want to stay here. Travelling is dangerous. Naturally, you'd want to remain where you feel safe.'

'And what is that supposed to mean?' Ruka's voice smouldered and Havisa did not miss the subtle shift in the council, the way their hands drifted towards knives and spears and other, less obvious, weapons.

'Only that I don't blame you for wanting to stay.' Eudon shrugged. 'After all, it's sensible, and if you're all too frightened to leave the safety of your village...'

Chairs clattering, the council rose, young and furious, and Havisa couldn't quite help the small swell of satisfaction she felt watching them juggle the insult, even as she edged towards the door.

'Enough,' Damiel finally spoke. He glowered at Eudon. 'We will not be insulted. You may fill your water skins, let nobody say we are not generous. But you will leave our village tonight. You are not welcome here.'

Eudon's eyes darted over the council. He licked his lips. 'I'll require a guide to see me to the crossroads at least. I don't know this country well enough to travel it after dark.'

'And this from the one who thinks he can save us from death magic? Are you too frightened to travel all alone then, little man?' Ruka laughed and the others joined her, the same, cruel cawing Havisa had endured for so many years. The same voices that snickered when her back was turned, that forced her to live all alone, that made the shame well up inside her until she felt as though she might burst with it.

'I'll go with you.' Havisa pressed herself away from the wall and willed her trembling leg to remain firm. 'I'm no coward.'

Some of the council snickered. Some of them seethed. She smiled at Eudon as if they were old friends. And why not? Eudon had tried to help her, after all, and he wasn't laughing at her now, was he? He simply smiled back at her, the expression slow and measured, as if he'd known all along she would volunteer.

The moon was already high, distant and milky as a cataract, when Havisa and Eudon began their journey. Havisa's silver had been enough to buy a snick of salted pork, a small bag of dried fruit, a heel of bread.

And five candles.

She wore them in the old style, strapped to her wrists and hanging from her neck in delicately balanced pendants, the flames surrounded by glass chimneys, perforated to let the wax drip. The longer those candles burned, the hotter the wax became so that when it fell, it would sear her skin. The pain would keep her focused. The flames would keep her safe.

There was a moment, when she lit the wicks, that her grief and fear swelled, the acrid smell of her burning home mingling with the clean wax. But there would be no chance of falling asleep while walking, and though she tried to convince herself she believed what she had told the council, she was not brave enough to venture into the dark – where death magic lurked and strange shadows waited – without those sacred flames to protect her.

Taking a deep breath, Havisa threw a final glance over her shoulder. Two of the council were backlit in the hall's open doorway. Ruka? Damiel? At this distance she could not tell, but their laughter was bright as it popped through the night-time air.

'Fools,' Eudon muttered.

Havisa turned to look up at him. He hulked beside her, swathed in black and stinking still, his face a pale, gaunt slash in the darkness. Perhaps he would have been handsome to her had she been younger. Perhaps she shouldn't have assumed he was trying to trick her earlier.

Havisa gathered herself upright as much as her hunched spine would allow. 'They're young.'

Eudon sighed and shook his head. 'The pace is yours to set, Havisa. If you need to slow down, just say the word. These paths must be treacherous in the dark. We wouldn't want you to lose your footing.'

'Worry about your own footing.' Havisa shrugged deeper into her cloak and adjusted the candles on her wrists. 'I grew up in these hills.'

Still, Havisa stepped closer to him as they began the long journey into the dark. It had been years since she had willingly travelled anywhere at night, and even when she was younger, she hadn't relished doing it. Since the curse of Shyish had descended, she had barely ventured from her house. The night seemed thicker than she remembered. She told herself it was her imagination, an old woman's worry, but it felt as though a damp blanket had been pressed over the world, making it difficult to breathe, making every movement feel sodden and heavy. The clear dryness of Aqshian night was gone. The moonlight barely reached the path as they ascended the foothills, the narrow way winding like an inky snake. A distant wind moaned. The air around them was still, and Havisa thought she heard the same low voices that once crept into her home at night, whispers she couldn't understand. Only here, in the open, they seemed rounder, fuller and infinitely more dangerous.

What business did she really have being there, after all, in the wide dark? To prove she wasn't a coward? To whom? Herself? Eudon? The council would never know one way or the other, and they'd already made their minds up about her years ago. Maybe they were right after all. She was old, her lungs still smoke-bruised. The day had been long, filled with tragedy and a long walk and fear.

Still, whether out of stubbornness or foolishness – she herself wasn't sure which – Havisa dug her spear into the earth and pressed on, Eudon beside her. Not once did he complain about her slowness. Not once did he mock her. He only followed patiently up the low, steady incline. Havisa told herself she was grateful for it.

Midnight had begun to ease over the foothills in slow, velvety shadows when Eudon finally asked, 'Why do you wear them?'

'What?' Havisa grunted as she navigated a skitter of loose gravel. They were nearly to the crossroads, which meant a chance to rest and catch her breath, a place to sit and ease the weight on her hip. From there, they could decide which path would be best to her nephew's village.

'The candles. I should think fire would be the last thing you'd want near you, after what happened today.'

She huffed and took another grinding step. Still, beneath the pain, Havisa felt a small swell of pride. 'I'm Aqshian,' she said. 'What else would I be wearing? The flames keep me focused.'

'But what if you burn yourself?'

'I'm not afraid of pain.'

Eudon jogged easily over a small rise, his eyes on the path ahead, the crossroads opening up to a wide, flat mesa before them. 'And to think the council called you a coward. They probably assumed you'd be easy prey here on the open road.'

'Easy prey? For what? That black dog you tried to frighten me with?' Havisa snorted a laugh and tried to ignore the way her heart quivered. What good would fear do now? Eudon had been the only one in that council meeting who hadn't laughed at her and called her a coward, after all. Even if she knew the truth, she wasn't about to act the part. She forced indignance into her voice when she said, 'I was on the battlefield before the oldest of them was in their father's ball sack. I'm twice the–'

There, again, from the corner of her eye, she saw it. That low shadow, black, hunched and canine. Havisa turned so quickly the candles on her wrists guttered out, the lanterns around her neck swinging wildly as she fixed her eyes on the darkness where that shadow had been and struggled to focus.

'You should be more careful.' Eudon was suddenly at her shoulder, too close, his breath sour and hot as he bent forward as if to examine the snuffed candle on her right wrist. 'You've already had one accident today. It would be a shame if you had another.'

Havisa twitched away from him, embarrassment and fear hurrying her over the uneven ground towards the brighter, moonlit intersection of the crossroad. Fumbling open one of the glass chimneys, she moved to relight the smoking wick. 'I know what I'm doing. I don't need you to–'

The shadow darted again across the pale earth, and Havisa dropped the chimney. The candle flickered and died. The two flames hanging around her neck suddenly seemed too small and weak. They weren't nearly enough to protect her from that shadow following her. They would never be strong enough to ward off the death magic.

Eudon crouched to pick up the glass, but his arm swung wide, catching one of the remaining chimneys. It clattered onto the earth beside him. The candle went out. And he was on all fours at her feet, the light from her sole remaining candle glancing across his long, pale face, the flames glittering crimson in his eyes.

Havisa backpedalled, the last of her flames wavering at her breast. 'What are you looking at? What do you think you're doing?'

The low moaning of the wind deepened, howling, and all around the edges of the crossroads shadows shifted, mercurial and menacing. Eudon didn't move. He remained crouched, his head cocked, his eyes bright even though her candlelight no longer reached him. Behind him it surged, that canine shadow, those four legs, that tail, the muzzle full of long, terrible teeth.

'Eudon!' Havisa clutched her spear. 'Behind you!'

And then he was moving, loping from all fours to two legs, one arm outstretched as he rushed forward, the shadow at his heels. Havisa braced herself, certain he was going to push her out of the way, to try to save her from that impossible, monstrous shadow bounding towards them both. But then the shadow swelled, bending around Eudon's long legs, writhing and snapping over his body, overtaking him until he had become a writhing mass of tarry fur, of teeth and wild, blood-red eyes.

Havisa had only just raised her spear when he slammed into her. The lantern around her neck shattered on impact, the flame a sudden, unbearable spurt of heat against her skin. Havisa fell to the ground, her arms braced between them, a shield against the growling, gnashing thing, the impossibly sharp teeth snapping at her eyes, lips and throat. Eudon's hands were claws, ripping into Havisa's shoulder and side. Her heart thundered. Blood soaked her tunic. Beyond the growling, the slobber of wet teeth and claws and her own shrieks of pain, she could hear the wind cackling wildly through the foothills. *Fool. Coward.* Even now, even at the end, mocking her.

Even in death, mocking her.

Fury blazed into Havisa. She would not die here. She kicked. Clawed. Screamed. She would not die like this. She bit him back, teeth sinking into the black shadow writhing around her. She elbowed his throat. She thrust her fingers into those red eyes.

Eudon yowled, and for one, precious moment he staggered up and off her. Havisa heaved herself upright, her hands closing around the shaft of her spear. Half blind and furious, Eudon lunged, his monstrous mouth slung wide enough to devour her whole. Havisa grit her teeth. She levelled her gaze. She slammed her spear home, driving the tip deep into Eudon's maw with a jolt and a wet squelch.

Eudon groaned, whimpered, convulsed, and crumpled to the ground.

Panting, Havisa jerked her spear from Eudon's throat. She looked down at the young man who had seemed so kind to her, the beast he had become, and she laughed, the sound giddy and desperate, before collapsing among blood and broken candles.

Her world faded to black.

This time, when Havisa woke, the sun was brighter and clearer than she remembered, the crossroads quiet and still. A thin breeze combed its fingers through her hair and along the crusted wounds on her face and throat. Havisa sat up with a groan. Her clothes were stiff with blood. Her shoulder ached and her arm hung limp at her side, a cold, deep pain in the socket. Everything, absolutely everything, hurt. She spat a mouthful of blood and wriggled a loose tooth with her tongue.

Wrapping a gnarled, stained hand around her spear, Havisa stood.

There, beside her in the centre of the crossroads, was Eudon, his mouth slung wide where she'd stabbed him, his eyes open and still glazed with red. Flies had already alighted on his corpse as if he'd been rotting for days instead of hours, but otherwise he was as she'd first seen him, a young man, long and lean – though still, now, his limbs splayed, his neck wrenched at an unnatural angle. His blood had spread outward from his skull, seeping into the pale soil until the darkness surrounded him completely.

It had flowed into the shape of a massive, black dog.

For a long while, Havisa stood there, feeling every one of her long years deep in her bones. But for once she wasn't ashamed. She had fought the Black Dog of Mhurghast and lived to tell the tale.

And that was something, wasn't it?

Slowly, Havisa gathered the remains of her shattered lanterns, her severed wicks and candle wax. It was a long way to the next village, and she would need every ounce of protection she could get. Maybe, when she arrived, her nephew would see her new wounds and the blood on her spear, and ask to hear her story. Maybe he would understand that though she hadn't burned bright when she was young, her fire was still smouldering.

TESSERAE

Richard Strachan

As soon as he stepped into the tavern, he saw the duardin hunched in the corner. His face was lined and drawn, weathered like old stone. His receding hair was flecked with grey, his beard tattered and sparse. He was clutching a mug of ale and sat on a low seat far from the fire, wrapped in a threadbare cloak. A dart of breeze followed the traveller inside. The flames licked and shivered at his passing, but the duardin didn't look up.

The traveller asked for beer and looked around while his mug was being filled – at the low beams stained with smoke, the stuttering aetherlamps, a stone floor covered with scattered straw. There were only a handful of customers on this bitter night, the air outside flecked with the hint of sleet – two old timers huddling by the flames, a couple of merchants haggling in hushed voices, their gestures as eloquent as any words… and the duardin, silent in his corner, tugging at his beard, staring into his mug.

'Make that two,' the traveller said to the barkeeper.

He brought the ales over and sat down next to the duardin. He pushed one of the mugs across the table and laid his travelling bag on the floor. The duardin peered up at him through bushy, grey eyebrows, his bottom lip slack and wet, the eyes darting down at the beer as if the traveller had just laid out a swatch of diamonds for him to examine.

'On me,' the traveller said, before he was asked.

The duardin's hand darted out from his sleeve, and the traveller was surprised to see it was as clean and well kept as any aelf's. The nails were bright and tidy, the fingers as steady as a pit fighter's knife. The duardin looked at him again and the darting hand stopped an inch from the mug.

'I'm not one to turn down a gift freely given,' he said, in a strangely clear and refined voice. 'As long as that's what it is?'

'Is what?' the traveller asked.

'Freely given?'

He nodded, but before the duardin could pick up the mug, the traveller put his palm across it.

'There is perhaps one condition...'

'Indeed,' the duardin said. 'There always is...'

'Nothing that will cost you, I promise. All I want in return is... your story.'

Something passed across the duardin's face then – a shiver of pain, an old dread freshly remembered. The traveller smiled.

'I know you have one,' he said. 'Everyone does.'

'You say it won't cost me,' the duardin said, passing his hand across his eyes. 'But my tale cost me everything I knew, everything I loved. Everything.'

'Come,' the traveller said gently, passing over the ale. 'Unburden yourself, friend. Tell me... *everything.*'

It was many years ago. Ten or more, perhaps. Longer than I care to remember.

Khelen is my name, Khelen Khar'nelian. Perhaps you have

heard of me? Well, in my day I was reckoned the best at what I do – or rather, what I did. I was famed throughout the city of Olhum as an artificer and an artist, a craftsman in stone and glass and precious gems. Folk came from far and wide to seek my services. Sigmarite priests hired me to design stained glass windows for their temples – scenes of Sigmar's wrath rendered in rippled, translucent crystal and polished gemstones, fashioned into place with strips of burnished silver. For rich merchant houses I designed great sigils and crests to hang above their doors, signs of their power and influence; filigreed gold laced around marbled stone, studded with jewels from all the trade routes across Shyish. I did a booming trade in precious jewellery and silverware, in decorative ornaments of surpassing beauty, engraved cameos – there was nothing my art couldn't master. Of course, Olhum was a wealthier place in those days, more carefree, not like it is now... Now, I find it a place of dark and empty houses, of streets that ring with no footsteps, black windows that look down on you like cold eyes. And the cold itself forces me from the streets these days, to seek shelter in places like this low tavern, although my coin cannot stretch further than an ale or two of an evening. The cold, and other things...

If I give the impression of success then let me temper it by admitting that I was not a businessman at heart. There are those for whom the turning of one coin into two is an art in itself, and my skill did not stretch that far. To make objects of rare beauty costs money, and no matter how much you charge for your work, there are always outlays to cover. Guild payments, taxes, the cost of materials – the list goes on. My son, Khadrick, looked after such affairs, but alas, his head was not one for business either.

Khadrick, my boy... Grungni, I pray, look after him in the underworlds where he rests now...

So it was that I found myself owing considerable sums to my creditors. With the threat of bankruptcy hanging over me, I found myself quickly accepting jobs that were beneath my station, and certainly beneath my skills. Anything to turn a coin, to provide for my son, and desperation makes anyone lower their principles. From designing stained glass for some of the greatest temples in the city, I became little more than a glazier, fitting simple windows of base silicate in taverns such as this. Instead of the finest ornamental art of the age, I turned my hand to baubles and trinkets and children's toys. It was a low time for me, one of shame and distress.

I still had my workshop, about the last thing I had to my name. I would not give that up, if I could. And it was just as well, because it was to my workshop one evening that he came – the man who was to change everything for me. Indeed, after I met him, I would never be the same again.

The evening was quiet, and the street outside was empty. Khadrick was upstairs working on the books. He was a simple lad, but he always wanted to be of use. Better we had dived head first into the poverty that was awaiting us, I sometimes think, than that I tried to carry on. I had worked hard to leave something for my son, but it seemed that I would in the end leave him nothing but debts. Alas, if only I could have left him that much…

But I digress. The evening was still, the shop was quiet. And then he entered.

It was hard to say what was wrong, at first. Certainly not his appearance, which was that of a well-to-do, young aristocrat; Azyr-born, if I didn't miss my guess, and with the customary confidence of that breed. I remember he wore a purple doublet of the most extraordinarily intricate brocade, and his cloak was lined with that shifting, rippling material that only comes from the finest Ghurite silkworms. He was tall, elegant, his face finely chiselled, his eyes dark and brooding under a heavy brow. I made obeisance at once, not daring to hope that he had coin to spend. As I said, Olhum was a wealthier place back then…

It wasn't his appearance that disturbed me, or his manner, which was as polite as could be expected. It was something intangible, vague, a hint of darkness that followed him into the room like a foul smell. It was as if he had trailed someone else's shadow in after him, if that makes any sense? He looked at me, and in that handsome face I saw only the lineaments of a mask. My fear was that behind the mask there would be nothing there at all.

Still, trade is trade. I forced myself to swallow my disquiet.

'Honoured sir!' I genuflected (hunger makes beggars of us all). 'You grace this humble establishment with your presence. Please, feel free to examine my wares, and–'

'It is not your wares,' he cut in, 'but your reputation that brings me, Khelen Khar'nelian. I hear there are none in this city with an ounce of your skill.'

'I am a modest artisan, your excellency,' I said with a laugh, hoping my heart wouldn't beat out of my chest, 'but I am not so humble as to deny the charge! I am, as it happens, reckoned of rare talent as a craftsman.'

'I make it my business to seek out the best in their field. Does your talent as a craftsman extend to restoration?' he asked.

'Most certainly,' I agreed. In that moment, I doubt there was a skill or trade in Shyish in which I wouldn't have claimed myself expert. 'May I ask the field in which...'

'Mosaic,' he said.

'Simplicity itself,' I said, beaming. 'Sourcing materials may, of course, take time, and... money, but I am confident that–'

'Money, I have. What I do not have is time. Come to this address tomorrow evening,' he said. He handed me a card, detailing an address on the other side of the city and bearing his name and title: Prince Cosimo. 'All you require will be there waiting for you.'

'Your excellency has thought of everything,' I said. I gave him my most obsequious smile. 'There is, of course, and I hesitate to raise such a vulgar subject in such august company, but there is still the somewhat delicate matter of the fee...'

Prince Cosimo smiled, and I could not meet his eyes. The gloom seemed to advance a shade; the air became a degree colder. Cruel fingers seemed to clutch greedily at my heart.

'Do not worry on that score, Master Khar'nelian. You will be well paid. You will be very well paid indeed.'

I arrived at the address he had given me the next day, in the late afternoon. Mhurghast Street... I had never heard of it, but from Prince Cosimo's directions I knew roughly where it was meant to be. I left the bustling streets of the merchants' quarter behind, and as I headed up into that more rarefied neighbourhood above the city, I found that the crowds soon melted away. This was an old part of town, I knew, once home to those grand families that had founded the city. The streets, once wide thoroughfares where gilded carriages passed night and day, now felt like empty canyons. Tall manses on either side cast their shadows into the street, and every other window was dark with vacancy. The aetherlamps stuttered their weak green flames. As the light in the sky began to dim with the onset of evening, I confess I felt a twinge of uncertainty. This silence, this emptiness, was perhaps a sign of the city's gradual degeneration that until now I hadn't noticed. Too concerned with my own issues, I hadn't realised that Olhum itself was on the cusp of depression. Shyish is a lonely place at the best of times.

I clutched my coat tight as a faint breeze whispered up Mhurghast Street, carrying with it a sliver of ice that spoke of the coming winter. I hefted my bag, the tools of my trade, and checked the address again on the card Prince Cosimo had given me.

The building was set back from the road behind an iron fence, with a strip of grey garden long since gone to ruin. It had been colonised by thorns and weeds, and there was a scattering of dead leaves across the greasy surface of a pond that was more scum than water. The building itself was tall and narrow, the pale paint on the clapboard starting to peel. It stretched up four storeys, culminating in a lopsided tower of black slate. The windows were narrow, like arrow slits, and all of them were dark. I imagined how it must have looked in happier days from this imposing position above the city, but the mansion of Prince Cosimo was now a drear and abandoned-looking place, wreathed in shadows. The city stretched out below was like a dark sheet, pricked here and there with fluttering lamplight.

I knocked at the door, fully expecting no answer, but it swung open before me. Prince Cosimo stood in the dim hall, quite as if he had been waiting there since returning from my workshop the day before. The hall stretched away into the darkness beyond him. I thought I could see in the gloom a flight of stairs leading to the upper storeys and, beyond it, another flight leading down into the basement. A lamp on a sideboard cast a faint and flickering light into the hall. Prince Cosimo smiled that smile at me, and I used the excuse of my new surroundings to look away, staring instead at the row of portraits on the eastern wall. Worthies of Cosimo's line, I presumed; a collection of hard faces with unyielding eyes, men and women who had carved out their influence in the city's earlier days, utterly without sentiment or pity. The shadows seemed to writhe around them.

'Master Khar'nelian,' he said. 'Welcome. My thanks for committing to the task at such short notice. Come, this way, please.' He took up the lamp and I followed him through the hall, our footsteps booming on the flagstones. 'Let us begin...'

He led me into a room on the left of the main door, a wide chamber that looked out into the empty street. He held up the lamp and I could see at once the remains of a large, circular mosaic in the centre of the floor, the design chiselled away, shattered in places – utterly ruined, in other words. Indeed, I noticed it because there was nothing else in the room to draw the attention; it was bare of furniture, the walls empty of pictures.

'Forgive the state of the house,' Prince Cosimo said, as if answering a question that I hadn't asked. 'It is undergoing some... *modifications* at the moment, and is not as it will be, in time.'

'I understand fully. This,' I said, indicating the broken mosaic, 'is the work in question?'

'Indeed so.'

I looked down at its remains. I found it hard to comprehend the design at first, but after a moment, in the quivering light of Prince Cosimo's lamp, I could see the suggestion of a lone figure in a landscape of some kind. The figure's face had been sheared away, as had much of the landscape for that matter. On the floor to one side of the mosaic, revealed as Prince Cosimo stepped around it, were several piles of tesserae, organised by colour.

He handed me a sheaf of papers. As I glanced through them, I saw that they were sketches of the final design – one displaying the mosaic in total, the others showing specific details.

'This should be sufficient for your purposes,' Prince Cosimo said. 'The materials are as you see them here. You should have more than enough to cover the entire surface. You have your tools?' I hefted the bag. 'Then, please – feel free to begin. There is but one stipulation,' he said. 'The task must be completed in one evening. It *must* be completed by dawn.'

I stared at the lamp in his hand. There were no other aether-fittings around the room, no candles that I could see. I laughed, but my laughter died as I saw the expression on his face, the dead light catching in his black eyes.

'Am I to have no more illumination?' I protested. 'This is delicate work, Prince Cosimo, work of great and particular detail!'

'Alas,' the prince said, 'as I mentioned, the house is in some disrepair. All I can offer you is this lamp. There is plenty of fuel. It should last you until morning.'

'And yourself, sir? Don't tell me you will sit in the dark all night?'

'I have business elsewhere in the city,' he said. 'You will have free run of the house. The kitchens are downstairs in the basement, should you desire refreshment during your labours. Do we have a deal then, Master Khar'nelian?'

He held out a pale hand, and to my shame I took it. I should have turned then, left and never looked back, but the press of money is a terrible weight for anyone to bear. I took that cold hand, and as I did so, Prince Cosimo drew me near and stared down into my eyes, his face masked in the lamplight.

'It is said that the duardin are an imperturbable breed?'

'We have that reputation.'

'Then I beg you... do not pay too much heed to what you may hear in the hours that follow. This is an old house,' he said, 'and it has its... peculiarities. Pay them no mind.'

I nodded, unable to break his gaze.

'There is one more thing,' he said before he left. He handed me a blue lacquered box and I took it in a shaking hand. 'I would ask you to reconstruct the face of the figure in the mosaic last of all, and when you do so to use only these specific tesserae. You will see why when you open the box. Do not disappoint me, Master Khar'nelian,' he said, as he strode for the door. 'I will see you in the morning, and I promise you handsome payment for your work.'

Of course, the moment he was gone, I opened the box to check its contents. Inside, gleaming like black pearls on a bed of velvet, smoky and dark and radiating a terrifying, subdued power, were nine small shards of Ulgu realmstone.

* * *

I'm sure I don't need to tell you, but just one of those pieces could have bought half the wealth in the whole city. Nine pieces together, nine shards from the mysterious Realm of Shadows, was a bounty that could scarcely be conceived. My hands trembled to hold them. I snapped the box shut, my heart pounding, sweat breaking out across my skin. Because, as I'm sure you have already guessed, to hold up such a temptation to the desperate is to ask only to be disappointed.

But, nevertheless, I set to the task, still convincing myself that I would complete it to my client's satisfaction. I drew up and opened the lamp, casting a green oval of light on the scene. I examined the sketches, checked through the piles of tesserae, made tentative sketches of my own. In truth, the job was not as daunting as I had at first assumed. The material had been well organised and the sketches were clear. They showed, as I had thought, a young man striding with confident and joyous expression through a rural scene, a newborn lamb in his arms. The image was rustic, naive and posed no particular difficulties. I filled in some of the preliminary outlines and was pleased with the effect. I progressed deeper into the scene, bringing out the tangled path along which the figure walked, the overhanging trees, the suggestion of grassy meadows in the distance – a perspective of Ghyran, perhaps, or the milder parts of Ghur.

Any artist will recognise the moment when the work captures the mind entire. Hours seem to die under the brush or the pen, or in this case under my tooling hammer and tweezers. I became thoroughly absorbed in the task, pleased to be working on something with real artistic merit after so many months of second-rate stuff. The inadequacy of the light didn't bother me. The questions of why such an incongruous scene was the subject of the mosaic didn't impinge on my thoughts at all, and it was only the rumblings of my stomach that drew my attention away from the work a few hours later. I stood up from the floor and stretched my back.

It was only then that I noticed her watching me.

I caught the gasp in my throat before it could escape, my heart leaping in my chest at the shock. She stood in the doorway, a black shadow on the edge of the lamplight. She was slender, small, her head turned slightly on its side. Her hair was lank, her dress no more than a pale, diaphanous shift. Her hands clutched at each other, wringing her fingers. I couldn't see her face, but I was sure she was opening her mouth to speak.

'Forgive me,' I stuttered, 'I thought I was alone, I–'

She screamed, a keening shriek that sliced through me like a knife. I raised my hand as if to shield my face, but... she was gone. I don't mean she moved away or turned to go; just that she was no longer there. She had vanished, as fast as the eye can blink. I rushed into the hall, but there was no one there; no sound of footsteps, nothing. A trick of the light, you may say. I would have agreed, but when I looked to the line of portraits on the wall, I saw that one of them was empty...

I gathered food and wine from the kitchen in the basement, looking over my shoulder the whole time. My blood pounded in my ears. My legs shook as I made my way back to the chamber. I ate quickly and addressed myself to the task once more, forcing my attention back to my work. I could not resist the urge to keep glancing at the doorway, but the woman did not reappear.

It could have been my nerves, I suppose – the shock of seeing that gheist, if that's what she was. But nerves alone do not explain what I experienced for the rest of that night. Piece by piece I put the mosaic together, and with every piece the temperature in that room began to drop. My breath smoked in the air. The light from the aetherlamp dimmed and stuttered, and as I leaned closer in towards the mosaic, carefully brushing each piece with fixative and angling it in place, I began to hear things that could not have been there.

The voice of my father, long dead, whispered from the cracks between the floorboards, muttering terrible things to me, curses that had tears prickling in my eyes. I heard footsteps across the ceiling from the floor above, in a house I knew to be empty. I felt the breath of some snuffling beast against my shoulder, could almost feel it dank and wet against my cheek, and yet when I spun around with a cry, the room behind me was empty. And once, I saw a pale, dead hand with bleeding fingertips reach across my line of sight from somewhere behind me, passing me one of the tesserae, and with a trembling hand, not daring to look, I took it.

This is an old house, and it has its... peculiarities, Prince Cosimo had said. *Pay them no mind...*

Well, I did my best. No depth of focus has ever been as profound as that which I displayed over the course of that night. I worked and I worked, until my head was pounding, and as dawn began to etch the sky with filigrees of gold, I came close to the end of my labours. The image was almost finished, the face of the figure in that rural scene only awaiting completion. I opened the lacquered box and gazed once more upon the shards of realmstone...

I admit that as duardin go, I am not sturdy of temperament, yet I felt I had acquitted myself well that night. But it was with a shaking hand that I touched those shards of Ulgu's most shadowy magic and fitted them into place. I needed no reference to the sketches, and the stones themselves seemed to guide my fingers. And it was when it was almost done, and when I had one final piece in my hand, that my courage snapped. Not the courage to complete the task, you understand, but the courage to deny my moral weakness; for after all, I had in my hand the wealth that a lifetime's labour wouldn't provide for my son. I had condemned Khadrick to poverty because of my failings; perhaps here I could redeem myself and give him the wealth and security he had always deserved.

There was still a quantity of tesserae left – Cosimo had more than provided in that regard. As the dawn deepened and the hour of the prince's return grew near, I scoured through the remainder and found a close match, quickly moulding it with my jeweller's pick and hammer into a near-exact likeness, fitting it into the eye of the laughing youth who sported along the rural track. Ulgu realmstone, as you may not know, can have a lustreless appearance, like unto the shadowy realm from whence it comes. Embedded there in the midst of its fellows, the facsimile was barely noticeable. I took the final realmstone shard and slipped it into my pouch, casting the box onto the ground. I gathered up my tools. The light was quickening in the sky, dispelling the horrors of the night just past. The apparition of the woman in the doorway, the dead fingers brushing up against my own, the voice of my long-dead father... they were no more than a terrible dream. But then, as I waited for the sound of Prince Cosimo's key in the lock, I glanced down at the mosaic and the blood turned to water in my veins.

At first, I thought it a flaw in my work. From a distance, the laughing boy looked more like he was screaming, the lamb in his arms contorted with terror. And then, as I continued to look, the scene began to slowly change. The rural track morphed and melted into a cobbled street, and the trees around the figure straightened and grasped upwards towards the smoky sky, becoming the rickety outlines of old tenements in a street that I recognised. The central figure began to shrink, hunching over, the expression on his aging face turning to one of utter despair and grief, the lamb in his arms transformed into that of a child, its body thrown back in death's grim repose. I stared in abject horror. I stared, and I recognised...

I don't have to tell you that the figure was me. The body of the child was my own son, Khadrick, and the space in the figure's eye where the shard of realmstone should have been was like a hole drilled into the void itself, peering into the outer darkness between the realms, into the place where the philosophers say all souls must one day flee, there to be extinguished in the light of unreason forever...

The duardin finished his ale and the traveller pushed over his own mug, untouched. With a grateful half-smile, the duardin took it and drank deep. He shivered and wiped the sweat from his brow.

'I ran home, of course. I had not the courage to confront Prince Cosimo, and my heart raced to confirm the safety of my son. Alas,' he said, and he passed his hand again over his eyes, stilling a sob. 'When I got back to the workshop and called his name, there was no answer. "Khadrick!" I shouted, but I knew what I would find even before I reached his room. There, as still as stone and twice as cold, lay the body of my son, passed from this world with not a mark on him. It was as if he had been taken in some aethereal grip and his light extinguished, a mere candle snuffed out... And if ever I had the courage to continue, it fled from me then. I ran, and I kept running, and I haven't looked back since.'

'And Prince Cosimo?' the traveller said.

'I never saw him again. If he looked for me, it was without success. Who knows, perhaps he was satisfied with my work and never even knew what I had stolen from him. Or perhaps my theft was punishment enough...'

'What do you mean?'

The old duardin offered a smile then – baffled, uncomprehending. 'The realmstone, the shard of Ulgu... I have it still, you see.'

The traveller nodded. 'So, you never sold it in the end.'

'No,' the duardin said. 'I found that I *couldn't*, somehow. I told myself that I feared discovery, that an artefact so rare was bound to draw attention, but...'

'Yes?' the traveller said, leaning forward. He rested one hand on his bag.

The duardin lowered his voice, and when he spoke his words were thick with either fear or grief – or something in between. A tear ran from the corner of his eye and dripped onto the table.

'It *speaks* to me...' he said. 'Whispering through the night, pleading, accusing, cursing. It speaks to me, and it is never quiet, and... it speaks in the voice of my son!'

The traveller nodded again, not unsympathetically, as if confirming a long-held suspicion. To the duardin's stifled sobs he said, 'I understand.'

He reached into his travelling bag and took out a wooden box, its surface glazed with a shimmering blue lacquer. He turned it towards the duardin and opened the lid, and the old artisan gave a muffled cry when he saw the contents.

'Grungni save me!' he wept. 'Is that...?'

'Yes.' The traveller smiled.

Nodding, the duardin reached into a leather pouch at his hip and took out the well-worn shard. He gazed down at it with the ghost of old longing; but then, wiping his eyes, he dropped it into the box's velvet interior, where it clinked as it struck its fellows.

The traveller snapped the box shut and replaced it in his bag.

'Thank you,' the duardin whispered, not daring to meet the traveller's eyes.

'Thank you, Master Khar'nelian,' the traveller said. He left two coins on the table, payment for the ale.

It was true what the duardin had said, he thought as he left the tavern. Olhum was a place of dark and empty houses now, of streets that rang with no footsteps. He turned to go as the wind muttered down the quiet roads, the bag heavy in his hand. Perhaps it was time he moved on.

GHOST PLANET

Steven Sheil

'This is the strangest story I ever heard,' said Joddrig.

He paused and looked from one face to the other – Mandelhahn, Oost, Padrine – while his cracked lips, hidden somewhere behind his grey, thickly matted beard, sucked on one of the stale strips of spiced meat that was close to all that remained of their rations. Oost sat back in her chair and registered his demand for her attention with a single arched eyebrow.

Clearly relishing the audience, Joddrig continued. 'It was told to me by an old hand on the first ship I ever crewed, a man of great wisdom and experience, a man who had seen all that the galaxies had to offer, a man–'

'For pity's sake, get on with it,' said Oost.

'What's the hurry?' scoffed Padrine. 'You can't be worried that we're going to run out of time.'

'Ha! The boy's right,' said Mandelhahn, who had worked in the kitchens, back when there had been food to cook. She was red-haired and badly fire-scarred on one side of her face, an injury she wore as though it were a medal. Oost looked at her darkly, resenting her laughter. Mandelhahn shrugged. 'We're going nowhere. What's the harm in a tall tale?'

'It's not the tale, it's his way with it,' said Oost. 'He never gets to the point. Grinds my nerves.'

'Then don't listen,' said Padrine. 'Go back to your cabin and your problem is solved.'

Oost shifted under their gaze. As much as Joddrig irritated her, it was comforting to be with the others. It helped the time pass more quickly. Kept her from thinking too much about the hopelessness of their situation. Better to listen to a tall tale than the gradually slowing hum of life support systems.

Oost grunted and waved a hand at Joddrig, signalling him, begrudgingly, to continue.

Joddrig nodded, took a moment or two to suck on the dry meat strip – a habit which Oost had become convinced was solely designed to conjure her irritation – then resumed.

'This man – Aendel was his name, a fine man, a worthy man – he told me of a creature, they call it a hollow flea, for it's as small as the head of a pin.' Joddrig held up two fingers, with barely any light showing between them to indicate the size. 'It lays its eggs in the latrine pipes of a ship. When they hatch, the young seek the closest warm place to grow. And if that happens to be the body of a man…' He sat back in his seat, shook his head.

'I've heard this before,' said Padrine. 'It's an old slicker's tale, same as all the sanitation crew tell. It's just a way to frighten the new boys. Nothing in it.'

'No?' said Joddrig. He leaned forward again, his gaze fixed intently on Padrine. 'Then how do you explain what Aendel saw with his very own eyes?'

'What did he see?' said Mandelhahn.

Joddrig's voice lowered. Instinctively they all drew in a little closer.

'A man in Aendel's unit,' said Joddrig, 'became home to one of these bugs. He didn't know it at the time, of course, but others began to notice the change in him. He began to move more sluggishly, as though he were stupefied, and he lost all his appetite. Then he began to lose the power of speech and his skin grew shiny and smooth, as though it had become tighter all over.'

They were all silent, listening intently now. As Joddrig paused to take a breath, there was the hollow thud of some piece of flotsam colliding with the ship's hull, like the low toll of a bell.

'Finally,' said Joddrig, 'one night in the mess hall, he let out a scream that pierced the souls of all that heard it, and fell jerking to the ground.'

With these words, Joddrig slammed the back of his hand down on the table in front of them, twitching his fingers violently to mimic a spasm. Oost felt her heart give a leap and cursed inwardly for allowing herself to be sucked into his tale.

Joddrig leaned forward, his voice now little more than a whisper, his eyes wide with sick delight.

'Then, in front of all of them, his skull split open from here' – he touched a finger to his hairline, then drew it down his nose to the point of his chin – 'to here. And what crawled out,' Joddrig licked his lips with relish, 'had a hundred thick legs of flesh, and no eyes, and a mouth the size of two heads. It had eaten the man alive from the inside, bones and organs and muscles and all, so that all that was left was his empty skin, like someone had thrown a blanket on the floor, soaked in blood and stinking guts.'

There was a moment of silence. Then–

'Psh,' said Oost dismissively. 'That's it? That's your big story?'

'It's grim enough for my taste,' said Mandelhahn.

'I thought it was a fair tale,' said Padrine. 'Better than most I've heard.'

'You know a better one?' said Joddrig. He fixed his eyes on Oost. 'Or are you just here to piss in everyone's porridge?'

'You want a strange tale?' said Oost. She rolled up her sleeves, leaned forward on the table. 'I'll give you one.'

Kaden could hear the others talking but his mind was somewhere else. He stood at the viewing portal of the standby comms deck in what remained of their craft – what once had been the small escort starship named the *Endless Wrath*. The starfield that stretched out in front of him was unfamiliar. He couldn't find it on any of the maps that had survived the blast, which meant most likely that they were drifting somewhere on the edges of charted space. He supposed they should count themselves lucky that they hadn't all been incinerated like the others when the explosion had ripped through their ship, that they'd all managed to find their way to this section with its still-functioning life support systems, that there was still hope that they might be found. But it had been a long time since the blast now. Rations were dwindling, along with the power they needed to keep the systems working. And being cooped up here, the five of them, with barely more than a handful of cabins to hold them, was fraying everyone's nerves. He wondered how much longer they could keep it up.

'Bog-bilge and bullshit!' Joddrig's voice boomed out across from the other end of the large cabin. Kaden turned to look at the others. Oost was sitting back in her chair, looking defiant while Joddrig shook his head in scorn. 'You heard this nonsense?' he said to Kaden.

'I wasn't listening,' said Kaden. 'Sorry.'

'Tell him,' said Padrine. 'Kaden's the comms-rat, he'll know if it's true.'

Oost looked over at Kaden. 'I was warning them of the Fireblood Scream. A comms-man on my previous ship told me about it. The sound that lives. It hides in the frequencies like a disease, waiting for silence. And when it finds it–'

'When it finds it, it fills it, bursting the ears of all who hear it, driving them into a rage of violent insanity.'

'You're saying it's true?' said Joddrig.

Kaden shrugged. 'As true as any story you hear out here, I suppose. Once it's passed through the mouths of a hundred men, who knows what's real and what isn't?'

'I've heard it,' said Mandelhahn. Everyone turned to look at her. She had taken on a solemn air, like she was recalling some deep-set trauma. 'The sound that when you hear it makes you want to kill? I know that sound.' She looked up at them and her face looked pale, haunted.

Oost put her hand on Mandelhahn's shoulder. Her tone was soft, solicitous. 'When did you hear it, Mandelhahn?'

Mandelhahn took a deep breath to set herself, then spoke. 'Just now when Joddrig wouldn't finish his blasted story.' She gave a big grin.

Joddrig cursed. The others burst into raucous laughter. Oost took her hand from Mandelhahn's shoulder and cuffed her playfully around the head.

Kaden turned back to the window, smiled to himself. It was good to hear laughter. There had been too little of it over these past days. With the situation they found themselves in, there was little to laugh about. He walked over to the comms console and sat down in front of it, made a routine check of the instruments.

'Distress signal still transmitting?' said Oost. She was hovering over his right shoulder. Kaden nodded, tapped one of the instrument dials.

'Full range, same as it's always been.' He turned to look up at her, shook his head. 'Still nothing.'

Oost nodded. Her jaw tightened as she looked at the dial. The distress signal was the only hope they had left. Either they'd be heard and found or–

'What about you, Kaden?' shouted Mandelhahn from the table. 'You got a story for us? Something to chill the bones?'

'You ask me, we don't need any more chilling,' said Padrine. He shivered a little. The life-support systems were on minimum levels to conserve energy and as the days had gone by it felt like the coldness of space was creeping ever closer to them.

Joddrig scoffed. 'You think this is cold? When I was on that fine old battle-barge the *Iron Fist of Strength*, the systems went down one time, and–'

'Oh, bite your tongue, Joddrig. We don't need another Fire-blood Scream out of you,' said Oost. She turned back to the comms-man. 'So, Kaden, you have a tale worth the telling?'

Kaden looked from one expectant face to another. Out of somewhere in the depths of his memory came a word.

'Valgaast,' he said.

'Valgaast?' said Oost. 'Is that a man or a beast, or...'

'It's a place, or so they say,' said Kaden, 'Truth be told, I've heard others call it different. Maybe it's just a word for something that there's no other word for.' Even as he spoke, he wasn't sure why he'd said the name, for even thinking of it made him uneasy. It had been one of the first tales he'd heard as a young boy taking his position on board *The Sharpasian*, a Class Two mining vessel, a tale told to him by his bunkmate, an old hand named Biksin, and one which had lingered long in his mind, though it had been nearly half a lifetime since he had last thought of it. He glanced towards the viewing portal and wondered if the fear of all that unknowable space that surrounded them had pricked his memory.

'There are planets, out there amongst the stars, invisible to scans, invisible to the eyes of humans, planets made up of the souls of the dead, where ancient, evil spirits rule. These spirits seek out passing crafts in order to steal from them new souls to populate their worlds, ever desiring to add to the endless, agonising cries of those that they have claimed. *This* Valgaast is one of these worlds – at least, so I was told. A ghost planet, drifting in space, moored to no orbit, undetectable. A place whose true horror you can only see once you have passed across the threshold of death, when your soul leaves behind its body and is sucked inexorably down to join the billion others in their eternal torment.'

As Kaden finished speaking, he was aware that a silence had settled around him. He looked up at the faces that surrounded him. The others looked pensive, their good humour replaced by a solemn introspection, as though something in his words had sucked away any entertainment that lay in their tale-telling.

'How do they claim you?' said Padrine, his voice quiet and low. 'These spirits.'

'No one knows,' said Kaden, 'not really. But some say that their trick is to enter a man's mind and turn his thoughts so that an easeful death comes to seem preferable to enduring the pain of living.'

His words fell like a blast of chill air over them all. Since they had found themselves stranded all those long days ago, the thought of death had been ever-present, so perilous was their situation. But it was one which they had each, in their own way, found a method of stifling, so as to allow them to continue to pass their days. Now the thought lay heavy in the air, and the thick shell of metal that contained them and kept them from the cold infinity of space seemed suddenly gossamer-thin.

Mandelhahn clapped her hands together and stood up, breaking the morbid spell.

'See,' she said to Kaden, 'this is why no one ever asks to drink with you.' She gave a wink to the others. 'And now I'm going to retire to my cabin and try not to think about impending death. Who's got first watch?'

* * *

Kaden lay on his bunk and looked at the ceiling. He was alone, as were most all the remaining crew. Another crew member's uniform still hung in the closet, but Kaden tried not to think about whose bed he now slept in, what had happened to them. Boiled alive in the explosion when the ship had first been ruptured by the warp storm? Crushed by walls that imploded in the sudden decompression? Or floating for long moments outside the ship's hull, gasping for a last, impossible breath?

He turned onto his side. He wished he'd never spoken about the ghost planet. It had put a pall across the evening, turned the mood of the others just at the point where they'd found some small respite from the hopelessness of their situation. Why had he done it? It was hard to say, except that their confinement and the desperateness of their situation did strange things to a man's thoughts, sometimes without him even realising.

He put the incident from his mind, tried to force himself to just give in to sleep. But just as he was drifting out of wakefulness, as he felt his taut muscles finally relaxing, a strident blast of sound filled the room.

'All crew to comms room,' came Oost's voice across the channels. *'All crew to comms room. Immediately.'*

Kaden leapt from his bed and rushed to the door. Could it be a rescue? Some passing ship noting their predicament? Or had one of the repair jobs they'd done to patch up this floating section failed? Were they now to be plunged into the final emergency?

When he reached the comms room, the others were already there, crowding round the viewing portal. Oost was at the front, looking intently at the glass, holding her arms outstretched to quiet the others.

'Keep watching,' she was saying, quietly but firmly, 'keep watching.'

Kaden joined the others, looking out at the vast starfield that lay in front of them. There was nothing there, no ship, no debris, no obvious danger. Then–

THUD.

A hand smacked against the glass from outside.

Kaden felt his heart jump. The hand was clad in a thick glove from a maintenance suit. There was someone out there.

'How do we know it's not just a body?' said Padrine. 'How do we know–'

But even as he spoke, the hand raised itself and came down again on the glass. Then a helmet came into view, and though no light shone on the face inside, it was clear that whoever was inside the suit was looking in on them.

'It's another survivor,' said Kaden.

'Impossible,' said Joddrig.

'Why?' said Mandelhahn. 'We survived, didn't we? Maybe he was in another part of the ship. We don't know what happened to the rest of the craft. Maybe there are more of them out there.'

The hand came again. THUD.

'The quickest way to find out is to get them inside,' said Kaden. 'Joddrig, you were a hull rat, you know your way around better than anyone. You want to take the lead on retrieval?'

Everyone looked at Joddrig. Taking trips outside the ship had been his daily grind for thirty years or more. But he shook his head.

'We don't know who that is, or what they want from us. You want to split rations between six of us now? You want to add another set of lungs to suck down this air?'

'We can't just leave them outside,' said Mandelhahn. 'If you won't go, I will.' She pushed past him towards the airlock. Joddrig grabbed her arm.

'I tell you, you're making a mistake.'

Mandelhahn glared and yanked her arm away. 'That's as maybe,' she said. 'Won't be the first time.'

As she walked off, Joddrig called, 'Aye, but it may well be your last.'

The five of them stood in a semicircle, looking at the survivor, waiting for her story.

'My name...' she said, and her voice was hoarse and croaking as though she was unused to speaking. She coughed, wiped her lips with the back of her hand, then started again. 'My name is Voll. I'm an enginseer, from deck five. I thought–' she swallowed again, wetting her throat. 'I thought I was the only survivor. I was trapped in another part of the ship, back that way.' She pointed to the damaged transit corridor that Joddrig and Padrine had blocked off during those first desperate hours to gain stability for the craft. 'But there was no way through. When my life support systems started running low, I decided to go outside, see if I could make it to another part of the ship, one that was still stable.'

She looked up at them now and the edge of a smile was on her face. 'I never expected to find all of you.'

She was a tall, gangling woman with a long, pale face and hair cropped close to her scalp. None of them ever remembered seeing her before, but that was no surprise – there had been hundreds on board the craft originally, and grunts like them generally kept to their own crew class.

'You got food? Rations?' said Padrine, eyeing the strongbox that Voll had been carrying with her on her jaunt.

Voll shook her head. 'I'm sorry, no. I ran out two days ago.'

Joddrig gave a dark laugh. 'So, you'll be wanting some of ours then?' He looked at the others. 'Just like I warned you, but you wouldn't listen. Just old Joddrig, talking his nonsense, aye?'

Oost flashed a look at him, and the old man gave a grunt and turned away. Oost nodded at the strongbox. 'So what's inside?'

'I thought it might help,' said Voll. She unlocked the box, pulled out what looked like a metal tube wrapped in a coil, dangling with cables at one end and fixed with a switch at the other. 'If I could find a working comms unit.'

'A signal booster,' said Kaden, who had recognised the object immediately.

'Yes,' said Voll. 'I couldn't use it where I was – the comms unit was destroyed in the crash. But I thought, if I could find a way to broadcast a rescue signal and I attached this...'

'It'd increase the range a hundredfold,' said Kaden.

The others looked at him. Hope flickered in their eyes. 'You mean,' said Mandelhahn, 'we just need to attach this to the comms unit and–'

Kaden held up a hand to stop her. 'It's not that simple. These units, they draw a lot of power. If we attach it, it will mean...' He hesitated. He was running all the scenarios through his mind.

'Mean what?' said Oost.

'It'll drain the life support systems,' said Voll. 'It'll cut the time you have left by two-thirds, maybe more.'

Her words hit them like a blow to the gut. The only thing that might give them a better chance of rescue might also increase their risk of dying?

'That's cruel,' said Oost. 'That's a choice straight out of the warp.'

'We should do it,' said Mandelhahn with conviction. They all turned to look at her. She shrugged. 'We all know that we're just counting down the hours and days until we die. At least this gives us a chance.'

'No,' said Padrine, 'time is what we need. The longer we can stay alive the better the odds on us being found. We hook that thing up' – he pointed at the device that Voll held – 'and we're signing our own death warrants.'

'The boy's right,' said Joddrig. 'We'd be fools to drain so much power.'

'We'd be fools not to try it,' said Mandelhahn. 'It might be our only hope.'

'It's too big a risk,' said Oost, shaking her head.

Mandelhahn laughed. 'I never knew I bunked with such a congregation of cowards,' she said. The others bristled at the insult, but Mandelhahn turned her attention to Kaden. 'You're the comms expert. Where do you stand?'

Kaden reached down, took the device from Voll, looked it over. 'We don't even know if it works.'

'So, test it, hook it up. Find out,' said Mandelhahn. 'If it does what she says it'll do, then we've got a choice. We can turn it on and take our chances. Or,' she said, looking back to the others, 'we can die slowly and painfully because none of us ever had the guts to take a risk.'

Joddrig threw his heavy boots into the corner of his cabin, where they clattered against the metal. Anger brewed and bubbled in him, like a cauldron on a furnace top. 'Coward, am I?' he muttered. The very mention of the word fired his blood. He had been through more than the likes of Mandelhahn ever had, more than she could hope to live through in ten lifetimes. He'd proved himself over and over, knew in his heart that he had courage, he had strength, he had resilience. He knew what kind of man he was. He was scared of nothing, nothing that lived or breathed or–

An image flashed into his mind and he shook his head, as though trying to dislodge a hook. *No*, he said to himself, *not now. Not that.*

He stood up from his bunk and paced the small cabin. He was right, he knew that. The signal booster would be too much of a risk. They were taking a chance even letting Voll inside the craft, cutting down their share of rations, using up more air. They'd have been better off leaving her outside, leaving her to–

Again, the image came, and this time it lodged in his mind. A memory, the day of the warp storm, the day the ship had been destroyed. Grejov's face behind the cracked visor...

Joddrig sat down heavily on the end of his bunk and rubbed his heavy, thick fingers over his face, feeling the scratch of his beard against his skin. He pressed the pads of his thumbs against his eyelids like a mask, but the image was still there, lurking behind them.

Joddrig had been on a routine maintenance assignment on the day of the storm, repairing a crack in the hull surface. Grejov had been his second – a tool-carrier, linked to Joddrig's void suit by a thick umbilical cord. It had been a task that they had undertaken a thousand times, and a thousand times before it had passed without danger. But the day the warp storm hit – with no warning, no chance to prepare – when the fabric of space itself seemed to rip open and tear apart anything in its reach, Joddrig and Grejov could do nothing but watch and try to survive.

Joddrig had desperately grabbed for a handhold on the hull, his fingers finding the crevice of an opening at the edge of an access hatch, allowing him to brace himself against the ship. But as he turned to see whether Grejov had found a similar anchor, he found himself almost yanked away from his place of safety. Grejov was floating beyond him, at the end of the taut umbilical cord, the waves of the warp storm twisting and bursting behind him. Joddrig tried to pull him closer, but the effort needed was more than he could spare, not without losing his own grip on the hull. Instead, he could only watch as the cracks that had appeared in Grejov's visor began to multiply and spread, crisscrossing the glass like a web, until finally the whole surface exploded, sending shards of the faceplate flying and exposing Grejov to the ice-cold airlessness of space.

For a moment, there was only shock and surprise on Grejov's face, then a flash of horror at the realisation of what was to come. Joddrig saw Grejov's lips open, expelling his final breath of air.

At the same time, Grejov's face began to swell and deform, the flesh around his eyes bulging and distorting as his neck began to distend, swiftly growing to almost twice its width. With no shielding against the energies of the warp storm, Grejov's skin began to blister and darken, like meat against a grill, then melt away completely, revealing the bloated and bloody flesh beneath.

The thing that had most horrified Joddrig, though, were his eyes, which showed every moment of pain, every escalation of agony. It was too much for Joddrig to bear. With his free hand, he had pulled the lever which released his end of the umbilical cord and watched as Grejov's body was pulled away from him into the depths of the storm, his bulbous, skinned lips gasping for a next breath that would never come.

Joddrig sat up straight, turned his face to the cabin ceiling and sucked in a lungful of the thin, stale air. His body was trembling at the memory of Grejov's last, suffocating moments. He was lying to himself when he said there was nothing he feared, for the prospect of succumbing to Grejov's fate terrified him to the core.

A single corridor linked the cabins with the door to the comms room, and Padrine paced the length of it from one end to the other like a guard on sentry duty, his boots pounding out a regular drumbeat on the metal floor – *d'dun d'dun d'dun d'dun*. A turn on his heels at the closed door and then he walked back again, *d'dun d'dun*, focusing his mind on the sound and the movement of his body, blocking out the other thoughts that were trying to crowd in.

Joddrig's right, was the thought that was hovering around him, *we should never have let her in*. He had nothing against Voll – he didn't even know her. But the last thing they needed was another body on board. It wasn't just the rations, or the life support systems, it was the lack of space. Ever since the explosions which had ruptured and torn apart the ship, when the five of them had been forced into this patched-up section of the craft, the sense of claustrophobia had been growing in him. He hated to be cooped up like this, kept like an animal in a cage, or like a–

Like a prisoner. He stopped walking, put his hand against the wall beside him. That was the savage irony of his survival from the storm that had wrecked the ship. The ruptures that had torn the fabric of the craft asunder had also freed him from his containment in the brig, where he'd languished for several long months. Just the memory of the cell in which he'd been held was enough to bring out a sweat on his brow. Four cramped walls, no room to lie down, barely room to sit, just his own mind for company. It had been enough to drive a man mad.

And for what? Because he'd taken a blade to that fool Tunt, carved him a new face full of holes, taught him that Padrine was the butt of no man's joke. Of course, he hadn't planned to kill Tunt, but in his enthusiasm to teach the man a lesson he'd been careless with the knife and severed an artery. When they'd found the two of them, Padrine was covered in Tunt's blood and the other man was gasping like a banked fish, and even though Padrine tried to convince them of his true intentions, there was no doubt that he was to blame.

None of the others knew this, of course. When he'd found himself free from his confinement and made his way along the collapsing corridors towards the comms room, he was just hoping to survive, and when he'd found the others and they'd put all their efforts into securing that section of the craft, there hadn't been time to talk. It was only later, when their immediate survival had been secured, that they began to share their stories. And then it was easy for Padrine to just omit his recent history of confinement, for what good would it do for them to know? If it came down to it, that they needed to sacrifice someone for the sake of their survival – to make the rations or the life support systems last – then why give them any reason to pick him?

He began to walk again, and as he walked, he felt in his pocket for the knife. It wasn't the same one that he'd used on Tunt. That had been taken from him. But it was a good enough blade, nonetheless. If it came down to it, as it surely would in these coming days, then he wanted to make sure that he was near the top of the pecking order for survival. And if that meant taking care of one of the others, then he was ready to do what had to be done. There was no brig to hold him now, after all – and no one to stop him.

'Are you awake?' said Mandelhahn. Oost was turned away from her on the bunk that they shared, but Mandelhahn could sense that she was not yet sleeping – something about the way she held her body, muscles tight as though in anticipation. Oost made a sound, neither a *yes* or a *no*, barely more than a grunt, and turned onto her back. She opened her eyes, stared at the ceiling for a moment, then turned to Mandelhahn.

'You have something to say? Are you going to tell me I'm a coward once again?' She scoffed, shook her head. 'Or is it a fool this time?'

'You're neither a coward, nor a fool,' said Mandelhahn. 'But you're more stubborn than any woman I've ever met.'

'Why? Because I won't take a needless risk that could damn us all?'

'Because you won't listen to reason,' said Mandelhahn, 'even when it's in your best interests. This device that Voll has – it could be our only hope.'

'Or it could kill us all,' said Oost.

'It's a chance we have to take,' said Mandelhahn. 'Can't you see that?'

Oost sat up on the bunk. In the dimness of the room, her eyes were just two glints of light. But they were bright, unwavering. Defiant.

'If you're in a hurry to die,' she said, 'there are quicker ways to get there.'

Mandelhahn held Oost's gaze for a long moment. There was going to be no convincing her. She swung her legs over the side of the bunk and stood up. As she reached the door and grasped the handle, she looked back at the other woman.

'Whether you die quickly, or die slowly, you leave the same corpse,' she said.

Voll stood at the viewing portal, looking out at the stars beyond, her head tilted to one side as though examining the detail of a painting. As Kaden emerged from beneath the comms desk, she turned to him and gave the same crease of a smile as before.

'Is it working?' she said.

Kaden grabbed a tool from the desk. 'It'll take a while longer,' he said. 'The whole craft was in a bad way when we first got here. We had to do a lot of patching up. Nothing's ever as simple as it looks.'

'But you can do it?' said Voll. 'You can fit the booster.'

'I can do it,' said Kaden. 'But I can't warrant that the others will want to turn it on.'

'They don't trust me,' said Voll. It was said as a blank statement of fact. 'They're afraid.'

'They have a lot to be afraid of,' said Kaden. 'It's been a tough stretch, being stranded here all these long days. Does things to a mind. Awakens superstition, sets nerves afire.' He looked at Voll, a curious crease in his brow. 'How did you manage it? Out there alone all that time, not even a crewmate to talk to? How did it not drive you to insanity?'

Voll uttered a dark laugh. 'I'm not sure it didn't,' she said.

'You seem sane enough to me,' said Kaden. 'At least no less sane than the rest of us.'

'I'll tell you something,' said Voll. 'When I first came across this section of the craft and looked in through the glass and saw you all gathered here, you want to venture what my first thought was?' She lowered her voice almost to a whisper. 'That you were ghosts, beckoning me to my death.'

Kaden gave a short laugh. 'That's no surprise,' he said, 'I've half wondered myself if we weren't already dead.'

Joddrig sat bootless on the floor, his right arm stretching into the gap between the heavy bunk and the wall. He strained to reach further, felt his fingertips touch the cold glass he was looking for. He fumbled to grasp it, felt it totter for a moment out of his touch and readied the mother of all curses on his lips. Then the bottle fell towards him again and he clasped it tightly in his palm, before drawing it out and holding it up to the light.

A bottle of amasec, a cheap but potent brew, the only alcohol left on board the craft. He'd found it on that first day after the ship's destruction, when they were inventorying their rations, and had managed to keep it hidden from the others ever since. In the early days, he'd taken a glug or two every evening, just to keep his spirits on an even keel. But as the weeks had worn on and he'd seen the bottle grow emptier and emptier, he'd decided to ration himself, and had interred the bottle in its hiding place behind the bunk as a means of staving off temptation. But now, with the memories of Grejov still swirling around his head, he needed a taste to quiet his nerves.

There was perhaps a finger of the golden liquid left in the bottle, and Joddrig was torn between the desire to gulp it down immediately or eke it out for as long as possible. He uncorked the bottle, raised it to his mouth, and as soon as he felt the alcohol touch his lips he knew that he would not be able to resist his first impulse. He drank it down in three large gulps, relishing the fieriness of it as it coated his tongue and slid down his throat, closing his eyes in satisfaction as the heat hit his belly.

He opened his eyes and licked his lips, seeking out every last taste of the liquid, cradling the empty bottle in his lap as though it were the dead body of a beloved pet. As the last faint specks of alcohol mingled with his saliva, he saw the cabin lights flicker, heard a buzz of energy around him, and then the room went dark.

In the comms room, Voll's silhouette stood out against the starfield beyond the viewing portal.

'What's happening?' she said in the darkness. 'Is there a problem? Is it the signal booster?'

'No,' said Kaden, from beneath the desk. 'No fault of mine. It's the powercells, they're on a cycle. It happens every night. A way to conserve energy. They'll be back on again in a short time.'

He took the torch out from his pocket, went back to work. Hoped that it was true.

With the lights out in his cabin, the only illumination came from the small round viewport which sat low in the wall opposite Joddrig. A circle of stars slowly rotated within the frame of the window as the craft drifted and turned, pinpricks of light glowing against the infinite blackness.

Joddrig watched the stars turn as the warmth of the amasec faded in his belly and the alcohol began to work on his senses, making him feel as though he were slipping into a dream. For a moment he wondered about the darkness, wondered what it meant, if he should be worried. Then something appeared, floating out there in front of the gleaming stars, something which robbed his mind of any other thought.

Joddrig's heart jumped and he scrabbled quickly on all fours across the cabin floor, dragging the empty amasec bottle with him as he went. He pulled himself up to place his nose against the viewport and looked out.

The figure of a man was floating out past the ship, a corridor's length away from him, but still close enough for Joddrig to know instantly who it was.

Joddrig's throat dried. He put a hand to his eyes to rub them clear, looked again. The man still hung there, suspended against the starfield.

Grejov.

It couldn't be. Too many days had passed since the storm, the damaged craft had drifted far from where Grejov had died. His body had been moving away from the ship when Joddrig last saw it. How could it be back here now?

But here it was, regardless. Joddrig recognised his friend's void suit, saw the long umbilical cord still attached, now hanging, useless. And even from this distance, he could see Grejov's face – flesh stripped almost to the bone, the eyes melted away into dark, empty sockets, the yellowed teeth exposed and set in a mocking rictus grin, the face that had been branded on his memory forever.

Those last moments came back to him again now – Grejov gasping for air, his eyes pleading with Joddrig for some kind of help. Joddrig, terrified for his own life, releasing the cord.

Joddrig pushed himself away from the viewport, scrambling back across the floor until he could no longer see the floating corpse of his friend. As his back hit the far wall, he realised that he was struggling to find his own breath, as though the air in the room had grown thin. A fear came over him. What if this was it? The lights going out, the life support systems failing – what if this was the end? What if Grejov's body was a sign of what was to come for him?

His heart was pumping hard against his chest and he could feel the panic rising. He sucked in one breath after another, but none seemed to fill his lungs. He crawled over to the cabin door, pressed the button to open it, but nothing happened. He pulled himself up to his knees and tried to yank the handle. It wouldn't budge.

This was it, he told himself, the craft was on lockdown. Systems failing, oxygen levels falling, it might be only a matter of minutes before he was dead. He looked again towards the viewport, saw Grejov's corpse even closer now. Saw the twisted and agonised grin on the near-skeletal face. The thought of a slow, suffocating death terrified him. He couldn't stand to die that way, there had to be something better. Cleaner. Quicker.

He felt the empty bottle in his hand and knew what he had to do. He swung it hard against the door, smashing away the bottom of the vessel, leaving a ragged, sharp edge. As he lifted the broken bottle to his throat, he was glad he'd drunk the amasec down in one. It might help to ease the pain.

As Grejov's corpse looked on from the window, Joddrig plunged the jagged edge into his throat and tore.

Padrine was in the store when the lights went out. He knew the place almost inch by inch – as part of the supplies crew it had been his duty to do so – but still, it disconcerted him. In the darkness every walkway felt narrower, every wall closer. He felt for the torch on his belt, but his fingers met an empty pouch. *Throne preserve us*, he muttered to himself. *What kind of fool goes without a torch?*

He walked slowly now, minding his step. On entering the store his aim had been to reach the furthest compartment, the one that held the hundred stacks of empty ration tins, all surplus to their requirements and therefore ignored by the others. It had been the place where he had secreted the last laspistol to be found aboard the ship, hidden away precisely for a time like this, when a firm hand may be needed to steer the group away from a ruinous path.

The more he'd considered it, the more suspicious he'd felt of Voll, the more certain he was that she possessed some malevolent agenda. The others were too trusting, especially that fool

Kaden – a by-the-book man if ever he'd seen one. If they weren't careful, she'd have them all going along with her lunatic plan. Drain the ship of power? It was madness. And he'd need to show them that.

He took a step forward and stumbled. As he righted himself, he felt a tug on his ankle, something tightening around the bone. Reaching down he felt something entangled around his boot. A stretch of cable, his fingers told him, and firmly knotted. He cursed to himself, then crouched down and worked his fingertips in between the taut rolls. He didn't know how many long minutes it took him to finally get his foot free, but by the end of his efforts he was sweating hard, and his head was pounding with the closeness of the air around him. All he wanted to do now was find the lasgun and get out of this dark and airless closet. He stood up quickly, went to move away – but then his other foot slipped on a loose strip of cable, and all of a sudden he was thrust forward, off-balance and scrabbling for a handhold.

His face hit a smooth, solid surface. He felt his nose crack and break, warm blood spattering his cheeks. At the same time there was a loud bang behind him, and something hard hit him in the back. When he tried to turn, he found that he was trapped.

With rising panic, he shifted his body round between close walls, to face back the way he'd fallen. He reached up his hands and felt smooth metal in front of him. He was in a containment locker, one of the ones that they'd already emptied of gear. It was barely bigger than the size of a man.

His hands scrabbled around the door of the locker, searching for some kind of latch or handle, but there was none. When he tried to push against the metal, bracing his back against the rear of the space, his hands found no give. It was as though there was no door at all, just a solid, impenetrable set of walls all around him.

He was sweating even harder now, and feeling his breath

growing short and more rapid as he struggled to find some hint of a crack in the walls that surrounded him. Memories flashed back into his mind – being locked in his cell, day after day, his legs cramped, his body aching – and now, somehow, he found himself in a situation that was even worse, even more intolerable.

He battered his fists against the door and the walls, but the thick metal sent back only dull sounds and he knew that the others wouldn't hear him, especially as he'd closed the store cabin door so as not to arouse suspicion while he retrieved the lasgun. Unless someone came into the cabin it would be hours before they found him, long hours confined in this space, trapped in this airless coffin...

The thought terrified him, and he felt his mind boiling to a frenzy. He couldn't stand it, couldn't make it through. It was too much to bear. He had to rid himself of the thought, drive it from his mind. He bent his head back and slammed his temple into the metal door. Bright stars sparked behind his eyes and pain shot through him, for that moment obliterating everything else – all thought, all memory. Bracing his arms against the door, he threw his head forward again, harder this time. Then again, and again, until blood coated his face, and he could feel the bones of his temple begin to crack.

Over and over again, he beat his head against the metal, until there was nothing left but blood, broken bone and oblivion.

Mandelhahn sat up on her bunk. She was in the cabin beside the storeroom, the one they'd been using as a medicae ward, where she'd been since her argument with Oost. There was banging coming from somewhere, a sound like a steady, ominous drumbeat. For a moment she thought it might be Padrine again, with his interminable pacing up and down the corridors. But this sound was duller, further away, like it was being transmitted through the very metal of the ship. Something in the sound disturbed her, but she didn't know why. She listened again for the sound, heard it once, twice, three times, and then no more. In the silence it came to her: the memory. The tale her father had told her of the great and terrible warrior, felled on the battleground, supposed dead and given a warrior's burial, only to be heard, days later, pounding his fist against the coffin that held him...

Kaden came out from beneath the comms desk, shuffling on his back in the darkness, the torch held between his teeth. The light hit Voll full in the face as he emerged.

'Done?' she asked.

Kaden turned the torch so that it was out of her eyes. 'Yes,' he said.

'The signal booster is functional? You've tested it?' asked Voll.

'It works perfectly,' said Kaden.

Voll nodded. 'Then we should call the others. Tell them it's time to make their choice.'

'Perhaps we should wait,' said Kaden, 'until the powercells–'

Even as he spoke there was a buzz and a flicker, and the lights on the ship came on again. Kaden blinked his eyes against the sudden illumination.

'You must be some kind of sorcerer,' said Voll.

Kaden gave a grunt. 'More cursed than conjurer,' he said. He looked at the switch which was now affixed to the comms unit. 'Before we bring the others in,' he said, 'there's something...'

A yell came from the corridor outside the comms room.

'Kaden!'

As Kaden and Voll turned to the sound, they saw Mandelhahn in the doorway. Her hands were smeared in blood.

'It's Padrine,' she said.

* * *

Padrine's body lay on the floor in the supplies cabin, his feet still inside the metal cabinet where Mandelhahn had found him, his lifeless face – nose broken, eyes swollen and dark, his forehead a crater of blood, pulped flesh and fragments of broken bone – peering up at them.

'That's where he fell when I opened the door,' said Mandelhahn. 'There's blood smeared inside the cabinet, front and back. Some frenzy he must have been in.'

'He did this to himself?' said Kaden.

Mandelhahn nodded. 'By all appearances.'

Kaden crouched to look closer at Padrine's face. Blood was congealed around the bone fragments that jutted from his forehead. 'Something was inside his head,' said Kaden, almost to himself. 'Something he couldn't get out.'

'It's not just him,' said a voice from the door. The three of them turned to see Oost. She was shifting nervously from foot to foot, her eyes hovering over Voll. 'There's something deadly come aboard this craft.'

The blood that pooled from the ragged hole in Joddrig's neck spread from his body almost to the door where they stood, its surface glinting with the reflection of the overhead lights, like stars twinkling in a dark pool, its stench – of plasma and amasec and death – thick in the stale air around them.

'What could drive a man to do such a thing?' said Mandelhahn. 'To harm himself in that way?'

'Perhaps it was the drink,' said Voll. 'Many have been ruined by it. If it finds you in a black mood, it can drive you down to the depths of–'

'It's not drink that's done this,' said Oost, cutting her off. 'Same as it wasn't drink that done for Padrine.' She was staring hard at Voll, her hands still clasping and unclasping as though preparing to make a leap. 'It's you.'

The others looked at Oost with confusion.

'Voll has not been out of my sight these past hours,' said Kaden. 'There's no chance that she could have had any part in this.'

Oost let out a hollow laugh. 'You don't know what she is, do you? You haven't discerned it yet. Not even you, Kaden.'

'You need to start speaking sense,' said Mandelhahn. 'We're not telepaths.'

Oost wiped a hand over her mouth. She was sweating, nervous, her eyes never leaving Voll. 'She's a spirit,' she said. 'One of those ancient ones, from the ghost planet.' She lifted her hand to point a finger in Voll's face. 'Valgaast,' she hissed.

'There's no such thing as spirits,' said Mandelhahn, her face blanching at Oost's suggestion. 'That's a heathen notion.'

Voll laughed, shook her head. 'You're losing your wits,' she said. 'Same as these others.'

Oost ignored her. 'She's here to take our souls,' she said. 'Take them down with her to the planet.' With a sudden movement she went past them over to the viewport, her feet making treads in Joddrig's blood. She peered through the glass, into the darkness beyond. 'It's out there somewhere, close by. It's how she was able to come to us. There's no other part of the ship that survived the blast. It's all a lie. A tall tale to make us trust her. And this bullshit about a signal boost – ha!' The laugh burst from her like a shot. 'It's just a way to get us to kill ourselves. To get inside our heads, same way she did Joddrig, same way she did Padrine.' She turned from the window, looked angrily at Kaden and Mandelhahn. 'Can't you see it?'

Mandelhahn shook her head, looked pityingly at Oost. 'That was just a tale,' she said softly, as though speaking to a child. 'There is no planet and she's no spirit.' She nodded over at Voll. 'She's flesh and blood, same as you. And she's not here to kill us, she's giving us a chance to survive. And it's a chance I think we should take, before this damned confinement makes lunatics of us all.' She turned to Kaden. 'Is it ready, the signal booster?'

'Yes,' said Kaden, 'but–'

Mandelhahn cut him off. 'Then we switch it on. Agreed?'

'No!' yelled Oost fiercely. She glowered at Mandelhahn. 'You'll touch that switch over my dead body.'

For a moment the two of them stood, eyes locked in mutual defiance. Then Mandelhahn turned, bolted and ran. As her figure disappeared from sight, moving towards the comms room, Oost let out a savage, manic scream and ran after her. As she passed, Kaden tried to grab her arm and pull her back, but Oost shoved him hard in the chest, sending him slamming against the wall, his feet slipping in Joddrig's blood. As Kaden hit the floor and felt the still-warm, half-congealed liquid smear across his face, he yelled out a desperate cry: 'Don't!'

Mandelhahn reached the comms room and ran for the desk. But even as she reached out her arm for the switch that would activate the signal booster, she felt a thud in her shoulder and an agonising pain went through her. She fell to her knees, reached up her hand and felt the knife that was embedded there.

Oost was at the doorway, pulling another knife from her belt. She glanced behind her as she saw Kaden and Voll running down the corridor towards her, then slammed her fist into the control panel, locking the door shut behind her.

With a rising moan of pain, Mandelhahn wrenched the knife from her back. Thick drops of blood hit the cabin floor and she felt a dryness in her throat. She had only minutes, she knew, before the loss of blood would make her too weak to carry on.

'Move away from the desk,' said Oost. 'I don't want to hurt you.'

Mandelhahn looked up, saw the resolve in Oost's eyes, saw the clean blade in her hand. Slowly, she stood up, wiped her own blood from the knife onto the thigh of her uniform and turned to face her.

Kaden pounded his fists against the door of the comms room. 'Oost!' he yelled, 'Mandelhahn!' He stabbed a finger against the control panel, but the door was jammed shut. He spun round to look at Voll, who stood behind him. 'Help me, for Throne's sake, help me!'

Mandelhahn and Oost circled each other, each holding their combat knife in front of them, each waiting for the other to make a move. With every step that Mandelhahn took, new smears of blood appeared on the floor beneath her feet. Her uniform was soaked from the wound in her back and she could feel a coldness beginning to spread across her body.

She wanted to say something to Oost, something that would quell her paranoia, something that would make her see that they had to take this chance, that nothing but madness awaited them otherwise. But looking into Oost's eyes, she could see that the time for talking was past. Whatever fragile bond they had shared before now as survivors, it had been severed and there was no going back.

As they moved around each other, Mandelhahn saw Oost's eyes flick over towards the comms desk where the signal booster sat, searching for a way to disable it for good. In that instant, she lunged forward, thrust her blade deep into Oost's torso, feeling the hilt push up against the flesh as the tip of the blade hit bone. Oost let out a gasp and her free hand grasped at Mandelhahn's back, pulling her in close as though in an embrace. At the same time, Mandelhahn felt Oost's blade plunge into her stomach, the serrated edge tearing a ragged split in her gut. The smell of her own exposed intestines hit her nose and she gagged.

For a moment the two of them stood locked together, eyes only inches apart, their blood mingling and spilling onto the cabin floor. A word seemed to hang on Oost's lips, but as the breath came to speak it, her eyes grew dim and the weight of her body pulled them both to the floor with a crash.

When Kaden and Voll finally forced the door open, Mandelhahn and Oost were both already dead, their bodies entangled on the cabin floor, their hands still holding the blades that sat deep in the other's body, making them seem like one single, twin-headed entity.

Kaden stared at the bodies for a long time, while Voll watched on, silently observing the agonies of thought which seemed to be traversing the taut muscles of his face. Finally, Kaden walked over to the comms desk and placed his hands either side of the switch, his head bowed as though in silent contemplation.

'I'm sorry for your crewmates,' said Voll, after a time.

Kaden nodded, keeping his head bowed, his eyes on the switch. Without seeming to hear her footsteps, Kaden felt Voll step forward to stand against the viewing portal beside him.

'The decision still remains,' she said quietly. 'The choice.'

Kaden took a deep breath and turned to her. 'There is no choice,' he said. 'All of this…' He gestured to the bodies of Mandelhahn and Oost. 'Joddrig and Padrine too. It was all for nothing.' He pointed to the switch. 'Your device works exactly as it should, yes. But…'

He turned to look at her. His face was ashen with guilt.

'There is no distress signal for it to boost. There never has been.'

A silence hung between them for a moment.

'You lied to them,' said Voll finally.

'There had to be some hope,' said Kaden. 'We had nothing else. What should I have done? Told them the truth? That we were doomed from the very moment we came aboard this craft? That only a miracle could save us?'

Voll nodded at the bodies on the floor. 'That's what hope did to them.'

'No!' said Kaden. 'That's what you did to them with your damned device. It drove them mad, made them lose their minds.' He looked at Voll, his eyes cold with anger. 'Joddrig was right. We should never have brought you aboard this ship. All you have brought is misery, all you have brought is…'

The words died on his tongue and he looked away.

'All I offered was a choice,' said Voll, quietly. 'That's all I've ever done.'

With Voll's help, Kaden moved the bodies of Joddrig and Padrine into the comms room and laid them out next to Mandelhahn and Oost. He covered them in sheets and muttered a ritual prayer for their souls, such as he could remember. Then, one by one, he put them into the airlock and opened it, sending their corpses into the airless depths of space.

'At the very least,' he said to Voll, as he stood at the door to the airlock, 'I can vouch that I got them off this prison of a ship. That, if nothing else.'

'I know that you mark yourself responsible for what befell them,' said Voll. 'But what's done is done, and there's no use in brooding on it now. And, in truth, the result of their sacrifice means that we now have more rations to share between us, and more oxygen too. Even if hope of rescue is slim, we have a little more chance now. Isn't that something to be grateful for?'

'Grateful?' said Kaden. 'No.' A curious look came over his face, as though something in his thoughts was crystallising. 'No, I won't be grateful for what they did. For their derangement and their delusions. I won't make my life on top of the bones of their madness. I should have told them the truth. I own that. But I'll be damned if I'm going to spend my last living days sucking down air that should have been theirs.'

'What then do you propose to do?' said Voll.

Kaden looked at the airlock. 'Make my own choice,' he said.

Kaden stood in the airlock and listened as the inner compartment door closed behind him. He faced the outer door, beyond which lay the vastness of space. He was ready. He had been since he had seen the bodies of Mandelhahn and Oost, Joddrig and Padrine, all laid out in front of him. They'd been through the worst of times together, the five of them. And they'd stay together now. He looked back through the window of the inner door and gave a nod to Voll, a signal to open the hatch. She nodded back and disappeared from view. Kaden took a last breath and then watched as two sides of the outer door slid apart and the star-flecked darkness appeared before him.

With a rush of air, Kaden was sucked out past the doors of the craft. Immediately he felt the coldness through to his bones, while his skin began to pulse and dapple with the energies that surrounded him. A rush of terror went through him, but also a feeling of peace. He'd done the right thing. He'd set the terms of his own death, no one else.

It was only as he expelled his last breath that he saw it appear below him, colossal and terrifying – the planet around which they had been orbiting. Continents of writhing, wraith-like masses, oceans of squirming souls all laid out before him, filling his vision in its immensity. Even through the airless distance of space he felt as though he could hear the cries of all the dead who populated this haunted, spectral world, their voices a cacophony of agony. In his last moments he knew that he'd been tricked, that he'd condemned himself and all his crewmates to an eternity of fathomless miseries. But there was nothing now he could do. His choice had been made. He felt the pull of the planet's gravity, as what remained of him left his frozen, bloated body behind and descended to the ghost planet's monstrous surface.

Back on the deck of what remained of the *Endless Wrath*, no soul remained to draw breath. As the ship drifted, unmanned, through the great vastness of space, silence reigned.

PENTIMENTO

Nick Kyme

The body stood erect and cruciform, naked and without modesty. Male, though the anatomical excisions made this difficult to define for certain, as did the general disfigurements to the victim overall. It appeared almost ritualistic. A statement of some kind.

Observation was Mabeth's art. She had an eye for it, or so Hakasto had joked. Gifted, some said. To her, the old artisan had been like a father. He taught her everything he knew, until eventually she surpassed him. Oka Hakasto's craft became Mabeth's craft, she his only student. Then, their work had been venerated around the world, as nobles and oligarchs clamoured for a sitting with the great Hakasto and his protégé. Coin, renown, they had been short of neither.

And now…

They say scent is the most powerful sense memory. Sitting in that empty church, the air thick with the reek of copper, Mabeth remembered her master. His legacy had ended with a knife in his neck and his arterial blood making a terrible mess of his otherwise fine robes.

Coin, renown... but also jealously and greed. She had wept and not changed her mourning robes for six days, her eyes thick with kohl, her lips inked black.

His death, for all its callous senselessness, was mundane. Not like *this*. This was art. Grotesque, unconscionable, but art nonetheless. And she knew art. Hakasto had not taught her that. That was innate. She *bled* art.

And there was much blood, lustrous and red.

Now, only the dead would sit for her, and they had little choice or awareness of the matter. As Mabeth sketched, she took in the arms that had been strung by the victim's own sinews. Hanging limply, as if some godlike and invisible puppeteer held onto them from above. *No, not a puppet*, she realised. She had misread the artist's intentions. She sketched splayed feet, their broken toes and bones distended, and the clawed fingers reaching like strange branches. And finally, the position of the body, utterly straight, rigid as any trunk.

'A tree...' she murmured aloud, pausing to regard it.

'What?' asked Levio. The proctor sounded gruff, his unshaven face further testimony of either a lack of self-respect or the lateness of the hour. Or both. He was badly dressed in a long coat and peacekeeper fatigues, one of several weary lawmen at large in the church. He worried at the aquila rosary wrapped around his wrist, half eyeing the shadows of the dingy church with only stab-lights to lift the darkness. He hid his irritation poorly.

'A tree,' Mabeth repeated, her charcoal stylus poised. 'He has been arranged in the manner and aspect of a tree.'

'There aren't any trees in the city.'

'I didn't say it was based on anything in Durgov.'

Levio took another look. 'I only see some poor bastard, tortured to death.' He turned, frowned. 'You said *arranged*?'

Mabeth nodded.

'What do you think it means?'

'Growth, rebirth... knowledge, maybe,' she said. 'A tree has broad symbolic meaning.'

'I don't see meaning. I see madness. City's infected with it.'

It had got worse. Ever since the sky had changed and the astropaths had died. No word out, no word in. Entire world had been affected. Something had happened, but no one knew what it was, only that it had. Powerlessness bred fear. Fear bred violence. And so it went.

'Why I am here, Proctor Levio?'

'Arbitrator wants a record.' He stalled to pick at something in his teeth. 'Doesn't want to come down here to see for herself.'

Mabeth gestured to the perturbed looking hunchback busying around a picter unit.

'Then what's he here for? Would a pictograph not capture a more accurate impression of the scene? Not to mention be much faster? I'm not complaining,' she hastened to add, 'I need the coin. Not much work for an artist when every patron has decided to start hoarding their wealth for the end of days.'

'I honestly do not know,' admitted Levio. 'So far, he's done precisely fuck all.'

The hunchback's dark robes hid several disfigurements, most of them cybernetic in nature. He was a sacristan, conversant in the utilisation and repair of machines. Right now, as he switched out parts from the picter or replaced powercells, he appeared only to be conversant in a varied lexicon of expletives.

'Here...' Levio pulled a folder from his long coat and handed it to Mabeth.

She opened it and leafed through several flimsies.

'They're all useless,' she said, frowning. 'Just blurred images.'

'Yep. Doesn't matter what that hunchbacked arsehole does, the picts won't come out. That's the sixth picter we've tried.'

'How long have you been in here?'

Levio rubbed his unshaven face and she had her answer.

Mabeth looked back through the images. They were obfuscated as if overexposed or smeared by a sudden jerk of the lens. But the subject was static, the picter secure and the light steady.

'This is very strange,' she conceded.

'I've gone from strange to irritating, and I'm circling livid. Or suicidal,' said Levio, 'it changes by the minute...'

Mabeth glanced down at her sketch. The rendering was good. The curve of the thigh, the overall musculature, the texture of the lank hair and scarred flesh... As vivid as she had ever been on parchment and almost more real than any pictograph...

'I see,' she said, handing back the useless flimsies.

'So, if you don't mind,' said Levio, 'hurry it the hell up. I can't get out of here until you're finished.'

He walked away to berate the sacristan, leaving Mabeth to it.

'Charming...' she whispered, but her work was almost done. Just a little detailing remained. She had a leather field case for carrying all her equipment and pulled from it a magnifying lens she attached over her left eye via a skull frame. Up close, even via the lens, the scene felt... *intimate*. Every knife stroke revealed. Every abuse. And it was neat murder, almost surgical. It spoke to obsession. Through her enhancing lens, she looked through a window into something dark. She lingered on the face, partly hidden by the hair. Something looked back at her from those cold, dead eyes. Recognition? Mabeth found herself drawn, though she wanted to recoil. The lips were barely parted, but she caught the suggestion of white teeth and then... they moved.

Paradise...

Like a lover's breath against her ear, warm and susurrant. The scent of cloying lavender filled her nose.

Mabeth tore away the lens, letting out a stifled cry.

Levio whirled around, reaching for his sidearm, until he realised the girl had shrieked at shadows.

'It's nothing,' she said, a little breathless, and out of instinct touched her neck. But there was nothing there. It just felt cold, like a strange absence.

Levio scowled, standing down as he went to light up a smoke and muttering some about the bad decisions that had led up to this moment.

Tentatively, Mabeth put the lens back on. Nothing happened. The body remained as it was, horrific but lifeless. There was no voice, no scent of lavender. Just old blood and musty prayer scrolls. She got what she needed and finished up, handing the parchment to the proctor on her way out.

'I expect prompt payment,' she said by way of a parting shot.

Levio's coarse laughter followed Mabeth until she had left the church.

Gethik was waiting for her outside, the servitor's dull eyes barely comprehending his surroundings and not so different from the corpse Mabeth had just sketched.

'Follow,' she uttered as she passed the brutish creature, hearing him fall into clomping lockstep behind her. The city had lost its mind since the killings, so it paid to have protection, even if Gethik was a piece of cyborganic shit better suited to the scrapheap than bodyguard detail. Intimidation went a long way though, and Gethik was big. He smelled of machine oil and rust, but at least it helped to banish the memory of sickly lavender.

'Must be tired...' she said and through the gaps in the overarching buildings caught glimpses of the sky. A blood-red blush coloured it, like paint clouding in water. Shouts echoed on the warm night air, a sign of the madness to come. She'd be gone before any of that. Mabeth turned away and headed for the mag-rail.

* * *

The other patrons in the carriage gave Gethik a wide berth, though the servitor barely noticed them and the late hour had thinned the crowds substantially so it wasn't hard to find a seat. Fires lit parts of the city, seen through a grimy window. The violence had started early tonight. It wouldn't trouble her here, Mabeth reflected, as the rattling journey played out in all its mundanity. Sat in her protector's shadow, she tried to remember everything she'd experienced in the church.

She must have imagined it, but it didn't feel imagined. She had *felt* his breath, *smelled* lavender… The voice had sounded old, but melodic. Definitely male. Not an accent she knew, though, and not from Durgov. From elsewhere. Her mind had conjured it from some remembrance, she reasoned. She rubbed her neck, her fingers gently caressing. The downy hairs felt soft to the touch, and her eyelids fluttered.

Paradise.

Mabeth sat bolt upright, suddenly aware of her surroundings. Perspiration dappled her skin, her fingertips tingling. A face looked back at her, reflected in the glass. Young and pale from a lifetime spent in her studio, shaven haired with a streak of violet running through it. A writhing serpentine neck tattoo, her own design. Jewellery on her wrists, gold and platinum. Good robes of warm cerise and a vermilion cloak with a silver artisanal clasp. Last season's fashions; she couldn't keep up like she used to, but her clothes and trappings were still finer than most. Affluent, it spoke to her success. She admired her reflection, pleased with what she saw.

And just behind it, another face.

Smiling and overlarge. Human and yet…

Mabeth turned around, heart pounding, but there was no one sitting behind her. A couple of factorum workers from farther back in the carriage glanced up at the sudden movement but quickly became downcast again as the day's labours grew heavy. When she looked back, the face had gone.

So startled was she, Mabeth nearly missed her stop and had to dash for the exit, her lumbering retainer in tow.

'I need to find a different line of work, Gethik,' she said, rubbing her eyes as they walked, her hab-tower close by.

The servitor did not reply, and merely shadowed her as always.

'What's that?' asked Mabeth, miming as if he had spoken. 'I'm in the wrong profession?' She gave a rueful shake of the head as Auric House came into view. Not so gilded any more with its tatty facade and chipped colonnade. 'Yes, you're right, I do need a change in fortune.'

Greeting the door warden with a tired wave, she went inside. He smiled as she passed, his mouth altogether too wide under the vision slit of his helmet, the teeth too white and too many. Mabeth recoiled, but the guard's sour look had reappeared almost immediately.

I'm losing my damn mind...

She hurried inside.

Her well-appointed rooms greeted Mabeth upon her return. Everything was as she had left it. The chaise, the hookah pipe, her silks and fine drapery, the ornaments and artist's lectern. Dark, on account of the hour, she instructed Gethik to light the lamps. The gloom lifted, shadows lengthened in corners and filled alcoves. The glass shades coloured the light, turning it into competing jades and crimsons. Mabeth collapsed onto a pile of plush cushions, her hand outstretched for the drink that Gethik then provided.

A sip of absinthe helped ease the nerves, warming as it passed down her throat.

'Leave me...' she uttered, reaching for the hookah as Gethik turned without comment and retreated into his alcove, out of her sight. Mabeth supped on the pipe, taking long draughts of *kalma* smoke. It had been hard to acquire and not a little expensive too. Worth every coin though. She imbibed and smoked until the bottle had drained and her eyelids grew heavy. Fingers slipping from the neck of the pipe, she drifted into a fitful sleep. As she breathed, the smell of over-sweet lavender lingered before something sharper replaced it. And she dreamed, of a forest – not of trees but of the dead, their limbs contorted in branches, their feet rooted to the earth. And the red, red sap of their blood.

Mabeth woke drenched in sweat, the lingering scent of warm copper already fading. Grey light surrounded her, the hour still early. Gethik must have doused the lamps. She started as she saw him looming over her, his dull bionic eye glowing like dirty amber.

'What are you doing?' she croaked, annoyed at her own skittishness. 'What are you doing, *slave*?'

Gethik didn't respond. Her throat felt hoarse like she'd been screaming in her sleep. The servitor's protection protocols must have kicked in.

'I'm fine,' she lied, deciding to get up. That's when she noticed the metal tube in Gethik's hands. He hadn't activated because of a protection protocol, he had taken receipt of a package. It came with an attached note. A snap of her fingers and Gethik lit the nearest lamp.

Mab, the note began, *I think I may have found the last decent paying commission in this entire shit heap of a city.* She knew the handwriting.

Yrenna was Mabeth's abettor, a seeker of work. It was she who had secured the contract with the peacekeepers. Hardly what Mabeth was used to but it kept the debtors at bay and her decanters full. There was a time when they'd enjoyed more than just a business relationship, but Mabeth's tastes had changed and so had her suitors. Still, old memories stirred at seeing her delicate script and provoked a frisson of lust. She turned over the parchment onto the opposite side.

Private contract. Three pieces, simple restoration needed. Yes, I know it's still low end, but it pays better than the peacekeepers and there are fewer dead bodies. She signed off 'Y', adding a postscript. *And that ugly golem needs a thorough cleanse, by the way.*

The note came with the address of the commissioner, and the fee amount her abettor had brokered.

Mabeth smiled and took the metal tube. 'Well done, Yrenna.'

The tube had been marked with an unfamiliar merchant's sigil that looked like a 'V'. Inside, she found three pieces of rolled up canvas. Unfurling each in turn, Mabeth laid them out on the floor, weighing them down with ornaments to keep them from curling back up. They were venerations, holy scenes from Imperial history, albeit faded and in need of repair. She didn't recognise the saints depicted or the other religious figures, the cardinals and the abbesses. She only saw the work ahead and began immediately.

Mabeth fashioned simple frames for each piece from which she could begin the restoration, and then placed them upon her artist's lectern, which was wide enough to accommodate all three. *Curious*, she thought, regarding them as a set, and wondering what interest a mercantile house would have in Ecclesiarchal relics.

A thorough assessment of the condition of the pieces preceded any actual work. The canvas was old, that much was quick to determine, although precisely *how* old she genuinely couldn't say. It had been preserved with oils or perhaps some synthetic equivalent, which made the canvas slightly stiff and flaky at the edges. After she handled each piece to clean them, she noticed a farinaceous substance layering her gloves. Again, she couldn't identify it and it only happened on that first occasion so she assumed the paintings hadn't been disturbed for some time.

She worked steadily, reinvigorating the tired pastels, giving them vibrancy and depth. Mabeth felt reinvigorated, not unlike the ecclesiarchs in the paintings. The brighter the image became, the lighter her mood, as if faith and protection radiated from it.

Hours passed without her realising, and by the time the fonogram started to drone, she had restored a cardinal's vestments and trappings. He was depicted standing upon some nondescript promontory, giving a fiery sermon to his flock.

The fonogram droned again.

She tried to ignore it but it began to irritate, and when she turned and saw the peacekeepers' ident she swore loudly.

Levio's gravel voice crackled through the receiver cup when she picked it up. *'Need your talents again.'*

'I have other work, proctor.'

'That can wait. Your contract gives the city unrestricted access.'

Fucking Yrenna, she thought, feeling less amorous towards the woman as Levio reminded her of that particular clause.

'Can it possibly wait? I am in the middle of something.'

'So am I... It's another one.'

And with those three words, Mabeth knew she would be leaving the hab as soon as the call was over.

'Same as last time?'

'Different...' Levio sounded like he was about to say more, but then swallowed audibly to clear his throat and gave her the address.

'Different how?'

'I'm not describing it over the fonogram,' he snapped, then quickly regained his composure. *'Just get down here.'*

He cut the feed and the fonogram line went dead.

'Arsehole...' Mabeth looked back at the paintings. They would have to wait. The dead, it seemed, would not.

Another dilapidated church, another depravity. The sacristans had returned, more out of hope than expectation, and they had just finished rigging a string of lumens to flood the scene with pearlescent light as Mabeth made her entrance.

She had to crane her neck to see. The victim had been suspended on wire – no, not wire, the veins had been pulled from its arms, woven together and used to hang it like a piece of art.

He's embracing it now, she thought, trying to remain analytical.

The victim hung in front of an immense window, its glassaic smeared in blood and other matter. Wan light streamed through, casting a ragged shadow. Entirely naked, the victim's arms were outstretched, its legs pinned together. But this was not what marked it out as different to the previous murder. The skin had been flayed from its back and chest, and then spread out like a pair of leathery wings behind it. Angelic. Horrific. The ribs were exposed, rimed with blood and glistening in the light. Intertwined organs had been heaped below, a rubbery tract unfurling from the abdomen like some gory streamer.

The face was untouched but for one detail – one of the eyes had been cut out.

'Throne...' uttered Mabeth, and swiftly covered her mouth. She smelled Levio as he sidled up next to her, the reek of sweat and cheap tabac pervasive. 'I understand why you didn't want to describe it over fonogram,' she said, recovering.

'An aquila,' he replied, gesturing to the victim's altered form, 'even I can discern that much. Who the hells does that?'

'I don't know, a religious fanatic? Aren't you supposed to work that out?'

Levio rubbed his balding scalp. The man looked paler and older since last night. 'I have no frame of reference for this.'

'It would take strength...' ventured Mabeth, 'and precision.'

'Still think it's art?'

'I think the killer does.'

Levio lit up a smoke. 'Paradise.'

Mabeth turned on him. 'What did you just say?'

From Levio's expression, she must have looked fearsome. He held up his hands. 'That's what the witness said.'

'What bloody witness?' She was livid, practically shaking. *The smile, the sickly scent of lavender…*

'Easy,' said Levio. 'Calm down.'

Mabeth stared, heart pounding. She felt feverish. A cold sweat clung to her body like a rotten bandage.

'Are you all right?'

She snapped back, hard as a spring. The fever ebbed. 'I'm fine,' she lied. 'I just… I didn't know there had been a witness.'

'Why does it matter?'

'Someone is killing people seemingly at random and turning them into grotesque anatomical works of art,' Mabeth replied, still a little shaky. 'I am both professionally intrigued and personally appalled. Of course it matters. Who's the witness?'

'An old curate. The church is mostly in a state of disrepair. He was effectively the caretaker until it could be restored. Though not much chance of that, given the state of things. He's back at the precinct house with the interrogators, who are trying to find out what he knows.'

'He didn't tell them?'

'Beyond saying "para–" *that* word, he hasn't said much of anything. Whatever he saw, he didn't like it. And it definitely wasn't him who did it, before you ask.'

'I wasn't going to.'

'Yeah, yeah, strength and precision and all that. Fancy yourself a peacekeeper, eh, artisan?'

Mabeth didn't answer. She'd had enough of Levio. She gathered her tools and began. The sooner she got started, the sooner she could leave.

The return to Auric House was conducted in silence. The rioting and unrest in the city had forced her to take a more circuitous route via maglev, and by the time she reached her studio again night had drawn in. It seemed perpetual now, and the memory of the 'flayed angel', as she had come to regard it, lingered like the aroma of decay. And no matter how hard she tried to mentally excoriate, it would not go away.

A long pulse shower when she was safely back in her domicile did little but leave her itchy and hot. She dressed in a gown, a glass of absinthe to soothe her fractious nerves. Every mirror shawled by a blanket. On the journey back she had assiduously avoided looking into any reflective surfaces, glass or otherwise, a silver snuff box held to her nose to keep any undesirable odours at bay. No visitations from the lavender man came to her.

'Am I losing my mind...?' she murmured.

Gethik, lurking in his alcove, offered no comment.

'Definitely losing it, if I'm trying to make conversation with a servitor.'

Perhaps she should call Yrenna for a rendezvous, but she didn't want to go out into the city at night, not with the curfew and the violence, and her domicile was in a parlous state so she couldn't invite her over. Empty bottles everywhere, the reek of kalma on her rugs and drapes.

She settled for another absinthe instead, before slumping onto a pile of cushions to regard the three paintings sitting on her lectern. *Subject matter in kind, but different artists*, she reflected.

The work remained, a refuge and a spiritual tonic.

Mabeth sighed. *It's not like I can sleep anyway*.

Putting her glass down, Mabeth took up her tools. It was late and the work painstaking but she threw herself into it, as if each small act of restoration cleansed a part of her soul. The images in her mind lessened in intensity, the imagined scent of lavender faded. Saints were brought to life on canvas. And it felt *good*. She made swift progress, an obsessive compulsive urge to be rid of the taint of remembering driving her.

Then she saw something unexpected.

She had begun to strip back the layers of ink and pigment, intending to rebuild them from the base up where the image was particularly degraded, when she noticed part of a second image, incongruent with the first, revealed beneath. A magnifying lens from her iris attachment brought it into sharper focus. She couldn't tell what it was exactly, but was certain it was not a part of the religious scene. A layer beneath a layer.

Hakasto had called it 'pentimento', when one image is subtly altered or a previous one painted over entirely. Though there was too little of the hidden image to discern much of anything about its subject, the rationale for hiding it was intriguing.

'Curious...' Mabeth muttered, and tried to reveal more. She reasoned she could repair the upper image later, but this one beneath, this *secret*, beguiled her. Her fingers ached, and while a heavy dose of stimms kept her going until the deep night hours, the scalpel eventually slipped her grasp and she fell into an exhausted sleep.

Mabeth woke to a feeling of disquiet, and the vague memory of a troubling dream that try as she might to grasp, dissipated like smoke. Sensations remained, of pain and pleasure, the instinct of peeling back the layers of her skin to reveal the dark places within. She shivered, despite the warmth of the morning and the blanket she had wrapped around herself.

Through the half-light streaming through the drapes, she saw the paintings and felt a moment of profound arrhythmia. More of the secondary image had been revealed. It was the same on all three canvases, despite the fact she could not remember working on the other two, but then she had taken a cocktail of alcohol and narcotics. She had lost time before.

'Gethik...' she slurred, still drowsy. The servitor lumbered from its alcove. 'Show me vid from last night.'

The servitor hard-linked to a cogitator sitting on a low table, and Mabeth waited for the device to warm up. A flicking projector cast the images from the servitor's gaping mouth onto the wall.

'Here we go,' she whispered as the vid-capture began to render and cycle. Then she frowned, and glared over her shoulder at Gethik. 'I said last night.'

'Confirmed,' he said in a mechanised rasp, the voice coming from a vox-unit in the servitor's neck.

'This is everything?'

'Confirmed.'

Her eyes narrowed, disbelieving. 'Are you certain, Gethik?'

'Confirmed.'

Perhaps she needed a sacristan herself. The vid units in her domicile, the ones she used to capture her artistic process for later review, had to be faulty. Blurred images filled her wall, like an overexposed pict, only in motion.

She caught snatches of... *something*. Mabeth drew closer as the vid continued to run, trying to see past the image flicker.

'What in the hells...'

Not her domicile. Definitely not that. It looked like... bones.

A hard rap at the door gave her a start. She cursed loudly, rubbing her eyes from staring so intently at the image now paused on her wall. She called out, already regretting it.

'Identify...'

It was Levio. 'Couldn't reach you via fonogram,' he grumbled through the door. He sounded even more perturbed than usual.

'So you came to my abode?' Mabeth snapped. She dimly remembered asking Gethik to cut the fonogram shortly after she had entered. A glance at the unit confirmed it.

'Abode?' Levio muttered something unseemly about artists and their ilk, then added, 'So, can I come in or do we shout at each other through your door?'

Mabeth was sorely tempted, but she gestured for Gethik to let the proctor in. He cut the image first, the wall turning blank again.

Even the sight of the proctor, dishevelled, pale, even *thin*... brought back the fear. He had become synonymous with it.

'Is it him?' she asked in a quiet voice. 'The lavender man?'

Levio nodded, and didn't challenge her. He had smelled it too. *Fuck*, that meant it wasn't in her mind. It was something else. She chose not to comment and instead looked through a gap in her drapes at the dawning sky outside, at the strange heavens that now fell over the city. And she wondered.

'Take me there,' she said, sparing a glance at the paintings, and went to get dressed.

It was different this time. In every way. Not a church or a temple. No glassaic or catechisms. A woodland with an overgrown esplanade running through it. In a clearing, a body had been staked out, its limbs meticulously and perfectly bifurcated, four becoming eight, and arranged in a star shape. Pale-white flesh, painstakingly exsanguinated, shimmered like wet marble in the rain.

No sacristans this time. They had learned their lesson, that their technology had no part in this, no purchase upon whatever *this* was. It was just Levio and a squad of peacekeepers wearing black carapace and carrying shotguns to ward off the curious. Mabeth counted herself among them, but she had been invited beyond the electro-cordon, her servitor waiting dully some distance behind her.

'Why?' she asked simply.

'Why what?' Levio answered. 'I'm not a damned mind-shriver, how should I know why the sick bastard is doing this?'

'No,' said Mabeth patiently, 'why do you need me to illustrate this?'

'It has to be captured. Known,' he said. Then added more quietly, 'Allegedly, certain parties are interested.' He extended his middle finger so it looked like the letter 'I'.

'Interrogators?'

'And worse, I expect.' He lit a smoke; Mabeth noticed his fingers trembled. 'Look...' He blew out a plume. 'If you don't want to, I can say I couldn't find you.'

'Won't your colleagues say I was here?' Mabeth gestured to the peacekeepers on sentry duty in the distance, partly veiled by the rain. She pulled up her coat collar but it wasn't much comfort.

'They want rid of this as much as I do. City's going to the hells, in case you didn't notice.'

She'd noticed. 'So they don't give two shits about you.'

'Reassuring.'

'You know what I mean.'

Mabeth stared at the body, so cold, so... *beautiful*. It was immaculate in every way. The work of a true artist.

'I want to do it,' she said, mumbling the words.

The weather soured further as Mabeth worked, a protective sheath over the vellum to keep the ink and charcoal dry. Levio sheltered her with a parasol Mabeth had brought to the scene, his face a picture of resigned annoyance.

'Is it a statement? Is that it?' he asked after a while. 'Is that what he's doing, do you think?'

Mabeth kept illustrating, her strokes deft and assured, despite the horrific nature of her composition. 'I thought you said I should stick to what I know, stop trying to be a peacekeeper.'

'I didn't say that.'

'Not in so many words.'

Levio grumbled his assent.

'I don't think it's as random as it appears,' said Mabeth. 'A tree, an angel... now this.' She paused to flex her fingers, tight after prolonged use of the charcoal stylus. 'It's almost as if he's recreating something. A ritual perhaps.'

The parasol shivered as Levio tried to stifle a sudden intake of breath. He bit his lip, and kept pulling at the buttons on his storm-cloak. He needed a smoke.

'Ever since the sky changed,' he said at length, 'the city changed. And us with it.' By 'us', he meant Durgov's citizens. 'It's always been bad here. Murder. Discord. The things people will do to each other… I've seen it all. But this is the first time I've felt such fear. Not just my own, but it's everywhere. It's like it slipped in through the cracks when the sky turned red and has been seeping into us ever since, in our air, our food, our bodies…'

'What are you trying to say, proctor?'

He rubbed his chin, the lip biting now chronic.

'Have you ever felt rain before it starts? You know, smelled it or tasted it on the air, and just *knew*?'

'Of course. Hasn't everyone to some extent?'

'It feels like that, like something is coming, only it isn't rain.'

He fell abruptly silent after that and Mabeth was glad to be rid of his company the instant she was finished. Levio gave a curt wave as she took her leave, a vacant look in his eyes not so different from Gethik. He looked almost hollow.

Something is coming… only it isn't rain.

The words followed her after she left the murder scene, and so too the scent of lavender, faint on the air. Levio must have smelled it too, but neither spoke of it. To do so would only make it more real.

The paintings would be her salvation. The restoration of the saints, and the cleansing of her soul. She returned to her domicile, the idea of indulging in such pious work soothing.

'No interruptions,' she ordered, and Gethik nullified the fonogram before retreating into his alcove.

Mabeth set to work, revivifying old pigment, giving it vibrancy and depth. Purification through art. The brush paused in her hand…

'I have to know,' she murmured as a deep obsession took hold.
I am a sailor, and they the siren. I shall go gratefully to their rocks.

A scalpel replaced the brush, and Mabeth's attention turned to the as yet unrevealed and the promise of the unknown, the image in pentimento. She worked feverishly, almost in frenzy, the scrapings like flecks of skin flayed from a corpse. Mabeth barely noticed. The work came easily, paint peeling away without resistance, as if what lay below wanted to be found. She would let it. She wanted it, too. More than anything.

After several hours, a fresh vista began to materialise beneath the veneer of the first. Not bones, but an Eden of lush and exotic flowers, of strange crystal and dappled sunlight... And something her eyes did not want to acknowledge. And in that stark moment of revelation, a sudden inertialess lurch seized upon her and she realised her mistake, her terrible mistake.

It was...

'Paradise...' rasped Mabeth, and fell into a deep, fathomless dream.

She is walking barefoot, the dew cold and refreshing against her skin. A grove had risen up around her, swollen with strange trees that are ripe with luscious, heart-shaped fruit. She is tempted to take a bite and reaches for the branch's bounty, but something stops her...

In the distance, thunder, or what sounds like thunder. And a white-noise susurration, like a cataract rushing over a cave mouth. She turns, a prey animal alerted to the scent of a predator, and sees him.

In shadow at first, the strange scented arbours of the forest hide him from her sight and she has to twist to see.

He is naked, apart from the modesty cloth around his waist. A study in anatomical perfection, almost deific. Unreal, a statue given perfect animation. His muscles are carved as if from pink opal, and a mane cascades around his shoulders like spun silver. Violet eyes glint and flash, alive. Amused? Desirous? She flushes at the thought, terror and arousal warring like belligerent nations.

In that instant of connection, she knows him. Or rather, what he represents.

He is the paragon of pleasures, a lord of excess, and he is here for her. I know you, *he says, though his lips are unmoving.* I am you. *And for a moment, it is bliss… until the blades unsheathe and the hooks unfurl and she is pinioned and torn. Undressed of her skin, it flutters away like taffeta, like flightless wings.*

And he smiles that over-wide smile, his teeth like pearls, and the scent of lavender overwhelms her…

She doesn't scream, she can barely breathe. Something heavy is pressing against her chest, a noose taut around her throat. She thrashes. A lamp shatters as she kicks it. Absinthe spills in a milky flood. The drapes tear at her grasping fingers and the sunlight crashes in.

Am I dying?

A hot poker in her chest, jabbing at the coals of her organs.

Please…

Then relief, her bindings loosed in an instant. The pain gone.

Mabeth stares, blinking in the harsh red morning. Its light brings revelation. The paintings are not three, they are one. Where the obfuscation of newer paint has been excised to reveal the old, she sees paradise stretched over each canvas. A triptych of pulchritudinous gardens. Vigorous, staggering, like a foreign country to her senses…

Seeded with bones and nourished with blood, Eden springing vibrantly from the slaughter.

The juxtaposition is so incongruous as to be almost indiscernible.

A familiar grove stands out, partially revealed beneath flaking pigment. Its strange trees are burgeoning with heart-shaped fruit.

No, not fruit. Hearts. Living, beating human hearts. And they are not trees, they are people, rooted and cruciform.

Mabeth recoiled, the scalpel she didn't know she was still holding clattering to the floor as she shuffled away on her backside, kicking madly, arms scrabbling. The wall was solid at her back, and she could flee no further. Her gaze was transfixed on the paintings, at the parts still to be scraped away. At horrors yet unknown.

For three days, she didn't move, didn't speak, didn't sleep.

Until Levio contacted her again.

Fires lit the city, the smoke thick but unable to hide the blood-red sky. It had turned a deeper crimson with the onset of night and echoed with the shrieking of desperate men.

Mabeth did her best to avoid the crowds. After alighting from the maglev, she and Gethik took side streets and lesser known byways. It scared her, the rioting, but that fear had been dulled by something darker. It called still, but she ignored it. An effort of will she could not sustain.

Levio looked skeletal as he waited with two armoured peacekeepers beneath the sepulchre's portico. Deep rings sunk his eyes, like small pebbles at the bottom of a well. He finished a smoke stick, crushing it beneath his heel where it joined a regiment of others, and lit another.

'Inside...'

Mabeth followed, leaving the two sentries outside.

The tomb had been made for a dignitary of the city, an ecclesiarch judging by the religious statuary. Something lay piled in one corner, folded neatly upon a stone seat. She assumed they were robes. *Perhaps they are symbolic*, thought Mabeth. A reliquary stood upon a plinth in the middle of the gloomy chamber, the bones of two saints entwined, their heads upturned to a light they would never see, their bony hands outstretched in faux supplication.

'I don't understand,' said Mabeth, frowning. 'Where is the–'

Levio ignited a lumen and the bones shone faint pink.

She gasped, as the awful truth revealed itself. 'Emperor…'

'He isn't here,' breathed Levio.

The robes, they weren't… And then the bones…

'How?'

Levio didn't answer, and that was answer enough.

Markings had been scrimshawed into the bone. Mabeth moved nearer for a better look.

Outside, the clamour had grown. Closer.

A word, carved into femurs and rib bones and clavicles. *Paradisum.* High Gothic, barely used now, but more common several centuries ago.

A warning shout alerted her. One of the peacekeepers. A coalition of voices answered.

Paradise…

'I can't do this…' Mabeth fled the chamber and stepped outside into chaos.

A mob had descended. They were afraid, like wild animals, running with fire and knives, desperate to quench their fear with blood. A shotgun barked, so close it startled her and the sound of it rang in her ears like tinnitus. The sepulchre was sunk into a natural valley, and there were men roaring down a ramp towards it. Towards her.

A second blast, no longer in warning. A man was cut down. The two peacekeepers stepped up, one kneeling as the other stood and braced. They bellowed their authority at the coming horde, but their words lacked conviction. Levio didn't join them, and stayed with the dead.

Breathless, terrified, her mind close to shutting down, Mabeth called out. 'Gethik,' she rasped, 'get me away from here.'

The servitor obeyed, his lurching, patchwork frame never more reassuring as it drove like a plough into the mob. Mabeth stayed close, a desperate hand clinging to his belt. Behind her, the shotguns spoke again. They spoke one more time, a press of shouting men around her unable to dull the shock of the sound. Then no more.

She was fortunate. The mob had no interest in her, though she would have been collateral if not for her slave. He must have killed a few in his headlong charge. She had heard bone breaking, cries suddenly choked off.

Gethik himself was torn, a dozen wounds spilling blood and oil, the whole mess of it congealing as it turned his boiler-suit black. He stumbled, slowing. A servitor is a cyborg, but it is still flesh. Mabeth knew his injuries were mortal. Dull-eyed, uncomprehending, Gethik got her as far as the only maglev out of the district before he slumped, a puppet left slack on its strings, and did not stir again.

Mabeth reached Auric House in a half-blind panic. The guard was absent his post, likely fled. Bolting up the stairs, she got to her domicile and fumbled with the locks, several nervous glances behind her revealing nothing but a dimly lit corridor.

Inside, the door slammed in her wake. Heart hammering, she lurched through the entryway and into the studio where the paintings stood, apparently innocuous.

And yet...

The old renderings of saints had been further scraped away, by her hand, by another; Mabeth no longer knew for sure.

She tried to raise Yrenna via the fonogram. She had a speech prepared, about demanding to know the provenance of the paintings and the identity of who had bought her expertise. She would reject them, reject the commission. Claim it was occult. Proscribed. She would threaten, mention the interrogators. Her blood was up, and she trembled with anticipation of the furore to come. But Yrenna did not answer and the fonogram returned only dead air.

Mabeth smashed down the receiver cup, partly shattering the plastek. She wanted to scream, anger a natural antidote to fear.

A snarl on her lips, she stalked to the lectern and snatched all three canvases, hastily bundling them under her arms. She recalled the patron's address in the city and, despite her best good sense, ventured back out.

I should burn them, she thought, but had no desire to add an angry patron to her woes. And the merchants in Durgov were not known for their forgiveness, particular in matters of property. It might not matter, anyway. The city was burning, at least in the slums and the poor districts. A fever had gripped it: fear, the great motivator for selfish men who hide their anxieties behind cruelty and wanton violence. Mabeth wanted nothing more than to shut herself away, but only when this last act was done and she was rid of the paintings could she hide again. She had been hiding for years, ever since Hakasto…

Ever since…

Lost in her thoughts, Mabeth almost didn't realise she had arrived at her destination.

A razor-wire fence surrounded a nondescript warehouse and offices. A faded sign declared the name of the merchant-combine who owned it, and answered the minor mystery of what the 'V' stood for on the metal tube.

Valgaast Exports.

The warehouse was burning, every inch of it wreathed in conflagration. Flames reached up into the sky, turning it a deeper red, staining it black with smoke.

Nothing else burned, only this property, and the mob had not reached this district yet. And the fire did not spread, as if dedicated solely to the destruction of Valgaast Exports. The oddness of it sent a spasm through Mabeth. Her grip tightened on the canvases still clenched in her shaking hands. She wanted to tear them, rend them into pieces and cast them onto the fire. Instead, she sank to her knees and wept.

It took a few moments for Mabeth to regain her composure.

She knew she couldn't stay here. She had to get back to Auric House. Maybe she could try Yrenna again. She hadn't realised how badly she needed to hear her voice. Any voice.

Stumbling through side streets, it wasn't long before a part of the mob found her. Mabeth thought perhaps they were bullet-makers, though their grubby overalls would suit many menial professions.

'Please,' she said, shivering like prey in a hunter's sights, 'I have nothing of value.'

The look on the men's faces suggested otherwise, and she had to stifle an involuntary yelp as she started to back away from her aggressors.

She had fine clothes, at least to the likes of them. Jewellery. Ostensible wealth. A noblewoman, abroad on unquiet streets and unprotected. Mabeth pulled the collar of her robes tighter. An alleyway she hadn't noticed before suddenly presented itself and she took it, bolting like a startled gyrinx. She dumped the canvases, to hells with the consequences. The merchants could burn like their fucking warehouse for all she cared. Behind her, she heard the grunting of pursuit and the tread of heavy, dirty boots.

Oh shit, oh shit...

They were closing, driven by something animalistic.

No, no, no...

And then nothing.

After a few hundred yards, Mabeth slowed and then stopped. The faint aroma of lavender pricked her nostrils and she whirled around in a panic, half expecting to see *him*. But the narrow byway she found herself in was empty, although rude tenements crowded on either side. Turning, she realised no one was chasing her either. The entire street was silent, as if shrinking back into itself and holding its breath.

Not questioning her good fortune, but trembling at so close a call, Mabeth found Auric House again.

* * *

She staggered inside, her breathing ragged, and began to shake. Trauma settled in now the adrenaline had bled away. A drink would ease the nerves. Maybe a bottle. Or two.

The absinthe veritably gulped into the glass, the edge *chinking* as it met the lip of the bottle. Mabeth drained it, poured another and drained that too. Slowly calming down, she took the bottle and the glass and went to find a place to slump.

As she passed the open archway of the studio, the bottle and the glass slipped from her fingers and smashed against the floor.

On the lectern were the three canvases. And as the paint began to fragment, flaking away like dead skin, Mabeth found she was drawn to them. To *it*.

A single vista, doggedly revealed for her to see.

Without knowing why, she took up her scalpel and began to scrape away the upper layer. And with every stroke, she uncovered greater and greater horrors. A scene of beauty and torture, of unparalleled human suffering so vivid she could almost hear their screaming. Tears streamed down Mabeth's face but she couldn't stop. It had her now. Perhaps it had taken her long ago, that first night. Perhaps it was inevitable.

The painting, the *true* image, was a conduit. Hakasto had always taught her that art is a voyeur upon the soul, its flaws and virtues laid bare upon canvas. Something from the realm of the soul had found its way through. The lavender man stood proudly amongst his depravity, his *paradise*, immortalised in oil paint. The artist, whoever it was, had captured his essence perfectly. And in a moment of stasis, caught between action and inaction, Mabeth wondered how much of it was actually paint.

A gentle touch nudged her hand back to the task and she shuddered, the scent of lavender stronger now and warm breath upon her neck.

I am here, the killer said without speaking, *as I promised I would be.*

She had done this. Her pride, her obsession... her excesses. It had brought her to his attention.

'Please...' she tried to whisper, but a soft susurration stayed any further objection.

Shh...

Outside her hab, the city had begun to eat itself. The rioting was everywhere, rising like a black tide to wash away anything good, anything pure. The structures would not hold. She bit her lip, using the pain to try to drown it out.

The cloying scent of his perfume made her gag, but she dared not stop. She felt the heat of his skin near her own, both a furnace and a glacier. Mabeth scraped away the above to reveal the below, knowing that as she did so, his foothold in the real would solidify.

A dead sky presented itself, blood red and terrible. A great wall thronged with desperate fighting in the distance. Gods and monsters vying for the fate of mankind...

The thoughts came unbidden, the memories and realisations not her own.

Terra... a voice in her head told her.

She knew it then, the vista revealed upon the canvas. An ancient war, the oldest of wars. The Great Heresy.

The Long War, the voice supplied, and could not hide its bitterness.

The last piece fell away, a nondescript corner but its style at odds with the rest, as if painted by a different hand. Two robed figures...

Mabeth released a gasp, for it was her. A perfect portrait. She had a red blade in her hand and before her on the ground was the second figure. Older, dying, a feeble hand pressed to the wound in his chest as blood poured from his mouth.

Mabeth was transfixed, the bare truth of her crime rendered as clearly as a pict, an impossible image as damning as any confession.

His perfumed breath broke her dark remembrance.

Perfection always comes at a price.

The hand upon her neck was firm but not painful. Not yet. It turned her head and she took in her abode. The indulgence, the trappings of wealth, desire and obsession.

Tell me, what did your master call it... that which is hidden beneath?

'Pentimento...' said Mabeth, almost beyond the ability for rational thought. 'It means redemption,' she added, a needless translation, her gaze now fixed upon the image of her murdering Hakasto. So she could be preeminent; so she could be perfect.

'A lie to hide another lie,' the killer answered, his organic voice as old as millennia.

Mabeth would find no redemption here, she realised, as the blades and the hooks bit into her flesh, and as she screamed they started to pull.

'But there will always be art,' the killer replied, as if reading her thoughts, **'and this my canvas.'**

BONE CUTTER

Darius Hinks

'They will not have you,' whispered Anava, pressing her face into the bundle of rags at her chest.

It was dawn. It was always dawn. The silver on the horizon never dimmed and never spread. It just waited. A dazzling splinter at the foot of a black, monolithic darkness. Anava turned Coryne to the light, letting it gild her face. She had spent so many hours like this, looking at her daughter's peaceful features. She never tired of it – watching her sleep and listening to the quiet, rodent snuffle of her breath.

She tightened her grip on the child and continued walking down the transitway. Every step was an act of will. Her boots had collapsed weeks ago and her feet were bloodied and raw, wrapped in so much cloth that they looked as big as her equally swaddled head. The toes inside the wrappings were bruised, frozen and numb. There was nothing she could do about it, so every time she felt a stab of pain, she thought of the horror she was fleeing from. That was enough to keep her walking.

Besides Coryne, she was carrying water skins, a combat knife, a backpack and, slung around her shoulder, an auto-pistol, prised from the fingers of a frozen corpse. The gun terrified her. She had got this far without using it but she was no fool. She knew her luck could not hold out forever. She had crossed hundreds of miles of earthworks, burnt-out gun emplacements and bunkers, scavenged food from abandoned hab-blocks and cowered in bloodstained snowdrifts. It was only a matter of time before a bone-cutter saw her. And when they did, she would use the gun, however much it scared her. The warm bundle at her chest would leave her no choice. *They will not have you.*

It took her an hour of slow trudging to reach the top of the next rise and see Valgaast Valley spread out below her. There were fires to the east, just a few miles from where she stood, blinking in the gloom. She crouched, took out her magnoculars and focused on the flames. It was a manufactorum, a big one by the looks of it. It had been set alight from end to end and she could see figures silhouetted by the flames. Bone-cutters. They had to be. No one else would stay out in the open. They were swarming over the snow like rats. There must be over a hundred of them. Her hand fell involuntarily to the blocky weapon at her side, her cold-clumsy fingers brushing its brutal angles. If a group like that saw her what would she do? How many could she stop before they reached her?

She looked the other way. The western end of the valley looked clear. It was a pit of darkness. Even the magnoculars could pick out no trace of heat or movement. The bone-cutters did not always give off heat signals though. As they rotted they became unaware of the cold, not bothering to wear coats or hoods. After a week or two they were usually clad in little more than rags, their bodies as cold as the snow.

She stared through the magnoculars, adjusting the lenses and muttering, unsure what to do. Then she shrugged and realised she had no option. Port Strabo was ten miles to the north. She *had* to cross the valley. And she would not be going anywhere near those fires.

She shrugged her backpack into a more comfortable position, kissed the rags around Coryne's head and began climbing down the slope. She had to move at a painfully slow speed. The rocks were coated in ice and the snow was equally treacherous.

Her breath coiled in the air, trailing through the blackness and catching the light.

After three hours she finally reached the valley floor and leant back against the rock face, struggling to catch her breath. Coryne was still asleep, but it would not be long before she woke for a feed. She had to find shelter before then, and ideally some new supplies.

Cut off from the perpetual dawn, the valley was profoundly dark. Anava crept on for a while, feeling her way over the rocks, but every few minutes she stumbled. It was only a matter of time before she fell. She was beyond worrying about pain, but a broken bone would be the end of her. Even a bad sprain might leave her stranded in the snow.

With great care, she took a lumen from her belt and clicked it on, aiming the beam directly at the ground in front of her.

The light was dazzling.

She snapped it off with a curse.

Coryne stirred, wriggling against her.

Not now, thought Anava, shushing the child and humming a gentle tune.

To her relief the baby settled.

She tried walking in the dark again but immediately stubbed her toe, staggering with a sickening lurch and nearly falling.

She shook her head, adjusted the lumen and snapped it on a second time.

The beam was fainter this time, but still bright enough to make her pulse quicken.

Holding the lumen in one hand, she grabbed the magnoculars in the other and looked up the valley at the distant fires.

The building looked unchanged, but there was no sign of the bone-cutters. Every one of them had vanished.

'Damn it,' she whispered, scouring the blazing building for signs of movement. 'Where are you?'

However hard she looked, she could not locate them. With a grimace, she trudged on across the valley floor, making for the opposite slope.

The lumen meant she could move faster but it made her feel like she was calling out to the bone-cutters, announcing her presence.

She was halfway across the valley floor when she saw a pile of bags, scattered across the snow.

She smiled. Her supplies were running dangerously low. This could be just what she needed.

Then she cast the lumen up and down the valley, checking that the bags' owner was not waiting to attack her.

There was another pile of bags a few feet past the first one, but no sign of any people.

She crept cautiously forwards, still flicking the light back and forth. It seemed to accentuate the darkness either side of the beam, making the night even more threatening. The harder she stared, the more the darkness seemed to roll and drift.

She reached the first pile of bags, reached out to them, then backed away with a groan.

It was a corpse.

It had been so brutally savaged that she had failed to recognise the shape. The limbs had been torn from the torso and the fur-lined coat was black with blood.

'Sweet Terra,' she whispered, recognising the remnants of a

face. The features were distorted and elongated, as if they had melted. Anava had seen it before. It was the pathetic shape of a body that has been robbed of its bones.

She stumbled on towards the second shape.

Again, it was a corpse. It was the body of a woman. It was lying face down in the snow but it looked to be intact. The bone-cutters must have missed it.

Anava slowed as she approached it, looking for weapons or food.

She dropped to one knee and turned the body over.

The woman groaned and grabbed Anava's shoulders, pulling her down.

Anava wrenched free, staggered back through the snow and grabbed the autopistol, struggling frantically to snap the safety catch with her bundled hands.

'Wait!' gasped the woman. 'Show some pity.'

Anava finally flicked the safety off and pointed the gun at her face, palsied with nerves and struggling to hold it steady.

The woman stared back at Anava, shaking her head, her mouth working silently.

Anava was so delirious with fear she almost fired. Then, with a gasp of relief, she lowered the gun. Bone-cutters did not beg for mercy. They did not stare in fear.

'You're not one of them,' she whispered.

The woman closed her eyes and sighed with relief, slumping back into the snow. 'No.'

Anava stood there, still gripping the gun. 'I can't help you,' she said, knowing it was a lie before the words had left her mouth.

If the journey had been slow before, it was agonising now. The woman had shrapnel lodged in her thigh and she struggled to walk. As well as carrying Coryne and the supplies, Anava now had the woman's arm slung over her shoulder as they trudged through the snow.

'What's your name?' she asked, casting the woman a sideways glance.

'Medunna,' she replied. Anava had refastened her coat and shared one of the self-heating ration packs with her. She seemed in reasonable health but, crucially, when she shone the lumen in her face, Anava saw no sign of the plague. It was always easy to spot. Within a few days of a person contracting the rot, their skin changed colour, turning a dirty green. A few weeks after that, growths began to appear: eyes, mouths, even whole limbs, sprouting all over the victim's discoloured flesh. Medunna looked half-frozen but she was untainted by disease. Since they'd started walking, the woman had remained silent, her eyes glinting deep inside her hood as she scoured the valley for movement. She looked even more terrified than Anava felt. Somehow, the idea made her feel better, braver.

'How many of you were there?' asked Anava, gesturing back in the direction of the corpses.

Medunna did not reply for a few seconds, and when she did, her voice was unsteady. 'Three.'

'Your family?'

Medunna nodded.

'Your child?'

Medunna nodded again.

They walked on in silence.

After a while, they reached a wide depression in the snow.

'Looks like there's a transitway under here,' said Anava. She was so used to speaking to herself that Medunna's reply was quite unexpected.

'It leads to Strabo.'

The two women glanced at each other.

They managed to pick up a little speed along the even surface of the road and finally started to approach the foothills.

'Is it a girl?'

Again, Anava was surprised by the sound of Medunna's voice. Instinctively, she held Coryne a little tighter. 'Yes.'

'I lost my boy,' said Medunna, her voice so flat it sounded inhuman.

Anava stumbled to a halt, then nodded and carried on.

A dark shape loomed out of the whirling snow clouds.

Anava grabbed her autopistol and pointed at the shadow. 'More bodies?'

'No, it's a building.'

Medunna was right. It was a watchtower. The snow had confused Anava's sense of distance.

Anava shook her head. 'Probably empty.'

Medunna nodded, but neither of them moved.

'I've come too far to stop,' said Anava. 'Can you walk by yourself for a while?'

'Yes.'

'Then wait here. I have a gun. You don't.' She took out her combat knife. 'Here. Take this. In case I don't...'

Medunna took the knife. 'You should give me the girl.'

Anava tensed. Then tried to calm herself. The woman was just trying to help. 'No. I'll keep her with me.'

Medunna said nothing and looked back at the tower.

Anava hesitated a moment longer, daunted by the ominous shape, then she started walking. Coryne was strapped to her chest and she was free to grip the autopistol in both hands, trying to calm her nerves with the weapon's pugnacious bulk. She had never even fired it. What if it was damaged? She had oiled it and loaded it in the way she had seen Guardsmen do, but there could be some flaw in the mechanism. It might do nothing. Or it might take her arm off.

She stopped and looked back at Medunna. The woman had dropped into a crouch, trying to shield herself from the wind, but she was still looking her way.

'I should leave you with her,' whispered Anava, stroking the rags around Coryne's head. But she could not do it. The woman had just lost a child. What if she decided to take a new one? Grief could turn to madness. Even *she* had been accused of losing her mind after Lade fell to the plague. And perhaps it had been true. Who could blame her? She saw the growths on his body, heard the shots that killed him. She knew he had to die. Plague victims left alive would eventually join the ranks of the bone-cutters. Collecting body parts to adorn their mutated flesh. But Lade's death still felt like a crime. She probably *was* insane for a while. It had looked as though she might even be impounded. And they were going to take Coryne from her. Then the rot took all of them and the matter became moot. Only she and Coryne had escaped.

Anger at the memory drove her on. She gripped the gun tighter and marched towards the watchtower.

The tower was a brutal slab of ferrocrete, hexagonal in shape and topped by a row of shattered machicolations. There was a single door, which had been blasted open at some point, leaving scorch marks around the frame and a dark, maw-like hole in the wall.

Anava crept towards it, gun held out before her as though she were trying to disassociate herself from the weapon.

She stopped a few feet away and waited, listening.

The wind howled through cracked walls. It sounded like the cry of a wounded animal. It was as though the tower had a voice and was pleading with her.

There were no sounds of movement within, so Anava edged through the doorway.

A little light was spilling through a window and she was just able to make out a small, hexagonal courtyard. The roof was still intact and Anava stepped onto something other than snow for the first time in weeks. The icy flagstones were littered with wreckage. One whole section of the wall had given way, scattering plasteel and ferrocrete in every direction. There were also smashed ammo crates and empty promethium tanks and a pile of broken weapons.

At the far side of the courtyard was a flight of steps. There must be another floor above her head, guessed Anava, recalling the windows she'd seen outside.

Coryne was stirring again. She *had* to feed her. This was the best shelter she'd find before they reached Port Strabo, but she would not be able to relax without knowing what was over her head.

She crossed to the stairs and began climbing, treading carefully and keeping the gun trained on the opening above her.

The next level was even more of a mess. There were engine parts piled everywhere and pieces of a large, dismantled weapon, some kind of anti-aircraft gun. And on the other side were dozens of rusted cables, stacked in a heap and partially covered by an old tarpaulin.

Anava was about to head back down when she saw a crate that was still intact. It was an old, battered trunk and the lock looked so rusty she thought she might be able to lever it off.

She needed to go and call Medunna in, but it would only take a moment to examine the crate. She walked over to it and began levering the lock. It moved, the screws sliding easily from the crumbling metal. The last corner would not come away, so she looked around the room to check she was still alone, placed the gun down next to the trunk and used both hands to pull at the lock.

It opened with a shrill creak that echoed loudly round the watchtower.

Anava winced, then lifted the lid and peered inside.

The trunk was full of bloody, human bones.

Anava backed away, gasping. There was a skull at the top,

covered in scraps of skin, and one of its eyes was still lodged in its socket, staring at her.

Her heart was thudding. Only a bone-cutter would keep such a collection.

Coryne chose that moment to wake up, announcing her hunger with a ferocious scream.

There was a clattering sound behind Anava.

She whirled around to see the cables shrug off the tarpaulin and rise from the floor.

They were not cables. They were rotten growths. They were the mutant limbs of a plague victim. He was so deformed he looked like an enormous arachnid. There was barely anything left of his human form, just a scrawny chest, surrounded by rust-coloured tendrils and his face, staring hungrily at Anava.

The mutant tried to speak as he staggered towards her but all that emerged was bile and flies.

Before the plague, Anava had never seen flies. Despite her terror, they mesmerised her, swarming around the mutant's head as he lassoed her waist and hauled her across the room, straight into his nest of thrashing limbs.

She screamed and grappled, straining to hold Coryne clear of the dreadful creature. Some of the limbs ended in bone-knives, sharpened hooks stained with blood. They flailed around her and then moved towards her chest, preparing to tear her open.

She tried to grab them with her free hand, but the flesh was moist and slippery.

As she struggled for her life the mutant never said a word, just gargling more flies as he brought his gaping mouth towards her face.

A loud rattling sound filled the room, like a drum roll.

The mutant tensed, loomed over Anava, then fell away, slapping down onto the tarpaulin.

Anava stared in confusion. The mutant's body had exploded.

Gaping wounds had appeared all over its mud-like flesh. Black blood was spraying into the air along with even more flies, columns of the insects that filled the air with a loud grinding sound.

The mutant shivered and then reached up with some of its limbs, grabbing hold of an overhead beam and trying to stand.

There was another loud rattling sound and more holes opened in its head, slamming it back against the wall.

Then it finally lay still, its ruined head lolling down onto its chest with a grunt.

As the flies began to clear, escaping through open windows, Anava saw Medunna standing by the chest, holding the smoking autopistol with a dangerous gleam in her eye.

Anava backed away from her, almost as wary of the woman as she was the still-twitching plague victim.

Medunna watched Anava closely. Then turned the gun around and held it out to her. 'We should stay together.'

Anava nodded and took the gun.

Medunna nodded to the screaming Coryne. 'You can feed her while I look for supplies.'

Port Strabo was under siege. Not by an army, but by its own people. As Anava looked down from the transitway she saw thousands of refugees swarming around its walls. There were lines of trenches and razor wire circling the whole starport and more Guardsmen than Anava had ever seen. There must have been hundreds of them, manning the walls and lining the single point of entry, a frozen track that was carrying armoured groundcars and personnel carriers through the baying crowds.

It was a desperate scene. People were holding up money and jewellery, begging to be admitted, but the Guardsmen were deaf to their cries. They were clad in an array of different uniforms and Anava guessed that some of the regiments had come from off-world, but they all had the same hard stare on their faces.

As Anava watched, a group of refugees managed to scale the razor wire and reach the track. Three Guardsmen opened fire, killing without hesitation.

Emitters were braying announcements from the battlements. *A relief force was on its way. The Imperial world of Jehudiel V was* not *being abandoned. Once the military were safe in high orbit, they would coordinate the counter-attack; they would cleanse the planet of mutants.* No one was listening. The truth leaked months ago: Jehudiel was beyond saving. The plague had spread too fast and too wide. Half the populace had been transformed into bone-cutters. Governor Scirion was pulling his men out and leaving everyone else to die. If the Imperial fleet ever did return to Jehudiel it would not be to save people, it would be to purge them with fire.

'There's no way in,' whispered Anava, horrified by the sight of so many desperate people.

Medunna nodded. 'The governor is no fool. If even one of those people turns out to be a plague victim, his evacuation will be pointless. If an infected person got onto the *Emperor's Sword*, everyone on board it would be dead. And then think what would happen when another ship finds them – the plague could spread across the whole sector.'

She looked down at the battlements. 'Maybe there's a way.'

Anava grabbed her arm. 'How? What do you mean?'

'I worked here, before the plague. I worked with the ground crews, refuelling and repairing the landers. I know where they load them into the *Emperor's Sword*. They might already have been towed into the embarkation decks, but if not...'

'If not, what? We could stow away?'

'Perhaps.'

'But how would we get in?' Anava waved at the wailing crowds below. 'They would shoot us before we reached the gates.'

Medunna stood up and started heading off into the banks of

snow, waving for Anava to follow. 'There is more than one way into Strabo.'

Medunna headed back onto the submerged transitway that had led them across the valley, then headed off it at another junction, moving away from the lights of the starport before finally approaching it again half an hour later, from a different direction.

'This gate is guarded too,' said Anava as they approached a much smaller entrance. There were no crowds of refugees here, but there was still an impressive scrum of Guardsmen around the doors, watching the surrounding hills carefully as freight-haulers rumbled past them into the port.

'There's another way,' said Medunna, waving her on.

They kept their heads down as they hurried behind snowdrifts, heading even further away from the main gates until Medunna pointed out a finger of rock, jutting out of the whiteness a few hundred feet from the walls of the starport.

'They built Strabo on the ruins of a native settlement. A temple complex or maybe even just a city that used to be above ground. We used to dare each other to explore it when we were drunk. The Guardsmen know about the larger chambers but not the smaller ones.'

As they reached the spur of rock, Anava saw that it was the remnants of a ruined wall. The architecture was clearly not Imperial. It was too crude and unadorned, devoid of the mythological beasts and ornate pediments that covered the rest of Port Strabo.

Medunna dropped down into a ditch and kicked away the snow until she was able to stamp her boot on something hard and hollow-sounding.

Anava dropped down beside her and gripped her arm. 'Why are you helping me?'

'Helping you? I'm helping me. I don't want to be left here. Why do you think I was trying to reach Strabo?'

'But you could have come here without me. You could have snuck away and left me at the main gates.'

Medunna looked at Coryne, sleeping in Anava's arms. 'Perhaps… perhaps she might have a better life than ours.'

The two women looked at each other in silence, thinking of the things they had lost.

Anava nodded.

Medunna reached for the gun and Anava handed it to her without hesitation.

There was a single, loud report, then Medunna handed the gun back and wrenched a rusty hatch open, revealing a flight of ancient, timeworn steps. She nodded at Anava and then vanished into the darkness.

Anava hesitated, thinking of the mutant in the watchtower. Then she whispered a prayer to the God-Emperor and climbed down the steps.

The *Emperor's Sword* was almost ready to depart. Anava knew nothing of space travel or voidships but, as she looked up at the spires and buttresses of the governor's ship, she could see that their time was almost up. There were columns of smoke and steam rising from its engines and the grand porticos that spurred out from its hull were almost empty, with just a few final crew members making their way into the light that spilled from within. Some of the smaller loading hatches were already slamming shut.

'They're not even taking the Guardsmen at the gates,' she whispered, cowering behind a fuel bowser with Medunna.

Medunna shook her head. 'Too risky. They spent too long with the refugees. Any one of them might be carrying a mutation.'

Anava felt no outrage at what was happening. She only felt numb.

'This way,' hissed Medunna, hobbling off through a doorway into an unlit blockhouse near the wall.

Anava rushed after her and, after closing the door behind her, she flicked on her lumen, lighting up the small room.

It was full of discarded uniforms and equipment, and Medunna handed her a suit of grubby overalls, studded with fittings for oxygen pipes and stitched across the chest with an Imperial eagle.

'Quickly!' said Medunna, grabbing another one for herself. 'That ship is ready to leave. We might only have minutes left.'

Anava carefully placed Coryne down on a pile of clothes, then donned the overalls. They were loose enough that she was still able to fasten them up once she had wrapped Coryne back around her chest. Coryne was still tiny but Anava grabbed an oversized jacket to help disguise the bulge.

Medunna looked her up and down and nodded. 'You'll do.' She looked around the room. 'No, wait...' She grabbed a small metal canister with a rubber pipe hung from its nozzle. '*Now* you look the part.'

Medunna limped back to the door, then paused to look at Anava. 'It's a long shot. Do you understand?' She looked at the bulge under Anava's jacket. 'I'm going to act like I'm still part of the ground crew and hope they are fooled by my familiar face. But if they don't know me, or they wonder who you are, we'll be shot.' She massaged her scalp. 'To be honest, the more I think about it, the more ridiculous this whole idea is. If they're being so thorough at the–'

'What other chance do we have?' said Anava. 'What other chance does my daughter have?'

Medunna nodded. Then she placed a hand on Coryne's sleeping form.

Anava tensed, but said nothing, aware of how much she owed this woman.

'We have to try,' said Medunna. Then she grabbed an empty flight case and left the blockhouse, doing her best to walk straight.

'Stay right behind me,' she said as Anava followed her. 'Our only hope is that they don't ask us any questions.'

Medunna led the way to one of the smaller loading ramps. There were only two guards watching it and they were clearly distracted, talking into a bulky vox-caster that was at the top of the ramp.

As they neared the Guardsmen, a terrific din rose up from the direction of the main gates. It sounded like gunfire and shouting.

The Guardsmen were speaking frantically into the vox-caster and then, when Anava and Medunna were still several feet away, one of the soldiers rushed down the loading ramp and headed away from the ship, yelling something at the Guardsman who had remained.

'They're going!' whispered Anava, unable to believe her luck.

'No,' replied Medunna, coming to a halt. 'That one is staying put.' Her tone was grim. 'And I do not know his face. He will want to see my identification and–'

There was an explosion on the far side of the main gates and a chorus of screams.

'They're trying to fight their way in!' said Medunna.

There was another roaring sound, but rather than coming from the gates this one came from the engines of the *Emperor's Sword*. All along its length, crewmen and soldiers began racing inside as hatches and doors clanged shut behind them. Loading vehicles careered across the docks, trying to reach the ramps before they slid from view.

'Now or never,' said Anava. 'They're leaving.'

'There's no way!' gasped Medunna. 'I don't know that man. When he sees we have no ID he'll shoot us on the spot.'

'I understand,' replied Anava, striding off towards the ramp.

The Guardsman saw her coming but most of his attention was still on the commotion at the gates.

Anava was halfway up the ramp when he finally looked at her properly.

'Throne knows how they think we'd get them all on here,' he laughed. 'Even a ship this big can't hold a whole damned planet.' His laughter was manic and his eyes were wide.

'Your papers,' he said, holding out his hand with a strained smile.

Anava gunned him down.

He slammed against the hull with a shocked expression, half his torso ripped away. Then he fell from the ramp and hit the ground in a heap.

'What have you done?' cried Medunna, staggering up the ramp after her.

Anava was staring at the gun, still feeling the reverberations of the shot. 'I killed him,' she said, her voice small.

Medunna shook her head, her face pale. Then she gently pushed Anava into the ship. 'You killed him before he killed you.'

Anava had never left Jehudiel before. As she cowered in the lander Medunna had led them to, she could see a reflection in its viewport – the curve of a world, gradually shrinking as the *Emperor's Sword* broke orbit and headed out into the system.

'They said they would wait in high orbit,' she said. 'They said they would coordinate the fight against the plague.'

Medunna frowned. 'Why are you saying that? You knew they were lying. The governor is never going back down there. He's going to leave all those people to die. No,' she corrected herself, 'it's worse than that. He's leaving them all to the plague. They will all mutate and lose their minds. They will become bone-cutters.'

Anava was not listening. Her thoughts were still full of the Guardsman's expression as he realised she had shot him. She could still hear him hitting the ground. *You're insane.* The words came back to haunt her. The words they used when they tried to take Coryne from her. 'They will not have you,' she whispered.

Medunna looked at her in confusion but stayed quiet. Then she looked up at the reflection in the viewport, watching Jehudiel shrink into the distance.

They must have been close to the enginarium. The lander was shaking constantly and the heat was becoming unbearable. As it grew hotter in the lander, Anava's head started to swim and she thought she might faint. 'Coryne,' she gasped, remembering that the poor child was still swaddled under her overalls.

She quickly undid the suit and lifted the baby out. Coryne was asleep and, to Anava's relief, she looked unharmed, her cheeks flushed with colour and her breathing calm.

She loosened the rags and allowed some air to finally reach the infant's body.

Medunna screamed.

Anava looked up in shock, expecting to see a Guardsman at the door.

There was no Guardsman. Medunna was staring at Coryne, her face drained of colour and hitching screams rocking her body.

'Plague!' cried Medunna.

'What are you talking about?' As Anava looked at Coryne, she had a dreadful vision. She imagined she could see what Medunna was seeing. She saw that, from the neck down, Coryne was a nest of rust-coloured tentacles, that she had been transformed by the plague. But, as quick as it came, the hallucination vanished, and she saw her beautiful, untainted child again.

'She's infected!' cried Medunna, scrambling at the access hatch that led back into the main ship, looking for the opening mechanism. 'The ship will be infected!'

Medunna finally managed to find the runepad that opened the door but, before she had managed to press any runes, she slammed against the door in an explosion of crimson, her body torn apart.

Anava lowered the autopistol and stood over Medunna's corpse with a blank expression. Then she looked back at Coryne.

'They will not have you.'

INTO DARK WATER

Jake Ozga

THE FIRST CIRCLE

The Unturning Wheel

The truth is revealed to you. Decline is stagnation, stagnation is decline. You are not safe. You will never be safe again. You will never know security again, nor the comforting delusion of hope.

You will never take another breath that is not stolen. You will never make another memory that is not rooted in sadness. Memories of better times are now memories of memories.

The path you are set on for the rest of your life only descends. Where once you felt it might raise you towards better things, know now that it will only decline. The path descends. You descend with it.

The wheel does not turn. Decline is stagnation, stagnation is decline.

You are not safe. You will never be safe again.

The man wakes to the sound of distant thunder. His body aches. He is no longer young, and he has slept poorly on stony ground.

It takes a few moments for his thoughts to find clarity through the fog of sleep and then he realises the sound is not thunder, but the crashing of waves against the cliffs below, loud now that the tide has turned. Loud enough to wake him. And there is something else, another noise.

In the city across the bay a tower topples from the cliffs and falls into the sea below. There is a cheer from the engineers working the demolition, a faint chorus carried by the wind. He climbs to his feet and wraps his cloak around him. It is coarse grey wool in a style unfamiliar to this region of Shyish, wet from sea spray and the morning dew. In the distance, great sandstone blocks tumble from the cliff into the churning waves, lost in the fury of the ocean. He stands there for a while longer, steadying himself against the wind; it is strong enough to snatch away his breath. The thunder of the waves along the coast is hypnotic. A primordial sound. A sound from before the ages of men and myth, when the land he now stands upon was thrust up from the depths of the endless midnight ocean like the clenched fists of a drowning god.

The people of this city were judged and found wanting. The Stormhosts commit holy murder against an enemy that appears more human than their executioners. Faceless giants born of thunder and lightning. The God-King's wrath made manifest.

We are sick, he thinks. There is some sickness in us, in all of us, even those who appear untainted by horrors. Rot and decay hides in the folds of a flower when its season has passed, and innocence is only skin deep. He has learned this harshest of lessons. Flesh can be deceitful, even your own flesh and blood. Chaos is a sickness upon the soul.

A flock of hundreds of small grey birds takes to the sky above what remains of the coastal city, disturbed by the devastation below. The sudden movement startles him and catches his attention through unfocused eyes, blurred and teared by the wind. He realises he is on the edge of the cliff, the very edge. Far below him the waves break against the shore in ceaseless crashing percussion. The winds buffet the tiny birds and yet they move as if with a single consciousness, like fish darting from a predator. Such small, fragile things. Such short lives. He has never learned what they are called. It does not seem worthwhile. He is leaning into the wind.

A voice calls out from somewhere behind him. He does not look around but steps quickly back from the precipice. He had heard no one approach.

'You are the historian?' the voice calls out again. A strong voice. The words carry above the noise of the waves, of the wind.

He does not reply.

'I seek Alessander Cellarius, the historian. They told me to come here to these ruins. To speak to the grey-bearded man who stares at rocks.'

He does not look around. He feels like he has been caught in the middle of a shameful act though he can't think for sure what that is. Instead, he feigns preoccupation with the ruins that surround him. They pre-date the city by hundreds of years at least. The stone is much darker than the pale pink sandstone of the distant towers, veined with tiny purple crystals, the edges worn smooth with the passage of centuries. Nature has long since reclaimed whatever was here. Buried among the long grass there are stones, ensnared in the amethyst ivy that is so prevalent in the northlands. He traces his thumb around the edge of the engravings. They are indistinct, their meaning lost to the ages.

'They said you would not speak to me, that you do not speak to anyone. And so, from your silence, I shall assume I have the right person.' The voice is clear and resonant. Confident, yet not unkind. 'I've travelled across the realms to find you.'

The man gestures at the rocks. 'I am... engaged with my work. Not to be disturbed.' His own voice is weak from disuse and his speech is croaky, his words mostly lost to the gale. How long has he been here, among these stones, he wonders? Two, three days? How long since he has last eaten? Since he last had something to drink? He fumbles at his belt, looking for the wineskin. It is not there.

A flask lands at his feet, thrown there by his visitor. He picks it up, removing the fired clay stopper, and takes a mouthful of the watered wine. He turns to face the newcomer.

The Stormcast Eternal stands half again as tall as the man. A giant, a soldier in the wars of gods and daemons. A man to be feared and worshipped, clad head to toe in golden armour forged by the artisan warsmiths of Azyrheim. Under his arm he carries a death-mask helmet. At his hip, a single-handed hammer of such size that no mortal could wield it. The old man hesitates.

'Do not be afraid.' The giant steps closer. 'You have met my kind before, I am certain. Ah, though perhaps not with armour of gold. My name is Ra'Xephael. I am a knight of the Hammers of Sigmar, foremost of the God-King's hosts. I have need of your help, historian.'

A distant rumble – the unmistakable dull thump of duardin munitions, felt as tremors through the ground. The Stormcast and the historian turn to watch as across the bay the engineers commence the demolition of another tower. The spire of the roof falls down into the crumbling levels below, swallowed by a cloud of pale, pink dust. Around the base of the tower, pulleys and cables tighten, controlling the angle of the collapse, and the building leans, then slowly falls over the cliff, into the churning sea below.

Clouds of dirt and smoke rise from the rubble, quickly carried away by the wind. Barely perceptible figures move through the ruins and begin casting anything that remains into the sea.

Soon there will be nothing of this place left, he thinks. They believe the stone of the land itself is tainted, that it must be reconsecrated. But there are always traces. These rocks… these stones are all that remain of a tower, long since fallen. A tower to watch over the bay. He pulls back the thick grass to reveal more of the ruins, half buried in the damp earth, blackened by the passage of centuries. His hands are shaking, black with dirt, his fingernails are bleeding. Foundations sunk deep into the cliff. Deep roots buried and remembered now only by restless spirits. The dead in this place are watching, but for now they tolerate his intrusions.

The giant takes the old man by the arm. There is concern in his voice.

'Come with me, historian. You are half starved. Let us find some food. These stones will still be here when you return.'

A gentle grip. The Stormcast guides him to his feet. He does not resist.

He walks in silence to the camps at the outskirts of the city. The golden giant follows, a pace or two behind, the heavy tread unfaltering despite the treacherous coastal trails – little more than goat paths – that skirt around the edge of the bay. The armies of Sigmar have already moved on, leaving behind earthworks and palisades as the only signs of the investment. Engineers remain within the ruin of the city walls. Of the people that once lived here, at first there is no sign.

After a time, they arrive at the first of the mass graves. The smell of freshly dug earth. Sods of loamy soil. Blackened vegetation where sometime in the night, fire has been set to burn those things that needed to be burned, because burial in Shyish is not always desirable and the dead are persistent.

In the bay there are more bodies that have fallen from the cliffs or have been thrown over. Eels thrash in the water, writhing coils of slick black rope tangled together in a feeding frenzy. Some days past he had seen an eel as thick and round as his thigh reach out from the surf to take a goat in its jaws and drag it into the sea. Now they have other food. Blood stains the foam pink as it washes up on the grey of the beach, and further out a black shadow moves beneath the surface, vast and sleek, trailing spindly legs behind it. An eater-fish venturing into the shallows, drawn by the scent of blood.

He sees the body of a young man, barely into adulthood, bloody and broken upon the shore. Limbs splayed unnaturally, tossed and turned by the rolling waves. From this distance it is not possible to make out any uniform or insignia. He watches for a time, standing at the edge of the cliff. The Stormcast beside him, towering over him. A mismatched pair. The stinging salt wind blowing in from the sea causes his eyes to tear.

'This is not a sight to linger on.' The Stormcast's voice is gentle; he is watching the historian with concern. Kind eyes, blue like electricity.

'You see him too? The young man?'

The Stormcast nods. 'There are horrors here,' he says.

The historian thinks: when Sigmar abandoned these people, hundreds of years ago... when the God-King closed the gates of Azyr, they had to find their own ways to survive. What choice did they have? What choice do any of us have but survival? And now the God-King returns. Like a disappointed parent, he returns to punish those that had the indecency to try to live without him.

The Stormcast is silent for a while longer, watching the old man.

'They say you travelled with the Anvils of the Heldenhammer,' he says. 'That you travelled the length of the Reach alongside them. They are known to be grim. Ruthless. And sieges are the worst of all the horrors of war.'

The historian says nothing. He watches the waves.

'I will not pretend that I have not participated in my share of horrors. But know this – we Stormcast Eternals are not all alike.' The Stormcast places a hand on the historian's shoulder. A golden gauntlet. He leads him away from the edge.

They follow the smell of cooking to the engineers' camp where a cauldron simmers on a crackling fire, the damp wood hissing and spitting. Eel stewed in bitter herbs, served in a wooden bowl with a piece of flatbread. The historian's stomach is too empty to be hungry and he does not know if he can eat. The cook stirs the pot with the haft of a broken ghostwood spear. He is bearded, his unwashed hands black with soot, a twin-tailed comet tattooed on his forehead and old scarring on his arms from alchemical fire. An engineer, a veteran. He serves the Stormcast with an expression of holy awe.

They eat in the shadow of the ruined city. They eat without speaking, and share wine from the flask, poured into wooden cups. The historian's strength is returning. The sun is waning in the misty sky, the light it casts is ethereal and sickly. Black-winged gulls and carrion birds feud with the eels on the shore at the foot of the cliffs, their grating cries and shrieks unwelcome but easily ignored. He has heard worse cries lately.

'You will not follow the Anvils as they continue their purge of the north,' says the Stormcast, and it is not a question. 'This leaves you without purpose or direction. A man must have a purpose.'

The historian says nothing. The Stormcast watches him as he eats.

'I am heading to Kuan'Talos,' he says. 'The Anvils have not yet reached that far. For now, it is a place undisturbed by Sigmar's great war of liberation. From there you could arrange for a ship to Sendport, then on to the Innerlands, or to a Realmgate. Journey away from Shyish, if that is what you wish.'

Again, the historian does not reply.

'They said you would serve as well as any local guide,' says the Stormcast. 'That you know the hidden paths and the history of this land. Did they speak true?'

'I have rarely been this far north,' the historian says at last, 'though I have lived most of my life in Ora.'

'I have wandered these lands for some time,' the Stormcast says. 'But I am an outsider and an agent of the God-King. Few will talk to me. Even fewer have anything worthwhile to say.' He pauses, gestures to where the sun is already beginning to set behind the devastated city, clouds of dust glow in the last light of the day. 'What can you tell me of this place?'

The historian sits with his back to debris that had once been part of the city wall, devastated now until only rubble remains. He thinks for a while. He is unused to talking, but it comes back to him: the role of tutor is familiar. He tells the Stormcast of the history of the land.

'It is a place much like any other in Shyish. Cities are born from the need for defence,' he says. 'Tribes gather, raise walls, try to keep the darkness at bay. Some places grow, some others are lost. Without Sigmar,' he says, 'some turned to other gods.'

His speech is halting, his voice rough. Behind him the skeletal remains of buildings cast long shadows across the scorched earth.

'They called this a free city,' he says. 'They resisted the worst of the depredations of the Ruinous Powers. No – I do not say all. They did not resist all.' The historian takes a drink from the cup. 'The history of this land is not unique,' he says. 'But these people kept their own records and they had their own libraries. That is a rarer thing. I had the chance to study some small part of these before they were thrown into the ocean. So much knowledge lost. We do not learn from history.'

'The books in places like this are forbidden,' the Stormcast says, 'along with all the works of these people, corrupted works. The knowledge contained within is dangerous.'

'All knowledge is dangerous when you have too little,' the historian snaps. 'I believed the risk was worth it, to learn of this place, these people. We have no other way to learn from the past. The Stormcasts, the Anvils – they choose to remain ignorant. To your kind, there are only absolutes.'

Nearby, men are lighting pyres so as to continue their demolition work in the half light of evening. They build fires made from driftwood and scavenged timbers from the ruins. The historian watches as they carry an ornately carved wooden centrepiece depicting some strange deity or daemon from a temple or shrine and heave it into the burgeoning flames. In the city countless small fires still burn. The smoke is lost in the darkening sky as the sun falls beneath the horizon.

'The people here survived for countless decades,' he says. 'They survived warring tribes, disease, famine... and each day they looked to the sea, dreading that they might see the sails of the plague fleets returning. And then instead, your kind arrived. To judge them and find them wanting. And so, this...'

'War is ever thus,' says the Stormcast. 'I did not seek to be admonished, historian.'

'No? What other lesson do you hope to learn from history besides admonishment? Look around you. You and your kind could learn from this. Or not. History does not care either way. I do not care either way.'

'You forget to whom you are talking,' says the Stormcast. 'Among the Stormhosts walk those who lived in those times, reborn now. If you seek lessons from the past you can ask one who was there.'

The historian thinks on this for a moment. 'And have you learnt lessons from your past?' he says. 'Will you share these lessons, or sequester them away in secret vaults? I was with the Anvils of The Heldenhammer for months. They are soldiers, not scholars, and for a solider knowledge is a weapon. They hoard secrets lest they provide some advantage in the prosecution of endless war. They taught me no lessons save for those in barbarity.'

They sit without speaking for a while, listening to the sound of the gulls and the wind and the distant shouts of the engineers in the ruins of the city. Dust from the demolitions blows through the camp, carried on strong winds so that it stings the historian's skin and he pulls his cloak up around his face.

'I concede that you are unique among the Stormcasts I have met before,' he says eventually. 'I never heard those bastards say more than a few words in all the months I was with them. I was to be their chronicler. In the end I was only a witness.'

The Stormcast smiles. It is a sad and gentle expression, incongruous on one dressed for war. The historian thinks it is the first kind thing he has seen for some time.

'They say that you mistrust others,' the Stormcast says. 'They say you would rather be out here alone, with nothing but dead things for company.'

The historian shrugs and wraps his cloak more tightly around him. Dead things. It is strange, he thinks, how you can make such meaningful choices, such important decisions. To entangle yourself in the life of another, to have a child, a family, a home. To build a life with love and purpose. And then one day it is all in the past and all that remains is the company of the dead. Dead things, and I among their number.

'You prefer the company of the dead,' says the Stormcast. His smile holds kindness and sorrow. His eyes are old and knowing, and within them there is perception and recognition. 'This is not a problem,' he says. 'I have died. Many times.'

A man must have a purpose, thinks the historian. Life has come to an end. Though I keep on breathing. Life is change and meaning and I have none of those things. Life is hope and love and I am without those things.

The Stormcast takes a book from his pack and offers it to the historian. Small, bound in red leather and tied up with twine. On the cover is an etched circle of thorns, embossed with flaking gold leaf. It is weatherworn, the leather faded to pink and orange along the spine and at the tattered edges. It is hard to glean its age.

'A gift for you,' he says. 'More forbidden knowledge. Something from a long time ago. I sense that you enjoy mysteries.'

The historian undoes the twine. The book is full of symbols in cramped handwriting. Each brittle page so densely inked as to appear almost black. Water has smudged the script in places. Old symbols that he knows, but not a language he recognises.

'Where does it come from?'

'A past life.' The Stormcast shrugs. 'Washed up on a shore. I do not truly know. I have had it for as long as I can remember.'

'What language is this? The symbols make no sense.'

The Stormcast shakes his head. 'My hope is that you are able to translate it,' he says. 'Some symbols are familiar, but the meaning eludes me.'

No, not a single language, but a pattern. The historian is lost in thought. A cypher. A common enough practice among the esoteric cults and sects of Shyish, the key to the translation would be a repeated sequence of symbols, most likely. Perhaps this first sequence. He turns each page carefully, engrossed. Eyes straining with the dense text in the half light of the pyres.

'There are mysteries in this land, secrets I would know,' says the Stormcast. 'I think you might be a key to those secrets, and this is a part of it. Read the book, historian. Tell me what you find.'

There is more to all this, the historian thinks. But for now, it is diversion enough. It is reason enough.

Kuan'Talos sits at the end of a peninsula, some leagues distant. The land curves like a skeletal finger, out into the sea. They walk a hidden coastal trail that winds along the edges of the cliffs, occasionally dipping down to skirt the beaches, and as they walk, the historian shares his knowledge of the area, gathered from books, from conversation, from exploration.

'The land here is poisoned,' he says. 'The local tribes claim some great daemon crawled this trail once, long ago, and now nothing will grow. The trees can sense such things. Even the dead stay away from poisonous places. Even so, it is far faster to travel than to follow the old roads, back inland and slowly out to the coast again. A journey that takes weeks.'

Where the coast is too broken, they head inland on a path through marshland and then a small forest. Skinny, leafless trees with partially exposed roots that cling to thin soil and sand. Dark, fibrous bark like the hair of a mangy dog. They stop infrequently. The historian is fitter than he knows he must appear; he is not truly so old as he looks with his grey beard and tired eyes. The Stormcast walks ahead. He seems like he could walk forever, even clad in heavy armour. He does not seem to get fatigued.

The historian's mind wanders, he daydreams, and the dreams turn sour. He thinks of the weeks he has spent with the Anvils on their campaign. To make a record, he told himself. We must document such things, record them in the annals of history. But it was the distraction that he sought, and a desire to... what... to see his faith in Sigmar made manifest? He has spoken little, but now he does to fill the silence. Anything that comes to mind.

'Do you ever take off your armour?'

'Yes. Sometimes, when it is safe,' the Stormcast says.

'Will you take it off here?'

'Here? No. We are not safe here.'

Ash from an unseen fire blows across the path. Something nearby is burning. A castle under siege. A village razed by the Stormhost. Ships burning far out in the mists. The ghosts and spirits know, but do not speak. This is a land at war, and they do not trust outsiders, not even him.

For a time, the coast path is grey with ash. He follows in the

Stormcast's footprints, much larger than his own. They quicken their pace and do not break. He ties the hood of his cloak around his face, in the style of the desert tribes from a faraway place. The Stormcast's fingers stray to the hammer at his waist. This is a man who has lived alone with danger for a long time, the historian thinks. Maybe longer than I can imagine. He tries to convince himself to take care, to be careful with his own life. This land of death welcomes the careless with open arms, he knows.

Would that be such a tragedy?

They do not meet any other travellers, nor see any sign of the unliving. The spirits of Shyish are quiet or preoccupied with the war elsewhere. There are hills further inland, overlooking their path; they loom large at night, shadows in the mist. He sees fires set at the summits, a blur of red and orange nearly lost in the blanketing brume that settles on the high places. Signal fires. Once, he thinks he can hear the mournful lowing of a great birch winding horn, but the wind changes and the sound is gone. *Someone has noticed our passage. What do we look like to the hill tribes? A broken old man and a golden god.*

In the evenings he studies the book. Pages of symbols that are at once familiar and frustratingly incomprehensible. Towards the end of the book there is page after page of diagrams, maps showing the stars. The centre point is surely Azyr. Maps of constellations with the Realm of Heaven a lodestone. A guiding light. But Azyr is not present in every illustration. In some, there is no star of heaven, no pattern that he can recognise.

At one time on the trail, the Stormcast puts on his helmet and takes his hammer from the leather loop at his belt. This is the only time he has seen him wear the death-mask helm. The Stormcast holds the hammer in his left gauntlet, and in his right, he holds a boltstorm pistol, a single-handed crossbow that the historian has seen before, used only by the Stormcast Eternals and too large by far for his own hands. They stand in silence for some time, the Stormcast tense and alert, looking towards the trees, and he feels useless, eyes searching, ears straining, but to no avail. Then in time they resume their walk.

'This place is not safe,' the Stormcast says; he repeats it, his eyes are ever restless, vigilant. They follow the path where nothing grows, the trail of an ancient daemon.

Each night they make camp beneath the stars, bathed in the purple light of aetheric storms beyond the horizon. Thaumaturgical phosphorescence illuminates the night sky, flaring with sudden brightness as the strange energies that gather nearer the realm's edge collide and coalesce. He watches them, for a time, before sleep takes him. The Stormcast does not sleep; he stands guard or sits and faces out to sea, his bronze-hued skin strangely blanched and pallid under the dancing light. You have your own thoughts to occupy you in quiet moments, the historian thinks. You carry your own ghosts.

He begins each new day with wine. Their provisions are sparse, limited by what they can carry. The Stormcast is nearby and the historian hears the rasp of a whetstone, distinct from the gentle lapping of the morning tide. There are ancient ruins buried in the loam not twenty paces from where he has slept; he did not see them in the dark. Another tower, he thinks. These ruined towers once stood sentry against the plague fleets all along this coast, but there is more to these ruins, an entrance concealed by ivy and scrub, a tunnel descending into darkness. A few paces in and the tunnel becomes flagstone steps that lead down, then are swallowed by murky, brackish water. Whatever was here has flooded, he can go no further. But the stones of the entranceway are engraved, less weathered than those he has seen elsewhere along the shore. He traces their outlines with his thumb, finds meaning in their shapes. Constructs a story from those pieces he can understand.

This was a temple, from before the Dark Gods ruled here,

before the Necromancer, before Sigmar. A temple to a spirit or lesser god, long since deposed or destroyed. Or simply forgotten. He has heard that there were many such, once, before the Necromancer consolidated his rule, but he doesn't know the truth of that. Some stories are too big to be rationalised in scholarly books, and the history of Shyish is constructed of myths and legends and impossible things. The Mortal Realms are a playground for the gods who rewrite history, rewrite the rules and natural order of the land to suit their whims. This is something he has learned to accept. To do otherwise would be to go mad, lost in the pursuit of understanding that is forever beyond the ken of mortal men.

His mind wanders, as it often does. Death is ever present in Shyish. There are rituals, ceremonies. There are ways that things must be done. There is not always room in these rituals for grief. The priest of Sigmar resembled a carrion bird with a shaved pate and hooked nose, and that is what he remembers the most. The priest had travelled for two days on foot to reach their cottage in the hills and to perform the rites, and he was riven with aches and sour with resentment at the inconvenience. There was no body to burn, just an empty space where a body should be. The priest did what he could or what he would, then returned back the way he had come, and so he had decided to leave as well. Pursue work, he had told himself. Occupy your mind. Find a purpose. There was nothing for him there. The priest had said, 'The study of history never reveals anything worth believing.' He thinks of these words often. There is some truth to them.

He shakes off the memory. He reaches reflexively for his flask at his belt, but it is not there. He believes his companion is hiding it.

'We all have our daemons,' he had said one day while sat beside the campfire, and wine was his.

The Stormcast had smiled, not unkindly. 'Ah, tell me more

of daemons,' he had laughed. 'Tell me of daemons, I have slain my share.'

Concentrate, occupy your mind.

The scenes engraved on the entranceway show images from the history of the land. They show the black sails of the plague fleets and the towers arrayed against them along a crude depiction of the shoreline. In one scene, flakes of blue pigment catch his eye. The sentinels positioned in the towers would throw handfuls of powder into the watchfire if they saw the dread ships approaching, and it would blaze with a blinding sapphire flame.

Above the archway there is a symbol, given more prominence than most. A nebulous form with many long and trailing arms. A spirit of the deep. A forgotten god. He has seen sign of this god before, a god of the sea – worshipped by fishermen and sailors and those on the coast that would pray to be spared from drowning, or for blessings of protection from the eater-fish and giant scuttlefish and worse things that made casting nets so perilous in the seas and oceans of Shyish.

He opens the red book, holds it close to his face to read in the half-light. Flicks through the pages. A symbol with trailing arms. A key.

The carrion-bird priest had said: 'Do you now worship death?' But he was a fool. Understanding you must die is not worshipping death.

A god of drowned men, its temple long since fallen to disrepair. Men will pray to strange and imagined things, he thinks. And strange things will ever welcome their attention.

We stand at the shore where the known meets the unknown, as the sun begins to set. We gather to watch the ritual, barefoot in the surf. Translucent crabs look like hordes of silver coins in the shallows. The sand is grey, the water as dark as blood.

In the tide pools there is a body. A boy, a young man. He

lies pinned beneath crushing stones, arms outstretched, held in place, the bones surely broken. They pile more stones on his chest, round and smooth, smaller placed atop larger to form a spire. With the weight pressing on his lungs he can no longer draw a full breath and his screams become gasps become groans. I wonder if his ribs are broken. He lies prone in the tidepool as the waves come back to the shore, lapping around our feet. We stand in the sea to witness. The waves come over the crest of the tidepool, white foam and swirling silt. The waves come in and the man cannot move. His hands held beneath rock, his fingers claw into the sand.

Dark water washes over him. His eyes widen and the cords in his neck bunch as he strains. But all he can do is raise his head a slight way and the water spills over his body, the silt swirls around him and his breathing is a ragged gasp and he strains, but broken bone has punctured his lungs and blood flecks his spittle until the waves wash it away and he spits and coughs and gasps to breathe as the water fills his mouth.

My queen looks at me; her feral eyes shine in the torchlight. This is necessary, she reminds me. I hold her hand and she holds mine and the warmth from her keeps me from trembling as the cool water laps around my waist and a tight fist of ice closes around my heart.

All along the shore, stone spires stand in the swirling waters and one by one they topple in the current. Falling soundlessly into the midnight tides. We stand together and watch until this last spire falls and all trace is washed away. All sign of his existence, undone.

A storm in the far distance, back along the coast. Lightning from a clear sky. The Stormcast watches, counting the flashes.

'They have reached Tor'Gar,' he says. 'The mountain keep. They say there is an idol to Dark Gods, sunk deep into the hollow core of the mountain, as tall as the tallest temple of Azyrheim. Made from the bones of those that defied the Plague God.'

'So I have heard,' the historian says. 'Lots of things are made from bones in this realm. They are an ever-cheap resource.' He doesn't look up from the book.

Over the next two days the temperature drops. The historian's breath steams and the steam wets his beard and the cloak wrapped around his face, and the moisture turns to crystals. His lips crack.

'Unnatural cold,' says the Stormcast. 'It will pass. Magical storms affect the weather in strange ways.' He shrugs. He has seen much stranger things, much harsher weather. He has travelled the Mortal Realms. He talks about how some realms are so hot that armour becomes like a clay oven and cooks you inside. The metal too hot to touch. A dry heat so intense it is painful to draw breath. In Ghur there is a wet heat so powerful that you gape for breath like a fish and yet may drown in your own sweat. 'Cold is better,' he says. The damp from the sea is comforting. He seems to like it here.

At night, the ground becomes frozen and treacherous. Black mud, black stone and black ice over it all. The wind is cold, cold so that the historian's bones feel like glass and he worries they will shatter if he falls, that they will break into shards. He steps carefully, each footstep a calculation followed by a sounding-out. There are no more fires in the hills at night. He finds that he misses them, misses the life that they represent. Life – at a distance – can be a comfort after all, he supposes. They make slow progress. The Stormcast is surefooted; it is as if he has walked these lands all of his life. He does not need a guide, the historian thinks. Why, then, am I here?

It takes two more days to follow the daemon trail to its conclusion. Or its origin. The path ends at the sea and it was here that once something either arrived or departed, beneath the ink-black waves. It is now only two hundred paces along the beach to the road, a broad road of amethyst slate, constructed by undying workers in ancient times of peace. The historian has walked that same road before, many leagues to the south, and it made him uneasy then. The industry of Shyish has ever been squandered on producing monuments to the egos of tyrants or yoked to the prosecution of endless war. Perhaps those are the same thing, he thinks. Out here in these remote parts he had hoped to escape the crushing weight of the world, a weight so heavy that he sometimes feels like he cannot draw a full breath, as if stones are laid upon his chest. The machinations of the Necromancer, the barbarity of the God-King. Old wars bleed into new wars. The wars of gods and daemons, with the lives of mortals seemingly only an afterthought, a distraction. He looks out upon the endless grey sea, rippled by the wind like hammered glass, white breakers under scattered whispers of mist. His eyes weep in the chill. The influence of the gods can never truly be avoided.

The next morning the Stormcast prepares food. He cooks on a small fire built from driftwood. Flotsam or jetsam. Many fishing boats are lost in this sea, to storms or to the creatures that live in the deep. Many ships too. There is a look of quiet consideration on his broad features. He is too large, too warlike, still clad in golden armour that catches the morning sun and gleams blinding white and silver. He moves with delicate precision to prepare the simple ingredients and guts a fish he has caught during the night. Three or four quick movements with his knife.

The historian watches for a few moments. Such meticulous actions might look absurd but for the skill and care of the giant, and the historian finds himself entranced as if he has stumbled upon a scene he was not meant to see.

The Stormcast looks up from his work and notices the historian's attention. 'I have lived many lifetimes. There are skills worth learning and there are some things worth spending time on,' he says. He smiles and shares out the food.

They sit on the beach and eat. Distant masts on the horizon, the fat-hulled merchant carracks on the trade route to Sendport and the Innerlands, hulls laden with salted fish, crab, eel.

'I have not been honest with you,' the Stormcast says.

The historian is eating, half listening. He has the red book open and he is able to read fragments now without pausing to translate. His mind is occupied with what he knows of rituals.

'I said you were a man without a purpose, a quest. And that every man must have a purpose.'

'And what, then, is yours?' the historian retorts. He is irritable after a poor night's rest. The cold spell has passed but sleep beneath the stars is taking its toll. 'Is there not a war you should be waging?'

The Stormcast flashes a smile. He seems immune to tiredness and irritability. 'Sigmar himself chose me from the ranks of the Vanguard,' he says. 'The God-King elevated me to the rank of Knight-Questor – a great honour – and assigned to me a special purpose. It is this mission that I now undertake and that I require your assistance with. This is my quest, historian – the God-King demands that I find the Szo-en-kur. I have sought it for many years, though what it is, I do not truly know. A mystery, set by Sigmar himself.'

'Szo-en-kur.' The historian sounds out the word. 'It would mean something like "heart of the sea" or "strength of the sea". Or possibly "egg".' He frowns. 'Ancient tongues are not my area of expertise. How do you expect me to help you? I have never heard of this... this thing.' He considers the book in his hands.

'The temple we saw on the trail, the shrine to the sea spirit,' the Stormcast says. 'I believe it is connected with that which I seek.'

'Then it was no coincidence that we made camp there,' says the historian.

The Stormcast bows his head slightly. 'I apologise for the deception,' he says. 'Please, tell me what you know of the history of the people of this land. I believe it is integral to my quest.'

'The people of this land?' the historian says. 'You think this book relates to them? This first chapter, this ritual – it is unlike any local ritual that I know of. It is more like the desert tortures of Aqshy, or perhaps a summoning rite from Ghur.'

He folds the corner of the page he is reading and sets the book down upon a rock, away from the fire and the sea-damp sand. He thinks for a moment.

'The history of this land,' he says, 'largely lost of course, during the Age of Chaos. We know that during the apocalypse the plague fleets from Black Nihil sailed in great force to the Innerlands, the more populous places. To Ossia, of course. Few fleets ventured this far north. Corruption spread to this land over the mountains and across the deserts. The conquered tribes pulled down their shrines to Sigmar and their old gods and in their place raised idols to the new dark powers. What choice did they have?'

The Stormcast – the Knight-Questor – listens intently. Bright blue eyes ever alert. Such old eyes for so youthful a face.

'When the followers of the Plague God came to these lands, there were refugees. Refugees in their hundreds of thousands,' the historian continues. 'An exodus from the Innerlands. Some sick, many too sick. Some sought to hide here in the north. Others would go further – to Coral, to Mhurghast and whatever fate awaited them in that cursed place. Some few cities and hidden tribes survived the apocalypse, one way or another. Most did not.'

'And to the castle at Kuan'Talos,' says the Stormcast. 'The so-called Amaranthe. You are familiar with that story? The sanctuary that fell beneath the sea.'

'The Amaranthe,' says the historian. 'A myth. It was said to be a place for refugees to take shelter from the coming apocalypse, protection against the coming of the Ruinous Powers. An ancient place. Improbable, impossible. The lord enacted a powerful enchantment intended to protect the castle, but it was a disaster. The castle collapsed and those that it sheltered were lost beneath the waves. They say that the lord was a pawn of the Dark Gods, that they made of him a daemon. They say the castle remains, beneath the waves, that he rules there still, dragging unfortunate sailors down into the deep.'

The historian sighs, suddenly weary. He looks out across the placid sea that stretches towards a distant horizon, above which the pale sun makes its languid ascent through a dismal, ashen sky. He is unused to lengthy conversation.

'I have walked a great distance in this realm,' he says. 'I have seen many impossible sights. A castle beneath the sea would not be the strangest thing among them. But this is local folklore, the superstition of sailors and fishermen. There have been efforts to find the Amaranthe. Treasure-seekers searched the shore for many leagues in each direction. There is nothing there. No ruins beneath the waves. No lost city. If that is where your quest lies, then the God-King has set you on a fool's errand.'

The Stormcast smiles. 'Let us discover the truth of that for ourselves,' he says.

Stones fall from a nearby spire. The ground beneath my feet shifts, a small amount. Birds take flight in alarm, small black shapes against the pale sky, their panicked flight turning to screeching argument. I watch, my queen's hand tight in mine. Far below the parapets on which I stand, the crowds of people stir to hastened activity. Their panic is apparent even from this height, as pale faces turn to the skies. And I watch them too, and I will them to be calm.

We are both barefoot and the stone beneath our feet is worn smooth by the passage of centuries, obsidian laced with violet. My queen and I are dressed in simple salt-crusted ochre robes. We wear crowns of spun gold, made to resemble the floating nests of the wader birds found along the coast, the great horned birds that weave their nests from sticks along with thorns and briar to protect against predators. We dress as did the Thalassiarchs of old, a vision of regality, of tradition. This is how my father and mother would appear on this same parapet when they were the lord and lady of the sea, as have all that ruled here since the times of myth. This is what the people expect and now it is our turn, now that the end has come. I fear the line ends here, that we are to be the last lord, the last lady, for the apocalypse has arrived. Does she regret coming here? How can she not? I hold her hand, she holds my hand.

In distant regions the plague fleets have been sighted. Most have turned south, heading along the Reach to the heartlands. But some sail north and travel further than we had hoped. Sigmar has no answer to this affront, nor the god of death nor the spirits of the sea. Prayer has not slowed the fleets. The Great Enemy comes, his advance implacable. The god Ner'gleck. The Plague God, the rot of men and beasts and the poisoner of the seas. He comes to the shores of Ora and now beyond.

The castle gates are open wide and through them comes a procession of refugees. A column of tribesmen. Fisherfolk. Villagers – their children and their elders, their scarce livestock and their wagons of possessions. Mounted warriors from the hills riding emaciated dox and elek, ducking their heads to fit their plumed helms beneath the teeth of the raised portcullis. Spirits and skeletal constructs carry the belongings of those families that can afford to barter with the undead of Shyish in the twin currencies of souls and thaumaturgical power. Many bring their dead with them, old bones and reliquaries, to keep them safe from the depredations of the despoilers and their dark magics. Guards in ochre livery watch this procession with hooded eyes.

Among the refugees are the sick and the weak. They are shunned because sickness is the precursor of the god of plagues, the tide of human misery driven before him like a vanguard. But they are accepted too, within the walls. They are infirm, unwell, but they are still human. My queen believes that to shun the sickly is to force them into the arms of the Enemy and thus strengthen him. To treat them, to cure disease, is to stab at the heart of the Enemy, to deny him. And none would doubt her in this for she has encountered the Plague God before.

We watch together in silence, noting every soul that passes through the great gate. And then when we have counted to the prescribed number, we bow our heads. And at this signal, the gates are shut. They are shut and they shall not be opened again.

Days pass. The sorcery begins.

They stand on the shores outside Kuan'Talos, half a league from the city walls. The sea here is violent, untamed. Waves twice again as tall as the historian crash against jagged black rocks.

'And yet, this is where the castle once stood,' he says. 'And there are no ruins, no remnants, or at least nothing conclusive. Nothing that stands out from the other ruins we have seen along this coast. The castle was said to shelter thousands. Nothing like that remains, not even below the waves. It is just a story. A work of fiction. I know not what else to make of it.'

'I have faith,' the Stormcast says. 'The quest does not end here.'

There are old stones, buried in the loamy earth, half hidden by long, dry grass and chaparral. The historian clears away the thorny brush with his hands. Here there is evidence, it is claimed, of flanking towers and the various structures that would have existed outside of the lost castle's walls. There is a channel said to be the remains of a roadway that leads to nowhere, terminating at the cliff edge. Most of the stone has been removed in ages past and reused for construction elsewhere. Nothing conclusive, nothing that hasn't been picked over by countless treasure hunters and scavengers a hundred times before.

Shyish is a land of ruins – fragments remain scattered across the realm – from the Age of Myth, or from the countless conquests and reconquests. To tear down the monuments of the defeated and raise your own monuments in their place, only to see them torn down in turn or succumb to the elements, or to the ravages of time in an endless cycle. No empire escapes these depredations, not even the empires of undeath. There is nothing special about these old stones, nothing unique about this place.

And yet there is one stone that catches his eye. One symbol graven prominently upon it. It has faded with time, but it is still easily recognisable. A barbed circle.

The Stormcast joins him. 'The same symbol as is upon the book,' he says. 'I have stood here countless times and looked upon it. It is repeated across this place, on countless stones. There is some connection. The stones, the book and my quest. If it is a fiction, then I am a part of it somehow.' He sighs. 'Tell me, have you discovered anything with your translations?'

'It is a journal of sorts,' the historian says, 'a collection of fragments, memories, stories. Transcribed by a single hand in an intricate cypher. Some words are incomprehensible. And then there are diagrams, maps of the stars, though these too make little sense to me. I do not know if the events recorded within are true or mere artifice.'

'The journal of one who witnessed,' says the Stormcast. 'I expected no less. The book is the key to my quest, and you are the key to the book. You are part of this as well, historian. The part I have been missing.'

There are revellers among the refugees, those who would sooner drink and dance than succumb to misery and despair in the face of armageddon. They slaughter those beasts that they cannot provide for and make of them a feast. I find such celebrations grotesque, but my queen tells me how denial of misery cuts at the poisonous spirit of the Enemy, because despair is the fertile soil in which his seed grows, for it is a seed that grows in the mind as well as in the body. Excise the rotten flesh and extirpate the poisoned seed. Cut at the heart of Ner'gleck thus and his power will wane in this realm.

Outside the gates the sight is enough to break all but the coldest of hearts. The moat has begun to flood, too wide now to cross safely yet some still try. The walls are unassailable, but some still try. The gate is unbending, unbreakable, but some beat upon it with the desperation of the condemned. There is nowhere for them to go. It is too late for them now to try the cities further along the coast. The last ships have sailed. There is nowhere to hide, nowhere that will stand. The lands behind them are burning. Rebellion, uprisings, madness. The tribes cast out their old gods and look to the invaders for mercy. Ner'gleck is a merciful conqueror if you pay his price: all he demands is everything you have.

We can take no more inside the walls, I say to myself. I repeat it over and over. Such are the terms of the compact. Such are the limits of our old god's power. Seven and seven and seven and seven. This is the number, this and no more.

At the gate there is a young girl. Dirty, lost and afraid. Someone has sacrificed everything to get her this far and now she is alone. I take off my crown and walk barefoot through the vast and empty courtyard. I harden my heart against the noise from beyond the wall, the noise of human suffering. And I close my heart to those within the walls. The sounds of revelry have continued late into the night and I am not sure which disturbs me the most.

I watch the masses beyond the walls. They are starving. They are sick. Plague spreads in such conditions as quickly as witchfire in the rigging when you sail through an aethyr storm.

Excise the rotten flesh.

I open the gate and take the young girl inside. She can share my rations, though I have the same rations as any other. She has no sign of sickness. It is a small mercy. Seven and seven and seven and eight, a breach of the terms of the compact. But our god is not cruel. Surely there is room for such a small one as her.

Even now the land tears and churns as the god's magic manifests. The bridge beyond the gate shatters and collapses. The land splits into chasms and the sea floods across the broken ground. Those within the walls will be taken into the god's protection, borne by the magic of the sea spirit. When our castle becomes an ark in truth. When the Amaranthe begins its voyage.

I spare one last look for those we leave behind. The waters already rise and there is nowhere for them to go. I tell myself it is a mercy.

'The Amaranthe did not sink beneath the waves, it sailed atop them. It broke free of the land – some magic, some sorcery – to drift away into the ocean. Or it rose above the waves like a… duardin sky-fortress – though that would surely be impossible. The entire castle, the land beneath it… They call it an ark.'

Can such a thing be true? The historian's mind is racing. A compact with a sea spirit, some ancient and powerful thing. Near eight thousand souls aboard. An ark – but more of an island than a ship. Impossibly vast. And no one has ever found it because it did not sink beneath the waves… at least, not here.

'How can it be that in all the years since it has never been sighted? And where is it now?' the Stormcast asks.

The historian rubs his eyes. They sit in the ruins where once the Amaranthe would have broken away from the shore if the journal is to be believed, where once all those that were not within the walls were washed away as the land split apart. He has been working for some hours, each new symbol a puzzle to be decoded. The journal talks of events he has heard of, though some names and words are in archaic local dialects that are hard to translate.

'There is no way we can know,' he says. 'Lost at the bottom of the ocean. Fallen off the edge of the realm. Or through some distant Realmgate. Gone. I fear this is a dead end.'

'I do not believe that, historian. I do not believe my quest ends here, in failure. There must be more secrets within the book.'

But the historian is despondent. 'This is not a puzzle to be solved,' he says. 'There is not a neat conclusion that awaits us. A hundred years ago this ark sailed into unknown oceans. It is lost, that is all.'

The Stormcast is silent for a long while, then he nods. 'I will wait here for a time,' he says. 'You should find an inn, for there is no need to spend another night outdoors.'

He hands the historian a pouch of coins from some faraway land. The edges are notched and on both sides there is only a symbol of a hammer. Aether-gold. It is a small fortune.

'Find a ship if there is one,' he says. 'I cannot ask any more of you.'

He leaves the Stormcast then, looking out across the endless grey sea. He walks the trail alone, down through the scrubland and desert where once, long ago, there had been farmland, then from the trail onto the road of amethyst slate. Kuan'Talos looms before him, sprawling, vast and empty. Once a thriving city, now a shell of its former glory, kept alive only by the trade ships and fishermen. Decrepit, empty buildings crumbling behind a partially ruined grey stone wall that encircles the city and carries out some way into the bay to form a sea barrier for the harbour.

A dead body at the side of the road. A young man, face buried in the sand. The historian quickly looks away, drinks from his flask of wine. He passes few other travellers on the road, and those he does see wear the colourless sackcloth garb of Shyishian peasants and keep their pale faces downcast as he walks by on the dusty path. They look stricken, he thinks. Devoid of hope. What do they see when they look upon me?

In parts of Shyish the dead and the living seem to grow ever closer, as if the walls between life and death are somehow thinner. The dead may work the fields, guard the walls and cast nets alongside the living, and in turn, those that live seem to share their strength, their vigour. It is as if they give away their vitality in exchange somehow, a sacrifice offered freely. This city feels like one of those places – a place where the concepts of life and death have grown indistinct. He wonders if anyone here is truly alive, if anyone is truly dead, or if there only exists a kind of half-life, a shadow of life. And if so, he thinks, will I be welcomed here, will I be recognised as one of their number? I could make a home in this necropolis, he thinks. A home devoid of comfort and warmth. A place to haunt. A place for old ghosts.

Those few that live here work the ships and the sea. Fishwives accost him as he walks the cobbled streets, hawking their wares. Translucent scuttlefish dredged from the seabed with great nets that take many days to haul, cast from a web of floating rafts like a seaborne shanty town. Fish and eels, sold from barrels at the streetside, packed in salt; the smell is overwhelming. Crabs and shelled seacrawlers, some the size of a small child. Chitinous legs as long as his arm. Hooked spidershark teeth sharp enough to pierce the thick skin of a seigewhale. Parts of countless creatures he cannot identify: hauls from the deep ocean, things found in nets or traps or skewered on harpoons by the deep ocean hunter vessels. The pale white flesh and bulbous black eyes of fish that have never before seen the light of day.

Ships and boats of all sizes fill the berths along the jetties that stretch far into the placid, inky water. The harbour itself is quiet, without the noise of larger ports like those found in the Innerlands or elsewhere in the Mortal Realms. There are a few undead workers that toil alongside pale-skinned natives. Lifeless golems and spirit constructs unload the rancid-smelling fishing carvels, hauling the carcasses of bloated sea creatures ashore onto the creaking timbers of the jetties, or across to the fat-hulled trade ships. Skeletal cats dart between their ankles, retrieving those fish that drop to the floor and taking them to the fishwives to be threaded upon monger strings.

He watches the workings of the port until he finds a ship that stands apart from the others, a sleek three-masted ship, rigged fore and aft, berthed away from the fishing vessels and traders. A messenger perhaps, or a merchant, but one laden with goods other than salted eels, and so this is the ship he seeks out. She is called the *Silenaita*, a name with an origin in Ossia, a desert queen from the Age of Myths. The ship is past her prime; patched grey timbers caulked with oakum bear the traces of faded red paint. The water in the harbour is calm and viscous, the surface oily, and the ship is reflected in the tepid water like a fading dream, ghostly and indistinct. Standing at the moorings he hails the crew as they work to make ready. A small crew, maybe only two dozen hands, but they work efficiently and expertly on their tasks and they are keen-eyed as they regard him and his coin purse. He comes unsteadily aboard across the swaying gangway.

'We are bound for Sendport,' says the captain. He is a short man, dark skin covered in tattoos, across his bare arms, across his weatherworn face and bald scalp. He has a friendly demeanour, but a multitude of criss-crossed scars and a crooked nose that looks as if it has repeatedly been broken suggest that this demeanour is changeable.

'We can take you along the coast. But you will have to share a berth with these,' he says, with a grin that is not entirely comforting. He gestures to a cabin where fish skins hang from every beam. There are skulls and bones of more exotic sea creatures, hung with fetishes and woven with beaded strings. Painted with charms and runes the historian does not recognise. 'Our holds are near full,' he explains. 'There is money to be made with such things. Used in magic, the skins made into leather and armour. Or fashioned into bone constructs that remember the deep places.'

The historian nods, his attention caught by one item among the bones, stowed away on a shelf and wrapped in dry seaweed. A skull like that of a man but deformed so that it has no hollows for eyes and the jaw is fused together, shaped into something more akin to the comb-like teeth of certain whales. The forehead is painted with crimson runes of warding, the paint peeling from the brittle, salt-weathered bone.

'Strange things wash up along these shores,' says the captain. 'Things from the deep, things from distant lands.'

They sit in the captain's cabin and drink wine.

'It is a month or more to Sendport,' says the captain. He has grey hair in his coarse beard, but youthful green eyes. An easy manner. The first person the historian has spoken to in some weeks – the first mortal anyway. They talk of inconsequential things. The historian's mind is elsewhere. He feels ashamed. It is a feeling deep in his gut and he cannot escape it. He thinks of the Stormcast standing on that grey shore and he tells himself that there is nothing more he can do, that only a fool would place any expectation upon him. Life is disappointing, he thinks, how could you expect otherwise?

The captain has maps and sea charts arranged upon what passes for a table in his small cabin. He plots a course that follows the length of the shore. The historian watches, but he remains distracted. They drink wine from the vineyards at Athanasia, flowery and surprisingly potent. The captain talks as he studies the charts, he talks of his trade and how few others think to come this far for anything other than fish. He explains that the fish trade in the north is essential to feed the Innerlands, that there is a wealth of fish in these remote seas and a good living to be made, but it is not a life for him. A man can get sick of the smell of fish.

The captain takes a device from a lockbox on his desk, an elaborate object like a large compass. He calls it an astrolabe, a device to navigate by the stars. Compasses become unreliable the closer you sail to the realm's edge, he explains, and even more so since the Stormcasts arrived, with their lightning and their sorcery. A compass needle will point towards magic, and even following the coast you can get turned around, lost in the mists. Once there would have been fires. Beacons along the shore. But now, the astrolabe is the only safe way. The star of Azyr is a constant in the night sky.

The historian thinks on this. The wine has slowed him, he has drunk too much. He fumbles in his pack to find the journal. *The star is a constant*, he thinks. He shows the captain the pages in the journal that are covered with drawings of the stars, annotated with numbers and symbols. He has translated what he can, his own notes are scrawled on the cramped pages. Endless numbers that make no sense to him.

'Astronomical readings,' says the captain. 'These are taken at intervals to record your position, and where you are heading. Taken with a device much like my own. See? The centre dial of the astrolabe turns to face away from the star of Azyr. There is a soul bound within that cowers from the light of that star, its craven nature turns the disc thus. The rest of the reading stems from that.' He twists the outer rings of the device; delicate, golden components slide and click mechanically into place.

The captain takes the book from the historian, flicks through the pages and compares the historian's notations to the charts on his table.

'The numbers show the year and even the day,' he says, 'determined from the position of the stars. Comprehensive, but...' He scratches his coarse beard. 'These readings make no sense. Some stars are missing, here and here,' he says, 'and these readings have no stars at all. And whatever ship this was barely made headway, for years and years. And then the readings stop, some decades past. Perhaps she sailed off the edge of the realm. Perhaps dragged down to the deep places.'

'With these readings, could you plot its course?' the historian asks. 'Determine where this ship was heading?'

'No,' says the captain. 'No indeed. You could take a guess taking the speed she sails and what we know of the tides and how they tug at her, but no. To do that you would need to know from what port she set out.'

The historian nods. He traces along the coast of the map on the captain's table with his finger until he finds the place he is looking for. 'Right here,' he says. 'Right here.' He thinks again. 'You say the readings stopped many years ago. But could you estimate where it is now? Could you take me there?' He empties the coin pouch on the table.

He sees the captain thinking it over. Calculating. The ocean is vast and unknowable, and time and the elements confuse and confound, but they could do it, the historian believes, they could find the ark.

'She is a lost ship,' the historian says. 'A strange ship to be sure. We have coin, and no doubt she carries strange and exotic plunder, and that is yours for the taking. But if you can take us – my companion and I – if you will try, I can offer you something better than gold,' he says.

He reaches out, and with one finger touches the captain's forehead, touches the twin-tailed comet tattooed there.

'I can offer you a mission from the God-King himself.'

THE SECOND CIRCLE

The Disenchanted Flesh

The second circle is the circle around a severed throat; a red circle reveals mysteries as simple truths. There is nothing hidden within, there is no godly essence within. Only meat, revealed in crimson certainty. The flesh, disenchanted. The inviolable, violated. You think it contains all of you, that it is sacred. Let us show you. There is no secret, the flesh splits and I am within, we are within, and you are without. You think your flesh is a vessel, that your body is the work of a god, your essence contained within. But you are like liquid, your flesh is like a pool and here is the tide to fill it. Your essence is a liquid to spill and mingle, to join with the tide. There are no edges, no limits to your container, your skin is our skin, your blood is our blood,

    your flesh
    is
        no

sacred
thing.

The *Silenaita* sails across the seas at the ends of the known world, beyond the scope of most reputable maps and charts. It is a voyage untroubled by storms and rough weather, nor is it imperilled by stray magics and thaumaturgical events, the likes of which can set ropes and sails ablaze in purple witchfire or transport a ship many leagues in the blink of an eye, to run aground on faraway shores. By day, the sea is an endless grey expanse, stretching to infinite perspectives. At night, the stars shine bright in a sky so black that it feels as if the *Silenaita* has become untethered from the Mortal Realms to sail through the endless void. Beyond the far horizon the eerie glow of the Starless Gates haunts them in all its dismal glory, an iridescent gyre burning in the night like a cyclopean eye.

They are borne by inconsistent and frivolous winds, and frequently need to spend a hard few days beating to windward to make any headway at all. The historian confines himself to his cabin, lying prone or curled like a babe as he retches at the gentle lurches and sudden jolts of the ship. He curses himself for a fool, having never sailed such a distance before, and wonders what madness made him undertake this journey. A voyage of many weeks to a vague destination on the uncharted seas of the realm's edge. Guilt, he thinks, or a misguided desire to please the Stormcast. Or perhaps it is just that he had nowhere else to go.

When he is able, he works on translating the journal, fascinated and appalled by the fragments he uncovers. He drinks wine and tries to sleep, his ears stuffed with wax balls against the endless creaks and groans, stamping feet and calls of the crew as they go about working the ship, their spirits high at the thought of plunder, and higher yet when in the presence of the Stormcast. The God-King's own emissary to bless their voyage.

The Stormcast lends a hand where he is able. The crew regard him with awe. He still wears most of his armour and it does not seem to be a hindrance even when the ship is caught by unexpected winds and tossed about. He is surefooted, like a man who has spent his life at sea. Never a slip or a stumble. He can heave the lines with the strength of many mortal men, and he is tireless, rarely sleeping even when the sea is calm and the ship is quiet. At times, he joins in with the shanties that the sailors sing, raucous songs of gods and mortals. He is quick to smile and laugh. He lives in the innocence of the present, thinks the historian, unburdened by the weight of the past, unconcerned by the threat of the future.

'You wear your armour even here?' the historian asks him one day.

The Stormcast grins. His hair is wet from the spray and his beard is wild and crusted with salt, but otherwise he seems unaffected by their situation, as if he has just stridden from the gates of Azyrheim. 'I do,' he says.

'And if you should be swept overboard, to sink like a stone?'

'That shall not happen.'

'If we should hit a rock and run aground?'

'We shall not run aground. Have faith.'

'And if this foul old ship should sink anyway?'

The Stormcast sighs. 'She is a fine old ship,' he says. 'But should she sink, and should I drown… Then I shall be reforged by Sigmar and reborn in lightning before your eyes. I will haul the captain up from the wreckage, and I shall demand that he return the coin that we have paid him.'

'You truly do not fear death?'

'There is nothing to be feared.'

'What about all that you lose? All that you leave behind?'

The Stormcast does not answer.

* * *

Fires still burn on the mainland at night. Not signal fires such as we once lit to guide the ships, nor warning beacons, but the fires of settlements aflame, of the old world burning. Are they fires set by the invaders, I wonder, or do those we left behind put their own houses to the torch as a last desperate act of defiance? Do they make of their cities great funeral pyres rather than suffer the fate of those that defy the Plague God? The coastal towns and villages of Ora were abandoned, and further along the coast even Talos – a city of many thousands – was all but empty when we commenced our voyage. Where those refugees are now, I do not dare think. I pray that they found a place such as this, a place to hide until Sigmar returns to drive the invader away, as he surely must.

Ner'gleck walks the lands now. Before him he drives pestilence and despair and naught but a devastating silence follows in his wake. Magical storms herald his coming in the west and in the south. Here in the mists we are hidden, too far from his dread gaze. I pray also that this is true. I will not let despair get a hook into my heart.

Despair is an invisible worm, borne on the currents of the wind. Like disease, it can seek you out and take root. Some aboard the ark have already succumbed. They have gone mad with despair or taken their own lives. They walk out on the shore at night, out into the ocean. They walk below the waves and do not appear again. We are adrift under uncaring stars. But I am not alone. I am not alone.

My queen is ever my source of strength and a source of hope for me and the people. She watches the seas through the eyes of a seahawk as it circles the island, alert for any sign of danger, or rides the spirit of the great albatross as they glide vast distances above the waves. She looks for any sign that we are pursued. She has seen the krakens migrating many leagues to the north and she described the spectacle to me, her eyes bright with joy at the memory. And each night she communes with the sea spirit, this old god with whom she has forged a compact. She tells me it is suffering, that we are a burden. But it will bear us yet.

Overall, the spirit of our people is strong. They have begun construction of a tower, taller than any other on the island, and plan to raise an icon to Sigmar so that he may find us here when the star of Azyr once again turns its gaze to this mortal realm. The star wanes, it seems more distant than before. But I believe it will not be long now before the God-King makes answer for these atrocities.

There is concern about the drinking water. It tastes of some impurity. There is a staleness to it that sits poorly in the gut and some young and the elderly refuse to drink it lest they become sick. The well at the heart of the island looks to be clean and there are no signs of foulness, but when it is drawn the water is somehow tainted. They blame each other, the guards have had to intervene.

There are some calls for another ritual from those that remember. An offering to the god. But we have already given enough. We ask much of the god below the waves, but we shall not be a burden for long. The God-King shall return. If not this year, then the next. We shall not travel these seas for long, I am sure. We will find safe harbour.

They are nearing their destination. The captain's charts show an area of sea some leagues across where they believe they may find the ark, should it truly exist, and should no sinister fate have befallen it. The historian is not sure what he believes, what he expects to find, but each day he climbs as high as he dares on the mast and looks across the endless sea for any sign. To rest his eyes, he tells himself; the cramped writing of the journal is exhausting to read. But secretly too he is excited about the prospect of discovery. Distant lights, seabirds circling, those are the things he searches for, though his eyesight is not half so good as the lookout in the crow's nest, nor the Stormcast who stands at the prow like a figurehead, golden armour gleaming like a beacon in the sallow light of the languid, ethereal dawn.

There is a sudden alarm from the lookout and a call from the Stormcast almost at once. No more than twenty paces from the starboard bow, a great shape breaches the water, twice the length of the ship. Dark grey, pockmarked skin slashed with ridges and creases that twist and spiral and glisten in the wan sunlight, coiling up from the depths like a length of rope passed from one hand to another, churning the water to froth. Whatever sea creature this is could shatter the *Silenaita* like kindling, the historian knows, and he holds his breath to wait for the crunch of impact. They are sailing close-hauled, and the sails luff then fill as the ship tacks, turning slowly, so slowly away. Some among the crew are praying.

'It is not a creature that destroys ships,' says the captain. 'At least not with intention. They are kraken, migrating. It is said they swim to the deep places where the skin between worlds grows thin.' He too is praying, to Sigmar, to Nagash. To the gods and spirits of the sea. He has a rosary in his hand, carved from shark teeth, scrimshawed with arcane symbols. A twin-tailed comet. A hammer. A form with many trailing arms. Two bells pass and still the leviathans continue to breach, the huge shapes receding now in their wake.

The next day, mist rises from the ocean, thick and absolute. Mist so heavy the ship seems to become mired in it. All progress comes to a standstill, the ship drifts without purpose or direction. All sound is swallowed – their lone bell peals a warning to any vessels nearby, but the ringing is muted and hollow and futile. The ship's compass spins endlessly, and the temperature drops until the deck becomes patchy with black ice. The historian can taste the magic in the air, coppery and musty. His teeth ache and the hairs on his arms stand upright.

They drift this way for many days and the historian is stricken with a sense of hopelessness that in turn becomes the achingly familiar degeneration into despair. When he is able, he works on translating the book, at other times he stares out into the whiteness, seeing nothing, seeking nothing. He sleeps fitfully and his dreams are bright and full of a radiance that is no longer there when he wakes, a light that he is not sure he has ever known. He sits alone in his cabin with the skulls and bones of strange fish and tries to remember the light from his dreams, but he cannot. All joy is now darkened, all purpose forgotten.

Some nights he cannot sleep at all. On one such night the Stormcast finds him standing at the taffrail, looking down at the faint ripples of the ship's silent passage through the ink-black sea, lost in private thoughts.

'You cannot sleep?' the Stormcast asks. His voice is low. Since the *Silenaita* has been in the mists, everyone has taken to speaking in hushed tones. It is as if all life must now adhere to new rules, the laws of a quieter place of existence.

'Bad dreams,' the historian says, and shrugs. He runs a hand across his face, through his wild beard. He is exhausted, his skin grey and sallow.

The Stormcast says nothing for a while, hands on the guardrail, looking into the water. 'I do not often sleep,' he says. 'It does not feel safe to do so, though I could not say why. But I am no stranger to bad dreams.'

They stand in silence for some time, then the Stormcast speaks again, his voice strangely distant.

'There is a dream I have, over and over. I have had it since my last death. Or maybe I have always had it. In this dream there is a great cat – huge and golden – the sort we had in the forests near Azyrheim, or that are found in the jungles of Ghur. It stands in a place devoid of all features – a void. It stands in darkness, or perhaps it stands in mists such as these, I do not recall this detail.'

The historian turns to regard the Stormcast now. He has never heard him talk this way. The Stormcast's eyes are downcast.

'The cat's great, broad head is bowed low,' he continues. 'Its breathing is slow. Its ears are flat back against its head and its teeth exposed. Something surrounds it. It does not move, it does not growl or roar nor so much as turn its head.'

The Stormcast pauses for a moment. There was a tremor in his voice, almost imperceptible. For an instant the historian feels his breath caught in his throat. A tremor, a crack in seemingly impenetrable armour.

'And then something bites it. Or... pieces of the cat are bitten away,' the Stormcast continues. 'Some invisible creature... I can do nothing to stop it. There is no sound, no tearing of flesh, no howl of pain. And no blood. It is like... it is as if the cat is made from clay.'

The Stormcast sighs. Straightens. 'I have seen terrible things, historian. I have fought daemons. Nothing scares me. I do not say this to boast. Nothing scares me because I do not fear death. I do not fear pain. I do not believe that any force in the Mortal Realms can stand against me when the God-King is at my side. But this dream... I fear that one night I will dream and there will be nothing left. Every part bitten away until nothing remains. Just an empty void.'

'Why are you telling me this?'

'Your dreams follow you into the waking world, historian. These ghosts, these things that haunt you. They are only real to you. Just stop believing in them. Just stop.'

'As easy as that?'

'No. No, it is not easy. You need faith. You need purpose.'

The girl, I should tell you of her. In her I have found a purpose. We are a family and our chambers no longer feel so empty. Though she is no longer really a child, she has grown – these last few years have not been easy and so she has matured quickly. She does not speak, the events of her past will not allow it, I believe. Whatever horrors she saw before she arrived here have taken from her the capacity for speech. We give her the best life that we are able; I hope it is enough.

My lady loves our daughter, I am sure, but I know also that she grows tired of this voyage. She spends little time with us and more time among the animals, seeing through their eyes, riding their spirits across the sky or beneath the waves. She walks the perimeter of walls in her shifted form. It makes the people uneasy. She cares less and less what they think.

I show the child the vast mechanisms of the star chamber where I measure the passages of time and the positions of the stars. A miraculous device forged of gold and brass that fills a room near the top of the keep. I spend many hours here, recording our progress aboard the ark. As the year changes, the discs and bars of the machine shift on innumerable, delicate gears and a needle moves along a track. We watch this together and she is entranced as the wheels turn and the needle moves along a single notch. The fifth year. The fifth year aboard this ark, and this salvation that feels now like a prison. Longer than I would have liked, but we have not given up hope.

The observatory has a glass-domed roof and directly above shines the star of Azyr, at the centre of all things. The star is so faint now, often lost in the mists for weeks at a time, and my readings grow imprecise. To catch a sight is a blessing, and yet the girl seems to shy away from it. She will not look at it. She is so thin, so fragile, it breaks my heart. It is such a sad thing to be abandoned by your god. I tell her, she must have faith.

The food stores and water that we brought with us have become scarce, we did not think our journey would be so long and those barrels of reserves that we do still have are often found to be foul when opened. We depend so much now on the sea, but the catch is frequently spoiled, the nets bring in such wretched creatures, soft shells full of black slime, translucent and deformed. The atmosphere has become one of despondency, hopelessness. More and more they walk into the sea.

Bells ring out across the island. They have built more towers, and at the top of each tower they have hung great iron bells, forged by melting down the icons to Sigmar. They say that the God-King cannot see us in the mists, but maybe he will hear us. I fear they toil in vain.

There is a sound. Once, twice. The distant ringing of a bell. They are on the foredeck together and quickly hush, ears straining in the silence. Then it comes again. Strangely flat and muffled but unmistakably a bell somewhere out in the mist. It is impossible to determine the direction; the sound seems to echo strangely, each time coming from a different heading. Then it is louder and there are more bells, each peal reverberating dully in the fog, a cacophonic chorus of discordant knells rolls and crashes around them and washes over them, from all directions and none. A pandemonium of rolling, thunderous bells that lasts for a hundred heartbeats and then suddenly falls silent. The historian holds his breath, straining to hear. The crew are similarly alert, standing at the rails or climbing the rigging, for surely it must be some hitherto unknown land or an armada of passing warships...

The island suddenly looms out of the mist, scarcely a hundred paces to the fore. It breaks out of the fogbanks like a giant insect pulling itself free from a spider's web, trailing wispy threads like ghostly shackles. The shadow of its immensity falls heavily across the *Silenaita*, obscuring the light of the moon and plunging them into darkness. Its jagged spires stand defiant against aged ruination, like unearthed bones dredged up from the ocean floor. Born in some cataclysmic event on the seabed then erupted forth, rejected by the depths. Waves break against encircling walls, walls like an oceanic trench, looming darkly, massive and inhuman. The sudden, impossibly close emergence takes everyone by surprise. The sailors shout and heave on ropes and climb the rigging in leaps. The sails are furled, and the captain and his helmsman pull hard upon the tiller before the ship can collide with the island.

The perimeter wall stretches away in both directions as far as the historian can see, before it vanishes into the night. It is black stone, cut precisely and set without mortar. Amethyst glitters in its shadows where it is infused with seams of dark purple. It is buttressed, crusted with barnacles to a height far above the ship's main mast and stained with green slime and guano. Above the wall, a score of towers rises from the island like branches of a tree, crooked and yearning for the light of an absent sun. The towers are jagged shards that scratch at the sky, the tangled teeth of a sea-bed predator.

The sailors are crying now in alarm as the *Silenaita* veers too close to the giant walls. The ship is turned but the island seems to move slowly to meet them, narrowing the gap so that the sailors reach for the sweeps to push the ship away. Oars splinter like matchsticks as they come ever closer, churning the sea between them so the ship rocks and then begins to groan and grate as the stone contacts the hull beneath the waterline. Then the Stormcast is there, standing at the gunwale, bracing himself, arms outstretched, gauntleted hands against the slick black stone. And it looks as if he must be crushed, but then he heaves, and the sailors heave along with him using the broken hafts of oars, and the grinding of stone on wood quietens as the *Silenaita* moves slowly apart from the island. Even the historian is pushing, his heart racing, fuelled on by the nightmare sound of cracking timbers. The Stormcast roars with effort, his arms straightening, then he is leaning, then staggering back to fall on the deck as the gap between the ship and the walls begins to widen. The span of a few arm lengths now, the sea calming, then the ship is steady, and the crew release a ragged breath that could be a cheer or a sigh of relief.

'The Amaranthe!' the Stormcast shouts. He is smiling, unfazed by the brush with disaster. 'I knew you would find it, historian!'

A stone bridge is spied in the mist some distance to starboard that would serve well as a jetty, and a team of men take out the ship's boat with a coil of stout rope and row down along the length of the wall towards it. They affix the rope around the bridge, half a bridge that leads to nowhere but is otherwise strong and does not crumble as the ship is pulled along the line, the rope wound about the capstan and the Stormcast pushing the wheel around and around with the strength of a dozen men. Timbers creak but the sea is calm, and they bring the ship within ten paces of the bridge, then drop a boarding ramp across the gap, metal hooks biting into the stone and holding fast. The historian observes the well-practised way the crew do this, too familiar by far, he thinks. Though this is not something they were expecting to find, they seem well prepared. Not a messenger ship or a merchant trader at all.

There is a chill wind and it carries on it a musty coppery smell; the cold permeates deep in the historian's clothing, wet from the spray, the mist and his sweat. The Stormcast helps him across as the plank shifts slightly underfoot. Five men wait on the bridge with oil lamps, cutlasses in hand. Gulls, terns and other seabirds shriek overhead, wakened from their nests in the walls and rocks by the intruders.

The castle is built on crusty black basalt that disappears beneath the waves as far down as they are able to see. It squats atop this jagged land like a vast parasite, with hooks sunk deep into the rock. From the bridge a paved road leads through an open portal in the wall, black and foreboding, wide enough for two carts to pass through side by side. The stone underfoot is obsidian, slick with green slime and crusted with barnacles and strands of seaweed like clumps of lank, wet hair. Small beaches of grey sand pocket the shore where the walls and buttresses plunge into the ocean. Beaches covered with dead, rotting fish.

Above the gate they see the castle's keep. It appears more solidly constructed than the multitudinous irregular towers, less spindly and twisted. Solid black stone with barred windows and arrow slits. No light can be seen within, no glow from a hearth or firepit. No sound can be heard save the lapping of the waves and the constant clamour of gulls, strangely muffled by the fog. The Amaranthe is dead. Long dead. He is not sure what he had expected, but it was not this. The island has been lost for a hundred years, but so many once lived here.

There is a cry of alarm and a flash of motion. The historian is pushed back and the Stormcast is suddenly in front of him, crossbow and hammer in his hands. Some type of eater-fish has emerged from the inky water. It is slick and lean, as purposeful and efficient as a spearhead, with three stacked rows of teeth like gutting knives and black, pinprick eyes. As it rises from the water the spidershark's trailing legs unfold and uncurl. Dozens of long, skinny, crab-like legs on each side instead of fins, so that it skitters across the sand, dragging its thrashing tail along behind it. One sailor is slow to react, and the creature is upon him before he can turn around. The multi-layered teeth shred clothes and flesh and the man screams as the fish shakes its head like a dog, pulling the sailor off his feet and tossing him effortlessly away before darting towards the others.

The first boltstorm quarrel pierces the shark's hide near its eye and it falters, skidding on the slick black stonework of the road. Its forelegs scratch futilely at the bolt as its tail thrashes, cracking stone and scattering shards of obsidian. It does not roar or screech but only wetly gnashes its blood-soaked jaws then turns to face the Stormcast, beady eyes focusing on the threat. The sailors scatter as it charges, their panicked cries answered with louder shrieks from the circling gulls.

The Stormcast drops his bolt weapon, switches his hammer to his right hand and braces to meet the charging creature. It closes on him, biting and gnashing its teeth, delicate, insectile legs propelling it faster than a galloping horse. And then it is upon him, and its jaws clamp down on the golden giant's left arm, teeth screeching across sigmarite. But the Stormcast has offered this arm, he has faith in the strength of his armour. He waits until the right moment presents itself, then brings the hammer down a single time with a dull crack on the beast's skull. It thrashes wildly then its legs give way, and it falls to its belly on the wet stone, scratching and scraping blindly. The Stormcast is dragged by his trapped arm, feet skidding on the slime, but he keeps his footing. He raises the hammer but does not strike again. Finally, it is still.

The courtyard beyond the gateway is a vast open space, almost large enough for an entire Stormhost to assemble. Behind them the monolithic wall blocks all sign of the ocean, the topmost reaches vanishing into the thick mist that smothers the island, draped across the battlements like a funeral shroud. Further along the wall another gate stands open, leading to a wide beach of grey sand. On the opposite side is the keep, and far above are the battlements where long ago the lord and lady would have stood and watched as the refugees arrived through this same gate. There are many smaller structures as well, most carved from the same black stone, but some are clearly later additions, fashioned in a more ramshackle manner. Some from wood largely disintegrated with rot, some from stone. They look like they have been formed by the tides, not by human hands, the historian thinks; time has worn the stone, so it looks organic. Among these structures dozens of towers rise like twisted stalagmites, wide enough only for a single ladder or winding stair, their topmost reaches lost in the mist. Everything is strewn with ribbons of seaweed and crusted with barnacles and limpets.

The entire courtyard is flooded ankle deep with oily water that glistens with silvery rainbows as they wade into it. Dead fish float in various stages of decomposition, and dead gulls, their skeletal flesh blackened with rot, their moulted feathers plucked and shrivelled by decay. There are larger remains too, whale bones brown with decay, fleshless and festering in the brackish water. The stench of old rot is dissipated by the breeze that ripples the surface of the false lake, and seabirds watch with agitation from perches atop the surrounding walls, but otherwise all is quiet and still.

There is no sign that anyone lives here still, and yet no sign of human remains either. The Stormcast is on guard, in case the island has been occupied by pirates or some other worse things. It is his nature to be vigilant. But nothing lives here, the historian thinks. It is his nature to expect the worst, and this is a place only of death and dead things. Even the birds seem reluctant to venture inside the walls.

The Stormcast leads the way, moving more silently than seems possible. The sailors follow several paces behind and the historian behind them. He carries a lantern as the rising sun of the early morning brings only a blanched and hazy light, and the great walls cast deep shadows. He is lost in his thoughts, his mind transported to other places, other times.

Diseases of the mind, carried by invisible worms that drift in the wind. This passage has stayed with him. He has read books that describe how these worms can carry diseases of the body, how they can be passed from one sick person to another without touch, travelling between their inhalations and exhalations, or lingering in stale air for days even once all evidence of the disease has gone, just waiting for a new victim to infect. It is possible that a disease of the mind works in this same way. He believes that these diseases seek out some weakness, some flaw that already exists in a mind or spirit; that they are a seed that grows from nothing. Like a weed that seeks out a crack to push through and find purchase, fed and nourished by the host, which then grows and blossoms into despair. And then in turn it spreads new seeds, passing from man to woman, from father to son.

I should have protected him from this, from all of this, he thinks. I should have paid more mind to that which I gave to him, that which he took from me. Corruption hides in the folds of a flower when its season has come to pass. It is so easy to miss signs in others, particularly if your thoughts are more often turned inwards.

The past keeps drawing him back, there is just so much of it. Too much to bear. The past is a weight that pulls him down beneath dark and cloudy waters. An image comes unbidden to his mind. A vision of a wheel, and the wheel no longer turns. It is not that I prefer the company of the dead, he thinks, it is that the dead are the only company I have, the only company I deserve. There is another existence, a wheel that still turns, and I can see it, but I see it as if through a veil.

He shakes his head, squeezes his eyes shut for a few heartbeats. To be here, here and now, is difficult for him. To exist so completely from moment to moment – like the Stormcast – is something he finds harder and harder to do. Concentrate on the here and now, occupy your mind. He repeats these words over and over in his head like an incantation.

Look around you. Take in the details.

And the more he looks, the more he realises that something is wrong with this place. The island appears far older than he would have imagined. The castle, made from ancient black stone, seems like it comes from some time immemorial, perhaps a relic from the time of myths, and that in itself is unusual, but there is something else that troubles him. According to the star charts and journal extracts he has translated, the Amaranthe began its voyage nearly a hundred years ago, during the Age of Chaos, and it held near eight thousand people. But this place has not seen any sign of habitation for... for how long? The heavy wooden gate was rotted through, fallen from rusted hinges as if from the passage of centuries, not decades. The spindly towers that are scattered around the island – several here in this courtyard – look as if they have been weathered by the passage of hundreds of years. Sconces on the walls drip with dark green slime. Rust peels away from iron barred windows like layers of dead skin.

The reinforced door to the keep is shattered inward as if it has been broken open and the remnants crumble into fragments as the Stormcast pushes through it. The air within is as stale and mouldy as the most ancient tomb or catacomb unearthed from the Age of Myth. He touches a wall with one bare hand. The black stone of the castle is cold and wet and coated in black slime and fibril spongy moss. Pockmarked in a way he has not realised before, as if every inch of the stone has been beaten and scoured by some desperate hand, faint veins of amethyst beneath the grime. Sea air and saltwater has a corrosive quality that accelerates aging, he knows, but he could swear this place has seen no living soul for thousands of years.

The captain of the *Silenaita* approaches them through the courtyard, wading with obvious distaste through the foul water.

'This is what you were looking for? I never thought we should find this place. Now that I am here, I wonder if that would have been preferable.'

'That which I seek can be found within. I am certain.' The Stormcast's voice is strange. Flat somehow, devoid of emotion.

'I, however, am less certain,' says the captain. 'It would be a rare and unexpected treat to find gold and gems here. I grow weary of collecting the skulls of strange fish.' He gestures and the sailors move to begin their search.

'What happened to the people?' the historian says to himself. 'And wherefrom came the ringing of the bells?'

The Amaranthe is rotten.

Rot has spread from the fish and the fouled water and it has spread in shrivelled hearts. It has crept into the very stone of this ancient place until our dream of sanctuary now feels swollen, black and bloated around us. Foetid water soaks into everything: into the houses they have built, into the well and the provisions and into their clothes and skin. And they drink it and wade in it and defecate in it and eat the fruits of the poisonous sea. I fear they have forgotten what it means to be men and women. Life is hope and love and they are without those things.

My lady views them with disgust. She sleeps in her shifted form and dreams the dreams of distant spirits. I fear that I too am diminished in her regard, but I cannot find the people vile. I pity them, that is the truth of it. I look at them, at what we have become, and my heart breaks. I stand above them on the parapet and look down at the mass of desperate humanity and I pity them as if I am not also one of them. The Amaranthe has sailed lost for seven long years, seven years where hope has dwindled to a distant memory, where lofty ideals have been replaced with only an exhausting need to continue, to survive. And it is too exhausting, too draining an existence for everyone to bear. And so they clutch rocks to their chests and walk into the sea, or they lose their minds and we have no choice but to lead them to the lower levels to wander lost and deranged in the sea caves and tunnels and bar the doors behind them and call it a mercy.

I place my hand on her shifted form as she sleeps. One eye opens slowly to regard me, two sets of eyelids retract to reveal an iris the colour of beaten bronze, the pupil a slit as black as jet. She does not talk to me. Our daughter is still mute, her presence that of a ghost that haunts our chambers. And so, I write, I record the passage of the stars. I dream of strange and terrible things. But I will not give in to despair.

Even now I hear the ringing of the bells and I know they gather in silent prayer. And at times I too feel the pull of those bells, the compulsion to go and stand with them shoulder to shoulder in the foul water and look up to the distant stars as they call out to a god that will not – cannot – answer because he is dead and we are alone.

The crew of the *Silenaita* begin their search with the buildings and structures that crowd the perimeter of the courtyard. They are methodical but most of these places are empty, the rooms and corridors within flooded and full of nothing but rot. The Stormcast and the historian head inside the keep, into a vast entrance hall with an expansive stone staircase. It leads up out of the water, circling round the black stone walls to multiple higher levels in the titanic edifice, each seemingly carved from living rock and supported by arches and buttresses that are at once both functionally unadorned and needlessly elaborate in their arrangement. Such is the skilful nature of the craftsmanship and the softening effect of the passage of time that the building appears almost organic. The historian is put in mind of an enormous honeycomb.

From the main hallway a large beaten bronze door crusted with corrosion stands ajar, and through it can be seen the start of a broad flight of steps descending into a great hall. The walls are of natural rock, partially formed of the jagged black basalt of the island's core and crusted with barnacles. The chamber is entirely flooded; it is as if this room has been carved out of the bedrock or fashioned from a natural sea cave, now submerged with the tides. The chamber is immense. Lantern light does not reach the far side but retreats weakly in the face of the impenetrable gloom. Some furnishings float in the murky water; fragments of chairs and table legs, among other debris, hint that once this hall would have seated many hundreds of people. Bones of fish and larger creatures are tangled in seaweed, scattered among the flotsam like the remnants of a discarded subaquatic banquet. From the ceiling, high above, black iron chandeliers hang from rusted chains.

The lower levels are all similarly flooded, so they begin with ascending the stairs. The Stormcast takes them in great strides – he seems eager in a way the historian finds disconcerting, at odds with his usual caution. Away from the seawater the floors are coated with thick grime and debris, the stone soft-edged and the damp air laden with motes of dust, suspended as if in syrup. Mist seems to seep through the walls, lingering like spectres around the edges of their vision.

They climb three flights of stairs, led by daylight leaking from behind a buckled and corroded metal door to a room with a vast, glass-domed ceiling. The room is full of ancient astronomy equipment, mostly rendered useless, with broken glass lenses that crunch under the Stormcast's armoured feet. The centre of the room houses a mechanical contraption, corroded beyond recognition. A brass orb twenty paces across is split into variegated hemispheres like the layers of an onion, each deformed with a verdigris patina that disguises their original purpose. Plates and discs pattern the floor and the historian recognises them as measuring devices, and the contraption itself as a vast form of something like an astrolabe. Directly above, the star of Azyr is visible, a pinprick of pure light in the milky whiteness of the mist, amplified somehow as if by lenses engineered into the glass of the dome.

'We are in an observatory of sorts,' says the historian. 'This device measured the stars, the passage of years.'

'It is familiar to me. I have seen its like before,' says the Stormcast. 'In the halls of Azyrheim perhaps, or the celestial orreries.'

There is something wrong. This equipment is corroded, rusted by saltwater. The room is protected from the wind and rain and yet the walls are damp. The historian is inspecting the machine. Corrosion flakes from it with his every touch.

'There is lichen growing here,' he says. 'And on the walls too, such as would grow in a tidepool. It is as if this entire castle was flooded.'

On the floor of the room around the machine there are tracks and markers and, on this track, there is a needle. The bronzework is green and crusted with patina like something dredged from the seabed. The historian clears away what he can with his hands until the numbers inscribed below are legible. Each notch on the first track marks the passage of a year, the second track marks decades, the third centuries. The notches are hard to read, and at some point, long ago, the machine must have broken down, corroded beyond repair. The historian counts for a moment, tallying up the numbers. He is holding his breath. The needle has recorded the passage of nearly two thousand years.

'How can this be?' the Stormcast asks. 'It is impossible. I had hoped we might find the... the children, the descendants, of those that lived here, but...'

'But there has been no living soul here for thousands of years,' the historian says. 'This place has been truly lost, lost in a way I cannot begin to understand.'

In my dreams I float beneath primordial seas, beyond the precipice. A place outside of time, outside of existence. I am adrift in the aether and naked as a babe. There are no stars above, there is no ground beneath my feet. I know not in which direction the stars should be found. In all directions, only darkness. There is terror in the core of my being, as if my fragile soul is bare and vulnerable and unseen monsters are circling.

It is then that I see the Unclean Ones. They grow in polyps that hang heavy and pregnant from the membranous belly of the aether. They are tumours, as if the realm itself is riven with disease. And they are parasites: they leech from the host, suckling and chewing. The sight is appalling, nauseating. There is one that chews and tears, a mouth full of milk and gore. I see it break the skin, pull itself through, to emerge into the realm in a flood of squalid afterbirth. I am drawn to this portal and carried along in the current. I try to cry out but my mouth fills with grey, viscous bile. It sees me and it knows me, and it calls to me. Its smile is sympathetic, paternal. Its appetites are obscene, its embrace promises an end to heartache. It knows me, it knows my sins and my misery.

It plucks at me like I am a flower.

The Unclean One burbles with mirth. I cannot comprehend what it finds amusing. It promises to show me.

I do not know if I can resist.

I no longer want to.

The floor of the room suddenly moves, lurching to one side as if the realm itself has shifted on its axis. The historian staggers and almost falls but the Stormcast catches him by the arm. The machine creaks and groans as new strains are placed upon it. There is a grinding, as of metal against bone, that comes from all around. And there is another sound: first a single bell, then more, a chorus of bells that peal out across the courtyard, the sound echoing all around them until the historian clutches at his ears. The discordant ringing of a hundred bells, clashing and rolling together like thunder. The Stormcast still holds his arm, drags him now to the doorway and to the stairs, pulling him along like a child.

'Something has happened, have we... collided somehow?' The Stormcast is shouting to make himself heard. 'Do you feel it? The island is moving, rising!'

There is a roaring sound from below; water is streaming from the lower levels, pouring out through cracks and passageways. This is impossible, the historian thinks, we are rising somehow from the sea as if borne upon some enormous swell or the crest of a monstrous wave. They reach the ground level. Water is streaming past their feet with enough force to almost pull the historian over. Bones and debris sweep past him, battering his feet and legs. The filthy water streams out through the doors to the courtyard, and down into the lower levels. The historian starts to head towards the courtyard but the Stormcast stops him.

'You will be swept away. Wait, wait, hold to me,' the Stormcast shouts over the thunderous cacophony of the bells. He has anchored himself somehow, implacable, immovable. He shields the historian with his body as debris breaks against his armour.

The great hall behind the copper doors is draining, the sea within frothing and churning as it pours away through underground cracks and fissures. The receding water reveals the true size of the hall, a vast and ragged void formed from the fusion of the castle foundations and the basalt sea caves beneath. The water level drops further, revealing the partially collapsed chamber floor covered in thick silt and encrusted with barnacles and lichen so that it resembles the seabed. Rubbery stalks of kelp and brown algae sprout from the craggy, broken floor, and these along with remnants of ancient furnishings, anemones, sea urchins and scuttling things are all swept along with the retreating water, caught by the torrential flood and sucked down into the lattice of pitch-black cave mouths that surround the room. The roar of the water and the howling of the air as the pressure changes adds to the deafening clamour.

The historian catches sight of something else revealed in the hall. White fleshy sacks the size of a man are uncovered, clinging to the basalt. Bulbous corpuscular growths with translucent trailing fronds like those of a jellyfish. They stream with water and he watches, appalled, as they begin to split like cocoons, peeling open and spilling out pink, frothy water that then becomes a thicker white liquid that oozes across the chamber, until the room is smeared white like the accumulated excrement of gulls in their nests.

Then from one of the ruptured sacks a figure emerges. A slender human arm thrusts out from the trembling membrane, fish-belly white, sloughing skin as if putrefied to the point of liquescence. Another figure emerges, then more. Arms and legs and skinny naked bodies, each and every one shivering and staggering, deformed feet sinking into the frothing seabed floor, stumbling and crawling, tearing themselves on jagged stone and spilling out briny waste and grey coils of viscera. For all their deteriorated appearance they move with purpose, and a thought comes to the historian, a thought that repeats over and over in his head at the expense of all others.

They hear the call of the bells; they heed the call to prayer.

There is a shriek from outside, audible over the sound of the bells. It cuts through the historian's fixation. Then the Stormcast is shouting at him to get back to the ship and he is running, slipping on the filth and silt that coats the black stone now the water has receded, leaving the entrance hallway thick with sediment and filth like a tidal flat. He looks back over his shoulder as he reaches the door to the outside. The Stormcast follows, weapons ready in his hands, wading through the mud. Outside, another cry.

Beyond the doorway the historian can see the same sludge now coats the courtyard, a graveyard of fishbones and carcasses half buried in the grime. Water streams in rivulets across this vista, cascading out through the gateway in the wall and down through sinkholes in the mud that even now widen to reveal previously hidden tunnels and cavernous openings down into the sea caves below. And from these holes more of the white figures emerge. Arms slick with slime and mud scrabble to find purchase as they pull their rotten flesh up from the depths, like the dead clawing their way out of the grave.

And, the historian realises, the island is still rising somehow. The constant thunder in the distance must be torrents of seawater spilling out into the ocean. Could the *Silenaita* weather such a storm? He looks for the sailors, but they are nowhere to be seen. The Stormcast shouts his name, urging him to run, and he staggers out in the bloodless daylight, splashing through the quagmire towards the gate.

Moments later he clings to the crumbling stone bridge and looks down at the *Silenaita* – now far below – as she is tossed and turned on the swells and frothing breakers, while the water spills from the Amaranthe in an endless swirling maelstrom. Spray lashes at him, whipped into a stinging, piercing assault by the confusion of wind and currents of rapidly displacing air. He calls out to the sailors running to and fro on the deck, but his voice is lost in the howling and crashing of wind and waves and the unceasing cacophony of the bells.

The *Silenaita* has torn free of her mooring and is now tethered by some few guide ropes and lengths of rigging that have broken free from their stays. The foremast has splintered, and ropes have become tangled in the looming black underbelly of the island, the lines becoming taut one by one as the island ascends, and then snapping as the ship lurches in the currents or gets tossed upon a wave and crashes back down. The crew hack at the ropes with their boat knives and cutlasses, hanging on against the bucking and the waves that threaten to sweep over the deck and wash them away. And then the foremast cracks and breaks and the lines that hold it snap and come free and the ship moves from the island with sudden speed, pushed away by the buffeting water. He stands and waves with both arms, and on the deck he sees the small figure of the captain looking through a glass and he waves and shouts to him until he can do so no more.

The island has stopped moving, he realises. The bridge he stands upon has now been elevated almost to the height of the *Silenaita*'s topgallants. Below, the sea churns and boils with spume as water continues to stream down from the jagged rocks. The *Silenaita* waits, pushed to calmer waters beyond the tumult, and the crew scurry to make repairs to the broken mast that hangs in a tangle of rope and sailcloth across the bow. They will wait, he thinks – they must put down a boat – and he lingers for a moment longer but there is no sign yet of a boat being lowered. The sea is too rough, he thinks, but they must wait, they must wait for…

He turns and scrambles quickly back along the bridge and into the courtyard, thinking to warn the Stormcast that this was no longer a route by which they could escape. He slips in the mud and stumbles through the gate, falling to his hands and knees, looking up through the tangles of wet hair plastered to his face. And in the centre of the courtyard, surrounded by horror and madness, he witnesses an avatar of thunder and lightning.

Electricity flickers around the Stormcast's unhelmeted head in a coruscating halo of power. Sparks trail from his eyes like tears. He is beset on all sides by creatures wrought of dripping, waxen flesh, dozens of them now. And more still come, clawing their way out of the mud on their bellies to writhe like maggots before staggering clumsily to their feet. And with deformed hands they reach for…

They reach for the heavens, the historian thinks. They reach towards Azyr. And the very island itself seems to strain towards the star of the God-King, pulling free of the ocean as if possessed of a will of its own.

Each bolt the golden warrior fires finds a target, piercing necks that bubble with red foam, or punching holes through chests and abdomens that resist the arrows no more than would sodden paper. Bones like rotten wood provide no resistance. The Stormcast aims at their heads. They have no features, no eyes or mouth, unless they are hidden beneath layers of slime. Bolts pierce skulls that crumple and tear and spill out grey liquids. He reloads and fires and reloads again until his ammunition is exhausted. Every bolt has struck true, bodies lie in the ankle-deep mud all across the courtyard. And yet more keep coming.

The Stormcast discards his crossbow, switches his hammer to his right hand. Electricity dances across the weapon, across the golden sigmarite armour, earthing in the quagmire at his feet. He wields the weapon as if it is weightless, as if he can never tire, never grow weak. Each swing of the hammer pulps flesh and crushes skulls. The historian can only watch. Can only witness. And he thinks, if I must believe in something, in the grandeur of some god, then believe in this. Believe in him.

The way the creatures move is not mindless, not without purpose and intent. They arrive in the courtyard as if compelled, but now move to encircle the Stormcast, stepping or crawling over the bodies of the fallen, wading through mud and the bones of fish. They are struck down or fall or stumble but there are too many. Limp hands reach for his armour, others reach for his hammer even as it shatters their bones. The Stormcast appears lost in the fury of the battle; his body works like a machine without the fatal hesitation of conscious thought. He responds to each attack as it comes, countering and retaliating. He presses every advantage that is afforded him. He does not make mistakes. Lightning seems to fuel him, makes him stronger than any mortal.

The bells ring out in a final crashing crescendo then fall suddenly silent. For a moment the absence of sound is disorientating, a sudden weightless feeling that makes the historian stumble again, even as he climbs to his feet. Then from all around there comes a deep and mournful groan as if the island itself is in pain. From every stone and every rock comes the sound and then, achingly slowly but with a ponderous sense of inevitability, the island begins to fall back down into the sea.

The historian realises he has become cut off from the Stormcast, with no escape possible through the gateway and the creatures emerging on both sides. Fear grips him now for the first time, grips him in a way that prevents rational thought. He needs to get down to the ship. And then he has no time for thought at all as the creatures reach out for him and he screams, stumbling back until he is with his back against the monolithic black walls of the castle and all he can do is retreat along it, wading through the mud as the creatures stagger after him. He sees the Stormcast, still fighting and unaware of his plight. He thinks to call out, but it is as if a hand has gripped his heart, gripped the machinery of his throat. And he realises he cannot do it, he cannot, because some part of him thinks he is undeserving of help, undeserving of the attentions of the godlike warrior. He cannot call out even if it means his death, and that realisation fills him with a flood of sadness that seems to radiate throughout his body, from his core to his extremities. And he comes to an understanding: that this is the limit of his own worth, that this is how he values himself.

He watches the Stormcast a moment longer. So many creatures lie dead and the golden warrior does not appear tired, does not falter. And yet, the historian realises with horror, he is beginning to lose. Even in death the creatures hamper the Stormcast's movements, slowing him down with the press of their bodies, fouling his attacks. Their broken fingers wedge into the joins between the sigmarite plates at his knees and waist and they are crushed but the flesh and bone remain, and his movements are slowed. Maimed bodies slither through the mud to grip the Stormcast's feet and will not let go and he has no time to free himself. His feet skid on mud and slime and viscera. The press of bodies surrounds him and then he can no longer bring his hammer up. He pushes forwards with both hands, seeking to make room, but there is no more room to be found; he is surrounded on all sides by a seething, crippled mass of rotten flesh. He struggles, he roars with defiance. Lightning arcs between his teeth. He stumbles. And then he falls.

And then the historian does cry out. The golden warrior is lost beneath a press of bodies. And now the historian too is surrounded – creatures close in on him, faceless and grasping. There is nothing he can do to help. There is a sinkhole in the mud at the base of the wall. A yawning black hole two arm spans across from which nothing now emerges save for the howling of wind and the distant churning sound of water far below. And having nowhere else to turn, he throws himself into the void.

The historian crawls through pitch blackness. He had dropped ten paces straight down, landing heavily on thick silty mud. Behind him the sounds of fighting have stopped but there are other sounds, sounds that seem to come from all around. The island is falling back into the sea, he thinks; this tunnel will be flooded. And yet what choice does he have but to press on, forward and downward?

Behind him come sounds of movement, of bodies crawling through the mud towards him. And now the tunnel is narrowing so that he is not sure there is room to turn around even should he wish to. He is forced onto his belly, crawling on his elbows and pushing with his feet, or sliding on the mud where he can, sliding onwards like a worm into the core of the island. The noise here is overwhelming, crushing. Around him the stone groans and the wind howls in the half-light and the rock around him feels immeasurable and primordial, like he has intruded on some ancient elemental truth writ in the language of gods and giants.

Tunnels branch off to the left and right, but none appear to head higher. He sees a wider opening and crawls through into a sea cave, splashing through icy pools and scraping his skin bloody on the craggy black rock. Below him the water is beginning to flood back up into the caves as the island sinks down into the sea, frothing and swirling as the caves and tunnels channel the water up from the depths. He can feel the island shifting, a sinking in his stomach and a trembling in the rock and mud beneath his bloody fingers.

Finally, there is a tunnel that leads up, and he climbs towards it, feet slipping on the wet rock, fingers straining for purchase. He crawls up a steep incline fuelled with a strength born of desperation. He can see daylight now and hear the torrents of spume as they crash against the great black stone walls, and the gulls crooning and squealing and circling in disarray as the island slowly descends into the churning sea. And then water is pouring in ahead of him as well and the space begins to fill until he is splashing through the rising seawater, coughing and spluttering. And then the water is all around him and he scrapes his head against the tunnel to take a long and panicked breath. Then he is submerged, pulling himself along towards that portal of light that fades and grows distant as if a veil has descended, and then he too seems to descend, drawn back and down through the tunnel, back down into darkness, and the thunderous reverberations of the water and the wind are washed away until he can hear nothing and see nothing and eventually feel nothing.

THE THIRD CIRCLE

The Portal

Consciousness returns to the Stormcast like the coming of a slow tide. The waves lap gently against the edges of his subconscious until he finds he can ignore them no longer, and following this initial recognition, more awareness begins to come to him, senses and sounds and feelings penetrate the mire of his thoughts, and chief among these feelings is pain.

Ra'Xephael, Knight-Questor of the Hammers of Sigmar, opens his eyes to an unfamiliar world. There is no light but a terrible dark radiance that seems to bleed from a stark and desolate sky. Water as black as old blood ripples against lichen-covered stone in an almost imperceptible rhythm. Grey sand, sharp black rock. A smell of electricity and brine.

He is lying prone. He cannot move and each attempt sends new floods of pain across his body. He is pinned somehow. He struggles to breathe and a momentary panic grips him as he cannot draw enough breath to fill his lungs. He wills himself to be calm. Pain is a barrier to all rational thought, and he wills that to subside, to fade, to become a presence in the background of his thoughts only. Pain exists only in the mind, he thinks. It is my body warning me of something, some damage or threat, that and nothing more. And through this force of will he begins to take control again, to take stock of his situation.

He can see nothing save for water, the jagged outcrops of rock and his right arm, pale and bare in the shallow brine. His head is pinned, turned to one side; some pressure holds it in place. He cannot feel his arms or his legs. He is naked. Water ice cold against his skin.

There is a sound. He is unable to move, even to turn his head, but he can still hear. Movement in water, the splash of footsteps. It is not safe. It is never safe. A grinding of stone. And then more pain. Pain in his leg. Broken bones or a broken spine. Weight all over his body. Crushing weight.

He can move his right hand. He feels the sand beneath his fingers, and he claws at it seeking some agency, some control. Around him there is more movement, the sound of stone grinding on stone and then more weight, weight on his chest that forces the air from his lungs, and he cannot draw it back. He is gasping for breath. Small rapid gasps. His lungs cannot fill. His chest cannot rise. He feels the weight on his chest and for a moment, all of his limited awareness, all of his constrained perception is focused on his lungs and his ribs, so that he can almost visualise them, almost picture it with perfect clarity when they crack one by one.

He thinks: I belong here.

Time passes, he does not know how long. More stones are piled atop him and with each new stone he loses consciousness only to wake moments or hours later. Then figures are moving through the lifeless water before him. Vertebrae grind against each other in his neck as he tries to turn his head to watch them. They stand in silence and face out to sea, as if waiting. The only sound now is that of his own laboured breathing. He feels on the verge of some revelation, some understanding, but it is just out of reach.

There is no tide in this place, no forces in the heavens to influence the movements of the ocean, and so the tidepool does not fill and he does not drown, and after a time the pale figures turn and wade back out of the shallow sea and he listens to their shuffling footsteps as they walk across the grey sand beach and down into the tunnels and caves to the dark places below.

There is no sun in the sky, no way to tell day from night. The Stormcast loses all sense of continuity. Every moment is agony and every snatched breath through broken ribs sends waves of pain so intense that he often blacks out, only to regain consciousness in an endless cycle of waking and sleeping that lasts for hours or days. Tiny transparent crabs crawl across his skin and he watches them as they walk along his outstretched arm, focusing on the sensation of the movement of their feet, tiny pinpricks on his flesh. He focuses on this to the exclusion of all else because the entirety of the rest of his existence is suffering, and so he must deny it or go mad. He watches them for hours at a time, waking and sleeping. Beyond pain, beyond the trivial considerations of cold or hunger.

Footfalls splash quietly through the water, waking him from his reverie. A huge golden cat walks through the shallows towards him, head slung low, ears back, tail flicking slowly from side to side. Its passage leaves barely a ripple in the breathless sea. As big as the great cats in the forests of Azyrheim that he has glimpsed while hunting in a previous life. A memory that has remained with him when so many others have not. The cat stops a short distance from him, its breath slow and even, visible in the cold air, its teeth bared slightly, each one the length of his fingers. It stands before him so he can look into its eyes. Eyes the colour of beaten gold. Feral eyes, wild and dangerous.

He reaches out towards the cat with his free hand which trembles as if palsied. He can barely move enough to raise his hand from the shallow water, sending crystalline shards of pain shooting back along his arm into his skull and tiny crabs scurrying away, back into the rocks. The great cat moves nearer, puts its head under his hand. His fingers rest atop its head and they stay this way for a while. The warmth of the cat keeps him from trembling even as a familiar cold takes a grip of his heart.

'I am sorry,' he whispers. 'I am so sorry.'

The historian wakes on a grey and lifeless shore where black water sits tepid and still under a sky that holds no colour and has no stars, but instead throbs with a dismal and profane glow. His last memory is of drowning, of vision fading to a single point and then that point extinguishing. This is some abyss, he thinks. Some deep place beneath the waves. He thinks he might be dead, trapped now for eternity in a haunted underworld.

The silence here is absolute. The roar of the wind and waves still echoes in his head, growing fainter, and he finds that he almost misses it, such is the totality of the silence. Behind him he sees the looming walls of the castle as they lean against the infinite void of the sky. The island sunk beneath the waves, he thinks. He should have drowned. Instead it has emerged in some other place, and he has been expelled, rejected by the sea. His hair and clothes are dry, his mouth tastes of salt and dirt, his skin and bones are bruised and scraped raw. He feels like he has been asleep for days, his body leaden and unresponsive.

Not knowing what else to do, he walks along the beach. Furtive, sodden footsteps in the grey sand. There are other footsteps here, hundreds, walking to and fro and then... down, into caves and sinkholes that riddle the shore like woodworm, and where the dark becomes darker yet and the silence is so dreadful that he looks away with haste, lest something should look back and take notice.

The strange light of this place nauseates him. It seems to tremble at the limits of his perception, at the corners of his vision, so that at times he thinks he sees all the colours of Chaos reflected in molten turmoil just outside of his comprehension. A rainbow of absolute darkness. A radiant abyss.

He comes across the column of stones in the tidepool, at the far end of the beach before it tapers off into the black basalt rocks and the foundations of the keep. Where the water is shallow, and the sand is thick like mud. And he sees the body trapped beneath, bones crushed by the weight of the rocks, wounds patterned on his flesh. His breath catches in his throat. Even here, he thinks. Even here my ghost has followed me. This time he does not look away, and as he approaches, he sees the figure is no phantom. He kneels in the water beside the Stormcast, takes his outstretched hand in his. The Stormcast is talking, his voice ruined and distant. He is saying that he is sorry. He whispers it over and over.

The historian cannot move the rocks save for a few smaller ones and these he topples into the sea. The larger ones would take several people to carry. Small colourless crabs scurry across the Stormcast's naked body. They gather at his wounds, at the cuts on his skin which glisten white and red and raw in the salty water. With tiny claws they trim away the skin and the historian watches in horror as they use their tiny mandibles like forelimbs to feed. They cluster like insects on a corpse, dancing their delicate dance as they work, and their translucent bodies flush momentarily with scarlet as they are sated and retreat back into the depths. He sweeps them away, but they come back again and again, and he can do nothing to stop them.

'I cannot free you. I am not strong enough.'

'You… you asked me once if I feared death.' The Stormcast's voice is a ragged, halting whisper. 'I am afraid of what I will leave behind when I die… I do not know how much of me is left.'

'Is it not better to forget this? Forget this place?' the historian says. He thinks of the promise of a life made anew, without ghosts, without the crushing weight of memories.

There is silence. The historian wipes tears from his eyes. He feels powerless.

'Look for the stars, historian, there are none. Sigmar cannot see us here. There is no rebirth for me.' The Stormcast's speech is faltering. He fights for every breath. 'And besides… I would not leave you alone in such a place as this.'

The historian sits in the icy water of the tidepool alongside the dying man. He wonders idly if the blood in the water will attract some larger predator and he thinks if that would be such a bad thing, because at least that would be an end to it, an end to the pain. He sits that way for hours or days, it is impossible to tell. How long have we been here, he thinks, how long has it been since we arrived at this cursed island? He does not feel thirst or hunger. His muscles cramp in the cold water and the pain fades to a dull ache. There is nowhere to go, nothing to be done. His mind wanders, sometimes to shameful places. He thinks: soon I will be alone here. And he looks at the Stormcast and he thinks: even as a ruin he is so beautiful.

Despite his wounds the Stormcast does not die. Crabs crawl inside him. Other creatures too, tiny black fish like eel spawn and translucent things like microscopic jellyfish. A feast for scavengers and parasites. The historian watches in horror as something like a flower blossoms on the Stormcast's bruised flesh, a white spot at first, and then a spreading pattern of crimson veins.

And when this suffering has lasted an eternity, finally a larger predator comes at last from the depths, drawn by blood or by ritual. The black water of the ocean swells as if pregnant as something vast emerges, and even this dark place seems to hold its breath at such a terrible birth.

And for a time, all sane and rational thought deserts the historian and the world loses meaning and coherency and is replaced instead by a confusion of naked panic and fear.

For a time, he loses his mind.

When he comes to his senses he is back in the observatory. His knees are pressed to his chest, he clutches them like a child, cowering in a corner away from the door. The room has been barricaded with the husks of broken telescopes. He has no recollection of having done that, no recollection of coming to this room at all. The last thing he remembers is...

An image appears unbidden in his mind's eye, the beach, the swell of the water and...

He shakes it hurriedly away, his heart pounding in his chest. He stands, he goes through various motions of life, of living. He finds his pack, discarded in this room when he had fled it earlier with the ringing of the bells. He sits and drinks water from his flask, he paces back and forth. He urinates, standing in the corner, staring at the black stone with tired eyes that become unfocused and then ache, and he realises he has forgotten to blink, and so he breathes and sits again and looks around until he looks up and he sees through the glass of the ceiling the trembling void and all the colours of uncreation.

He thinks of the Stormcast. He thinks of the pale, faceless figures. And he thinks of the creature that came ashore. He thinks of these things in silence, with his eyes screwed shut and his head in his hands, his mind wide and screaming and open. There is little light in the room, only the leaden light from the sky above that gives the room a ghostly complexion devoid of depth and shadow.

A small sound wakes him from this fugue. Among the debris

of the barricade there is a compass that has not suffered the same extent of decay as the other items. He watches the needle as it spins around and around, though bent and wretched with rust. He explores the rest of the equipment. He looks for something to use like a knife but there is nothing that will do. There is a telescope sealed in a waxed hide case that still seems sound though the glass is cracked, and he cannot find a replacement among the scattered lenses that cover the floor.

He stops. He has cut his hands on the broken glass and he looks at the blood and does not recognise it. He thinks he is going mad; he has dreamed of uncreation, of unexistence, and now it has come to pass that he is to be unmade and his consciousness is to diminish like the dying embers of a fire and his body is to collapse or maybe fade away, and now that it happens he is afraid.

Hours and days pass, and he would not know it but for the motes of dust that drift across his vision like moons in their orbit and the blood that drips and pools like the birth of a primordial ocean, and all else is still and silent.

The historian climbs to the top of the tallest tower, up steps roughly hewn from stone that eventually become little more than niches carved into the wall, and then a single rail ladder when the space becomes so narrow and so crooked that he feels like he is back in the caves below the island, and that at any moment the water will rise and he will drown, and he finds that this thought does not trouble him – and that if he was to stop to allow himself to think on it, he might even find the idea a comfort.

At the top of the tower a cramped bell chamber contains seven rusted iron bells of various sizes. The largest is as tall as he is, suspended from a black stone headstock by a heavy chain that looks like it could once have served as a ship's anchor rode. The bell is deformed with age, disfigured so that the engravings that cover its surface are no longer legible. He traces their outline with his fingers, looking for a pattern he recognises. There is a twin-tailed comet, though it has been defaced, gouges hacked into it so deeply that the clapper can be seen through the holes.

He stands at the balcony, knuckles white as he grips the stone rail. There is no wind, but the height is such that the tower seems to sway, and his movements send showers of dust and stone tumbling down to the courtyard far below. He looks through the cracked telescope, glassing the impenetrable horizon where the black of the ocean meets the emptiness of the sky. In all directions there is nothing. He has looked out in this way many times before, as the days and weeks blur into one, periods of wakefulness marked only by infrequent sleep and constant nightmares. He looks from all sides of the tower save one, the side that faces towards the grey sand beach. The beach itself is hidden from sight by the walls of the castle but he still will not do it.

When he is not sleeping, he walks the length and breadth of the castle, even venturing to the mouths of the caves and sinkholes that cover the courtyard and the lower levels of the keep. He sits at those dark entranceways and listens with his heart pounding in his chest, waiting for the sound of rushing water, or the scrabbling of fingers through silt and mud. There is no sign of the bodies of the creatures that the Stormcast had slain, just tracks where the corpses had either been dragged or had crawled away, slithering through the thick mud to return to the dark places.

He walks the corridors and passages of the keep, opening doors where he is able, to search the rooms – though they are invariably bare of anything of value. He walks the ginnels and alleyways of the strange hovels that surround the courtyard and takes it all in with a historian's eye, and imagines what it must have been like when these cramped places were filled with men and women, and for the children who grew up here and for whom the walls formed the limits of the only world they had ever known. Each hovel would have housed several families, the floor perpetually flooded with filthy water. Nothing dry, nothing free from disease.

He never ventures close to the beach.

The bones of fish litter the island, and crabs and small creatures can be found where the silty water has formed pools. There is a well, but it is fouled with brine. He neither eats nor drinks and does not find he needs to. Without wine the world has become a place of sharp edges. The scrapes and cuts on his hands, arms and legs have swollen and turned lilac and brown but he does not feel a great discomfort. He is sick; he retches and brings up nothing but traces of seawater. He sits now in the observatory and coughs until his throat is raw and his spittle is bloody. He turns the pages of the journal. He does not know what he is looking for.

I am in a deep state of perpetual despair. The ark is a poisoned place. The nightmares haunt me even in my waking moments. It is as if I am trapped in some other place, a darker place, from which all my senses work as if through a veil. When I touch it is as if my hands are not my own, my skin is not my own. When I look upon my queen it is as if I see her from far away, the colour faded. There is a whirlpool of black water at the centre of my being that draws everything inwards and downwards towards an inescapable terminus. All joy has faded in the presence of this abyss.

And yet in this condition I find I can examine myself with a terrible clarity. My thoughts are stripped clean of sentiment, and of the comforting delusion of hope. And now, free from these things, I am motivated by a strange and morbid energy.

Despair is in itself a rejection of Sigmar. It is a determined belief that the torment of your life is beyond his ability to repair. That you are too broken, too unworthy. You think yourself beyond salvation. And if you are beyond salvation you must conclude that there are limits to his power and thus you reject him, you reject his claim of omnipotence, of godhood.

To accept Sigmar is to believe that your life has value and purpose, to believe that you are worthy of salvation. Yet with the clarity of vision found in my despair, the limit of the God-King's power is revealed: change is a lie. All things decay, and so there can be no value to life. There is no true growth in this life, no potential for salvation. It is a dishonest god that pretends otherwise.

The strange energy that enervates me does not lie about the purpose and reality of life. It offers no salvation, only acceptance. The path I am set upon goes only ever downwards, unchanging for eternity.

Should I write such things? I do not think the God-King still lives but if he does then he cares not for our fate, or he has not the power to change it. The star of Azyr has not been seen for twenty years. I cast my dreams of salvation into the abyss.

This most recent entry affects him deeply. He realises he has been clinging to the story found in the journal as if it offered a chance at salvation, as if through the author's unwillingness to succumb to despair, he too could find strength. He rubs his eyes. His vision is suffering, and translating the journal puts a strain upon him so that he finds it difficult to read for long. The writing has become more erratic, the language less coherent. And his translations suffer too, his once steady hand develops a near constant tremor.

He wakes in the night to fits of coughing. He feels himself wasting away, though a yawning fullness in his belly concerns him more; it is as if he is sustained by some parasite. His teeth are loose – he tests them with his fingers and then stares blankly at the bloody, rotten molar in the palm of his hand. His head throbs, his bones ache and the cuts and scrapes on his skin do not heal or scab over, but rather appear sickly, as if festering. But with it all comes a sense of lightening, as if a burden is being removed, piece by piece. Each day his wounds appear worse upon inspection, but the pain is lessened.

He knows that he is dying but he also knows, with some certainty that he cannot rationalise, that true death is not possible in this place, that he exists now in a place somehow outside of the normal confines and structures of time, beyond the reach of all gods, and that even the god of death has no power here. He thinks of the creatures in the places below the island and he wonders if that is the fate that awaits him – in a hundred years, or in a thousand years – if he will crawl to those dark caves, crawl back down through the tunnels on his belly like a worm to find some hidden corner and there remain until his flesh rots away, to wait for the ringing of the bells.

Each day he walks the castle, sifts through the debris and the bones. He sorts through those artefacts he can find, cleans away grime from old stone to search for secrets hidden within. His hands shake and his fingernails are black and brittle. He does not feel the eyes of the dead upon him, he does not feel the presence of those spirits that watch his intrusions. He wants to believe in the lessons of the past, of the value of knowledge, but it is becoming harder to do. The study of history never reveals anything worth believing, he thinks. He is disillusioned, cast adrift.

He sits and watches the grey water as it stretches away to nowhere, repeating nonsense like a mantra to keep his mind devoid of thoughts. His prayers are bitter. He thinks of the carrion-bird priest who had prayed with him that day. He clings to resentment because otherwise he would have nothing. He knows he should think of the Stormcast. He rarely sleeps. His dreams are full of violence and ghosts.

* * *

I rarely sleep any more. The nightmares are constant and overwhelming. I am exhausted but I know we are not safe. At night I sit and wait, my sword at my side, and I stare into the darkness at the barricaded door of our chamber and I try to keep the nightmares at bay. Those nightmares that are real and those nightmares that are unreal. Perhaps there is no difference any more.

The people are sick, they are stricken with plague. They gather to ring the bells, but the sound is unholy. They go to the places beneath the castle and I do not know what they do there in the darkness, but the screams that rise up from the caves to echo through the castle at night... I fear they have given themselves to Dark Gods.

Sometimes she twitches so that I know she is dreaming of some hunt perhaps, back in the Realm of Beasts. Before she fled for the first time, before she left her life behind to escape the Enemy and to be with me. Sometimes she is so still that I have to check that she is still breathing.

And my daughter. She looks at me with haunted eyes, pallid and weak with hunger. I have failed her, and I have failed my queen, and I failed our first child who we gave to the god beneath the waves. We paid such a price for this existence. The guilt is too much to bear.

And with these thoughts repeating in my head I fall asleep, if only for a moment. And that is all the time it takes for the nightmare to be made manifest.

When all else has been exhausted, the historian thinks of his own son.

Little more than a boy when he went away to fight in the endless wars. A young man when he died in some distant land. They did not know the manner of his death. They did not have a body. A battle fought between the armies of the God-King, and those that would call themselves free people. He does not know where his son's allegiances lay.

So he had explained to the priest of Sigmar who had performed the funeral rites, and the priest had arched his brows and blessed the empty casket. Hidden in his voice and manner had been a hint of disdain, and it was this that had proven to be more than the historian could take, more than his old life could endure.

He thinks of all that he gave to his son. This burden he placed upon him, this weight that he had thought was his alone, but which in truth he spread to the other people in his life and did not even notice. I inflicted this upon him, he thinks, this gift of life, this curse of conscious thought. And further than that, my own weakness. It would be better to plant a seed in a place devoid of all light and sustenance so that it may never have grown at all. Not a flower, to wilt and rot as the beauty of innocence fades. Not even a weed.

The Amaranthe has not infected me with despair, he thinks, it was not here waiting to poison me. I have brought my own. I have made of this place a home.

Hands black with disease pin me to the ground. They take my daughter and she does not resist. They scream as my queen awakens and her shifted form tears them limb from limb. But they have spears and nets and they cut into her, they cut into her with rusty iron blades and cleave great chunks of her flesh until she staggers and falls and they set upon her and sever every limb and pull out every claw and the last thing I see is her amber eyes fading to lifelessness as they carve away her head.

They take me to the dark place. They draw a circle in the dirt. This circle is the unturning wheel. All time is as one, all time is decline and all decline is stagnation.

They draw a second circle beside the first and this is the disenchanted flesh. They reveal to me the secrets of my flesh; there are no mysteries within.

They tell me what they have done, with voices cracked with emotion. They are begging me to understand. They do not pray to the god of disease; they pray to keep him away. They pray to keep him away.

I could almost laugh. I fear my mind is broken.

The third circle they draw above the others. It is a barbed circle. They place the crown upon my brow. The three circles in the dirt form the symbol of the Plague God. They tell me that I am the Undying King and they have built for me a throne. The third circle is the portal and it draws me to it, and I shall open the way.

I see the abyss within me, aglow with dark radiance. And from the heart of this oblivion the Unclean One rises, emerging from dark water. It knows me and it speaks to me in a voice that echoes in my head, in a voice that wounds me like the death of children, and it tells me at last what it finds so amusing.

I have eaten your god.

Movement catches the historian's eye as he stands on the parapets of the keep and stirs him from the torpidity of his thoughts. Movement in this lifeless place, so rare a thing that his heart races. Some new phenomenon has reached this afterlife, and the once-empty skies shift and ripple. Vast shapes emerge from the swollen sky, shapes that swim through the air as if it was the depths of the ocean. Each form is the length of the island, and they wind like coils of rope, intertwined so that it is impossible to count their number. Dozens, hundreds maybe. Grey skin covered in ridges and creases like the vast whales that swim the oceans at the edge of the realms, or like...

Krakens, he realises. Krakens such as those that nearly sunk the *Silenaita* all those weeks or months ago now swim through the skies of this void in defiance of all that he knows of the laws of nature. It is a beautiful and terrifying spectacle. He watches in awe.

He thinks of what this signifies, this change in a place where there is no change. And then, though his heart pounds in his chest and his legs threaten to betray him with their weakness, he descends the stairs of the keep and walks out into the courtyard, then to the gate at the far end where through the darkness of the archway lies the grey sand and listless waters of the beach.

He steps onto the grey sand, crouched low in the shadows, as silent as he is able. He hides among the basalt outcrops around the buttress of the wall. Overhead the skies have become still once more, as if the huge creatures breached this place and then returned, diving back into the depths of the starless sky. The beach stretches away before him, the ocean black and unmoving as oil. His eyesight is weak, and he searches the tide flats for the pools where the stone spire had stood, but it is not there.

At the far end of the beach he sees the daemon that he knows to be the god-eater. The Unclean One is a vast and appalling shadow, and though only revealed in silhouette it is a presence that offends and horrifies him beyond his ability to comprehend, some primal revulsion. And it moves, slowly and slightly, to wade in the midnight ocean, and so steps from darker shadows to be revealed in the faint coruscations of the otherworldly radiance.

And in this movement is revealed a new horror, for the daemon holds to its breast another figure. A figure so small in comparison that it is cradled in the crook of the daemon's arms like a babe, like a broken doll. A figure ruined beyond human endurance. And the historian watches, wide-eyed, hands clasped over his mouth. Watches as new details are revealed in every passing thunderous heartbeat and the figure moves, though just a fraction, to raise one arm before it is crushed again against the bosom of rotten flesh.

Somehow, impossibly, the Stormcast is still alive.

In the absence of hope, fear disappears. Now the worst is not a possibility; it is a certainty. There is nothing to fear any more. There is nothing worse out there than already exists in your head.

I give up on hope. I discard it. And I find that the absence of hope is not the same as despair. I see now that hope is the cause of despair, it is the root of all suffering. I give up on the false promises of hope and I take strength from this absence. I take strength from this void at the core of my being.

We are told to defy the dark, to hold a light against it. But if you extinguish that light and wait in the dark for the horrors then you can master the darkness, you can confront the monster in your head.

And you can reach out and break its neck.

He thinks on these words as he sits in shadow and watches. Some power has invigorated him, not the clarity of despair, but a new purpose. He thinks on those words again as he paces back and forth in the observatory and when he walks the corridors and secret passageways of the keep. He feels powerless, as he has always done in this cruel world of gods and daemons, but now the worst is here, he no longer feels afraid.

Above him, the star of Azyr can be seen, revealed flickering and fading in the churn of dark heavens. The barrier between this place and the Mortal Realms has thinned and things pass through. And he thinks: once I would have seen this as a sign my faith was rewarded. Once I would have wept at this portent. But I have had my fill of gods and daemons.

Rain touches his skin, and then the caress of wind and he could almost weep to feel these things again. Ripples on the water by the broken stone bridge. He watches for a time and thinks about arriving at this place, so long ago. And then a thought comes to him and he turns and searches in the alcove near the bridge, in the shadows and the jagged rocks until he finds one carcass among many. The spidershark, its skull caved in by the Stormcast's hammer, salt-bleached bone revealed through rotting flesh. He cuts at it with a knife of broken glass, held in a swaddle of cloth. He cuts until he has made a ragged hole and then plunges his hand into that hole up to his elbow, and he feels around inside the rancid meat until his fingers close on a bolt from a quarrel and he pulls it free and holds it up to be cleansed by the rain and he sees that it is straight and true.

He returns to the beach with the crossbow, loaded with a single shot. He has never fired a weapon like this before, a boltstorm weapon made for Stormcast Eternals. Made to be held in one giant gauntlet but impossible for him to hold unless he braces it against his chest and holds it with both hands. His hands tremble, the trigger is too large, he is unsure if he has the strength to pull it. He hides in the shadows of the rocks, waiting in the darkness.

The daemon is huge, fleshy and pale as a corpse. There is something wrong with the way it acts as it stands in the shallows and looks out towards the deep. The monstrous form twitches as if tormented. It seems damaged somehow, deformed. It convulses with sudden violent spasms as if its body is at war with itself. White skin like a tattered cloth barely conceals the rotten meat and muscle within, and this skin shimmers and shifts in a way the historian cannot comprehend until he realises it is covered in living creatures. Tens of thousands of translucent crabs that crawl across and under the rubbery flesh, emerging from blisters in the skin, then eating and becoming engorged only for the flesh to regenerate around them in a perpetual cycle.

Tentacles trail from the daemon, writhing as if with a mind of their own. They wrap around the daemon's arms, hindering its movements. They grope from the wound of its mouth like the feeder parts of some strange insect, tasting the air. They trail behind it, thick and covered in sucking, suppurating mouths that pucker and ooze as the tentacles seem to somehow work against the daemon, as if seeking to drag it back into the deeper water. There is movement within the daemon's guts and the historian realises that what he had taken to be grey ropes of intestine is really a writhing mass of eels. Eels that coil and twist within it and chew on it from within.

This daemon is a broken thing too, he thinks. It is abandoned here, away from its god, away from its purpose, whatever hellish thing that may be. Can such a monster die? Is this a form of daemonic undeath, such as the undeath of those wretched creatures that came up from the dark places? He is fascinated, unable to look away though its very presence appals and sickens him. It is like the urge to bear witness to a terrible injury, to lift the bloody shroud and see the ruination beneath.

He had not realised the most important detail. It does not hold the Stormcast. He forces himself to look away, to scan his surroundings. It is like looking away from a pit as you fall into it. Its presence will not be ignored. There is so little room left for thought on other things, as if nothing of consequence can coexist with the daemon, as if it is the centre of all existence.

In the gloom of the craggy rocks of the breakwater at the far end of the beach he sees a prone figure. He skirts along the beach, staying low and moving from shadow to shadow, though he does not know if darkness is an impediment to the daemon. The body of a young man lies on the lifeless shore. He does not look away.

The Stormcast does not see him, not at first. His eyes are shut, the corners crusted with tiny shell-like growths. Something moves beneath one eyelid, a sandworm-like squiggle. His bones are broken, crushed repeatedly only to heal, to fuse together in grotesque misalignment. His chest is caved in but still rises and falls. Barnacles grow in clusters from wounds on his skin, their structures raised from his marrow, their roots graven in the wreckage of his flesh. This, then, is what I choose to believe in, the historian thinks. This broken man, this ruin. Not a god, not salvation. He weeps, silently. The Stormcast is speaking.

'I was born when I met her.'

The Stormcast's voice is scarcely a whisper.

'I was born when I met her,' he says again. 'I was alive only when she loved me. And when she died, when she was taken from me, my life also ended. Though my body lived on, my life also ended.'

The historian wipes his eyes with the back of his hand.

'This is enough,' the Stormcast says. 'I have had enough.'

The historian has the crossbow. Now the time has come he doesn't know what to do. The weapon feels clumsy in his hands, overlarge and absurd. He tries to raise it, to hold it to the Stormcast's head. But he cannot do it.

The Stormcast places one hand atop the weapon, pushes it aside. His hand shakes, his fingers bent and broken. He takes the quarrel from the groove, tests the point with his thumb. Draws a bead of sluggish blood the colour of sea-worn rust.

'Leave this place.'

The historian nods. He has nowhere to go.

Across the water, in the obscurity of the horizon where a grey and morbid sky bleeds into the black and lifeless ocean, there is a light. Faint at first, then growing brighter. Then more. Pinpricks of blue light on a distant shore.

The historian returns to the gateway that leads to the courtyard. He does not remember his flight across the beach. He can go no further now; his lungs burn and now he stops to spit up blood and coughs until he gasps for air. He can see his breath, misting in the gloom. The temperature has dropped and the air smells of copper. He looks for the star of Azyr, but it is not there, hidden behind some nebulous cloud or retreated back into the mire of the night sky.

'But you will watch,' he whispers. 'Sigmar, do you hear? You will watch. What sort of father would turn away, would look away from the death of his son?'

The daemon wades ashore. It is a blacker shape against the blackness, a thing devoid of light. Trailing tentacles seem to try to anchor it to the sea, to drag it back, and it pulls and tears its own flesh. It returns to the beach, like some primordial sea creature venturing onto the land for the first time. Water sluices from its ruined body. It reaches the Stormcast, picks the limp figure from the sand like a toy, shakes it, holds it to its breast in a crushing embrace.

Lightning splits open the sky with sudden, terrifying ferocity. A sound like the world tearing in two. A single bolt from the empty and starless sky. No, not quite starless. All is cast in sudden, fearsome incandescence and there is only black and only white and nothing in between. The lightning touches, for the briefest moment, the broken body of the Stormcast.

The historian's vision is cauterised by the white-hot light. Afterimages are writ across the inside of his eyelids in a confusion of shapes and darkness. He blinks until vision returns and tries to make sense of what he sees. The lightning has claimed the Stormcast, but in its descent it has passed through the daemon, and this passage has wrought devastation, it has wrought the wrath of the God-King.

The headless Unclean One staggers and smoulders. Smoke like the burning of corpse-piles, black and acrid. It bubbles in a molten scream then retches, spilling milky effluence like a punctured bladder. And it seems to be losing the fight now, the fight that its own body wages upon it, as the groping tentacles find there is now less resistance, and the wounded daemon is dragged backwards by these grasping limbs, dragged into the water where it thrashes in the surf until the sea is thick with white slime, as if the daemon has collapsed to the point of gelatinous disintegration. And then beneath the water in a froth and then gone, gone until there is nothing but a trail of bubbles leading away towards those distant blue fires.

He sits in silence on the beach. Rain falls heavily now, kicking up divots in the grey sand. He has not the strength to go much further, he knows. Whatever journey this is, he has not the strength to carry on. With faltering steps, he walks to where the lightning has fused the sand into glass. The rain has washed away most of the evidence of the daemon's wounding, soaked away the dregs and the bile. But there on the sand is the object he seeks. An egg, no bigger than his fist. Blue skinned and leathery, trailing delicate strands like arms. It is still covered in the daemon's mucus, which he wipes away with the hem of his sodden cloak. All that remains of an ancient spirit.

He places it in his mouth, feels the stringy appendages search down his throat. He swallows, it works its way within him. And then he sleeps.

Waves lap against the shore, flecked with white surf. The sea is a deep azure that swells and shifts under a wide blue sky where seabirds circle and the pale sun rises to bleed ghostly and cold from behind a heavy blanket of mist. The historian's sickness has passed, and his wounds have healed; his health returns with unnatural rapidity. There is no sign of the fires on a distant shore, no sign of a shore at all, only an endless expanse of blue that fades and then vanishes in the haze of the horizon.

He has built a raft from flotsam that has washed up on the beach, the main part of which is the *Silenaita*'s broken foremast. Once he would have prayed that it would see him to safety but now, he does not, and instead he checks and double checks the knots where he has lashed the structure together with lengths of untwisted rope and strips of canvas, and he trusts in himself and himself alone. He has in his hand a compass. The needle no longer spins endlessly, but instead seems uncertain, facing first one way then another and now he discards it. Throughout my life, he thinks, I have put my faith in unnecessary or undeserving things, rather than risk being lost.

There is one thing left to do. He returns to the sinkhole in the courtyard, stares into the blackness. A distant roar of waves, echoing and echoing again until it is only meaningless noise. It is dark, yet still he enters. Down into the winding tunnels, through portals eaten in the rock like the passageways and corridors of worms and then further still, into the sea caves and the dark places where pale figures wander without purpose or direction, blind in the darkness. He walks among them and they do not touch him. There are so many of these creatures, stumbling, falling. And even as he watches one of them turns and walks into the sea and does not emerge again.

He stalks these dark places until he comes to a new chamber where the stone beneath his feet is worn smooth and a shaft of faint daylight seeps through bedrock to provide meagre illumination upon a desolate scene. Here there is a throne of driftwood set upon tumbled rock, made up with faded ochre cloth and shrouded in shadow. It is unoccupied, but at the foot of the rotten dais there are bones, and among the bones is the skull of a great cat. It is ancient and brittle, flakes of bone crumble in his fingers as he traces them across it. Degraded by the saltwater but still whole. And he collects the skull up and wraps it in his grey cloak. He carries it where he is able and pushes the bundle ahead of him through total blackness when the tunnels tighten, until eventually mottled daylight and a misting rain finds him, and he reaches the surface again and does not look back.

Stones fall from a nearby spire. The ground beneath my feet shifts. I stand alone on the parapets, and far below the crowd of monsters wail and surge in panicked frenzy. They ring their bells, their pale faces turned to the skies. And I watch them, and I will them all to drown.

They have taken my daughter and drowned her as an offering to madness and despair. They have... they have murdered my queen and all her feral glory is extinguished. There was never enough life here for her and now she will never leave, never return home. They have fed the old god to a daemon.

And they have made of me a portal... they have made a riddle of my flesh and my life now drains away and spills across these ancient stones that I once called a home. I hold myself together with broken hands.

I hear them even now, breaking down the doors I have barricaded. They will seek to bring me back to the daemon's embrace, to be their undying king, but they are too late, and I am falling apart. I hold myself together only because I have one more thing that I must do.

They think me broken. They have made of me a portal and the abyss consumes me from within. But a portal works both ways and with this final act I shall send this place down into dark water, I shall send these people to the heart of oblivion.

The Amaranthe begins to sink beneath the waves. There is no escape for me. I belong here. But I shall watch them drown. If you read this, know that I watched them all drown.

I feel the life leaving me, but there is one more thing I must record. As I lie here, I see a light in the forlorn heavens, I see the star of Azyr, a white eye watches me through the mists.

The God-King has returned.

The torn pages of the journal flutter in the wind that comes in with sudden intensity from the sea, sharp with chill and the sting of salt. The sea breeze catches the scraps, plucks them one by one up in swirling currents and eddies and carries them away to vanish among the rocks and crashing waves, where the shoreline winds along towards a distant horizon. He stands on the very precipice and listens to the footsteps as they approach, heavy footsteps as of a man in armour, surefooted on the mossy rocks of the clifftop path and barely perceptible over the rumble of the ocean far below.

'I seek the historian,' a strong voice calls out to him.

He does not look round nor reply.

'I seek Alessander Cellarius, the historian. Are you he?'

'I am no historian, not any more,' he replies. He steps away from the cliff edge and turns to face the Stormcast. A giant, resplendent in golden armour. There are similarities and there are differences.

'Nevertheless, you are the man I seek? They said you washed up in these parts near death some weeks past. They said you claim to have been to the lost castle of Amaranthe.'

'I am he. And those things are true.'

'I am a Knight-Questor of the Hammers of Sigmar. I am set upon a mission from the God-King himself, to seek an object of great power, the Szo-en-kur. Some say it lies within the mythical Amaranthe.'

'I know that of which you speak.'

'Then you can tell me where it may be found?'

The old man thinks for a moment then asks, 'This object – do you know what it is?'

'It is a weapon,' says the Stormcast without hesitation. 'A weapon with which to crush the God-King's enemies. Or perhaps an aegis, a ward that protects the bearer from the Dark Gods. It is a most valuable thing and I have sought it for longer than you can imagine.'

'What is your name?' asks the old man. 'Why do you not remove your helm?'

Lightning crackles behind the empty eye sockets of the golden death-mask helmet. The giant does not answer.

'You truly have been to the Amaranthe?' There is doubt in his voice. 'What did you find there?'

'I'm sorry,' says the old man after a moment. 'This thing you seek was lost. It was eaten by a daemon that then fled beneath the waves somewhere far away, or long ago…' his voice trails off as he looks out to the ocean.

The Stormcast watches him for a time. They stand in silence as waves break against the rocks and the wind whistles around them, as distant gulls circle and fight over scraps on the shore below.

'Tell me,' says the Stormcast. 'When did you last eat? Come, walk with me to the village. There is an inn there, you can be warm.'

The old man smiles. It is a smile full of warmth and when he smiles he looks much younger. 'I am well, thank you, my friend.'

The Stormcast waits for a moment longer. He seems uncertain. Then he nods once and turns to leave.

He hesitates. He crouches to look at the skull of the great cat where it lies atop a thorny nest of woven sticks, the bone salt-bleached and pitted. He places a gauntleted hand gently atop the skull, fingers resting there for a moment.

'What creature is this?' he says. 'I have never seen its like before.'

'She was from Ghur,' the old man replies. 'I intend to return her to that place. In a day or two I make the journey. By land, I think.'

'Ghur.' He nods and slowly stands. 'Safe travels to you then, old man.'

He watches the Stormcast walk away, back down the cliff path towards the distant smoke that rises in faint swirls from the fishing village, one of many on this stretch of the Ora Coast, each the same as the last. He thinks of a life forged anew without the weight of memories and the presence of ghosts and how all it costs is everything that you have.

Further down the coast, three or four days distant, there is a cottage in a bay where he once whiled away the hours of a lifetime.

Sheltered from the winds and rain and the notice of strange ships and the predators of the land and sea. Beneath the notice of gods and daemons and the wars that they wage in vainglorious monument. It is a place where the concept of life and death has grown indistinct, a place devoid of comfort and warmth. It is a place where old ghosts wait to welcome him back among their number. But it is no longer a place for him.

ABOUT THE AUTHORS

Graham McNeill has written many titles for The Horus Heresy, including the Siege of Terra novellas *Sons of the Selenar* and *Fury of Magnus*, the novels *The Crimson King* and *Vengeful Spirit*, and the *New York Times* bestselling *A Thousand Sons* and *The Reflection Crack'd*, the latter of which featured in *The Primarchs* anthology. Graham's Ultramarines series, featuring Captain Uriel Ventris, is now six novels long, and has close links to his Iron Warriors stories, the novel *Storm of Iron* being a perennial favourite with Black Library fans. He has also written the Forges of Mars trilogy, featuring the Adeptus Mechanicus, and the Warhammer Horror novella *The Colonel's Monograph*. For Warhammer, he has written the Warhammer Chronicles trilogy *The Legend of Sigmar*, the second volume of which won the 2010 David Gemmell Legend Award.

Lora Gray lives and works in Northeast Ohio. Their fiction has appeared in various publications including *Shimmer*, *The Dark* and *Flash Fiction Online*. When they aren't writing, Lora works as an illustrator, dance instructor and wrangler of a very smart cat named Cecil. Lora's short stories 'Crimson Snow' and 'He Feasts Forever' feature in the Warhammer Horror anthologies *Maledictions* and *Invocations* respectively.

Richard Strachan is a writer and editor who lives with his partner and two children in Edinburgh, UK. Despite his best efforts, both children stubbornly refuse to be interested in tabletop wargaming. His first story for Black Library, 'The Widow Tide', appeared in the Warhammer Horror anthology *Maledictions*, and he has since written 'Blood of the Flayer' and the Warcry Catacombs novel *Blood of the Everchosen*.

Steven Sheil is a writer and film director based in Nottingham, UK. His films include the features *Mum & Dad* (2008), winner of the *Silver Méliès* at the Leeds International Film Festival, and *Dead Mine* (2012). His short fiction has previously appeared in *Black Static* magazine.

Nick Kyme is the author of the Horus Heresy novels *Old Earth*, *Deathfire*, *Vulkan Lives* and *Sons of the Forge*, the novellas *Promethean Sun* and *Scorched Earth*, and the audio dramas *Red-Marked*, *Censure* and *Nightfane*. His novella *Feat of Iron* was a *New York Times* bestseller in the Horus Heresy collection, *The Primarchs*. Nick is well known for his popular Salamanders novels, including *Rebirth*, as well as the Cato Sicarius novels *Damnos* and *Knights of Macragge*. His work for Age of Sigmar includes the short story 'Borne by the Storm', included in the novel *War Storm*, and the audio drama *The Imprecations of Daemons*. His most recent title is the Warhammer Horror novel *Sepulturum*. He lives and works in Nottingham.

Darius Hinks is the author of the Warhammer 40,000 novels *Blackstone Fortress, Blackstone Fortress: Ascension* and three novels in the Mephiston series, *Mephiston: Blood of Sanguinius, Mephiston: Revenant Crusade* and *Mephiston: City of Light*. He also wrote the audio drama *The Beast Inside* and the novella *Sanctus*. His work for Age of Sigmar includes *Hammers of Sigmar, Warqueen* and the Gotrek Gurnisson novel *Ghoulslayer*. For Warhammer, he wrote *Warrior Priest*, which won the David Gemmell Morningstar Award for best newcomer, as well as the Orion trilogy, *Sigvald* and several novellas.

Jake Ozga is a lifelong Warhammer fan and horror fanatic with a particular interest in exploring the dark corners of the Mortal Realms. He lives in Leamington Spa with his partner, Abi; his dog, Freya; and his cat Horobi. His first story for Black Library, 'Supplication', featured in the Warhammer Horror anthology *Invocations*.

YOUR NEXT READ

WARHAMMER HORROR

THE REVERIE
by Peter Fehervari

Three travellers are drawn to the Reverie, the wound in the world of the Angels Resplendent. Knight, poet, scholar, each will face their shadows amidst a deeper darkness…

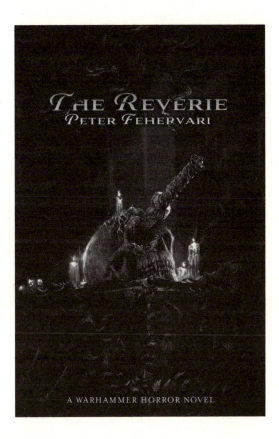

Available from **blacklibrary.com**, **games-workshop.com**, **Games Workshop** and **Warhammer** stores, all good book stores or visit one of the thousands of independent retailers worldwide, which can be found at **games-workshop.com/storefinder**

YOUR NEXT READ

WARHAMMER HORROR

THE DEACON OF WOUNDS
by David Annandale

In the harshest of times, even the most faithful can walk in dark places – as Arch-Deacon Ambrose discovers when drought and plague sweep through his city.

Available from **blacklibrary.com, games-workshop.com, Games Workshop** and **Warhammer** stores, all good book stores or visit one of the thousands of independent retailers worldwide, which can be found at **games-workshop.com/storefinder**